“Erica Vetsch has outdone herself in *A* ... *at Carlton Hous*...
ating the perfect blend of swoony romance, historical intrigue, and page-turning suspense. It’s a mystery that’s as fun as it is clever, with enough twists to keep you guessing, and richly drawn characters you’ll be rooting for all the way. Perfect for anyone who loves a good caper and a story that lingers long after the last page.”

—Misty M. Beller, *USA Today* best-selling author of the Sisters of the Rockies series

“Erica Vetsch is my go-to Regency mystery author, and *A Thieving at Carlton House* is packed with all the deliciousness one might expect from a queen of entrancing subterfuge in the era of Jane Austen. Twenty-five hundred gold stars from this fangirl!”

—Jaime Jo Wright, author of *Night Falls on Predicament Avenue* and Christy Award–winning *The House on Foster Hill*

“When I want a riveting story with characters that will feel like friends, I pick up a novel by Erica Vetsch. The wit, charm, and intrigue are the perfect combination for a fully satisfying mystery. I can always count on Erica for a brilliant read.”

—Jocelyn Green, Christy Award–winning author of *The Hudson Collection*

“Erica Vetsch has masterfully crafted another page-turner full of mystery, adventure, sparkling dialogue, and shimmering Regency details! Compelling faith arcs met me right where I needed them most, and Philippa might just be one of my favorite heroines. Whether you’re a longtime fan or first-time reader of Erica’s work, you’ll love this one!”

—Amanda Wen, Carol Award–winning author of *The Rhythm of Fractured Grace*

"A clever detective story with intelligent characters and a twisty whodunit! Erica Vetsch is back with a fascinating new Regency detective series where the multilayered mystery takes center stage. With her signature blend of authentic history, beautifully drawn characters, and delightful intrigue, Vetsch draws you right in and keeps you hooked until the end. Murder, corruption, and redemption—and a hint of true historical happenings—make this a memorable story that'll resonate with readers. Vetsch is in her element with this series, and her fans will adore this new adventure!"

—Joanna Davidson Politano, award-winning author of *The Lost Melody*

"Fans of Masterpiece's *Miss Scarlet and The Duke* will eat up *A Thieving at Carlton House*. From the very first page, Erica Vetsch's characters sparkle with purpose and gumption. I found myself repeatedly cheering for Philippa's heartfelt vision of creating a place of refuge for those who need it most. With satisfying faith elements woven throughout and likable characters who linger in your mind, this solid start to the new Of Cloaks & Daggers series will undoubtedly leave readers ready for more!"

—Heather Kaufman, author of *Up from Dust*

A Thieving at Carlton House

OF CLOAKS & DAGGERS

A Thieving at Carlton House

A Scheming in Parliament

An Accusing at the Old Bailey

THORNDIKE & SWANN REGENCY MYSTERIES

The Debutante's Code

Millstone of Doubt

Children of the Shadows

SERENDIPITY & SECRETS

The Lost Lieutenant

The Gentleman Spy

The Indebted Earl

Joy to the World: A Regency Christmas Collection

A Thieving at Carlton House

Erica Vetsch

A Thieving at Carlton House

Published by Kregel Publications, a division of Kregel Inc., 2450 Oak Industrial Dr. NE, Grand Rapids, MI 49505. www.kregel.com.

Published in association with Books & Such Literary Management, www.booksandsuch.com.

The character chart on pp. 7–8 was originally created by Rebekah Firmin, www.mockingbirdartiststudio.com.

Library of Congress Cataloging-in-Publication Data
Names: Vetsch, Erica, author.
Title: A thieving at Carlton House / Erica Vetsch.
Description: First edition. | Grand Rapids, MI : Kregel Publications, 2024. | Series: Of Cloaks and Daggers ; book 1
Identifiers: LCCN 2024020125 (print) | LCCN 2024020126 (ebook)
Subjects: LCGFT: Detective and mystery fiction. | Christian fiction. | Novels.
Classification: LCC PS3622.E886 T55 2024 (print) | LCC PS3622.E886 (ebook) | DDC 813/.6—dc23/eng/20240502
LC record available at https://lccn.loc.gov/2024020125
LC ebook record available at https://lccn.loc.gov/2024020126

ISBN 978-0-8254-4862-1, print
ISBN 978-0-8254-7192-6, epub
ISBN 978-0-8254-7191-9, Kindle

Printed in the United States of America
24 25 26 27 28 29 30 31 32 33 / 5 4 3 2 1

To Peter, as always, with my love.

CHARACTERS *in the* HAVERLY UNIVERSE

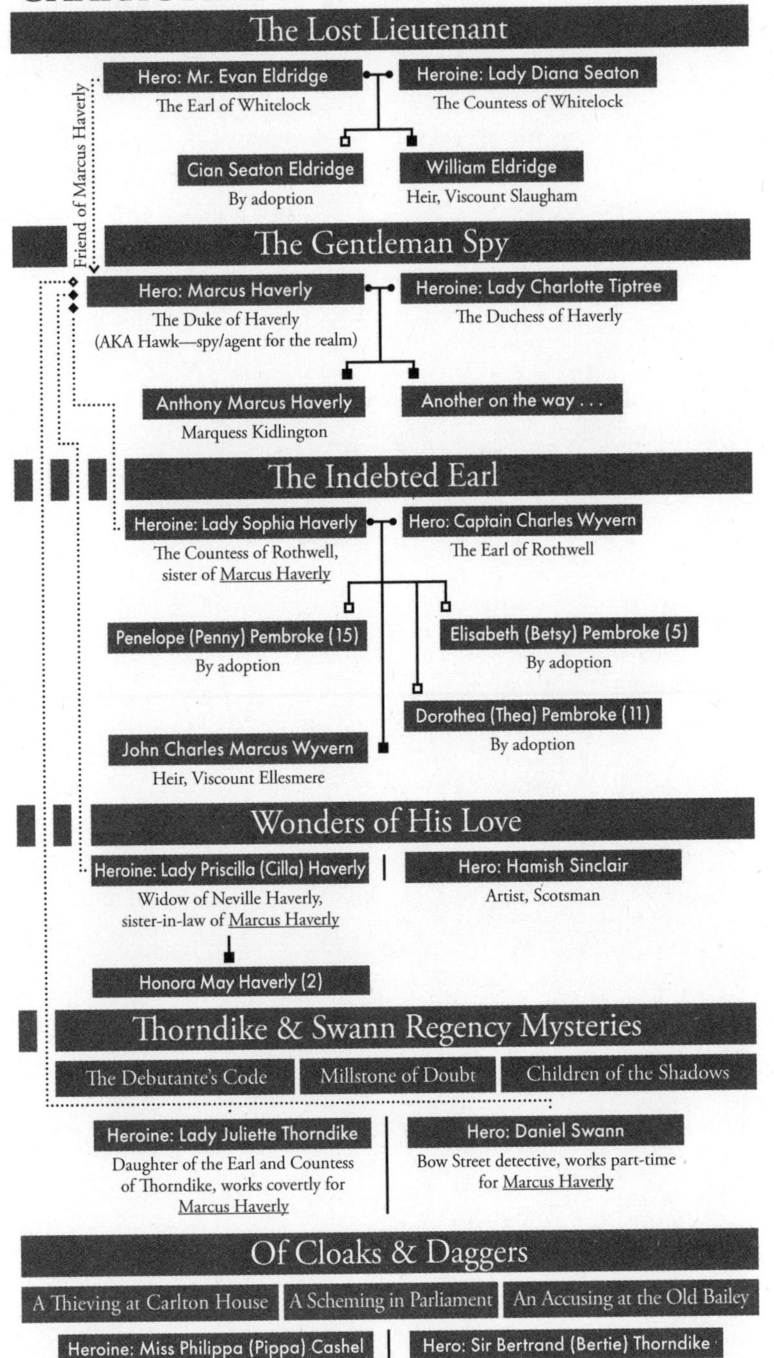

Chapter 1

June 5, 1816
London, England

"ARE YOU CERTAIN YOU KNOW what you are about with this venture?" Mr. Asbury tapped the head of his walking stick into his palm, slanting a glance at Philippa Cashel, all his reservations in his expression. "It is quite unorthodox for a woman to take on such an endeavor without a male representative. I expected the duke to be here to negotiate terms."

Philippa clenched her laced fingers, certain her gloves would be a creased mess by the time she finished dealing with this pious, pompous man.

I do not need a male representative to speak for me. Men have burned every bridge they've ever tried to cross as far as I am concerned. The only man I trust is Marcus, and I will not lower my guard to any other man, ever.

She kept her voice level. "I can appreciate your caution"—Lord, forgive her that lie, for she had no appreciation for it whatsoever—"which is why, upon my brother-in-law, the duke's advice, we sent you a complete prospectus. Our plans, our means, our schedule, and more. We *are* ambitious with our goals, but the need is great. We hope to set about another fundraising campaign as soon as the location for the school is secured."

Soliciting funds. The worst aspect of charity work. Philippa loathed it. She would rather scrub every pot in the scullery than ask for money from people who thought they were her better merely because they were well funded. But without money, there would be no school. With no school, the women now forced to sell their bodies to survive would have no recourse and no way to reform and change their lives.

They stood before a rather seedy-looking manor, vacant for the last decade but owned by the Asbury family. The property had been for lease for some time, probably because of its proximity to the Horsemonger Lane Gaol. She had been certain they could secure the tenancy but had not considered the owner's reservations about their occupancy.

It was as if, from her birth, God had decided her path would be obstructed and she would have to fight for every inch in this life. She would spend the rest of her natural existence striving to atone for her past, overcoming hurdle after barrier—yet it was a past He had a part in subjecting her to.

She had long ago given up expecting life to be fair.

Philippa considered Mr. Asbury, what she knew about him, his fussy mannerisms, his foppish dress, the way he looked at her as if not quite able to forget what she had been.

Time to lay on some charm.

"Your generosity toward charitable causes is approaching legendary status, and we are honored that you would consider our humble project. When you said you might allow us to rent your property with the option to purchase, why, my heart just soared. It is a most magnanimous gesture and will surely aid those who are in such great distress." Just enough flattery to appeal to him, but not enough that he might suspect her of being disingenuous.

Mr. Asbury adjusted his cravat, touching the mother-of-pearl tie pin, then smoothed his lapels and adjusted his cuffs. His prissy movements irritated. He was the one skittering about, but it was Philippa who felt uncomfortable.

Pedantic and peculiar.

But he, like most men, could be flattered and cajoled around to her way of thinking, and often in the end, the men thought the entire enterprise their own idea.

He ran his hand along his watch chain, as if counting the links, rocking on his toes. He tucked his walking stick into the crook of his elbow and his thumbs into his waistcoat pockets. "I was not aware when I responded to your inquiry that you had . . . well, such a checkered past, Miss Cashel. I merely believed you to be the sister of the Duchess of Haverly." His face reddened. "Can you assure me that your efforts with these fallen women will be successful? That your behavior and those of the women you help will be above reproach? I am not interested in having my name or my property attached to a failure. Or anything salacious. If you can avow that the vast majority of those you bring here will leave with changed hearts and with enough skills to make their way in the world without giving in to their lascivious or baser natures . . ."

Philippa clenched her teeth, railing inwardly against this prevalent notion that women involved in prostitution did so willingly because they could not control themselves, rather than the truth, which was that most women were forced into the life through sheer desperation because they lacked any other means of support. They were victims of men who could not control *their* desires, not the other way around.

As to his learning of her history as a former courtesan, she had never sought to hide it. She had earned a living by working in a disorderly house, but that was in the past. Thanks to the efforts of her sister and brother-in-law, and Aunt Dolly, she now had an honorable occupation, a purpose that added to society and would help many others . . . if this annoyingly fastidious man would only give them the chance.

She calmed her voice and features. "We have shown excellent results in our efforts thus far. With the help of the Dowager Duchess of Haverly, Mrs. Stokes and I have been able to rehabilitate and educate nearly a score of young women who are now gainfully employed as domestic servants, shopworkers, and seamstresses. We've even placed a pair of young women into service at Carlton House with the prince. We hope to continue the work we've begun while adding more to our curriculum in the way of education, vocation, and spiritual nourishment." All this was laid out in the prospectus. Had the man even read it?

Aunt Dolly—Mrs. Stokes to the pupils—Philippa's friend and partner in the charity, rounded the corner of the manor house, an eager expression smoothing some of the hard-worn lines of her face. Her lace cap fluttered in the early summer breeze. "It's perfect, I tell you. Though there are some much-needed repairs, they should not take long. The house could hold as many as fifty pupils easily. And the cow byre will allow us to both train those with a desire to become dairymaids and to provide for the needs of the kitchen. There is an excellent fowl house for chickens and geese too. And a walled kitchen garden that could use a bit of attention." Her voice held enthusiasm, something Philippa hadn't heard from her mentor in some time. "When do you think we might take possession of the property?"

Mr. Asbury removed a snuffbox from his pocket, seemed to remember how vulgar it would be to indulge in front of ladies, and returned it to its hiding place. "There is much to be decided yet. It has been on my conscience to somehow use this property for the good of my fellow man, or in this case, women, I suppose, but still, my mind hesitates. Is this the correct charity to which the land and buildings should be devoted?"

Why on earth would he hesitate now? The property had been to let for months. If he didn't lease it to them, then what would he do with it?

"I actually have another party interested, who wishes to use the manor and grounds as a reform school for children at risk of becoming delinquents. The gentleman hoping to start the school has a fine prospectus and grand plans, and he has a prestigious board of directors already in place. He also has funds in the bank to begin right away."

Philippa pressed her tongue hard against her front teeth. She had thought the conclusion to the matter so near, and here he was, bobbing about in purpose like a cork in the ocean. Another interested party? Was Mr. Asbury telling the truth, or was he hoping they would increase their offer of monthly rent? What would it take to convince him to show them favor? She and Aunt Dolly and the girls must find a place soon and remove themselves from the Haverlys' house. They had been a burden for long enough. She could not impose herself on her sister's family any longer, especially given that she and the Duchess of Haverly were only half sisters, and she was baseborn.

Charlotte had been kindness itself, never looking down on Philippa's illegitimacy. From the moment Charlotte had learned of her existence, she had welcomed Philippa into her home, rescuing her from her life as a high-fashion courtesan and treating her as if they were equals, though Charlotte was a duchess of the realm.

There was nothing Philippa wouldn't do for her sister, and that included removing her charity from Charlotte's house at the earliest opportunity.

Carriage wheels on gravel drew her attention. Glossy black paint, gleaming brightwork, the family crest on the door, pulled by two magnificent bays . . . Philippa's heart sank. The dowager had arrived. She had hoped to have procured the property before that particular wind gusted in.

Mr. Asbury blinked. "I thought you said Her Grace could not attend today."

"We were not certain if she could fit the appointment into her schedule. She has a very full social calendar. We are blessed to have her as one of our patrons." Philippa spoke the truth, though the dowager's involvement could be challenging at times. At least Philippa wasn't related to the woman like her sister Charlotte. Imagine having the dowager as one's mother-in-law. It took every bit of tact and patience Philippa possessed not to give the dowager a scold for her interfering, outspoken ways. Yet there was no doubt having such a high-ranking aristocrat as a partner in the charity was a boon.

Charlotte assured her often that though the dowager was dictatorial, she meant well. She harped because she cared.

The dowager must care a considerable amount.

Asbury hastened to beat the coachman to the carriage door and helped the dowager alight.

Her Grace took one look at the manor house and shuddered. "A bit of a hovel, isn't it? Though what else I expected, being so close to the prison, I don't know." She tugged at her gloves, appraising the gray stone of the front elevation. "Still, it will do, I suppose, if the inside is even remotely functional. One cannot hope for too much when one is getting a bargain."

Bite your tongue, Philippa Mary Cashel. Momentary satisfaction at confronting the dowager will not blot out the backlash. There must be no hint of discord between us, else the opportunity will slip away.

"Your Grace." Philippa smiled through tight lips. "May I present Mr. Asbury? He owns Reeding Manor and has not yet decided whether to allow us to rent the property." If the dowager tumbled in now and extirpated this offer with her high-in-the-instep ways, Philippa really would give in to temper, consequences notwithstanding.

"Well, are we going to wait in the sun until I'm faint from heat? Show me the property." The dowager leaned on her cane. "We cannot know if the place is suitable until I see it."

Those words epitomized the dowager's view on life. Nothing worth noting could happen unless she were a part of it and approved.

And yet, she *had* been helpful with the women they had brought into her house for training. Well, perhaps it was a stretch to call Haverly House or the country estate the *dowager's* property—they belonged to her son, the duke. She lived in the dower house on his estate and in his London house when they were in town for the Season. Still, it was her home, and she had opened it to the first students.

Her instruction to the ladies could be exacting and abrasive, but she held the students to the same high standard as would their future employers. They would not be accepted as rehabilitated and ready for the workforce unless they were willing to maintain the level of excellence required by the aristocracy. Trial by fire might describe the dowager's instructive methods.

Mr. Asbury sidled toward the manor, ushering the dowager. "I believe, though there are some repairs necessary, the house should suit your needs. Mrs. Stokes and Miss Cashel have been through the place, of course. I let them explore, not knowing you would be coming, else I would have waited and allowed you to be first."

Philippa caught Aunt Dolly's eye behind the dowager's head. This appointment would now take more than twice as long. Yet if Asbury was flattered by the dowager's attention and it resulted in him choosing them to occupy the property, Philippa would grab firm hold of her patience and go along.

The heavy, iron latch stuck, and Asbury put his shoulder against the front door to get it opened. The gouge in the floor showed how lax the hinges had become.

Their footsteps echoed in the entry hall, and Philippa looked to the gallery above, admiring how the dust motes floated in the shafts of sunlight coming through the oval windows high on the front facade.

"Humph. This dark woodwork is so out of fashion. I'd paint every bit of it white, and these plaster walls . . ." The dowager grimaced. "Perhaps some pale green or even yellow coloring would brighten this space."

Again, Philippa and Aunt Dolly locked eyes. Where did Her Grace think they would secure money to decorate? Essential repairs only would be the order of the day, as their budget was paper thin.

"I believe we should concentrate on beds, tables, and kitchenware to begin. Aesthetics will have to wait." Mrs. Stokes spoke gently but firmly. "There are some broken windows upstairs, and one or two places where the roof is leaking. Those areas must take priority over paint and wall coverings, I'm afraid."

"How long has the manor been empty?" The dowager ignored Aunt Dolly and spoke to Asbury. Another tactic of which she was fond—changing the subject when she heard something she didn't like.

"Coming on ten years. My father purchased it just before his death, with an eye to bringing it back to its former glory. After he passed, the house and grounds went unoccupied and uncared for."

"And how old is the original manor?"

"It was built around 1480. Though it's been added to and renovated several times through the centuries. This room was the first baronial hall. There are some stunning Tudor-era murals in the royal chamber, the oratory, and the book room. Of course, when the manor was built, the owners were Catholic, but the oratory was kept as a sort of storeroom when the Church of England was founded."

"The oratory would make a fine classroom," Philippa offered. "With desks in place of the benches."

"And you do not need to bother about a place to worship, as there is a church building on the property." Asbury patted his lapels as if he alone were the one who had thought to provide such a luxury. "When I first perused your prospectus, I did some investigating as to whether London truly needed more than one establishment for the reclamation of the fallen. After all, there is the Magdalen Hospital which has been in existence for half a century." Again, that speculating glance knifed Philippa's way. Judging eyes, remembering her history.

He could find nothing to cavil at in her current appearance. She never dressed to remind people of her past. For this encounter, she wore a fichu the dowager would be proud of, a long-sleeved navy spencer, and had her hair covered by a sensible straw bonnet, as chaste as any maiden walking with her chaperone in Hyde Park.

"That is true, and they are doing a fine work. Some of our policies and procedures will be based upon what has worked so well at the Magdalen." Though she wanted the freedom to structure the school in her own way, patterned after her own experiences rather than the strictures of a bunch of well-meaning but obtuse men who had no notion what it was like to live as she had and little clue how to help a woman such as she had been.

"Hmm, yes, but what I was saying is that a steady source of income for the Magdalen Hospital is their ticketed Sunday morning services. By charging admission, funds are raised to keep the place open. I would suggest you follow that example, and once the chapel is repaired and you are holding services, you charge admittance."

Philippa's stomach tightened. Charging people to attend church?

Was that even proper? One aspect of the Magdalen Hospital that Philippa wasn't keen on was that the "Magdalens," as they were called, sang in a choir on Sunday mornings as part of the church experience. Put on display to the public. Objects rather than people.

And Philippa had cause to know that women who made their way in the world as prostitutes had been objectified enough for a lifetime.

Asbury wasn't finished. "I have just the man in mind for the chapel services. I shall have to insist, as part of the rental agreement, that you use the services of my friend, Mr. Simon Todd. He's garnered quite a following recently as an ardent preacher, and in fact, was just appointed as one of the Prince Regent's personal chaplains. He will bring in crowds, which will bring in money. I owe him a great deal of gratitude. He helped counsel my son when he was struggling with some private matters and helped him see sense. I will do anything I can to advance the career of Mr. Todd. Having him associated with the school will help ensure you can cover the cost of your rent each month."

A celebrated preacher, and one favored by the Prince Regent? No, thank you. She would not be dictated to by this man, nor his lackey of a parson. But before Philippa could say anything, the dowager exclaimed, "How wonderful. I agree to those terms. Once we finish with the house tour, we can visit this chapel where Mr. Todd will speak."

Barging in where angels feared to tiptoe. Her modus operandi.

"Let us not be too hasty. The charity board for the school has yet to be formally assembled. Should not the board be the one to make such a decision?" Philippa tried to head the dowager off tactfully.

"If this Mr. Todd is good enough to advise the Prince Regent on spiritual matters, surely he's good enough for this new school." The dowager leaned on her cane, head tilted as if she doubted Philippa's ability to reason. There was a glint in her eye, however, that told Philippa she would not be dissuaded from her course.

Aunt Dolly put her hand on Philippa's arm, gently drawing her to the side. She whispered, "Let us not fight this battle here, in the territory of strangers. There will be time enough to go over everything we've learned today and make a sound assessment. If this is the location God has for us, He will make the way plain."

Philippa nodded, her lips pressed together to hold back the tide of frustration. Did God even take a personal interest in their lives? In her experience, God was remote at best. If He cared so much about people, why was there so much suffering in the world?

Was this how the leopards in the Tower Menagerie felt, crammed into a cage, itching to pace? Sir Bertrand Thorndike surveyed the tiny, cramped, dark room. Why did Haverly insist upon keeping this little bolt-hole, barely bigger than a closet, with no ventilation beyond a few patterned openings in the brick high in the wall? The duke owned one of the most beautiful houses in London, with a private meeting room on one of the upper floors. Yet he kept this box of an office, his secret meeting place as an agent for the Crown, hidden upstairs in a bookshop in St. James.

This room smelled of smoke, ink, paper, leather, and dust. The only illumination came from oil lamps and candles. The walls seemed to close in on Bertie every time he visited.

"Not three years ago, I sat in that very chair, getting yet another new assignment from my supervisor, but one that changed my entire life. It led me to Charlotte, to capturing a spy, and to the attention of the Prince Regent. You knew the former director, Sir Noel St. Claire?" Marcus, Duke of Haverly, leaned to the side in his desk chair, propping his elbow on the armrest and dropping his chin to his fist.

"I did know him, though I did not work with him myself. I was never high enough up the chain of command to receive orders personally from the director. I did not even know of this room until a few years ago." Bertie resisted the urge to lounge in the soft chair. Somehow, in this place, where so many crucial things were planned, where so much important information changed hands, and in the presence of his superior officer, he could not bring himself to relax. Though he and Haverly were friends, he was accustomed to the hierarchal nature of their relationship, both in society and in their work.

"It has its uses, though I could wish it was a bit less like a cell in the Tower of London." Marcus studied the aesthetic with a shrug. "Still, I could not bear to part with it, because it reminds me so strongly of Sir Noel and my early days as an agent."

Bertie would not have associated the duke with sentiment, but he supposed every man had his weakness. Bertie had long ago learned to steer clear of sentimentality. If one let one's heart become involved, one made poor decisions.

"Tristan and Melisande are in Brighton for a few more days, are they not? Have they sent word when they expect to return to town?"

"Within the week, though I do not have a specific day for their arrival."

"You've been a good mentor to Lady Juliette, but for the foreseeable future, I believe your niece and her parents will be better served if I do not send them on any missions. Your brother and his wife can concentrate on their daughter's nuptials, and Lady Juliette can focus on her newly betrothed and newly minted earl."

Bertie nodded, receiving the compliment on his mentorship. And he agreed with Marcus. His brother and sister-in-law had been away from their daughter far too much since Lady Juliette had returned from finishing school. She deserved their attention as she prepared for her wedding.

"So the Thorndikes will be heading to Worcestershire almost immediately, then?"

"Yes, the house will be in an uproar with packing and planning. They will be on the road within a fortnight." Bertie had long ago ceased to be surprised by the depth and breadth of Marcus's information network. The man seemed to collect and collate facts like a miser collected and counted coins.

"And you are not traveling with them?" Marcus asked. Though he posed the question as if he already knew the answer. Which he probably did.

"I am not. As you said, they need time to be together as a family, and honestly, I find the wedding talk tedious. They'll be detouring to Swann's new property to assess what they will need to make the house habitable. I've heard they're sending to Whitehaven for some of the earl's workforce to make improvements to the place. Whitelock's idea of training veterans as builders was brilliant, and Tristan wishes to make the renovations of Aylswood Manor a wedding present to his daughter and her soon-to-be husband."

"And as Juliette's uncle, do you have a wedding gift in mind?"

Bertie shook his head. "I told Melisande to take care of it, find something they either need or want, and let me know so I can reimburse her. As I said, I find all this wedding hubbub exhausting. For some unaccountable reason, before she left for Brighton, Juliette consulted me on place settings, stemware, linens, even items for her trousseau. And honestly, every charger and champagne glass looks identical to me, forks look like forks, and why on earth would I care which soup tureen she selects?" He threw his hands up. "Does she not understand I am a confirmed bachelor with neither the enthusiasm nor the expertise for which she's looking? I am a dilettante, and in the eyes of the *ton*, a sot. I cannot be bothered with wedding planning."

Marcus smiled, giving an understanding nod, and yet, a calculated, pensive look in his eye set off a tiny warning bell in Bertie's brain.

"You've been a good asset these past few years, especially as a member of your brother's team. Due to recent circumstances and your not inconsiderable abilities and talents, I believe it is time to give you more responsibility in the agency."

Bertie lifted his chin. Suddenly the room didn't seem quite as confining. More responsibility? He liked the sound of that. Bertie had often felt underutilized, but perhaps that would change now. He had been a cog in everyone else's wheels for a long time. Playing roles in other agents' missions, hiding behind his facade as a drunken cad. He felt as if he were a caterpillar kept too long in the cocoon, aching to break out. Was this perhaps his chance, at last?

"There are a few things I think we should change about your cover, however. With Tristan and Melisande out of action for the foreseeable future, I would like you to form and head your own team. I have a new mission in mind for you, which will require you to leave a different impression than half-sotted dilettante. But the new mission, which will wear a public front, cannot be the reason you leave your drinking habits behind. You will need an obvious motivation for such reform before we embark upon this mission."

Bertie's mind whirled like one of those new kaleidoscopes being sold in Vauxhall Gardens. What new mission? What public front would he assume with a hidden motive of spy work going on behind?

Marcus studied him, then said, "I can think of no better reason for cleaning up your bacchanalian ways than that you've found a love interest. Nothing like the love of a good woman to reform a man. People will believe that easily."

Bertie gaped, even as he shook his head. "With all due respect, Your Grace, no, thank you. I am heart-whole and free, and I intend to stay that way. Do not attempt to disrupt my contentment."

Haverly steepled his fingers, pressing them against his lips. Eyes sharp, he considered Bertie. "Are you? Heart-whole? Content? Or are you just wary? You've nursed a broken heart from a boyhood infatuation long enough."

Bertie's jaw hardened, and the muscles in his neck tensed. Yet he could not overreact, for that in and of itself would be telling. How did Marcus know any of this, something so far in the past? Bertie had locked away that part of his heart long before he had ever heard of Marcus Haverly or been introduced to the world of spies and agents. There were some things a man had the right to keep private, even from Haverly.

"If there ever was such a woman, it is, as you have said, so far in my youth as to no longer matter. It is only that I like being free." He trotted out all the reasons he had given Tristan and Melisande in the past when they tried matchmaking. "The work for the agency is both perilous and time consuming. I, more than most, am available for dangerous assignments, with only myself to consider. I cannot imagine the distraction having a wife and children to care for would be in the situations in which I have found myself. I would not like the burden of knowing at any moment my wife could become a widow, my children orphans."

"I appreciate your candor, though many men in your position manage both a family and the job. Give it some thought. As Sir Noel told me not so long ago, a wife gives a man a certain stability and can provide great cover for his more clandestine work. I, too, was skeptical at the time and resisted his suggestion to marry, but I have to say, he was right. My wife is an asset to my work, not a hindrance. Look at your own brother. Tristan is a much better agent because he has Melisande at his side. And they're passing their knowledge and abilities down to Juliette who will marry soon. You, yourself, have played more than a casual role in her training. She's the closest thing you have to a daughter, and yet, caring for her well-being has not compromised your ability to do your work."

"Juliette is an exceptional prospect, and now that Triss is going to remain in England for a spell, he can take over his daughter's training. I only stepped in because he was absent. And of course I am fond of her, but should I perish in the line of duty, her life would go on much the same because she has her parents and soon a husband to look after her."

"You think yourself so dispensable to them? I believe Lady Juliette would care very much should you disappear from her life." Marcus shrugged and flipped open a folder on his desk. "Give the search for a bride some thought. The mission I have in mind for you—a wife would be an excellent backdrop. 'Whoso findeth a wife findeth a good thing, and obtaineth favour of the Lord.' You'd be quite a catch on the Marriage Mart if you let it be known you were looking to set up your nursery. Knighted, from an aristocratic family, and wealthy enough in your own right. Yes, quite a coup for some matchmaking mama."

"What is this new mission?" A change of subject was called for here, and Bertie was frankly curious. What could Haverly possibly have for him to do that would require being sober and married? Surely not entering the clergy?

Marcus shook his head, his eyes tensing a bit, as if ordering his thoughts. "There are still plans and preparations to be made before I can reveal the nature of the assignment to you. Suffice it to say, a new team, headed by yourself, needs to be in place before you can begin this particular task. I would not ask you to change your life so radically if it were not important and if I did not think you would be the better for it."

Bertie frowned, but he knew not to press. Marcus would share the information when he felt the time was right, and pushing would only earn his displeasure.

"Now, about your new team. I had intended to put Daniel Swann under your tutelage, but his new role as supervisor of investigators at Bow Street means he will not be in a position to do much spying. He will still be a great asset, but I would prefer him to focus on the informational and criminal side than the espionage or diplomatic fronts. That and his new title and lands and bride will keep him occupied for some time."

Bertie cast about for who he would like to work with. He'd never had the luxury of choosing his colleagues. Would he have the opportunity now, or would Haverly already have them assembled? His contact with other agents had been limited to only a handful of men for the safety of all concerned. If one did not know the extent of the spy network, one could not be forced to or inadvertently divulge their identities.

"Of course," Marcus continued, "Juliette has been thrown into deep water right from the outset, and she deserves leave from spying responsibilities. In any case, she will, for the foreseeable future, be considered a member of her parents' team." He picked up a quill, dipped the nib in an inkwell, and wrote something on the bottom of one of the pages. "Therefore, I am going to make Mr. Partridge, my own right-hand man, your lieutenant. He's been a valuable part of my team, but with my increased administrative duties, I feel his considerable talents are being wasted. He's got a wealth of experience, great contacts, and he is absolutely fearless."

Bertie nodded. He had long admired the taciturn yet very effective Mr. Partridge. They would do well together.

"As to a third member, I do not wish you to make any snap judgments, but rather to *consider* this person. Do not reject out of hand."

Wariness crinkled Bertie's scalp.

"I'd like you to consider Pippa Cashel. Well, Philippa, as she now wishes to be known."

Bertie blinked. Pippa Cashel? Not long ago, she had been the most desired courtesan in London. How could she possibly be an effective team member when she was as recognizable as Sarah Siddons? Was Marcus tossing out her name because she was his wife's half sister and needed something with which to occupy her time now that she was no longer a lady of the night?

Marcus cleared his throat. "I know what you're thinking, but she provided valuable information for me on many an occasion. She was privy to the secrets of powerful men."

Uneasiness hitched up his windpipe. "But—" How did he put this delicately? She was Haverly's family after all. "That was in her former capacity, was it not? She has left that life, and therefore the access to those same powerful men. Isn't she fundraising for a charity hospital or reform school for women who are seeking to leave her former line of work?"

"She is, and yes, she no longer practices the particular profession that brought her those same sources. However, she is the best I have ever seen at detecting when someone is lying. She can read people better than anyone else, without exception. Anyone who can judge people as well as she can would be a valuable team member. And she's adept at disguise. She had the ability to become whatever her client wished, and she is remarkably skilled in hiding her own feelings. With a bit of training, she could be an excellent agent."

Bertie had encountered Miss Cashel a few times at various social events. She was stunningly beautiful, with a touch-me-not expression and watchful eyes. She reminded him, in her self-possession, of his sister-in-law, Melisande. Melisande was never discomposed and had mastered the art of putting people in their place with grace and ease.

Unlike Melisande, however, Miss Cashel's situation in society was tenuous. As a former courtesan, she had attended the opera, the theater, the symphony . . . but always in the capacity of a paid paramour. It was widely known she was the illegitimate daughter of the Earl of Tiptree, though unacknowledged by him. She had no entrance into society except that her half sister, the Duchess of Haverly, Charlotte, both acknowledged and invited Miss Cashel into her life. Miss Cashel currently resided at the Haverly mansion, attended various functions with her sister, and as a result, society, which would not dream of insulting the duchess, perforce had to accept her.

The duke waited for Bertie to respond. What could he say? Haverly was his supervisor and had the final say in the composition of Bertie's team. But if Bertie wasn't confident in his team members . . .

"I shall consider the matter as you have asked. Have you approached her about the possibility? Is she aware of what you do, or did you obtain your information from her in the past without her knowing the uses to which you might put it?"

"She only knew me as Hawk at first, my cover persona when I was in the field, but now, of course, she knows both identities. I once was a frequent visitor to King's Place where she worked, though never as a customer, only in my role as a spy." His mouth twisted wryly. "You can imagine the stramash when, early in our marriage, Charlotte found out I visited there, though she did accept my explanations eventually. I urge you to give the matter serious consideration. Once Miss Cashel gets this school up and running, she will have access to women who were like she once was, and the information they may be holding."

Marcus butted the papers on his desk together and stood, signaling Bertie that the meeting was over.

"There is a gathering at my home tonight, and I would appreciate your attendance. Nine o'clock. If there is time and opportunity, you may confer with Partridge. And possibly Miss Cashel, who will be there as well. Think over what I've said. I believe she would be an asset to your team. And cast about for some likely candidates for marriage. Seeking a bride would make an excellent, plausible reason for you to slow down on the drinking and start the transition to the role I am considering for you."

Bertie nodded, groped for the doorknob in the gloom, and slipped down the stairs into Hatchard's bookstore. The door to the sanctum was in a small cul-de-sac, and no one lingered nearby. Bertie moved the Wollstonecraft book from the top shelf to a lower one, to indicate to other agents who might come calling that there was no meeting in progress in the stuffy sanctum upstairs. Stepping out onto Piccadilly, he inhaled the light summer air, grateful for its freshness and warmth.

His own team. No longer in the shadow of his elder brother.

A new mission. Something that sounded quite ambitious and challenging, just what he had been longing for. But to give up the persona he had so carefully curated? What mission could possibly require that drastic a change?

The ludicrous notion of finding someone to marry aside, he looked forward to the challenge.

Chapter 2

Philippa's mind raced with ideas and hope, but her heart fluttered. So much effort had already gone into getting to this point, and yet, taking on that property would mean another tremendous amount of labor, money, and planning. But oh, the possibilities. What positive effects might they accomplish once they had the proper facilities?

Her thoughts and emotions swayed more than a tall case clock's pendulum.

They must concentrate on the essentials in the beginning. Bare necessities only. Though safety, warmth, and food would seem palatial to many of the girls they rescued.

The dowager, rocking across from Philippa in the carriage, had plans and schedules of her own. "The church is in utter disrepair. Until the new roof is complete and the ceiling retiled, the place is a hazard. It could take several weeks to finish. Until then, where do you propose holding services?" She stacked her hands atop her cane, and her mouth pinched like a miser's purse strings. Her puckered mouth hadn't stopped her though from commenting on every inch of the grounds, the problems they faced, and her displeasure at the prevarications of Mr. Asbury. "His dithering is irksome. The very idea that our charity may not be 'good enough' for his dilapidated property. I'm of a mind to ask Marcus to purchase the place outright, just to put an end to his hemming and hawing."

"Please do not, Your Grace. Marcus has been more than generous already. If we are to make this school work, it must be funded by others than just Marcus and Charlotte." Philippa could not burden them with such a responsibility, no matter how generous they were inclined to be. It wasn't as if she were legitimately Charlotte's sister. Charlotte may have accepted her as such, in spite of her past, but Philippa would not trade upon that relationship. She was well aware of the sidelong looks and whispers every time she accompanied Charlotte to a social event. She was tarnishing Charlotte's reputation, though she only went with her sister in order to speak with possible donors for the school. The sooner she moved out of the Haverlys' house, the better for them all.

"Once we have secured the property, we can set about implementing ways for the school to support itself—a dairy, a laundry, making goods to sell," Mrs. Stokes said. "We will not be as dependent upon donations once we are installed in a proper school."

The dowager nodded. "Not to mention the funds from the chapel services. I think Mr. Asbury had a good idea there. We can pattern ourselves after the Magdalen Hospital in that way." She touched her lace cap as her iron-gray curls bounced against her cheeks with the movement of the carriage. "I shall attend one of the Magdalen's services soon and make observations. I am certain I can improve upon their efforts." She tapped her cane with supreme confidence.

"I am of two minds about holding services at the school at all, much less inviting the public to pay to attend. It seems wrong." Philippa gripped her hands in her lap as the carriage crossed the Westminster Bridge. "Can our pupils not attend a local congregation without utilizing the chapel on the grounds for our own church? We must husband our resources and concentrate on the manor house repairs."

"What church would have you? I cannot imagine a local congregation would rejoice to have a score or more unfortunates filling the back pews. And Mr. Asbury seemed adamant that including this Mr. Todd would be a requirement to reaching an agreement on the lease."

The dowager's question about who would accept their students into a congregation flicked Philippa on the raw. It was true they would have to sit in the back of any church they attended, but to be considered unwelcome wholesale angered her. Wasn't the church meant for sinners? Didn't Christ come to heal the sick?

Who should cast the first stone?

But the dowager wasn't finished. "In any case, you will not be asking patrons to *pay to attend* services. They will be making a donation. In exchange, they will hear excellent preaching, beautiful music, and feel good about doing their bit for charity. Singing in a choir is a wonderful discipline to teach the students. How is accepting donations for a service different from hosting a fundraising concert or subscription dance?"

"There's a vast difference between a dance and church service. Church should be free to attend."

Not to mention the idea of putting the girls on display for all to see. It felt not unlike some of the *ton* who had visited the soldiers' hospitals just to gaze at the wounded during the war. No help, just gawking and whispering. Philippa would have hated that had she been one of those injured veterans.

She well knew what it felt like to be on display because of what had happened to you in life. Many men had taken her to the opera or theater to show her off with no care for her as a person.

The dowager sniffed. "If you can think of a better way to bring in funds, Miss Cashel, I am willing to listen, but it will take a great deal of money to keep the school operating. Food, firing, clothing, linens, supplies for the schoolroom, and materials for the vocations you are hoping to train them to do. The resources must come from somewhere. Perhaps if we had a steady stream of income guaranteed in the future—such as the donations from a weekly church service—we could ask Marcus to advance money to start and pay him back gradually as we have means."

Philippa winced. Truth be told, despite her best efforts at fundraising, only about a hundred pounds of what she had in reserve had come from someone other than Marcus and Charlotte. The goods and dairy products the school might be able to produce would not be enough to keep the larder supplied, much less any of the costs it would take to make the place habitable.

Still, charging admittance to church?

She was caught betwixt and between because subscriptions to the church service might be the only thing that kept them afloat. Not to mention that Asbury's preacher came with the lease. A man she had never met. How might he treat the type of women who needed his help? Was he compassionate? A dictator? More concerned with appearances or with souls? Or a lecher? He wouldn't be the first man of the cloth with lascivious motives.

She shook her head, dispelling such thoughts. He might be a perfectly upstanding gentleman. As much as she hated to be judged by someone who didn't know her, she should refrain from doing the same. Time enough to take his measure when she finally met him.

How had she gotten caught in a predicament where yet another man would have sway over even a part of her life?

"It will all work out to our satisfaction. I shall ensure it." The dowager was both as plain as a pikestaff to read and perplexing as a Chinese puzzle box. Half the time she acted as if they should be grateful that she would even consider helping with such a controversial charity, and the rest of the time, she acted as if she were the originator of the idea and should have sole charge of the endeavor.

Philippa helped the dowager up the steps to the Haverly's London house. The elderly woman had taken a tumble last autumn and broken her ankle, and it gave her trouble from time to time. Charlotte had speculated that the break had not healed well, but Philippa thought perhaps the dowager used the injury to her advantage.

The butler opened the black lacquered door, and Philippa was struck by the absolute chaos in the foyer. Boxes, bags, trunks, and people. So many people.

"Sophia!" The dowager gasped.

A slender young woman turned, removing her bonnet to expose her pretty brown hair. Pink rode her cheeks, and her eyes glowed. "Mother, you look so surprised. Surely you got my letter?" The woman came forward, arms outstretched, and pulled the dowager into a hug. With a laugh, she kissed the dowager on both cheeks. "You're looking well."

"As are you, Sophia. I received no missive from you. Are you certain you sent one? And is this cacophony strictly necessary? A street fair could hardly be more chaotic."

Sophia laughed. "I suppose I've become accustomed to it. Let me introduce you to everyone." She clapped her hands, and the movement stopped.

"Mother, these are our wards, Penny, Thea, and Betsy Pembroke. Girls, this is Her Grace, the Dowager Duchess of Haverly, my mother."

Penny, a girl of about sixteen with glossy brown hair, wide brown eyes, and a porcelain complexion lowered herself in a perfectly executed and graceful curtsy. The middle girl, Thea, with red, curling hair, a smattering of freckles, and an impish look, bobbed lightning-quick, her bright eyes missing nothing.

The littlest one, Betsy, a cuddly looking little beauty with wide blue eyes and brown hair, blinked, moved closer to stare up at the dowager, and reached out to take the old woman's hand. "Are you our grandmother?"

The dowager gasped and sputtered, and Lady Sophia laughed. "There is no sense in trying to remonstrate with Betsy. She adopts who she will. Darling, you may address her as Your Grace until given leave to do otherwise. Which I suspect will not take long under your charms." She cupped the child's head fondly.

A tall man with graying temples and a narrow face emerged from the study. He had a military bearing. This must be Charles Wyvern, Earl of Rothwell and Lady Sophia's husband, a former captain in the Royal Navy.

"Madam, a pleasure to see you again. We seem to have made landfall like an invading force of marines. I do apologize for the lack of discipline. We'll have everything shipshape in double time." He bowed to the dowager.

She sniffed. "I had no idea you were arriving today, else we would have been more prepared. It seems your missive indicating your plans has gone astray."

Charlotte hurried down the stairs as fast as her pregnancy would allow. "Actually, madam, I did receive their letter only yesterday, and I forgot to tell you. Sophie, the bedchambers are all arranged, though we'll be a bit cheek by jowl. Penny shall have your old room, and Thea and Betsy can share the nursery with Anthony. I've put you and Charles in the Bamboo Room. I know you will want to be close to Lady Richardson, so I've put Mamie in the Rose Room next door, and of course, the baby will be in the nursery under the care of our baby nurse."

Philippa's head whirled at all the people. She knew of Charles and Sophie, of course, and their baby boy, but three young girls, and a Lady Richardson? The Rothwell family was larger than she'd realized.

The dowager's face lit. "Where is the child? I am eager to meet him."

Betsy still held the dowager's hand, and she scrunched her shoulders. "His name is John Charles Marcus, but Mama calls him Johnny. He squawks a lot."

"Babies tend to do that." Sophie motioned toward the back of the entrance hall, and a woman with an age-lined face and a lace-trimmed apron and cap stepped forward, her arms cradling a blanket-wrapped bundle.

"I'll leave him with you, Lady Sophia, and go tend to Lady Richardson."

"Thank you, Mrs. Chapman. Mamie will be disconcerted being in a strange place. Thank you for accompanying us. She is always comforted by your familiar presence." Lady Sophia took the baby and turned to her mother. "This wee gentleman is Master Johnny." Sophie bent a maternal, loving gaze on his tiny face. "Johnny, this is your grandmother."

The dowager didn't take the child, but leaned on her cane, released her hand from Betsy's, and eased back the blanket to look at her grandson. "He is well? The birth went well?"

"Yes, we are both quite fit. I think the birth was harder on Charles than on either of us." Sophie sent a teasing glance at her husband.

Mrs. Stokes edged around the baggage and headed toward the back of the house, and as she went, Charlotte shook herself. "Where are my manners? Mrs. Stokes, wait." She made quick introductions, informing the Rothwells that Mrs. Stokes was a guest. "And this is Philippa, my sister."

Philippa found herself shaking hands, accepting hugs, and to her surprise, Betsy seemed to transfer her fascination from the dowager to herself. "You're very pretty. I like your dress."

"Thank you. I like your dress too," Philippa replied, all seriousness. She had little experience with children. Charlotte and Marcus had a young son, of course, but Philippa hardly saw him. He spent his days in the nursery, under the care of the baby nurse, or with Charlotte and Marcus in their private sitting room.

Colleen, a young girl Philippa had rescued off the streets in the Haymarket a few weeks ago, hurried through the entryway with a tray laden with tea and treats. She paused, meeting Philippa's eyes, uncertainty clouding her expression. She wore a house servant's uniform—somber black dress with pristine white apron and cap, from which a lock of her blonde hair escaped at her temple.

"Go ahead, Colleen. You're doing well." Philippa urged the girl, knowing she needed affirmation so early in her training.

The girl bobbed her head and eased through the drawing room door. The housekeeper must have started the tea tray first thing when the Rothwells arrived.

"Girls." Charlotte put her hand on Thea's shoulder. "Let's have tea and give the footmen an opportunity to get everyone's things to the correct rooms."

"Mama lets us have tea with her, but she said when we came here, we'd have to eat tea in the nursery." Thea crossed her arms and frowned.

Philippa studied her. The child was so skeptical, as if mistrusting everyone's motives. How had she come to be so suspicious? Philippa was accustomed to such looks from shrewd urchins who had to bring themselves up on the streets of London, but not from wards of earls.

Then she paused. Lady Rothwell had introduced the girls as her wards, but Thea had just referred to her as Mama.

It seemed that Charlotte was not the only Haverly to adopt strays and treat them as family.

Charlotte laughed and cupped Thea's cheek. "Sometimes, if the dowager is entertaining, you will take your tea in another room, but when it's just family, we'll eat together. As long as you mind your manners." She turned to Philippa. "How did the tour go? Is Mr. Asbury amenable to renting to you?"

Philippa shook her head and shrugged. "It will keep. Marcus has invited a few people over tonight for a meeting about it. I'll tell you more then. For now, enjoy your family. I'm going to change and go to Mrs. Bell's Milliner's Shop and check on Annie. She's been working there a week, and I want to satisfy myself that she's settled in well."

Charlotte nodded. "We'll talk about it tonight then, and I hope Annie is well."

So did Philippa. If so, perhaps she could mention the fact to Asbury, and he would see a "success" that might help sway him to favor their cause.

Bertie checked his timepiece. Two minutes to nine. He winced and hurried under the maples across Berkeley Square toward Haverly House. Being late might be fashionable for a ball or soiree, but not for a meeting called by the duke.

Haverly had not given specifics as to why he'd called the meeting, though this was not unusual for him. He never shared unnecessary details. If Bertie needed to know, he'd be told at the proper time.

Still, one couldn't help wondering.

Several carriages waited at the curb, and he threaded his way through them toward the steps.

If this meeting involved a new assignment, why were there so many other guests? Or was Charlotte entertaining in another part of the house? Haverly had not said it was a social event.

He checked his appearance, straightened his cravat, and knocked on the door, hoping he had worn the right attire for the occasion.

"Good evening, sir. This way." The butler was the picture of unemotional propriety.

They passed the drawing room door, and Bertie spied Charlotte and several guests, but the butler did not stop.

Typically, when Bertie called upon Haverly, he was led upstairs to a private meeting room, but this time, the butler guided him to the dining room. Dinner was over and the service had been cleared, but several people gathered around the table.

He noted those he knew and waited to be introduced to those he didn't. Of interest, Miss Philippa Cashel sat midway down the left side, serene and beautiful. And as remote and cold as Polaris.

Haverly really thought she would make a good member of his team? Trust was so important among agents. She was impossible to read. Was she trustworthy? Would he be willing to put his life in her hands? As she nodded his way with a single lifted brow, the question might more rightly be: Would she willingly put her life in his?

He brushed off the thoughts. It was certainly early days for that sort of thinking. She hadn't even agreed to be an agent as far as he knew. Perhaps he should consider her an occasional source of information. Would Haverly be satisfied with that?

"Good evening, Sir Bertrand. Please, come in." Marcus waved him to a seat directly across from Miss Cashel.

Introductions were quick, and Bertie took special care to note the names. At any time, Marcus could be setting him up on a case, and his quarry might be in this very room.

Sir David Button from the Bank of England and Mr. Moody, a solicitor from the firm of Coles, Franks & Moody. The Earl of Rothwell, Marcus's brother-in-law, completed the strangers to Bertie, and he assessed the man's lean face, sharp eyes, and naval bearing. Though dressed in civilian garb, Bertie could imagine the bicorn and shoulder epaulets. The dowager eyed Bertie sharply but said nothing. A woman he had met before, Mrs. Stokes, completed those assembled.

"We're awaiting the arrival of one more."

Odd. If this was about agency business, why have the women and the banker and lawyer? But if this was a social gathering, why the dining room? And why was Charlotte entertaining elsewhere? Marcus never did anything by accident, so there was a plan in there somewhere, but what? And how did it involve him? A footman placed a glass of wine before him, and out of habit, Bertie raised it to his lips.

He caught Marcus's eye at the same time the dowager gave her customary sniff of disapproval. He was supposed to be curtailing his pseudo drinking and changing his image. He took a sip of the sharp wine, rolling the tangy liquid over his tongue before returning his glass to the table.

The butler brought in another man. "Mr. Todd, Your Grace."

Bertie took in Geneva bands and somber black attire, thick chestnut hair, and the florid good looks of a man in his midforties. A clergyman?

"Good evening, Mr. Todd. Won't you sit down?"

"Most kind of you to invite me to your home, Your Grace." He bowed with a flourish and took the empty chair near the foot of the table. "Rothwell, so good to see you again. It has been many years."

The earl smiled and rose to shake the preacher's hand. "It has been many years since you were the chaplain aboard my ship. Civilian life seems to suit you. You are prospering, I hope?"

"I'm doing well. Just appointed to be a spiritual adviser to the Prince Regent, and he's given me free run of his library at Carlton House. A scholar's dream. You seem to have adapted to living on land as well."

Rothwell, as if suddenly aware that they were holding up the proceedings, indicated his chair. "We'll reminisce later. So good to see you."

Marcus rose, leaned forward, and rested his fingertips on the polished tabletop. "I have called you here tonight to invite you to join my duchess, myself, and my sister-in-law in forming a board of directors for a new charity hospital. We thought it best to select a panel with persons of varying talents and viewpoints, including legal, financial, spiritual, and practical abilities."

A charity hospital? Bertie refrained from rolling his eyes. This was the sort of thing his brother was invited to be part of, not himself. He was the dilettante bachelor. Even his knighthood had been conferred upon him as a bit of a favor, or so the *ton* assumed. In actuality, he had been knighted for services to the Crown, but those services were clandestine. But a man of charitable good works? That would undermine his reputation for certain.

If he wasn't careful, Marcus would turn him into a respectable citizen, a staid, sober, married man. He shuddered at the thought of becoming so . . . boring.

"Miss Cashel was able to tour a facility today that is suitable to our needs, and I would like her to describe what she saw." Marcus yielded the floor to his sister-in-law.

All eyes turned to Miss Cashel, and Bertie couldn't refrain from noting her regal bearing, the tilt of her chin, and, surprisingly, underneath all that beauty, a sharp intelligence that shone from her eyes. Intriguing.

He had always admired intelligent women who were more than ornamental, empty-headed chits obsessed with clothes and gossip and idle pursuits.

"The manor will need a thorough cleaning, and there are no furnishings in the place. There are some broken windows, and a few places where the roof is leaking. The cow byre and fowl house can be put to use almost immediately. There is a large brick oven as well, so perhaps we can take in local baking to help make ends meet. There are several opportunities for revenue that come with leasing the property. The church on the grounds is in the worst repair, with work needed to the roof and some of the ceiling masonry."

"However," the dowager broke in. "Once that is finished, we can sell tickets to the Sunday services like the Magdalen Hospital does, and we will have steady revenue to help support the school without having to solicit donations constantly."

Miss Cashel flinched and made a small noise in her throat.

"I don't mean sell tickets." The dowager backtracked. "I mean ask for donations from those who come to the services. The money raised will go to the upkeep of the school."

"An excellent idea." Mr. Todd nodded. "I've preached at the Magdalen several times, and I would like to offer my services for your, er, services." He grinned at his little joke.

Miss Cashel spread her hands—a gesture of frustration, perhaps? "I'm afraid the landlord, Mr. Asbury, has insisted upon that stipulation, Mr. Todd. If he leases us the property, you are to be the chaplain for our school."

The dowager sniffed and nodded, settling back in her chair as if quite pleased with the arrangement.

"I am truly honored. As you may know, the Prince Regent recently requested that I become his personal spiritual adviser, but that position does not require my constant presence at Carlton House. Might I ask if there is separate housing provided at the school for the chaplain? It is quite a drive from my current lodgings to the property, and I feel I will be needed there more often than in the city."

Marcus looked to Miss Cashel.

"Yes, there is a manse beside the chapel that will be made available for your use. It will need cleaning and furnishing. Again, this is all contingent upon Mr. Asbury looking favorably on our application."

Bertie sensed she would rather not have the added expense of preparing the preacher's home. He didn't blame her. Todd gave the impression of being entirely too impressed with his own importance, while also appearing humble and willing to serve. Twice he'd mentioned his new role for the Prince Regent. Of course, if he could make any headway in the spiritual life of His Highness, he'd have the gratitude of a nation.

Marcus had resumed his seat, and he leaned forward, drawing everyone's attention. "For tonight, I would like us to agree on the formation of the board of directors for the school. If you are willing to serve, when I call your name, please indicate so." Sir David, Mr. Moody, Mr. Todd, Miss Cashel, and the Earl of Rothwell along with Marcus all assented.

The dowager agreed, and Mrs. Stokes.

"Charlotte will also sit on the board, though her hostess duties have taken her away from the meeting tonight. Sir Bertrand?" Marcus asked.

Serving on a board of directors. He'd rather not. After all, what good could he be to a charity? This really was more of his brother's purview. And yet, how did he refuse the duke?

"Thank you, Your Grace. It will be my honor."

He caught a flash of something in Miss Cashel's dark brown eyes. Marcus had mentioned that she was unparalleled when it came to sizing people up, detecting the truths of their words. Did she sense his reluctance?

Of course not. He was a trained spy, used to schooling both his features and his voice. He smiled blandly at her across the table, and she looked away.

Exactly as he thought. She could not read him.

"Philippa, do you think Mr. Asbury will be convinced to rent us the property? Aside from Mr. Todd, did he have any other stipulations?" Marcus asked.

"He did. He is quite adamant that we must show a high success rate of rehabilitation and that at no time will there be any scandal associated with our school, staff, or the property under our care. If we violate those rules, the lease will be terminated, and we will be asked to vacate the manor immediately."

Mr. Moody tapped the table, his brows lowered. "Who decides if something qualifies as a scandal, and how will success in rehabilitation be determined? The language is vague. I would hesitate to sign any agreement that left such things to arbitrary interpretation."

Spoken like a true solicitor. Bertie nodded.

"I agree," Sir David said. "And do you have any language in the lease that speaks to the work and funds needed to bring the property into a habitable condition? Also, what happens if subsequent repairs are required? Who is responsible for maintaining the property?"

Miss Cashel frowned. "Marcus has the lease agreement. It was given me to look over. Perhaps those with experience in such matters can advise us?" She looked from the lawyer to the banker. "Mr. Asbury mentioned twice that he was unused to dealing with women in business matters, and wouldn't it be better to finalize things with a gentleman?"

Bertie winced. Her tone made it plain what she thought of someone treating her in that fashion.

Mr. Moody wasn't so foolish. "I will be happy to go over the contracts with you, and you may present our revisions to Mr. Asbury, Miss Cashel. I am at your service to attend that next meeting, but I am more than certain you can handle it on your own if you so choose."

She inclined her head to him, no doubt recognizing his tact.

"Let us comb through the lease agreement and come up with our own recommendations. Mr. Moody, you and Sir David would be amenable to helping Miss Cashel with that process?" Marcus asked.

"Yes, of course."

The dining room door opened, and the duchess entered, waving for the gentlemen to remain seated, even as they were halfway out of their chairs. She walked the length of the room, her dress swishing, and the slight bulge of her unborn child more noticeable than the last time Bertie had seen her. She bent to whisper in Marcus's ear.

His head came up, and he reached for her hand. "Ladies and gentlemen, I thank you for your willingness to serve with us in this worthy cause. We will need to meet frequently in the coming weeks, but I expect once things are up and running, our gatherings will be quarterly or as needed. For now, there is something to which I must attend, and I will have to bid you good night." He rose, keeping hold of his wife's fingers. "Philippa, if you could remain behind?"

Bertie took his time, pushing in his chair, letting others go before him. Before he left, he asked, "May I be of assistance in any way?"

"It is a private family matter. Thank you, Sir Bertrand. I will be in touch." Marcus tilted his head toward the door, and Bertie nodded.

As he settled his hat atop his head outside the front door, he blew out a sigh. He was now a member of a board of directors.

For a charity.

To rescue fallen women.

Tristan and Melisande would never believe it. He hardly believed it himself.

Philippa remained seated as Marcus had requested, reviewing the meeting in her mind as the guests filed from the room.

The charity now had a board of directors. While elated that things were rounding into form, it was a tad bittersweet that what she and Aunt Dolly had brought this far was now in the control of so many others. Though she had left the choosing of the members to Marcus and most were quite logical, she had to question the inclusion of Sir Bertrand Thorndike. The man was an idle lush. He had no power, no social standing beyond being the second son of an earl. Why would Marcus consider him an asset to the charity? Had he some special influence of which she was unaware? His name had certainly never come up when she had lived on King's Place, neither as a customer nor as an enemy of the women who worked there. His offer of assistance surprised her. Did he have more substance than he let on?

Charlotte, once they were alone in the dining room, reached for Marcus's hand. "I am sorry to interrupt your meeting, dear, but the messenger said there was no time to lose. He's suffered apoplexy."

"Do not fret, my love." Marcus touched her cheek. "We had nearly finished. I am only sorry that your father is unwell."

Philippa heard the news but could muster no sympathy. So their mutual father, the earl, had suffered apoplexy? The cold core of her being, ice that had formed there the day he had abandoned her and her mother to fend for themselves, shook.

"They've called for the physician, but the situation is dire. Mother says to come at once." Charlotte's face was drawn, the skin around her eyes tight as she leaned into her husband's caress.

"I will take you now if that is your wish," Marcus offered.

It pleased Philippa that Marcus was leaving the choice to attend the earl to Charlotte, not forcing her to go.

Charlotte crossed the ends of her shawl over her middle, hugging herself and her unborn child. "Mother seems to believe that if I desire to take my leave of him, I should not tarry." She turned to Philippa. "You will come as well, won't you?"

She blinked. "Me? Why would I want to see that man?" Why would Charlotte believe she would wish to ever see the earl again, especially in his opulent home, where he displayed all he had denied Philippa and her mother?

Charlotte's green eyes reproached her. "Pippa, I think he's dying."

"My attendance will not forestall that event and perhaps might hasten it." The frost in her voice surprised even herself, but she would not under any circumstances attend that man's deathbed. She owed him nothing and would not pretend a grief she did not feel.

"No, but for your own sake, you could go and make your peace with him." Charlotte lifted her hand, imploring. "Tis the reason I must go, though you know there was no love lost between my father and myself."

"Make your peace if you must, but there is no peace to be made on my behalf. It is you who has been summoned, not me. I cannot imagine he will wish me to attend. He made his feelings on the matter quite clear when he rejected my mother as his mistress and disowned any knowledge or care of me." He had ceased all support without warning, forcing them out of the home he kept them in for years. They had been cast out to fend for themselves however they could.

In her case, that meant the worst way possible.

Charlotte's lips trembled. "I know the hurt he caused, and I wish he had the heart to be ashamed of his actions as I am ashamed for him. I cannot excuse what he did to you. Will you not go for my sake? Will you not stand beside me while I take my leave of him? Marcus will go, and I will lean upon him, but you and I share this unique bond. We are sisters. Please? For me. Even if you do not wish to speak to him, I would appreciate your support while I do this."

Philippa considered her sister, remembering all Charlotte had done for her, how she had never condemned her as the by-blow that should not be named. Instead, with warmth and openness, even when it shocked society, Charlotte had brought her into her home. She, Philippa Cashel, illegitimate and a Cyprian, treated as the sister of a duchess.

Hadn't she told herself just today there was nothing she wouldn't do for Charlotte?

"I will go, but do not make me speak to him."

Marcus had the carriage brought round, and Philippa went to change into something suitably somber. Even as she returned to the foyer, she vacillated. Everything in her screamed "don't go!" She loathed that man for what he had done to her, to her late mother. She had sworn never to lay eyes upon him again.

Yet, for Charlotte, she would go.

When they were in the carriage, Philippa turned her face to the window, staring at the street lamps and houses whizzing by but not really seeing them.

Joseph Tiptree. The earl. The man who had segmented her life into three distinct parts.

Three days in her life, his presence loomed large. The first was on Pippa's eighth birthday. Her mother had hectored her father into taking her out for the day and treating her like a true daughter. Most of the time, when her father came to the house, he ignored Pippa, but for some reason of his own, this time, he had chosen to do as her mother asked.

It had been the best day of her life. A day she had relived many times in her memory.

It was the first day she had felt that he might possibly, just a tiny bit, love her.

It had also been the last.

He had taken her on a long carriage ride. At the time she had thought it grand, but now she knew he only wanted to get far away from where anyone he knew might see him and have questions about her. In the town of Richmond, they fed the ducks on the river, and then, on the market square, they watched a traveling acrobatic troupe perform. Her heart had been in her throat the whole time as they juggled flaming batons and balanced on a high rope. Her father had even indulged her by purchasing a little wooden man suspended on strings and slats, who flipped and twirled when she pressed the bottom of the toy together.

Then there was the sweet cake from a bakery and home again. Though he hadn't been exactly warm to her, he hadn't reprimanded her or pretended she didn't exist.

However, the moment they arrived back at the house, he had lifted her from the carriage and directed her to the door. He had left without a word to her or her mother, and when next she saw him, he was back to ignoring her.

That bit of attention had needed to suffice for a long time.

The second impactful day he'd had on her life was the day she realized she was an illegitimate child and that her mother was a kept woman. She was twelve, almost thirteen. Her mother had protected Pippa's little-girl heart from the truth. She thought her father was merely Mr. Joseph Tiptree. Her mother called her Pippa Tiptree and referred to herself as Mrs. Tiptree. But one day, Pippa overheard the neighbor women who were washing clothes in the courtyard by the well.

"That Cashel woman, putting on airs when she's no better than she ought to be. Imagine being a loose woman with a by-blow child and thinking she's better than us. Calling herself Mrs. Tiptree. I suppose we're lucky she doesn't go about calling herself a countess and expecting us to curtsy. She might be the kept woman of an earl, but Tiptree is just like any other man when it comes to his baser instincts, breaking his marriage vows before the ink is dry in the church records. If she thinks she can keep him forever, she's barmy."

"Not to mention the girl will most likely grow up to be no better. Amelia Cashel still thinks she can persuade the earl to acknowledge her daughter. Perhaps educate her and provide for her. Ha! She probably even thinks he'll find a match for the girl."

Their laughter at the absurdity of the notion had cut Pippa's heart.

She had run back into the house and spilled everything she had heard to her mother. That was when her mother explained their situation to her. The first seeds of hatred toward Joseph Tiptree were planted that day.

The last day that the earl loomed large in her life was not the day he abandoned them, cutting off his support for his mistress and his daughter, though that had been traumatic. No. That day paled in comparison to the worst day of her life, entirely caused by Earl Tiptree. The day when, hungry, cold, desperate, and without hope, Pippa had first sold herself to survive.

Her mother was ill; they were living in a wretched alley, filthy and starving. Though her mother had pleaded with her not to and had insisted she just let her die, Pippa had done what she felt she had to do. Sixteen years old. Horrified, terrified, and certain she was signing her own eternal damnation papers, she had crossed the line she could never uncross.

But the coin she had earned had bought them food, and a medicinal draught from the apothecary that had helped her mother.

From that night on, she had safeguarded a fierce hatred toward him, holding it deep in her heart, feeding it, nurturing it, ensuring it never waned.

Now she was on her way to the deathbed of the man who had fathered her, abandoned her, and ruined her.

As the carriage stopped at the curb, she wanted to leap out and run as fast as she could away from the memories, the pain, and above all, the shame she wore like a brand on her soul.

Marcus, ever the gentleman, helped them alight, and she wished she had worn a cloak or cape, something to wrap about her as a shield. But the night was soft and warm, and she wore only a spencer over her dress.

So this is where he lived—where Charlotte had lived when they came to London each season. A modest townhouse, narrow fronted in a row of similar structures. Charlotte had described a bit of her life growing up to Philippa, but mostly they avoided the subject.

Charlotte described her marriage to Marcus as her rescue from all she had suffered at their father's hand.

I'm glad you got away, and that you met someone who loves and cherishes you to a degree that makes me jealous. Not of Marcus himself, but that you've found such happiness.

Nothing like that would ever happen to Philippa. She, because of the life she had been forced into by the man who lay dying upstairs, would never be worthy of the love of a gentleman like Marcus Haverly. No man of quality would forgive her past. She would never be good enough.

Nor did she have the capacity to love. That part of her had been cauterized long ago. And a loveless marriage was beyond consideration. She would stay a spinster and stay free.

A chill rippled through her as she stepped over the threshold of the earl's house. The foyer had a reserved nature. Not ostentatious but clearly showing signs of wealth in the polished wood and carpeted steps. A maid led them up the staircase, and here, the trappings became more Spartan. A single candle burned on a table at the end of the hall, and no carpet covered the floor. Charlotte, in her description of the house, had mentioned that the ground floor rooms were for show but the rest of the abode displayed her father's parsimonious leanings. Nothing wasted, nothing unnecessary.

A man opened the bedroom door. "I'm Dr. Peters." His gray side-whiskers swooped outward from his face to an alarming degree, and on the end of his hooked nose, a pair of rectangular glasses perched as if preparing to leap to the floor.

"Is that you, Charlotte?" A woman's frail, warbling voice.

"Yes, Mother." Charlotte entered the room. "Tell me what happened."

Marcus and the doctor consulted in low tones, leaving Philippa to edge around the doorway. But she refused to look at the man in the bed. She concentrated on the woman, the Countess of Tiptree, Charlotte's mother. So many conflicting emotions crashed through her, she couldn't seem to grasp any particular one.

This is the woman who held the position Philippa's mother never could. This is a woman betrayed by her husband . . . and in a way by Philippa's mother too.

The countess had been forced to live with him, even knowing his philandering ways. She could not ignore the fact or pretend she didn't know because Philippa's mother, Amelia, had confronted her with the truth one day, in public, and quite loudly.

Mama, who had passed away last winter. Unmarried, unloved by anyone but her daughter, and with hardly a cent to her name. Philippa had tried to give her money when she was working as a courtesan, but Mama had refused it. Said she would rather die than live off her daughter's suffering.

It wasn't until Philippa escaped the life, thanks to the generosity and provision of her sister, and found a new raison d'être rescuing others out of her same situation, that Philippa's mother had allowed her to provide any support. A small place, food, clothes, and peace of mind. At least she had been able to make her mother's last months comfortable. Yet she knew the hard times that had befallen them, the privation, the cold, the worry, all caused by Joseph Tiptree's abandonment, had shortened her mother's life.

And now Philippa was here.

The countess dabbed her eyes, and Charlotte put her arm around her mother's narrow shoulders.

"This is my fault. I made him angry. Again. I brought the household accounts to him after dinner, and he queried every expense. Groceries, lamp oil, wages for the cook—everything cost too much, and he said I was going to put him into the poorhouse. I was so weary I forgot myself and said what I thought. I told him if he could do better, perhaps he should take over the running of the house."

Lady Tiptree raised her hand to her cheek, and even in the dimness of the room, Philippa noted the slight swelling under her eye. Many a time Philippa had worn that same mark, having been slapped by an angry man. A tiny bit of sympathy leaked out of her heart for the woman.

Charlotte's eyes met her husband's over her mother's bowed head, and the sorrow there kindled Philippa's anger anew.

"He threw the account book across the room, and then he froze. For a moment, I thought perhaps I was losing my senses, but then he grabbed his head, staggered, and fell to the floor." The countess demonstrated, plastering her palm to her hairline, smashing her lace cap against her curls.

The doctor cleared his throat. "I believe he's suffered apoplexy—bleeding in the brain. He was still on the floor when I arrived, and though he was somewhat conscious, he could not speak. He was in a great deal of pain, so I dosed him with laudanum. There are no menservants in the house, so I was forced to knock next door to get help carrying him upstairs."

Too tightfisted to keep a butler or valet or even a footman on staff. Probably because berating and bullying female employees was easier.

Charlotte assisted her mother to a chair.

Marcus went to his wife, taking her hand. Together they walked to the bedside. Philippa remained by the door, her feet like millstones. Charlotte stood beside the bed, and Marcus took up station behind her, his hands on her shoulders, no doubt trying to imbue her with his strength.

Charlotte had said she needed Philippa to accompany her, but in truth, she had everything she needed in Marcus.

If Philippa approached the bed, it would be alone, with no one to bolster her courage but herself. She felt the countess's eyes on her, and she turned her head to face whatever the woman might wish to express.

But her father's wife did not appear angry or shocked that Philippa was there. She seemed puzzled as to who she was. Philippa stepped a few inches into the room, emerging from the shadow cast by the door and allowing the weak candlelight to illuminate her face.

"You," the countess breathed. The whites of her eyes gleamed in the darkness as her shock showed.

She gathered her dignity about her, the armor she rarely let slip. *That's right. Me. Pippa Cashel.* She stopped short. No, not Pippa. Philippa.

She was no longer the helpless child, Pippa. She was a woman grown, a different person from the urchin abandoned by her father.

"Philippa is here at my request, Mother."

Charlotte beckoned her to the opposite side of the large bed.

No. No. No. I won't go over there. I have no desire to ever see that man again.

The candlelight flashed in the jade of Charlotte's eyes, and then Philippa caught Marcus's expression. With an infinitesimal movement, he raised his chin, his stare challenging her. Not a hint of pity or embarrassment. Only a request for courage.

And she realized he was giving her strength too.

A special man, Marcus Haverly.

Thick, green curtains—plain rather than brocade or velvet—hung from the bed's canopy, and Philippa slowly made her way over to stand next to one of the tall columns. Stomach knotted so hard it quivered, she forced herself to look at the man she hated.

He was propped on a bank of pillows, his face ashen, his mouth slack. Eyes half closed, insensible to those around him. His chest barely moved the sheet and coverlet as he breathed. She glanced at his hands, those hands she had watched so carefully lest they strike in anger. Hands she had feared.

They were lax, unresponsive, as if abandoned on the bed.

She had nothing to fear from him now. No abuse, no disdaining glances, nor the behavior that hurt the most, purposefully ignoring her existence.

The great Lord Tiptree, laid low.

Charlotte touched her father's shoulder through his cotton nightshirt. "Can he hear me?" she asked the physician who stood at the foot of the bed.

He shrugged. "It's possible, but we cannot be sure. Not enough is known about apoplexy. The symptoms and severity vary greatly. However, if there is something you wish to say, you should." His tone vibrated with finality.

She bent over him. "Father, it's Charlotte. I am sorry this has happened to you. If you can hear me, please know, I am sorry I was a trial to you at times as a girl. I want you to know I forgive you and bear you no ill will. I pray your soul is right with God and that, if it is your time, you will depart this world in peace."

Blinking rapidly, she stepped back, and Marcus pressed a white linen square into her hand, even as he drew her to his side, his arm around her shoulders.

They waited, Charlotte dabbing her eyes and looking at Philippa.

Speak now or forever hold your peace?

No words would come. Especially none of forgiveness or apology. She had nothing for which to apologize and certainly no forgiveness to impart. She would not lie nor pretend either, for she would choke on the attempt.

Her conscience niggled her to be charitable, but she stuffed it into silence. If charity began at home, it should have begun with him. She wasn't responsible for his being laid low. Perhaps it was God's judgment on him for his mean ways.

"Do you wish privacy to speak to him?" Charlotte finally asked when she said nothing.

With a slow shake of her head, Philippa turned away. She crossed the room, keeping her chin parallel with the floor, her shoulders straight, not hurrying but walking as she had so often walked through the vestibule of the Royal Opera House when on the arm of a gentleman—one who was paying for the privilege. Protecting herself with the armor of remoteness.

She did not look again at the countess, her father's lawful wife. Instead, with every step, she saw her own mother's dear face.

Chapter 3

BERTIE WHIPPED AROUND, SLINGING HIS knife at the sawdust-filled bag hanging from the rafter by a tatty rope. The knife blade struck true, but he had thrown it so often at the target that the burlap had weakened. The knife not only pierced the bag but cut through and clattered into the wall behind.

Sweat dripped from his temples, and he snatched a towel. He wore only his breeches and boots, having discarded his shirt an hour ago, before beginning his training. Lifting sandbags, pulling himself across a set of elevated bars, balance drills, knife skills . . . he had only the sword work to complete now. He took up his blade. *Lunge, parry, riposte, lunge, parry, riposte.* He practiced the movements over and over, working on his balance, his aim, his dexterity, switching hands and repeating the elements.

When his shoulders burned from the effort, he lowered the sword and rolled his head, loosening his neck.

Not a bad afternoon's work. Now to bathe, change, and head to White's for an evening's card playing and pseudo drinking. He hadn't visited the club in some time, and he wanted to catch up on the latest *on dits.* Gossiping at White's often gleaned more useful information than infiltrating an enemy nation's embassy.

An hour later, he checked his reflection, straightened his cravat and adjusted the points on his collar. Fairly dashing, if he did say so himself.

A commotion below caught his attention, and he looked away from the mirror.

Exiting his suite, he hurried down the hall and leaned over the banister to see into the foyer below.

Tristan, Melisande, and Juliette stood to the side, removing hats and bonnets as footmen carried their trunks and baggage into the house. Juliette spied him on the landing and hurried up the stairs.

"Uncle Bertie, you're looking well. Did you miss us?"

He gave her a quick embrace. "How was Brighton? Prinny show you a good time?"

She grimaced. "Too much food, too much drink, too much everything."

"Too much Daniel?" he teased, delighted when he caught a hint of color in her cheeks. Her darker complexion often hid her blushes, but he had become adept at both provoking them and detecting them.

"Never too much Daniel," she rallied. "The Prince Regent took quite an interest in him, showing Daniel off as if he had invented him . . . which I suppose, in a way, he did."

"How is our young man taking to his new role as Earl of Aylswood?"

"Bertie," Tristan called up the stairs. "Come and tell us what you've been up to while we were gone. We missed you in Brighton, didn't we, my dear?"

Bertie's elder brother slid his hand around his wife's waist, and together they moved into the salon.

Bertie offered his arm to his niece. "Shall we join them?" He mentally jettisoned his plans to go to his club.

"Yes, and to answer your question, Daniel is growing accustomed to being an earl, but it isn't natural to him. He has the most hilarious observations, which he whispers to me in situations where it would be improper to laugh, and I have to stifle my mirth. Then he gives me a look that says, 'Pull yourself together. I cannot take you anywhere.' And I am off again."

Bertie patted her hand, feeling a twinge. He had always been the one who could make Juliette laugh at inopportune moments.

Melisande, his lovely sister-in-law, sat in a Hepplewhite chair, letting her wrists hang limp on the arms. "I don't know what's more exhausting, keeping up with the Prince Regent's revelries or that awful, rutted road from Brighton to London. It does feel nice to stop moving and bouncing and just sit."

Juliette hugged Bertie's upper arm briefly before letting go. He stifled a wince. That was the arm in which he had received a bullet graze a few weeks ago, and though it had healed, it was still a fair bit tender.

"If you think that journey was long, consider our next. The miles to Pensax have to be covered sometime in the next fortnight." Tristan went to the table along the wall and leafed through the stack of correspondence his secretary had placed there. "I for one am eager to get to the estate. I've spent too long in the city and on missions and away from Heild House."

"The next fortnight?" Juliette asked. "What about the shopping? And the wedding preparations?"

"Do not fret, my dear." Tristan tossed down the letters. "Your mother has everything under control." He smiled fondly at his wife. "It should not surprise you that Melisande has made plans."

Bertie dropped onto a sofa, letting his head rest against the upholstery. He had exhausted his capacity for wedding talk long ago.

"And with my daughter's wedding well in hand, I believe it's high time I turned my plans to you, Bertie," Melisande said. Her dark eyes held humor and intent.

Bertie frowned. "What do you mean?"

"I believe it's beyond time for you to consider setting up your nursery. You've remained a bachelor for far too long." Melisande tilted her head.

"We've had this discussion. I have no intention of getting married. I refuse to have my work hampered and my life disrupted." He spoke firmly. Had Marcus discussed this topic with his family? Was that why she was bringing it up again now?

"Every bachelor says those things until they meet the right one. I want you to be happy, Bertie. I don't want you to miss out on the best things in life because you're so devoted to your work, or even worse because you can't be bothered to bestir yourself enough to look for a bride. If you let it be known you are in the market for a wife, you'd be nearly overrun with prospects."

He gave a mock shudder. "Who wants to be overrun? Melisande, I assure you, I am happy. I have been happy, I am happy, I will be happy as long as you keep out of my affairs. You and Juliette are caught up in a whirlwind of wedding preparation and think everyone else should be seeking romance as well." He could not think of anything more humiliating than having Melisande arrange a match for him. Talk about salt in an old wound.

Mr. Pultney entered the salon. "Sir Bertrand, there is a message for you." He held the card on a silver tray.

"Thank you, Pultney."

"Is the foyer cleared?" Tristan asked the butler. "All the luggage toted upstairs?"

"Yes, milord. And Cook has dinner preparations well under way. How many should I tell her?"

"Four, I should think. Unless Daniel will be attending?" he asked Juliette.

"No, he was going to Bow Street to check in with Mr. Beck." Juliette made a moue.

"Make it three for dinner." Bertie studied the card again. "I've been called away."

Tristan's head came up. "Business?"

"I'm being summoned to Carlton House." So much for a quiet evening.

Dusk was falling, and the lamplighters were out when Bertie arrived at the second-most prominent address in London.

Carlton House. The residence of the Prince Regent.

Bertie had never been inside, though a few weeks ago, his brother, sister-in-law, and niece had all attended a meeting there. Mr. Partridge met him at the lodge gate.

The burly agent sketched a quick bow. "Was told to wait for you here."

Partridge was a man of few words, but Marcus Haverly had complete trust in him. And now he was seconding Partridge to Bertie's new team. Did that mean Haverly had complete trust in Bertie, or that he was sending Partridge along as a minder?

Where was his usual confidence and sangfroid? Since being informed of his imminent promotion, Bertie had been dithering about his abilities in ways he hadn't since he was a schoolboy.

"Do we know why we've been summoned?" He tried to infuse his voice with command.

"Nay."

Bertie sized up their options. Should they present themselves at the front entrance or to be shown in the back? As he considered, a liveried footman descended the front steps and hurried toward them.

"Sir Bertrand Thorndike? His Highness is expecting you." The footman was perhaps three and twenty, and he wore a harried look, as if he had far more tasks than time. "This way, please."

The gold braid on his livery gleamed dully in the setting sun, and his stockings were flawlessly white. He strode ahead of them back to the front entrance of Carlton House, holding the door for them.

In the hall, if one could use such a pedestrian name for such a space, the arched and coffered ceiling soared above to a glass and ironwork dome. Ionic columns flanked every opening, and about an acre of marble stretched across the floor. Their footsteps echoed in the cathedral-like space. The footman did not pause to gawp as Bertie wanted to do. Though Bertie was quite accustomed to luxurious houses, this was far beyond his scope of experience.

Partridge seemed to take no notice, and yet, Bertie had reason to know of his observational skills. The man may appear disinterested, but later, if questioned, Partridge would recall every detail.

They crossed the hall into an octagonally shaped room which evidently had no function but to serve as a sort of vestibule. Light green walls, impossibly ornate ceilings, marble statues, and a chandelier that must have been assembled in the room, for it was far too large to have fit through any of the doors. To their right, a magnificent dual, curving staircase showed through a doorway, and ahead of them, yet another opulent room. Through the windows on the far side of this room, the gardens and lawns faded into dusk.

The footman stopped before a pair of pocket doors. On either side, two more men in livery stood at attention. Another man, in a dark coat and white linens, nodded to their escort. "Thank you, you are dismissed."

"Yes, sir." He bowed and turned away.

"Sir Bertrand? We were told to expect you and your"—he paused to inspect Mr. Partridge, who looked as out of place in the prince's residence as a tin cup at a tea party—"associate. I am Mr. Lingfield, secretary to His Royal Highness. If you will come with me, he's waiting." He nodded to the remaining footmen who opened the pocket doors.

Lamplight shone from a dozen or more wall sconces, and another massive chandelier reflected that light in a thousand or more crystals. Deep carpet muffled sound, and the entire room was awash in pink satin. Drapes, wall coverings, furnishings. Huge paintings in gilded frames covered much of the wall space, and marble statuary, decorated plinths and stands between every window.

On one particularly large sofa, the Prince Regent reclined, his right foot on a plump footstool.

Bertie had on occasion seen the prince before, but never to speak to him. The slightly bulging eyes, the large, fleshy lips, the well-padded features and frame were all familiar, though hardly as pronounced as in the caricatures by Gillray or Rowlandson.

When Mr. Lingfield bowed, Bertie did as well, catching from the corner of his eye Partridge following suit.

"Your Highness, Sir Bertrand has arrived."

The prince studied Bertie through skeptical eyes. A red, cracked flush covered his round cheeks, testament to his overindulgence in both food and drink.

"Leave us, Lingfield. I want privacy."

The prince waited until the man had bowed and retreated before speaking again. "I wanted Haverly himself, but he persuaded me that his presence in the house would draw too much attention. He's correct, of course. This situation must be handled discreetly. You are discreet, are you not? Haverly says you can keep your own counsel. Can you?"

"Yes, Your Highness." Bertie held his wrist with the opposite hand before him, trying to appear relaxed but not too informal in the presence of the regent.

"Haverly also says you're the best man for what I need. Are you?" He all but barked the question.

"Perhaps if I knew what your needs were, I could better judge," Bertie answered truthfully, with what he hoped was due reverence. The man was every bit as pompous, self-centered, and rude as he had been led to believe.

"Ha, a quick tongue, haven't you? I'll tell you, I'm sick. And angry. And tired. And in a considerable amount of pain. I do not need this aggravation in my life. I have too many responsibilities to be subject to this sort of mistreatment."

None of which gave Bertie even the slightest hint as to why he had been summoned.

"I have recently been in Brighton, arriving back in London only today. I find a few weeks at the seaside in late spring is good for my health."

Bertie shuddered to think what the man might suffer should he not have those few weeks, if this was him in better health.

"Before I left for the coast, I made a purchase. A parure of sapphires and pearls. Exquisite stones, and perfectly matched, lustrous pearls. It was to be a gift."

To whom would the prince gift expensive jewelry? Not to his wife, whom by all accounts he loathed and who was on the Continent at the moment. No, such a gift would most likely be for yet another of the prince's parade of mistresses.

"They were delivered here to Carlton House two days ago, received by my secretary. And now they are missing. Stolen. I want you to find them."

Bertie frowned. "Your Highness, with all due respect, do you not think this is a matter for the constabulary? Though the items are no doubt valuable, at its core, this is a simple theft, an action that does not fall under the purview of myself or Haverly."

Fire sparked in the regent's eyes. "I want this situation handled discreetly and rapidly. If Bow Street gets involved, it will be all over the newspapers in a trice. I am at a delicate stage in my negotiations for a trial to obtain a divorce from my wife, and public sentiment is already running well against me. I cannot see why the people wish to support that cow I married—she's a smelly, petulant tramp, but there you have it. There is no accounting for the behavior of the common man."

Bertie flicked a glance at Partridge, who stood as impassively as the Tower of London, but who slid his eyes sideways and quirked one eyebrow.

"You will take charge of this investigation. You will resolve it quickly, and there will be not one word of it breathed outside these walls, is that understood? Lingfield will assist you in questioning the staff and directing you through the house. I do not wish to be troubled by this matter unless or until you have found my jewels. I will then decide on punishment for the thief."

Though whoever was caught would deserve a fair trial, Bertie had no doubt that if the acting monarch wished the entire incident quashed and the culprit punished without due process of the law, it would happen. Bitterness coated his mouth. This lascivious fool made his skin crawl.

"Your Highness, we will do our best. It might be wise, however, to enlist the help of Lord Aylswood discreetly at Bow Street. He has considerable acumen when it comes to solving crimes, and you must know he is able to hold his own counsel."

"I have thought of that, however Lord Aylswood is soon to depart for his new estate, and he will be distracted by his forthcoming nuptials. If you cannot make any headway on the issue, you may consult, but I do not wish Aylswood to be unnecessarily burdened at this time."

Odd for the prince to be considerate of anyone else. He really must have been taken with Daniel during their time in Brighton. He had heard the prince was a man of whims and caprices. He showed a particular fondness for those he brought into the peerage for services rendered.

"Very well, Your Highness. We shall begin immediately. Perhaps we might have a word with Mr. Lingfield. But before we do, is there anyone in particular you suspect? Someone who might be capable of the theft or have a reason for it? Was anything else stolen or just the jewels?"

"Just the jewels. The case was found empty." He waved his hand to a polished wooden box with veneer inlays of seashells gracing the top. "Look for yourself. As to my suspicions . . . if I thought I had employed a thief, they would never have been allowed in the house. Of course I don't know who could do this. If I did, the man would be in Newgate Prison, regretting his life's decisions."

Gently, Bertie raised the lid on the box. Velvet-lined, it bore the imprint of the jewels it should contain. From his recent experience stealing an emerald parure—purely in the line of his work as an agent of the Crown and in time duly returned to its rightful owner—he could make out where the various pieces should rest. Earrings, brooch, bracelet, necklace. But there was one half-circlet he couldn't fill.

"What belongs here?"

"A tiara."

Of course. As if tiaras were as common as snuffboxes. Though to be fair, perhaps in the Prince Regent's world they were.

"Leave me now. I tire of this nonsense. I expect results quickly and privately." He flapped a pudgy hand, wincing as he readjusted his foot on the footrest. Bertie had heard the royal suffered from gout due to his overindulgence in wine and sweets. An agonizing ailment if what was told be true. No wonder he was short-tempered.

"Your Highness." Bertie bowed and backed a few paces before turning with Partridge. When they stood in the anteroom and the footmen had closed the doors once more and moved away, he looked at his new team member.

"Where should we start, sir?" Partridge asked, his voice low to keep inquisitive footmen from overhearing. Though why they should bother with secrecy puzzled Bertie. In all likelihood, there wasn't an employee in the house who didn't already know. Gossip spread like an epidemic amongst the staff in a big house. If the prince thought he could keep this quiet, he was in for a rude awakening.

"Let's find Mr. Lingfield." Bertie had little enthusiasm for this new task. This was a matter for the police, not a trained agent for the Crown. So the prince had lost a few baubles. From the ostentatious decor and size of this dwelling, he would hardly miss the expense.

The secretary awaited them in the atrium.

"Show us where the jewels were kept and tell us who had access to them."

By then, nightfall was upon them, and the corridors and rooms were shrouded in darkness. Mr. Lingfield motioned to a footman, who lifted a candelabra and carried it ahead of them up the curving staircase. They passed several servants, pages, footmen, and maids, lighting wall sconces, carrying linens, each stopping to lower their heads until the small cavalcade passed by.

"How many are employed here?" Bertie asked.

Mr. Lingfield shook his head. "It depends upon whether His Highness is in residence, what time of year it is, and if any special events are planned. On the night of a royal ball, there could be as many as two hundred working, from the lowly pages to the master d'hotel. There are several divisions of servants. The housekeeper is over the maids and laundresses and seamstresses, the chef oversees all the kitchen staff, and the butler has charge of the footmen and pages. Then there are the stable staff, the grooms, drivers, postilions, tigers. Not to mention those who are appointed and come as needed. The farrier, the dentist, the apothecary, and the chaplains. I suppose only the comptroller who pays the salaries would know exactly how many at a given time."

Discouragement at the massive suspect pool settled into Bertie's chest. He would have to narrow the list down and quickly.

Lingfield led them down a long corridor. He stopped at a door, motioning the footman to hold the candelabra high. "The case was placed in this room when it arrived from the jewelers. The clerk of the house and I both checked the contents of the case upon delivery. It was recorded in the clerk's ledger, and the bill sent down to the comptroller's office. The comptroller had the funds for the jewelry couriered to Rundell & Bridge on Ludgate Street. They are His Highness's preferred jewelers."

"Who has access to this room?" Bertie asked as they entered. Neat boxes lined shelves, cards in holders labeled the contents of drawers. More clothing than he'd seen in his lifetime, haberdashery, ranks of boots and shoes, powdered wigs on faceless stands, hats, linens, and cravats. The room was near to bursting with the Prince Regent's wardrobe. All organized, but plentiful to the extent of avarice.

"Many people, I'm afraid." Lingfield went to a long drawer on the left side of the room, skirting a plush, round ottoman covered in red velvet and upholstery buttons. Where the prince sat during his daily robing? "It takes many people to look after the prince's wardrobe. The valet, the seamstresses, the laundresses, maids of all work who come in to dust the shelves, the boot boys who polish the shoes. His Highness's equerry, his courtiers." He shrugged. "Any of twenty people come and go, not to mention the tailors and vendors who deliver new items constantly. His Highness demands personal service from his vendors and suppliers. No sending round a shop boy with a new waistcoat or stockings. It must be the proprietor himself. They are all directed to this room to make their deliveries. Though never left unsupervised." He pulled open the drawer.

The footman held the candelabra high, and the flames picked out gold, diamonds, and other precious stones. Rings, cravat pins, stick pins, cape chains, bejeweled daggers, medals on ribbons, watches, and chains. Nothing seemed out of place, and the only space left on the velvet bed was a square at the end that bore a faint imprint the size of the parure case.

"Why would the prince store the item here? There are no other women's jewels in the drawer." Did he not have a safe or strongbox for his more valuable items? Leaving them here was practically asking someone to take them.

"His Highness wished to gift them to someone upon his return to London, and he requested they be close to hand." Lingfield glanced at the footman and leaned toward Bertie. "His Highness has a new mistress, and the parure was a gift for her."

Bertie resisted rolling his eyes. If the gossip of years was to be believed, Carlton House saw a steady stream of mistresses for the prince. His Highness's disdain for his wife, the Princess of Wales, was no secret, nor apparently her dislike of him. Their daughter, Princess Charlotte, appeared to be the only bright spot in the marriage.

But Lingfield wasn't finished. "If you were to ask me who I thought would take the jewels, it would be Mrs. Una Bascome."

"The new mistress?"

"No. The new mistress is a Mrs. Frederica Wye." He shook his head, eyes round and serious. "Mrs. Bascome is the one he kicked out to bring the new one in."

"I take it she wasn't amenable to leaving?"

The footman made a sound in his throat.

"Do you have information?" Bertie asked him.

"His Highness sent instructions that she be put out of the house before his return from Brighton, so we gave her the word yesterday. I was tasked with carrying her things downstairs as the maids packed them, sir. Mrs. Bascome was carrying on something awful. Screaming, throwing things, using language that would surprise the devil. The last thing I heard her say was that she would make His Highness sorry. He'd regret tossing her out for another woman."

"And she had access to this room?"

"Yes, sir. I went downstairs with another trunk, but by the time I returned, she had run into this room and was tossing things about. She'd opened drawers, tipped over stands, and stomped on the things she had strewn on the floor." He shook his head, as if the memory dumbfounded him. "She could have taken the jewels and secreted them about her person or stuffed them into some of her baggage. It took two footmen to escort her out of the house, and that with considerable force. Harold received a black eye from her flailing elbows for his trouble, and her screams would break glass, they would. The room was in such a state, we did not notice the jewelry was missing until we began straightening the chaos."

Mrs. Una Bascome moved right to the top of Bertie's suspect list.

Pray the case was as simple as a spurned mistress looking for revenge.

Chapter 4

"I MERELY ASK YOU TO consider it, that's all."

Philippa regarded Marcus, trying to assess his level of intent. "I would not be an asset to any such team. I am no longer in that world and therefore no longer have access to the information I once passed along to you. And in any case, I must put my focus toward the charity. If Mr. Asbury agrees to lease us the property, I will be busy getting it ready for occupants. If he does not, then the search continues for another residence." Though no place she had looked at up till now would suit as well.

Neither he nor Charlotte had mentioned the visit to the Earl of Tiptree's bedchamber the evening before, nor had they chastised her for showing not a hint of forgiveness. The ordeal had so tired Charlotte that when she had taken her leave of the house, she had fallen asleep against Marcus's shoulder on the carriage ride home. Philippa had sat in stony silence, staring out the window, and had retreated to her room the moment they had returned to Berkeley Square.

Philippa had spent this day with Aunt Dolly, making lists and ideas, with occasional input from the dowager. Now that dinner had ended, she had commandeered the dining room table, her notes and lists for the school spread before her.

She forced herself not to think of her father, lying in bed, or possibly even now dying, and kept her mind focused on all the exciting prospects and potential of the somewhat run-down manor house she had viewed yesterday.

"I realize the school must have priority on your time, particularly in these early stages, but I'm asking you to consider joining Sir Bertrand's team on a limited basis at first. He has never led his own team before, and you could be helpful to him. Especially in your ability to sense when someone is lying. I always thought you would be a devastating card player. No one would be able to bluff you."

A bit of warmth feathered across her skin. All her life she had sought sincere praise, someone who valued her for herself and not what she represented or could give them, but rarely had she found it. Her father had nothing good to say about her, and her mother had nothing left for Philippa after lavishing her attention on the man who kept her. As for her former customers, they had flattered but with their own agenda, not because they saw or cared about the real Philippa.

But Marcus never pandered to her vanity. He spoke plainly, whether in approval or chastisement, a quality she had always appreciated in him. And she owed him so much, more than she could ever repay, because it was through his kindness to his wife that Philippa had been able to break free of the prison of her former life. Marcus had allowed Charlotte to give Philippa a safe haven, had encouraged her to follow her newfound passion in rescuing women, and had funded much of the enterprise to date.

"Perhaps if the school is in dire need of funds someday, I shall have to frequent the gambling clubs," she said dryly, then conceded. "I will consider the idea of working with Sir Bertrand on a limited basis, but I cannot commit fully until the school issue is settled."

She knew nothing about Sir Bertrand Thorndike other than his weakness for strong drink, and Marcus's suggestion puzzled her. "I have not often been around Sir Bertrand, but how can you give him a team to command when he cannot stay away from the liquor cabinet?"

"I'm certain if you spent time with him, you would see through his cover. What people perceive as drunkenness is but a ruse. If everyone thinks him an idle dilettante, they will not be as careful around him with their words. No one takes him seriously when they think him a lush, but he is truly the best agent I've ever trained. However, he is on the brink of a new mission, one I have been considering for some time that will require him to change his persona. He will have to give up the bottle act, though he is reluctant after spending so much time cultivating that role." Marcus stroked his chin in a way that said the wheels of his mind were turning.

An act? Sir Bertrand must be very good indeed at his pretense, for she had never suspected a sham. Perhaps he would be an interesting man to work with.

With, not for. She would never work for a man again.

But alongside?

Perhaps. In a limited capacity.

"Speaking of the school . . ." She would put off giving him an answer for now. "Your lady mother has an appointment with a builder tomorrow afternoon at the grounds to see about which repairs are vital and which can be held off until we have the funds. Mr. Todd is joining her, I understand."

"Even before Asbury agrees to the lease?"

"You know the dowager. When she is on a mission, nothing can deter her."

"You know I would be happy to bring my influence to bear with Mr. Asbury. We could have the papers signed by noon tomorrow." He crossed his arms and rolled his neck, signs she had come to recognize as fatigue.

"Thank you, but no. You have been more than generous already. If I'm to be taken seriously by the community, I must do this myself and not always be leaning on you and Charlotte. I must make my way in the world. As you and Charlotte and Mrs. Stokes have all said, if God is behind my efforts, things will fall into place. Mr. Asbury will let us the property, funds will come in to furnish and supply, and we will become well established."

"Do you not think that if God is behind your efforts, he might use the likes of Charlotte or myself to accomplish His will?"

"He has shown He is behind *your* efforts. It is now time for Him to prove He is behind mine." And if He did, and she worked hard enough, perhaps she could blot out some of the stains of her past and become more worthy of God's attention. Perhaps she could feel as if there was a hope of true forgiveness for all the bad she had done, the bad she had become.

Marcus let his arms drop. "You speak as if God cannot be behind both you and me, and as if He hadn't intertwined our paths for a purpose. Please know that I stand ready to help when you are ready. I will not act without your consent, as this is your undertaking, but if you should change your mind, I will do what I can to aid you."

She nodded her thanks, cherishing the assurance that he spoke truthfully, not because he wanted anything from her but because he cared. Marcus Haverly was one of the only truly good men she had ever met.

He took his leave so she could work, but so much had happened over the last couple of days and she had so much to consider that she couldn't concentrate on her lists and plans. She gave up and went to bed.

At the next day's breakfast, a quiet affair to which members of the household came and went, Philippa sipped a cup of chocolate, planning her day. She'd spent a restless night, waking frequently from dreams of being pursued through the city by a faceless man. Such dreams were a common occurrence for her, seeming to come after an emotional day. She was grateful to be alone at the moment to sort out her thoughts.

Marcus strode into the room, purposeful as always, and her brows rose. He was usually the first up and out of the house in the morning, and she had not expected to see him midmorning.

Sir Bertrand Thorndike followed him into the room.

Having been apprised of the true nature of Sir Bertrand's intoxicated bouts at society events, she now looked at him more closely. He showed no signs of dissipation or the aftereffects of such indulgences. His brown eyes were clear.

He sketched a bow in her direction. "Miss Cashel."

"Philippa, Sir Bertrand has come to ask your assistance."

She raised her brows. "Indeed? In what capacity?" She had told Marcus she would *think* about aiding Sir Bertrand from time to time, but this was a bit much to ask, a mere twelve hours after he'd proposed the notion.

Marcus went to the sideboard to pour himself a cup of tea while Sir Bertrand took the seat across from her at the table. "Tea? Or coffee?" Marcus asked.

"Nothing, thank you. Miss Cashel, Haverly has given an indication that you might consider playing a role on the team I'm heading for the agency."

"I told him I would consider it." She held herself composed, giving away nothing. It was the way she must treat all men, lest they labor under the gross misapprehension that she would be willing to give of herself as she had in the past. Too many times since she had left that life, she had been propositioned, even at society events. On one occasion at this very table, sotto voce, by a dinner guest one evening—an act guaranteed to have Marcus tossing his guest from the house, should she have told him. Nothing surprised her when it came to men's behavior, and she must always be on her guard.

"I had hoped to ease you into any work with me and my team, but a need has arisen in which I think you could be most helpful. Haverly says you can be trusted to keep your own counsel?"

She turned her cup in the saucer, looking into the milky-brown liquid. Then she looked him in the eyes. "I know more secrets than an alchemist."

His mouth twitched and a flash of humor went through his eyes. "I appreciate your candor. For the purposes of my current assignment, I will consider you a part of my team, and therefore I can inform you of the particulars. Last evening, I was called to Carlton House to investigate the theft of a pearl and sapphire parure from the Prince Regent's dressing room. I've barely begun to even get a complete list of who was present in the house at the time, much less question them, but we have reason to suspect his recently rejected paramour has taken the jewels. While Mr. Partridge, whom you know, is conducting a thorough search of Carlton House in case the jewels have been secreted somewhere inside by a staff member or guest until they could be removed safely, I am tasked with questioning said rejected paramour about the theft." He spread his hands on the table. "When I made my report to Haverly this morning, he suggested I take you with me to her new residence."

She looked to Marcus.

"As I said last night, you seem to know instinctively when someone is prevaricating. And, as a woman, this Mrs. Bascome might be more inclined to speak with you than with Sir Bertrand."

"Mrs. Una Bascome?" Philippa asked.

"Do you know her?" Sir Bertrand leaned forward.

"I know *of* her." Gossip in a brothel being what it was, many of the most sought-after courtesans were known to one another at least by reputation. "When I knew of her, she was not the prince's paramour, however." She appreciated that Sir Bertrand neither flinched nor showed undue interest in her speaking of paramours. Genteel women did not even acknowledge they knew of such things, much less allow the word to cross their lips.

"Would you accompany me—with a proper chaperone, of course—to her temporary residence? As Haverly says, she may be more willing to speak with you than me."

Was he asking her as a woman, as a former courtesan, or because Marcus thought her capable of sensing deception? Or all three?

She looked to Marcus, who held his teacup to his lips, his gaze steady. He wanted her to say yes. If he had asked her to go along with himself, she would not hesitate. But to go with Sir Bertrand, to be under his leadership? Rebellion at the notion dug in its heels.

"Who would be conducting the interview?"

Sir Bertrand blinked and leaned back. "I had supposed I would," he said slowly. "Did you think to?"

"I shall go with you, but I would like to ask Mrs. Bascome the questions. I would require you not to interfere or interrupt." Would he acquiesce to her terms? If he thought she would go as an ornament, they were off to a bad start and she would tell Marcus an association was not possible.

"May we discuss the nature of the questions you would ask while on the journey over?" he proposed.

"I am amenable to that."

"Very well, you will question Mrs. Bascome."

Philippa's stomach muscles eased. He had passed her first test. Perhaps they could work together harmoniously from time to time.

"Your terms are acceptable. We must go in the forenoon, as I have a very busy afternoon scheduled." She pushed her chair back, and both men rose courteously to their feet.

"I shall wait here for you to be ready, if you would like to go at once."

A hackney carriage waited at the curb when she had changed into visiting clothes. Sir Bertrand handed first her maid and then herself into the carriage before entering.

Her maid, Mary Rush, had been with her only a short while, having been admitted to their reformation program not a month ago. In that time, her coarseness had toned down a bit, and her rather flamboyant manners subdued, at least in company. She kept her eyes down, her hands folded in her lap, and made no overtures or even appeared to notice Sir Bertrand. Progress indeed.

Philippa had no desire to completely quash the personalities of the young ladies receiving training, but often they did require deportment lessons to learn what was and was not acceptable in polite society. Mary Rush was intelligent and eager to fit in. She was doing well, for she had no desire to go back to walking the streets.

"Where are we going?" Philippa asked. "To the townhouse in Clerkenwell?"

Sir Bertrand looked at her sharply. "You know of that place?"

"It is common knowledge in certain circles. The prince keeps a piedà-terre for his most recently rejected mistress. They're allowed to stay a few weeks until they find another residence or another man to keep them." And if what she had heard was true, one woman was shuffled out the back as the next went in the front door of the place.

He shook his head. "I am not doubting your word, only that I had no knowledge of the place myself until yesterday. Gossip being what it is at society functions, I would have thought someone would have mentioned it."

"I, too, am surprised, given the proclivity of the *ton* to indulge in *on dits*, especially about the prince's less savory behavior."

"Did you not want me to question Mrs. Bascome because you believe she would not talk to me, or that you will make a better fist of it than I can?" He did not seem upset, only curious.

What if I told you it was because I was testing you, to see if you would give me rein to operate how I wish?

"Perhaps it is because I can sympathize with Mrs. Bascome in a way you cannot fathom. She will be in a precarious frame of mind as well as position. She knows that the sand is running through the hourglass, and she will have to vacate the property soon. The prince set her up in the townhouse with servants and most likely an allowance for running the household. That all stops, probably at the end of this month. Unless His Highness was particularly generous, she will have little property or money of her own. Perhaps she will have trinkets or possessions she can sell to get funds, but that will depend upon how long she was the prince's mistress and whether he liked her well enough to lavish her with gifts. His typical pattern of behavior is to woo a new paramour with something extravagant, but once he is sure of her, those gifts taper off. I've heard he has even taken back items from a mistress when he's put her on the street."

Often Philippa awoke in a cold sweat, caught in a nightmare of memories. The very real fear of being turned out of her position in the house at King's Place and forced to once more live on the streets invaded her dreams. For too long she had been only one day—one whim of the owner's—away from being destitute.

"I wish to treat Mrs. Bascome gently. If she did take the jewels, part of the motive, other than revenge or jealousy, could be to provide for herself. Women in that life, at the end of the day, must rely upon themselves. No one else can be trusted." She folded her arms, looking out the carriage window.

Her maid, Miss Rush, had nodded at every statement. She, as a former kept woman, would know the jeopardy.

Philippa shook her head. Two former prostitutes in the company of a gentleman, going to call on another prostitute. The *ton* would never approve.

Sir Bertrand said nothing more until they arrived before the townhouse, one in a row of identical dwellings.

A wide-eyed housemaid answered their knock, showing them into a spacious but sparse sitting room. Several boxes and valises cluttered the foyer, testament to the speed with which Mrs. Bascome had been evicted from Carlton House.

Mary Rush remained on a bench beside the stairs in the foyer while Sir Bertrand and Philippa waited in the salon. In a moment, Mrs. Bascome joined them. Red rimmed her eyes, and her cheeks held a high color that had nothing to do with rouge. Philippa had expected her to be downcast and fretful, but instead, she was furious.

"Yes, what? Have you come from His Royal Pompousness to oust me from even this mean corner of his realm?" She bit off every word as if cracking each one in two as it came from her mouth.

"Not at all." Philippa smiled. "Please, we have come to ask a few questions, if you will indulge us."

"Questions about what? Who are you? Do I know you? And who is this man?" She scowled and crossed her arms. She wore a rather low-cut dress for this time of day, but perhaps she had no other clothing.

"My name is Philippa Cashel. This is Sir Bertrand Thorndike."

"Cashel?" She tilted her head. "From King's Place? I thought you were called Pippa." Suspicion coated her words, and she backed a step toward the door.

"I was once an occupant on King's Place, and I was once called by the pet name Pippa. My given name is Philippa. You may call me Miss Cashel, and I will call you Mrs. Bascome." She spoke with firm dignity. She would not shy from her past, but she would not apologize for it to this woman who was no better than she.

"And is this gent looking for some companionship? Is that why you brought him? He look after you, or do you want a fee for making the introduction? Are you a procurer now? Coming up in the world?"

Philippa's cheeks burned. "Sir Bertrand is not keeping me, nor is he looking to acquire a mistress. He is here in an official capacity for the Prince Regent."

At the mention of Prinny, Mrs. Bascome's jaw set. "I got nothing to say about him beyond he's a lying, treacherous weasel, and if he wasn't the heir, couldn't get a woman to look at him cross-eyed. Ugly, mean, fat old toad."

For having nothing to say about him, she certainly packed in plenty of words and sentiment.

"There is a set of jewelry missing from Carlton House, and we have come to rule you out as a suspect."

Her jaw slackened. "Missing jewelry? You mean stolen? And you think I had something to do with that? Isn't that a fine thing? Thrown out, and now accused of thievery?" Her lip quivered, and her face crumpled. She sagged onto the sofa.

Sir Bertrand stepped back, his brows rising at such a display of emotion.

But Una Bascome wasn't finished. "Why? Why would he do this? What did I do to displease him? If he tells people I stole from him, what defense will I have? I'll be thrown into prison or shipped to Botany Bay." Her descent from defiance to despair came with a wail as she buried her head on her arms on the back of the sofa. "Or hanged."

"Please, Mrs. Bascome, do not distress yourself. I said we had come to clear you of all suspicion. If you will but gather yourself and answer our questions, we will be on our way and leave you in peace." Philippa kept her voice kind but firm. If she indulged the hysterics they could go on. She had no idea if the woman was guilty of the theft or not, but if she said that, they would get no cooperation from her.

Their hostess lifted her damp face, blinking. Sir Bertrand stepped into the hall where the housemaid waited. "Perhaps you could fetch your mistress a cup of strong tea?"

Philippa inclined her head to him. Thoughtful for a man.

"Mrs. Bascome," she said. "You did not accompany the prince and his court to Brighton?"

"No," she shook her head, her ornately curled hair looking a bit worse for wear. "That's when I started to worry. He said I should remain at Carlton House, and when he was ready, he would send for me. Only he never did. And before he even returned, he had a missive delivered ordering me from the house. He no longer had an interest in me, to pack my things, and he would accommodate me here for a few weeks. I'm to find myself another patron. He gave me a coin purse with twenty pounds. Twenty pounds. After all I did for him, being at his beck and call night and day, pandering to his every whim—"

"Mrs. Bascome, please. Stay on the germane issue. Were you aware of a pearl and sapphire parure from Rundell & Bridge that arrived at Carlton House while His Highness was in Brighton?" She hoped she had that information, given her by Sir Bertrand in the carriage, correct.

"I saw it, and like a fool, I thought it might be for me. A peace offering for leaving me behind while he went to the seaside. Is that what's missing? He thinks I took it? Ha, I didn't, but good luck to whoever did. May they thoroughly enjoy the wealth that comes from them."

"Did you see where the clerk put the case in the house?"

"No. I never saw it after it was delivered, and even then I only chanced to see the clerk and Mr. Lingfield examining it with the jeweler. He likely put the set in the prince's dressing room or maybe kept them in his office below stairs. The clerk's office door looks out on the silver cleaning room and the silver storage room. He has a lockbox there where he keeps money for household needs. Seems a good place for them till the prince returned. I never said anything about seeing the jewels because I believed them to be a gift, and His Highness would wish me to be surprised by his generosity." Enough sarcasm dripped from her words to make Philippa taste their bitterness. "And all the time, they were intended for another woman."

"We were told you created quite a scene before you left Carlton House?" Sir Bertrand asked the first question, but obliquely.

Philippa frowned. He wasn't supposed to interfere.

"I did. I wasn't going to take being tossed aside lightly." A shadow passed over her face. She wasn't young, not past her prime, but near to being so. With broader hips, a generous bosom, and wide eyes, she favored the type of woman who had held the role of mistress to the Prince Regent, but other men might prefer someone younger with fewer encounters in their past. "I suppose I should have gone meekly. Perhaps if I hadn't been so caustic, there might be a chance he would turn to me again, once he is over his fancy for the new one."

Philippa wasn't surprised at the vacillation. Women who made their living as this one did—as she once had—were a maelstrom of emotions—self-loathing, anger, absurd hope, optimism, jaded philosophies. They could feel repugnance and longing in the same moment for the same man. Despising the ways he used her and yet yearning for some word of approval, some sign of genuine caring.

"When you threw your tantrum in the prince's dressing room, did you open the box with the pearls and sapphires?" Philippa asked.

"I didn't even know they were there. I certainly didn't see them when I stormed into the dressing room. I was in a fit of madness. I wanted to smash and break anything that belonged to him, but I would never steal. If I had found those jewels, I would have thrown them down and stomped on them, but I would not have taken them." She addressed her answer to Philippa, but her eyes slid to Sir Bertrand.

Philippa could detect no subterfuge in her words. Though all successful courtesans were practiced liars, they worked their wiles on men. They seldom bothered to lie to women, especially other courtesans.

She looked to Sir Bertrand and gave the merest shake of her head, the tiniest shrug. He stepped away from the fireplace where he had taken up station.

"Madam, I will have to search your belongings. You may be present or delegate one of your servants to be there." His tone brooked no argument.

"You would not dare. Go through my personal things?"

"Please, madam," Philippa said. "If we do not find the jewels in your possession, suspicion of you will reduce greatly. If you did not take them, you have nothing to fear. If you prefer, I would search your more intimate bags or trunks myself. If you resist at this point, Sir Bertrand will have no choice but to call in court officers and perhaps to remove you to Newgate to await a more thorough investigation."

Newgate, Coldbath Fields, even Retribution Hulk, the shipboard prison that sat moored in the Thames until a sufficient number of prisoners were collected for transportation to the Antipodes. Those names struck fear into the heart of every Cyprian, for the crime of prostitution was considered theirs and theirs alone, no blame falling on the men who procured their services.

Mrs. Bascome balled her hands into fists, arms straight, her frame shaking at the futility of her choices. "Very well, but only you may search through my things. I won't have a strange man riffling my belongings."

Philippa bit her tongue on the sarcastic thought that shot through her mind, and she did not make eye contact with Sir Bertrand.

With the help of Mary Rush and Mrs. Bascome's housemaid, Philippa searched every box, trunk, and drawer. She found several pieces of jewelry, but nothing of any great value and certainly not a parure worth many thousands of pounds.

When she had finished her search, she said, "Mrs. Bascome, I understand your current predicament. I want you to know that there is a better option than finding another man to keep you. I am opening a school to teach women skills to look after themselves. There would be a place for you, a place to learn, to be safe, to become your own woman making your own decisions about your life."

Mrs. Bascome laughed. "What skills could you possibly teach me? What do you expect me to do, become a milliner or a governess or a music teacher? Who would hire me, a woman with my past? I'm damaged goods, and you well know it."

It was an attitude Philippa came up against often amongst the jaded women she approached. One she understood all too well.

"Reformation is possible, you need only reach out for it. We try to educate women in a trade or skill that suits them, one that will allow them to either secure employment—with our references as to character—or begin a business of their own with which to support themselves. If you are brave enough, you will call upon me at Haverly House on Berkeley Square or later at the school itself, which will most likely be at a property in Southwark."

She took her leave, hoping her offer would be well received.

Chapter 5

"I MUST STOP AT CARLTON House to check in with my associate. Mr. Partridge will have concluded his search of the property last night and was to meet me there to go over his findings. No doubt he will have drawn some conclusions of his own." Bertie readjusted his hat and tugged on his gloves.

Miss Cashel had conducted herself well with the questioning, though her sympathetic approach wasn't one he would have chosen. However, she would know better than he how to handle someone like Mrs. Bascome. Just being in that house had discomfited him.

Miss Cashel was a curious puzzle. So remote, so cool, but with keen intelligence behind her lovely eyes. She could have stepped out of any masterwork painting, flawless skin, the perfect shape to her nose, high cheekbones, a soft curve to her neck.

A former courtesan. He hated to think of her in that situation, to know she had been used—and most likely abused—by powerful men, expected to please them, but having no real place, no standing in society. A pity.

"I will send the carriage on for you, to return you to Haverly's."

"Actually, I would prefer to visit Carlton House, if I may. I would like to check on two young maids who were recently placed there after completing their training." She addressed the carriage wall beyond his shoulder instead of looking him in the eye. He'd noticed that about her. There were no flitting or flirtatious glances. She either bored through him with her stare or avoided eye contact altogether.

"Certainly. I didn't realize you had any young ladies at Carlton House. How did that come about?"

"The housekeeper is an acquaintance of my friend and fellow reformer, Mrs. Stokes. The girls were originally in Mrs. Stokes's house on King's Place, rescued at a very young age. The Carlton housekeeper took the girls in as a favor and promised to look after them. Nell and Lydia. They're each about fourteen now, though they came to Mrs. Stokes five years ago. Before I knew her."

They must have been mere babies when Mrs. Stokes had manumitted them. He grimaced. How easy it was for people to ignore such tragedy, especially wealthy members of the *ton* who most likely could not imagine committing desperate acts in order to survive. He had his brother and sister-in-law, and his work as an agent to thank for his broader views. Tristan and Melisande were well known for inviting people from all walks of life to their dinner parties, and he had often posed as a dockworker or street thug or ostler in his work as an agent, bringing him into contact with other lifestyles and experiences than the second son of an earl would usually encounter.

He composed his thoughts, ordering them on the task ahead.

"We will enter through the gatehouse courtyard. I understand the housekeeper's sitting room and maid's dining room are close to the basement entrance." He reached into his pocket and withdrew a folded paper. "The prince's secretary gave me one of these. Imagine living in a house so large one needs to hand out maps." He pointed to the labeled rooms.

Once they were inside, the Carlton House housekeeper, Mrs. Evans, sent for the girls, and Mr. Partridge was retrieved from the footmen's dining room where he was sharing a meal with some of the men who had helped him search the residence.

"Will you be all right if I leave you here for a bit?" Bertie asked Miss Cashel.

"Certainly." She gave him a puzzled glance, as if his asking if she could look after herself was laughable. She had her arms around the girls' waists, and they appeared glad to see her, their thin faces wreathed in smiles. "We shall have a nice natter, and I will be here when you are ready to leave. With the housekeeper's permission, of course. I would not like to pull them away from their duties, but I wish to check on their welfare and their progress."

"Come into my sitting room. I'll have tea brought, and we'll chat." Mrs. Evans, though she had a severe countenance, had a kind, almost indulgent, voice.

As Bertie and Partridge walked up one of the many servant staircases to the first floor, Partridge, ever a man of few words, said, "Found something."

"The jewels?"

"No. But something curious." He led them to a small room off the prince's dressing room. There was a narrow bed in one corner, a wardrobe, and a table full of medicaments and lotions in glass jars. A truss hung from a peg on the wall, and clothes and hairbrushes, an assortment of snuffboxes, and other accoutrements sat on shelves.

"Whose room is this?" Bertie asked.

"Valet to the prince."

Which explained all the paraphernalia. The means to pamper His Royal Highness day or night.

Partridge went to the wardrobe, which, when opened, revealed well-tailored clothing but not royal garb. "The valet's things. But if you notice, the inside doesn't fit the outside." He moved aside the waistcoats and jackets and tapped on the back of the wardrobe. An odd hollow sound. With a quick movement Bertie didn't see, Partridge removed a false panel. "Take a look."

Four bottles of French wine, a silver candlestick, and at the bottom, a velvet pouch. Bertie picked it up, hearing the clink of metal. He opened the drawstring and tipped the contents into his hand. Seven guineas. A tidy sum, and more than a personal valet, even a valet to the Prince Regent, was likely to have in his possession.

"Did you question him?"

"Nay, thought you should do it. Didn't tell anyone I found it." He waited for Bertie to return the coins to the pouch and the pouch to the hiding place before he reinserted the panel and adjusted the clothes. "Might be a reasonable explanation. Might be he keeps this little cache for the prince. Doesn't have to run downstairs for wine or a coin if he needs it."

"How do you explain the household silver? Why would the prince need his valet to hide a candlestick, and a silver one at that?" Bertie asked.

Partridge rubbed his chin. "Mayhap you should ask. Found this hidey-hole late last night. Didn't consider it urgent as the jewels weren't there."

"I shall see if Mr. Lingfield can be present when I question the valet." Bertie studied the rather humble room. Wood floor with a strip of carpet down the middle. A single candle in a holder on the windowsill by the bed. A far step down from the opulence next door in the prince's chambers.

Bertie ran Mr. Lingfield to earth by inquiring of every footman he passed on his way to the basement. The prince's secretary was conferring with two men in what Bertie's house map said was the clerk's office. He glanced at a door marked Silver Scullery and another marked Silver Office—just as Mrs. Bascome had said, situated where the clerk could watch them at all times. She hadn't mentioned the door directly across from the clerk's office labeled Wine Storage.

Mr. Lingfield noticed them in the hallway and came out. "I didn't realize you were in the house, Sir Bertrand." He seemed shocked that Bertie should be in the basement. "I was going over some expenditures with the comptroller and the clerk. How may I be of service, and wouldn't you prefer to leave your man here and go upstairs where you will be more comfortable?"

If Lingfield knew of some of the places Bertie's work had taken him, dangerous, dark, filthy places, he wouldn't worry about Bertie being offended by servants' quarters now.

"There is no time. I need a word with you about one of the household staff. Is there somewhere nearby where we may speak in private?" He had no desire to go traipsing back through the labyrinth to some secretary's aerie three stories up.

Lingfield took them into the room marked Silver Office. A whale oil lamp hung from the ceiling, and the light revealed shelf after shelf of salvers, platters, ice buckets, tongs, tureens, and more, all in silver, all gleamingly bright.

The change in Lingfield was startling when Bertie informed him of the valet's hidden compartment. The secretary went from businesslike and cordial to irate, his face hard, his movements brisk. He stuck his head out of the Silver Office and shouted for a footman to fetch the valet. While they waited, he paced. "This is an outrage. There is no reason for those items to be in a hidden compartment in the valet's possession."

When the valet, a man about fifty with a hangdog expression arrived, he paused in the doorway. "You wanted me, Mr. Lingfield?"

"Indeed, I do. These individuals have made a thorough search of the house, including your quarters. They've made a most interesting discovery."

The valet swallowed, eyes wide, a sheen of sweat emerging on his brow.

"I can explain." His voice croaked.

The secretary towered over the valet. "What is the meaning of this? Stealing from His Highness? When he gives you everything you could ask." His voice boomed off the metal around them and no doubt carried down several halls. "His Highness will see you swing on the gallows!"

The valet flinched, and his back straightened. He'd been caught red-handed and must have felt he had nothing left to lose. "Everything I could ask? You must be quizzing me. He never thinks of a soul except himself, and well you know it. Serves him right to lose a few light things he'd never miss in a month of Sundays. A little wine, a few coins."

"A silver candlestick?" Lingfield said, his voice silky with anger.

"You reported that candelabra damaged. You took it to the silversmith's yourself."

"No damage. Just found a fellow who would exchange it for silver plate." The valet sneered.

This was getting Bertie nowhere in his own investigation. "Sir, did you steal the pearl and sapphire jewel set?" he asked.

"What receiver's shop would take that from the likes of me? I'd be in Newgate before the coins hit the bottom of my pocket. I only took what I could fence easy. Man would be a fool to steal something as unique as those jewels."

Which begged the question as to who would and could steal the jewels? Where might they sell them?

Bertie caught Partridge's eye and motioned toward the door.

Before Lingfield could berate the man further, Bertie said, "We'll take our leave. This is clearly a matter between you and a staff member. We'll see ourselves out."

In the hall, they could not help but overhear the shouting.

"Valet's right. If the thief got the jewels out of the house, they're probably dismantled and being sold individually." Partridge rubbed the back of his neck. "Worth more as a set, but risky to sell as such."

"If it's broken down, it will be harder to track."

"What do you want me to do now?"

"Go collect the stolen items from the wardrobe, then when Lingfield's finished, escort the valet to a magistrate and then on to Newgate if necessary. Start canvassing the receivers' shops and jewelers. I'll speak with Haverly so he can tell his network to watch for anything suspicious that might tie into our case. Especially any fine sapphires or pearls individually coming on the market."

"Aye, guv. Where do you want me to report? Your brother's house? The duke's?"

"My brother's place." Hmm, perhaps, if he was now to lead his own team, he really should give some thought to acquiring his own residence in the city. Rented rooms would not do. Too conspicuous as to the comings and goings of his team. A house. Yes, that would be the ticket. "Give Pultney, the butler, the password, and he'll show you to the War Room. Tell him, 'the White Horse.'" The pub in his hometown of Pensax, a place Bertie had whiled away many an evening in his youth.

The first time he had seen Melisande, he had been standing on the mounting block outside the pub, preparing to seat his hunter, jesting with his older brother who was already astride his horse. Melisande had been stepping out of a coach.

A woman to take one's breath away, and his young, impressionable heart would have been hers for the asking in that moment.

Less than three months later, she had become his sister-in-law.

He shook his head, rueful at the memory. What a callow lad he'd been all those years ago.

"I will see you tonight. After ten." Bertie did not know if his family had dinner plans, but he could get away if he needed to. For now, he must retrieve Miss Cashel and go to Bow Street.

He found her and the girls and the housekeeper, Mrs. Evans, seated pleasantly together in the housekeeper's sitting room. A spacious area, with a fireplace, small dining table, and a bank of cupboards.

"Was that shouting I heard?" Mrs. Evans asked.

"Yes, I'm afraid so. There seems to be a bit of a row going on between Mr. Lingfield and one of the servants." Bertie sent an "are you ready to depart" look at Miss Cashel, but his attention was drawn away by the two girls, who stiffened and looked at one another.

"What is it?" Miss Cashel asked them.

Mrs. Evans, who had begun worrying the hem of her apron, answered. "Mr. Lingfield has a terrible temper, and when he gets riled, he takes it out on the entire household. He's good at his job, for it isn't easy managing His Royal Highness's affairs, but he has a sharp tongue, and he isn't above striking someone who displeases him."

Bertie frowned. It was one thing to be a bit of a tyrant verbally, but to strike out in anger?

The housekeeper rested her fingertips on her cheek. "He won't be pleasant to encounter if there truly is a problem with one of the staff."

The girls nodded. One with light brown hair, one with dark, dressed in navy fabric, with white aprons. Bertie had no notion as to the duties they performed, but he was grateful the little mites were no longer on the streets.

Miss Cashel, who sat between them, again put her arms about their waists. "You are both doing well, if Mrs. Evans is to be believed, and I am proud of you. I cannot wait to report back to Mrs. Stokes. Continue in your work and listen and learn everything you can. Before you know it, you'll be out of the scullery and perhaps working above stairs."

Seeing the hope in the girls' eyes caught Bertie by surprise, but he suppressed the emotion, reminding himself that he wasn't concerned about such things as maids in the Prince Regent's household. They were fed, clothed, making honest money. He needn't worry about them.

Yet, how low had their lives been that they considered a promotion to a chambermaid a windfall?

Though she had spoken favorably to the girls, it seemed Miss Cashel had other ideas out of their hearing. As they trundled along in the hackney, her maid silent beside her, she said, "I wish I could find another household for those girls. The prince is a terrible example for them, so interested in his own appetites, and Mr. Lingfield clearly frightens them. Mrs. Evans herself seemed cowed by his temper. I wonder if he slaps employees regularly."

"Is there another place for them?" His brother had recently taken in a boy, rescued by Daniel and Juliette in Daniel's most recent investigation. Was there room for the girls at the townhouse or on the estate?

"Not at the moment." She pinched her lower lip, her eyes pensive, staring out the carriage window.

He reminded himself again that they were not his concern. He had no say in whom his brother hired, nor should he be clouding his mind with anything other than finding the prince's jewels.

He stirred himself, putting some heart into his voice. "They're hardly likely to encounter the prince, working in the scullery, and I believe if it came down to a choice, Mrs. Evans would protect them from anything

Mr. Lingfield might rain down. We caught Lingfield off guard with the information we uncovered in our search for the jewels, and he reacted. I'm sure, once the offender is removed from the house, things will return to normal."

Bertie turned his leads over in his mind. The jewels hadn't been discovered in the house, and the spurned mistress seemed an unlikely culprit now. "Anyway, isn't it good advertising for the success of your school to have placed two girls in a royal household? That should satisfy Mr. Asbury as to the worth of your efforts."

She seemed to consider this, but an indentation between her brows told him she was still concerned.

But he should not be, at least not about those girls. He had an investigation to complete, jewels to find, and a future monarch to placate. Enough to be going on with.

"Ah, Philippa, just in time. You have guests." Charlotte met her in the foyer. "There have been some developments."

Philippa did a quick gallop around her mental calendar. She hadn't missed an appointment. She was not expecting callers.

Charlotte's eyes bore a bit of strain. Worrying about their father? Though the physician had not been hopeful when they had visited, the earl continued to linger. Philippa removed her gloves and hat. Were the visitors bringing news that he had finally expired? But if so, why would Charlotte refer to them as Philippa's guests?

"Is it the earl?" Did she want to know? She'd shoved thoughts of her father to the back of her mind, where he deserved to be.

"My goodness, no. There's been no change there. It's Mr. Asbury and Mr. Todd." Charlotte tucked a blonde curl behind her ear. "They've brought paperwork. Marcus is with them, and he's sent for Mr. Moody. They want to lease you the school, and Marcus wants your solicitor to be present." She smiled, though a shadow remained in her eyes.

A surge of hope burst through Philippa's heart. "Is Mrs. Stokes here?" Aunt Dolly should be present for this. "I won't bother to change." If her dress was fine enough for Carlton House—even if just visiting the servants' areas—it would do for a meeting with a landlord and a preacher.

"Mrs. Stokes is in there with everyone." Charlotte squeezed her hand. "I'm very happy for you, Pippa. Though I will be sad to see you move to the school. I've truly enjoyed having you here." She turned to go up the stairs, and Philippa stopped her.

"You're coming into the salon, are you not? It would not seem right for you to not be there after all you've done for me . . . and the charity."

Again, the smile transformed her sister's face. "I would be honored." She looped her arm through Philippa's.

The men rose at their entrance, and Philippa caught the glint in Marcus's eye. He nodded fractionally and gestured to the settee beside him for Charlotte.

"Ah, Miss Cashel, I apologize for calling unannounced, but I am leaving London for several weeks, and I wanted to formalize our arrangement." Mr. Asbury sketched a bow.

Before he could resume his seat, the dowager arrived like a ship in full sail. Her cane rested in the crook of her elbow, and she brought it down on the carpet with a thud. "Why did no one tell me we had guests? I wanted to be present at such a momentous occasion."

She stared from one face to the next, finally lighting on Philippa's.

When you move to the new school, she will not be underfoot each day. Keep that in mind. Philippa fought the sinking feeling in her chest. The dowager would dominate the proceedings as only she could. Unless Marcus quelled her.

A clattering in the hall announced the arrival of Mr. Moody. He bustled into the room with a footman in his wake, shedding his hat and walking stick as he went. Philippa marveled again at the respect Marcus Haverly commanded. The world was divided into two types of people, it seemed. Those who made appointments to see solicitors and those to whom solicitors came at a beckon.

"Your Grace. I made all haste." He surveyed the room.

There were too many people here, her instincts told her. How could she control the situation when there were so many individuals here to put their oars in? The dowager and the reverend, in particular, were unnecessary to the proceedings.

Why had Mr. Todd come? His role in the school was yet to be determined, and if Philippa had her way, he would have none. If she must accept his presence in order to obtain the lease, she would do it, but not forever. There must be language in the document that would provide for a parting of the ways. She did not intend to be saddled interminably with his presence, especially as she had no notion of how he would treat her girls. Would he breathe fire and brimstone, ladening them with guilt too heavy to carry? Or would he be too lenient, not requiring true change?

Though she had no reason to distrust him, she was wary. Preachers varied widely in temperament and abilities, in her experience.

Philippa gripped her friend and mentor's hand. This had been Dorothy Stokes's dream longer than it had been hers.

"I'm so glad this day has arrived." It was Mr. Todd who spoke. "When Micah Asbury informed me of your organization and the role I might play in helping, I was flattered and eager to join you."

I imagine you were. A soft place for any preacher to land, with free room and board. But why are you speaking when you should have no say in the proceedings here?

"Micah conferred with me on the lease agreement, and I think you will find the terms are very generous. I insisted upon that, as I know what a struggle the first few months, and possibly years, will be. Of course—and I may be flattering myself here—but I believe once we are able to begin church services, donations will flood in." He smoothed his waistcoat front.

"Of course, Simon." Mr. Asbury nodded. "That was my thinking too. And I will admit, quite influential in my coming down on the side of the ladies' reformatory school over the other petitioner. It is most important to me that this property be put to good use, a use that will honor God and better our society."

Suddenly we're good enough for you? Philippa's fingers tightened. Had the reverend that much sway over Asbury, or had Marcus been at work in the background?

Marcus's face gave nothing away, but then again, he was a master at secrets.

"Perhaps we could see the documents?" Mr. Moody asked. He had set up station at the desk against the wall, his quill and inkwell at the ready.

"It's a standard lease, for a term of five years." Asbury handed over the pages. "Five years should be long enough to determine whether your charity will make a go of an independent school."

Five years. Philippa had never had the luxury of planning anything five years in advance. Her whole life had been day to day, week to week, trying to avoid looking too far down the road. A woman in her former way of life, if she lasted long, had a terrible spiral of descent to look forward to, so most didn't, preferring to live only in the present.

Five years. The prospect both terrified and thrilled her.

Mr. Moody read the pages silently, slowly, carefully, and while the wait was tedious and a bit awkward, Philippa was grateful that he took his time. She wanted no surprises leaping out at the wrong moment. The dowager filled the time conversing with the reverend, drawing out of him, and not at all reluctantly, about his position as spiritual adviser to the Prince Regent.

It appeared, like most men, the reverend had little difficulty talking about himself.

The solicitor looked up as he finished the last page. "A few salient points?"

Asbury blinked. "Yes?"

"On behalf of my client, I, along with the dowager and Mr. Todd, have inspected the property, taking with us an architect, Mr. Isaiah Hoffman. He is of the opinion that while the manor house and most of the outbuildings are structurally sound, the chapel itself needs considerable repairs before it will be safe for occupation. Nowhere in this document does it say who is responsible for those repairs. If you are making it a condition"—he flipped back to a previous page—"that the school employ Mr. Simon Todd and hold regular services in the chapel, it seems only appropriate that you, sir, are responsible for making that chapel usable."

Asbury's mouth dropped open. "I do not believe that should be the case. It is in the agreement that the lessee is responsible for all repairs and updates to the property."

Her heart sank. If that was unchangeable, they would not be able to take on the lease. It was one thing to make the manor house serviceable. They could scrimp and get by, but the chapel was a hazard. She had no idea how much stonemasons and builders would cost, but she knew it was unfeasible if those costs fell to the charity. They had barely any budget at all, and certainly none that would run to ensuring the church was in a safe condition to use.

Marcus leaned forward. "Sir, what you are asking is unrealistic at best." He shook his head. "I must advise the charity board against signing such an agreement. The advantages are all on your side rather than the charity. They would have to invest in the upkeep and modernization of the property at considerable expense to themselves, and in five years, when the lease expires, you would have a renovated manor and chapel, and they would have nothing to show for their investment should you not renew their lease. Either you must make the church building habitable, or you must remove the clause requiring them to hold services there under the direction of Mr. Todd."

Todd frowned. Mr. Asbury tugged on his chin. The dowager looked from one face to another as if she hadn't quite kept up with the turns in the conversation.

"What is this?" she asked. "How much could it cost to repair the church? A few rafters, a few bricks? I would imagine, with a thorough cleaning, which the entire place needs, things won't look so dire."

Mr. Moody shook his head. "Your Grace, Mr. Hoffman is a leader in his profession, an architect of great renown, with nothing to be gained by exaggerating his estimations. He assures me the repairs will be extensive. The transept's roof is ready to collapse, and the foundation under the bell tower is crumbling. Those repairs alone will run to several hundred pounds, not to mention replacing the windows. Even if you use standard glass rather than restoring the stained-glass panels, it will be quite costly."

Was this the way to jettison Mr. Todd? Convince Mr. Asbury that the chapel was beyond repair, therefore unusable for his friend's services?

"Surely there is some compromise here." Mr. Todd's eyes sharpened as he stared at Mr. Asbury. "I have not yet mentioned to you that I have made inquiries to my superiors. They are much in favor of this enterprise and have promised some funds toward opening the school."

"Your superiors? In the church?" Marcus asked.

"Yes, of course. The bishop of London, William Howley, has pledged church funds, and he's sent out a missive to the parish churches of the west London area. Each will take up a special collection toward the costs of repairing the chapel. And each of the church leaders will be looking in their parishes for those they feel would benefit from inclusion in the school." Todd had gotten to his feet, delivering his information as if he stood in a pulpit. "With the help from the greater church, surely we can reach some form of compromise on the repairs."

"Would the contributions be enough to cover the costs of fixing the school chapel?" Marcus asked.

"I believe we can realistically expect to receive five hundred pounds through these efforts. That would stabilize the building and the roof, surely." Todd looked to the solicitor.

Mr. Moody nodded. "That would take care of many of the repairs, I believe. At least the ones necessary to maintain the safety of the parishioners."

"There you have it. The problem is solved." Todd took his seat again, practically purring.

Why was he so eager to become the spiritual leader of a charity, when he was climbing the rungs of the Church of England so effortlessly? Was he truly altruistic, or did he think it would appear well to others that he was charity minded and thus hasten his ascent to higher office?

Perhaps you should put your mistrust aside and accept that he wants to help. Must you look for impure motives where there may be none?

Aunt Dolly squeezed Philippa's hand. "Your Grace, if the bishop is willing to contribute to see to the restorations, do you recommend our signing the lease?"

Marcus looked to the solicitor, who gave one small nod.

"Before we do that," Philippa said, "the term of five years is acceptable, but at the end of the lease, I would request that all points of the agreement are open to renegotiation before renewal." Which would rid them of Todd's presence should it become necessary.

"Of course." Mr. Asbury nodded.

"There is one further point on which I would like clarification," Mr. Moody said. "You've a 'morality clause' here, if I can use that term, that was not in the original lease documents. 'If at any time the occupants of the property are deemed to have brought disrepute or dishonor on the school or the landowner, the lease will be terminated.' Might I ask what the parameters are here? Who decides what is dishonorable, or what that threshold is?"

Mr. Todd cleared his throat. "I believe I can answer that. Mr. Asbury has put me in charge of the spiritual condition of the school, therefore, I believe that I, in conjunction with Miss Cashel and perhaps the dowager might form a tribunal, as it were, to review any case that might be actionable. I do not foresee having to convene often on that case. I believe the work and our spiritual guidance will be enough to rescue these women from their depraved ways and set them on the correct path."

"I agree." The dowager tapped her cane. "You and I are certainly equipped to know when someone has been dishonorable, Mr. Todd. I would be happy to lend my expertise."

Philippa stifled laughter and groans at the same time. Did the dowager realize what she had said? That she was tantamount to an expert on dishonorableness?

Depraved ways, indeed.

"That should satisfy everyone." Mr. Asbury put his hands on his knees as if he would like to rise. "As I said before, I am leaving London for several weeks, and I need this business accomplished sooner rather than later. If we are all agreed, can we sign the papers?"

"Allow me to make the amendments, and if all parties are in agreement, signatures will follow." Mr. Moody dipped his pen into his inkwell and began to write out the particulars and changes.

This was really happening.

The solicitor paused. "What is the name of the institution so that I may fill it in?"

Philippa looked to Charlotte and then Aunt Dolly who nodded. "Eleos School."

The dowager sniffed. "Eleos? What kind of word is that? I've never heard it before." As if a word could not exist if she had not encountered it.

"Eleos is the Greek word for mercy." Charlotte tilted her head. "This charity will be about mercy, compassion, and forgiveness. Philippa, Mrs. Stokes, and I have discussed this at length, and Philippa asked me to find a word that encompassed those ideas. Eleos School"—she spelled the word for Mr. Moody's benefit—"will be a place of refuge and restoration for women in need."

"Humph." The dowager frowned. "I thought it might be called the Haverly School, considering how our efforts are driving its creation."

"This hospital is not about us." Marcus took Charlotte's hand. "It's about doing what is right by those who need our help. We've been blessed by God to hold the positions and possessions we have, and we are told true religion is judged by what we do regarding widows and orphans, and I believe that also extends to those most in jeopardy in any society. Eleos is a fine name." He winked at his wife, and she rewarded him with one of her beautiful smiles.

Marcus signed the lease on behalf of the hospital, since women were not permitted to make contracts. But when he had finished, he handed the first copy to Philippa.

"Now the real work starts," he said.

Chapter 6

"How many more servants can there be? We've talked to half of London, it seems." Bertie leaned back, tapping his fingers on the table in the pages' dining room at Carlton House. He and Partridge, or mainly he, since Partridge asked few questions, had been interviewing the staff since nine that morning. It was gone three, now.

Mr. Lingfield consulted his list. "It's not been easy on us, you realize? We've had to work around everyone's normal duties, including my own. We're in the process of packing and preparing for His Highness to travel yet again, and everyone is pressed. We have only a handful left to question, and truly, I cannot imagine they had anything to do with the theft. Most don't even have access to the house. It's largely the stable and garden staff remaining."

Bertie considered this. "Perhaps my colleague could question the outside staff. As you say, they had no access, but they may have seen something, someone leaving the property at the time in question." He raised one eyebrow to Partridge, who nodded.

"Aye." He rose, as if eager to get out of the house. Bertie couldn't blame him. No one had seen anything, no one knew anything, everyone was mystified, and to be honest, cowed by the presence of Mr. Lingfield. The Prince Regent himself had insisted Mr. Lingfield be present during the questioning, so as to act quickly when the culprit was discovered. Bertie couldn't excuse him from the room, but he did tell each employee if they later remembered anything that might help, they were to contact him personally.

"I would like to see the dressing room once more." If he could plot the routes to and from the room, perhaps he could determine how long it would take to get the jewels out of the house, and the various ways in which the thief might have accomplished it. Unless the culprit was bold enough to walk out the front doors, the egress had to have been made through the basement.

On their way up the staircase, the secretary moved aside for the man coming down. "Good afternoon, Mr. Todd. Have you been with His Highness?" Lingfield asked.

"Yes, I've just left him now. He's given me permission to borrow more books from the library here. I shall speak with Mr. Powell as the head librarian, and then be on my way." He paused. "Sir Bertrand." He sketched a bow. "You must be delighted with developments concerning the new Eleos School. I look forward to serving on the board with you. It was a privilege to be present when the lease was signed yesterday."

Eleos? He'd had no idea that would be the new name for the hospital. Greek for mercy, if his lessons at university were reliable. Fitting. Bertie had received a missive from Haverly that the lease had been signed and inquiring as to whether he wished to sit on the committee that would interview applicants. What in his past history gave Haverly the notion that he would have anything substantial to contribute to such an endeavor, both the governing of a school as a board member or the judging of the fitness of applicants? But Haverly had his own reasons for everything he did, and he kept his own counsel. Bertie wouldn't know until the duke decided to tell him.

"Do you have a meeting with His Highness? I should give you fair warning, he's a tad irascible at the moment. His foot is hurting him dreadfully, and it has soured his mood." Todd shrugged and nodded, as if allowances must be made for someone suffering so greatly.

Lingfield raised his chin. "Sir Bertrand is here as a personal favor to the Prince Regent. There's been a theft, and His Highness has asked

Sir Bertrand to look into it for him. As one of the new chaplains, you are now a member of the household and should be informed."

Bertie winced. The prince had wanted the investigation kept quiet, but at this rate, it would be in bold type on every broadsheet in the city by nightfall. Every servant had been strongly warned against speaking about the subject outside the house, but it had been unrealistic to believe news wouldn't leak. He was only surprised it hadn't already.

"A theft? Someone nick some silver then? Perhaps we should arrange for me to preach to the staff about the state of their souls." The preacher shifted his weight, running his hands down his coat sides. "His Highness mentioned his vexation at finding his valet was stealing from him."

"This is more than the theft of port or a few coins. Someone has stolen a very valuable parure the prince had commissioned as a gift. Just took it right out of his dressing room. The house has been searched from cellars to rafters, and nothing has turned up, but we're going to search again."

Bertie put his arm out to shush the secretary, but it was too late.

"Are you certain it wasn't the valet who also took the jewels? If a man will steal coins and port, he would surely steal jewels." Todd's eyes widened.

"The valet wasn't here when the jewels went missing. He was with the prince in Brighton," Lingfield offered.

"It's odd that the prince did not call in someone from the magistrate's court to investigate. That new earl, Aylswood, for instance, now in charge of Bow Street."

"His Highness wishes it all to remain secret for now, so he called in Sir Bertrand to find the jewels." Mr. Lingfield jerked, as if just now realizing he was contributing to the spreading of the news. "You mustn't say a word."

"I've built my reputation on maintaining my own counsel. You can rest assured I will not breathe a syllable."

Bertie nodded. "Sir, we must be about our work. I will no doubt encounter you again in our efforts for Eleos School."

"Indeed. I wish you success in your search for the thief, Sir Bertrand. If I may be of assistance, please call upon me."

It took Bertie and Lingfield several minutes to arrive at the prince's dressing room. *This house is ridiculous. If the occupants of St. Giles rookery could see this gaudy, ostentatious display of wealth, they would riot in the streets. The décor of one room could feed a poor city block's inhabitants for a year.*

While destitute women in the city were doing the unthinkable to keep body and soul together for themselves and their dependents, the prince was indulging in velvet cushions and gold plate. It was one thing to enjoy a certain amount of comfort that wealth brought, but the carnality on display here was beyond what Bertie could stomach. Did His Highness give anything to charity? Did he consider anyone but himself?

Bertie felt an itch of guilt. Perhaps he should increase his own subscription to the new Eleos School.

A footman approached. "Sir Bertrand, Mr. Lingfield, His Highness requires your presence." He bowed slightly. "He is in his bedchamber."

Bertie straightened his cravat as he hurried after Mr. Lingfield. The secretary led the way past the robing rooms and wardrobes to a pair of double doors. With a very light tap, he twisted the right knob and held the door for Bertie to enter first.

"Your Highness," Lingfield said as he bowed. "What is your pleasure?"

Too many people asked that question, Bertie surmised as he bowed deeply from the waist before clasping his hands behind his back.

"My pleasure is to know the progress you've made. Where are the jewels, and who has taken them?" The prince reclined on a chaise, his foot submerged in a basin of ice water on the floor. He raised the limb, puffy and red. "Why can the physicians not find a cure for this dreadful gout? Numbing my foot appears to be the best option, but that only lasts so long, and I must be careful not to freeze these poor digits right off."

Perhaps backing off his vices of food and drink might help, but it was more than a physician's life was worth to say so, most likely.

"Your Highness, we're continuing with our inquiries. The house has been searched, and nearly every staff member has been questioned. There were many people who had access to the jewels while they were in the house, but we have narrowed the window of time for the theft. They were last seen by Mr. Lingfield when he brought the haberdasher to your dressing room with new cravats midmorning on Wednesday, June fifth. They were discovered missing five hours later when new shoe buckles were delivered."

At the rate new clothing items were brought to the house, how had anyone had time to steal anything? The prince's wardrobe was astonishing. Bertie could understand the need for so many people to care for the clothes and accessories. Master of Robes, Deputy Master of Robes, Clerk of the Closet, valets, dressers, seamstresses, laundresses, the list went on and on. Bertie was only spared having to speak with all of them because at least half had been with the prince in Brighton at the time of the theft.

"That is not good enough. You were to handle this quickly and quietly. How can I present a gift to a friend if the gift remains missing?" His Highness scowled.

"We must be certain that the correct culprit is identified. I will continue my inquiries, but I would again recommend bringing in Lord Aylswood and his investigators at Bow Street."

"No, no. That would mean word getting out to the public. I leave for Tunbridge Wells midweek next. My physicians seem to believe the waters there might be good for my health. I will not tarry, however, and will return to London in a fortnight. If you have not found the thief before that time, I will remove you from your position and shall inform Haverly of my disappointment." He stared at Bertie, his meaning clear. If Bertie did not solve this case, his work as an agent for the Crown could be finished.

His heart sank to his boots, anchored in the plush carpet of the prince's bedchamber. This pompous, self-indulgent fool would end his career as a spy on a whim? "Yes, Your Highness. I shall make every effort."

"See that you do. Lingfield, send for a glass of port. In fact, bring a bottle. I'm parched." The prince waved a pudgy hand, dismissing them both, and lay back against the pillows as he returned his foot to the freezing water.

Half an hour later, after having walked every route he could find from the dressing room to an outside door, Bertie was more puzzled than ever. Each path he took, he encountered at least half a dozen servants. How had the thief gotten out of the house without being seen?

How would *he* have done it? After all, quietly removing valuable items from wealthy places was his specialty.

Was that why Haverly had given him this job? Because it took a thief to catch a thief?

What would happen if Bertie couldn't find the jewels? Would the prince have a word with Haverly, having him removed from service in the Home Office? The prince was a man of whims. He could end Bertie's career without warning.

Stop muddling about. Think.

He would have perpetrated the theft at night. Fewer people, obscurity of darkness, higher chance of success. Because the house was so closely guarded, there was a greater likelihood that the thief had been allowed in or worked here.

But this crime had been committed during the day. The parure had been in the dressing room before Mrs. Bascome's tantrum, when Lingfield and the haberdasher had entered, and gone when the shoe buckles had been delivered. That left a time of about five hours when the theft could have occurred.

Whoever had stolen the parure had to have concealed it in something innocuous and ordinary to get it out of the house. No pocket or apron would be large enough to hide a tiara plus all the other jewels. Unless the jewels were still in the house despite the search.

People carried things in and out of the place constantly. It stood to reason the jewels were no longer here. With as many people who worked in the house, someone might accidentally stumble across the stolen goods in the course of their duties if they had been hidden in a cupboard or some such. Getting the parure out of Carlton House would be the thief's highest priority.

Bertie and Lingfield reached the basement once more, only to be met by the assistant cook. Her knotted brow and fist-mangled apron alerted Bertie. She had been serene and confident when he'd questioned her earlier that day. One would hardly think it was the same woman, such was her emotional state.

"Sir, you won't believe it. I don't know how it got there. It wasn't me, I promise you." The ruffle on her cap trembled as did her lower lip.

"What is it?" Bertie asked, as she'd addressed him and not Lingfield, who received only a glancing blow of a look.

She withdrew her hand from the wad of her apron and opened it. There on her palm sat a brooch, pearl and sapphire, the size of a damson plum.

Clearly from the stolen set.

"Where did you find it?" He took the piece, which was heavier than it looked, due to the gold setting, no doubt.

"It was in a soup tureen in the scullery. I went to fetch the tureen for the upper servants' dinner table, and I heard a clink. I thought perhaps one of the scullys had left a spoon inside, so imagine my surprise when I found that." She pointed at the brooch.

"Show me."

They went into the scullery, off the kitchen. The two girls Miss Cashel had visited sat on a bench along the wall, arms around one another, eyes large in their pale faces.

The smaller one looked away.

"It was in this." The assistant cook picked up pieces of broken porcelain. "I'm sorry, Mr. Lingfield. I was that startled, I dropped it."

Lingfield scowled but said nothing as he surveyed the woman.

"I can see where you might." Bertie looked at the shelf where an opening showed the previous location. Shoulder-height to him, a bit of a reach for the assistant cook, and a tiptoe job for the scullys, though there was a stool handy.

"I cannot imagine how this got here, Sir Bertrand," the housekeeper,

Mrs. Evans, said from the doorway. "I was in this very room when your man Mr. Partridge searched it. There was no jewelry here at that time."

"Who has access to this room?" he asked.

"Me, the head cook, our assistant cook, the pastry chef, the still room attendant, and of course, the scullery maids here. But honestly, anyone could have come in, because the door is never locked. We only keep pots, pans, and lesser quality porcelain in here. The items in the scullery are never seen above stairs, so there's no reason to lock them up."

Something about the smaller scullery maid's demeanor bothered Bertie.

"The ones who have the easiest access to this room, however, are the scullery maids?"

The girls tensed, leaning into each other on their bench.

"I'd like to speak to them, please." He considered their surroundings. "Perhaps in the upper servants' dining room?"

The bigger girl shook her head, eyes wide. "We don't know nothin'. I swear."

"Then let us discuss what you don't know." He motioned toward the door. "Mrs. Evans may come with you."

"I shall also be there. I'm responsible to answer to the prince for his employees." Lingfield scowled at the girls.

"That is acceptable, but you must not interfere with my questioning." The secretary had stuck his oar in far too much already. And he clearly put the staff on edge.

Once seated across from the scullery maids, Bertie tried to relax them by giving a reassuring smile. "Now, I don't think either of you stole the jewelry, but you may have seen something or someone and not realized the significance." He had not questioned the girls earlier, them being so young, and not really having access to the prince's dressing room. He hadn't thought it necessary. Perhaps he had been remiss. "What time do you begin your daily duties?"

"I wake them at five-thirty every morning," the housekeeper said.

"Thank you, madam, but if you would let the girls answer. And do forgive me, I don't remember your names." Bertie removed a notebook from his inner pocket, along with a pencil, a habit he had picked up from watching Daniel Swann during police investigations. His friend and soon-to-be nephew-in-law always carried those implements with him.

"I'm Nell, and this is Lydia." The bigger girl took the lead. "We get up frightful early to help prepare breakfast."

"And what are your primary duties?"

"We mostly wash dishes, sir. And fetch and carry for the cook and housekeeper. We help with laundry when we need to, and we run errands for anyone on the staff."

Bertie looked up from his notes. "Anywhere in the house or just here on the ground floor?"

"Anywhere in the house, but we must use the servant stairs. We aren't to be seen in the areas where guests could be." Nell moved her hand, and Bertie suspected she was gripping Lydia's beneath the table edge.

"Did either of you have an errand that would take you to the prince's dressing room on Wednesday morning?"

The girls looked at one another.

"You must tell the truth. If you had such an errand, perhaps you saw the thief and didn't realize it."

"I was sent by Mr. Green, one of the footmen, with a can of hot water up to Mr. Lingfield's room." Lydia said. "And Nell came behind with some hot coals from the kitchen fire, because the fire in his room had gone out." These were the first words he'd heard the girl speak. She had a low, husky voice that went well with her pretty face. Dark curls clustered beneath her cap, and her wide, dark eyes were older than her age.

Bertie consulted his memory and his map of Carlton House. Lingfield's room was on the floor above the royal apartments, but the servant's staircase would take the girls very near the prince's dressing room. He looked to the secretary, who shrugged.

"I did not hear the delivery of the water, nor of the coals to start the fire. I am a sound sleeper, especially when His Highness is not in residence."

Bertie nodded and returned to his questions. "You went together on your errands?"

Nell shook her head. "Lydia went first with the water. I met her coming back down. I had to finish setting the table for the upper servants, right here in this room, before I took the coals upstairs."

"Did you see anyone on the stairs, or in the hallway leading to the prince's dressing room? Did either of you go anywhere near that room?"

Nell closed her eyes as Lydia shook her head.

"Nell, what is it?"

She kept her gaze down at the table edge. "I saw several people. There are always people about, but I cannot remember who they all were. I was carrying hot coals. I needed to pay attention."

Bertie could understand that, but why did he sense evasion?

"Did any errand take you upstairs later in the day?" The jewelry had been taken well after they had run their early morning errands, but he wanted to get a view of their entire day.

Again they looked at one another, and Bertie began to wish he had separated them for these questions. They were saying volumes to each other with their looks, messages he could not decipher.

They nodded in unison. "We were ordered upstairs to help clean Mrs. Bascome's room after she left the house. We had to wait in the hall until her belongings were finally removed. She caused a bit of a stir."

Bertie raised his brows. He had, indeed, been remiss in overlooking the girls as witnesses. "You saw her leave?"

Lydia shrugged. "We did, sir. And those who didn't see it most likely heard it, for she was quite loud."

Lingfield rolled his eyes, and Mrs. Evans nodded.

"Did either of you see anyone carrying anything when you went about your work? Who else was present?"

"Mr. Todd was in the hallway, trying to calm Mrs. Bascome." Lydia shrugged. "One of the footmen carried a crate upstairs. He said it held a pair of candelabra just come from the silversmith. But there were a good number of people rushing about carrying things. Mrs.

Bascome's possessions were packed up quickly. Lydia and I were carrying dusters and mops and buckets to tidy the room because Mr. Lingfield wanted it turned around quickly. The laundress had stripped the bed and pillows, and two of the upstairs maids were already rolling up the rugs to be taken out and beaten."

Bertie nodded. It was as he feared. Too many people with too many opportunities.

The clerk, the reverend, Mrs. Bascome, any number of footmen and maids who had assisted with the removal of the paramour from the house. Yet none of them seemed a likely candidate for jewel thief.

How did the brooch end up in the tureen?

"Have you had use of that tureen since Wednesday?" he asked the housekeeper.

"I do not believe so. The girls would know because they would have washed it up."

Both girls shook their heads. "It's sat there until this morning."

"Did you see anyone in the scullery who shouldn't have been there?"

Again their eyes dropped to their laps, but they shook their heads.

"What aren't you telling me?"

"Girls, you mustn't keep anything back. Tell the man." Mrs. Evans clapped once, sharply, making the maids jump.

"I don't want to get into trouble. It wasn't my fault. I didn't invite him." Lydia bit her bottom lip. "Mr. Sloan came in this morning, and he asked if I would go to church with him of a Sunday and to dinner at his mother's home in Whitechapel. Please don't tell Miss Cashel. She said we was too young to be walking out with any men, and that we couldn't be getting into any trouble, not with the school just opening and that Mr. Asbury being so fusty about how we used to live and not calling bad attention to the place."

Mr. Sloan, a footman who had been present when Mrs. Bascome left. Had he secreted the jewels into the lady's luggage somehow to get them out of the house, and then . . .

But why put the brooch into a soup tureen?

It made no sense.

Mrs. Evans and Mr. Lingfield both wore stern expressions. Bertie hoped no sharp discipline would come to the girls. As far as he could tell, they'd had nothing to do with the theft, and Lydia was guilty only of garnering the attention of a young man who had offered to take her to church and home to see his mother. Hardly a crime or motive for theft.

He closed his notebook.

Was this the only secret Lydia hid? He sensed there was something else, but she would most likely not tell him, or at the very least, not in front of the housekeeper and secretary.

A thought trickled through his mind. Had she been working with the footman on the theft, and the brooch was by way of a bribe? Her portion of the snatch?

No, that couldn't be true, surely.

Do you reject the idea because you don't want it to be true, because you know it will be a blow to Miss Cashel and her efforts with Eleos?

"I will keep the brooch for the time being." Bertie slid back his chair. "I will most likely have more questions for you both on the morrow."

Before then, he intended to call in another team member for help.

Philippa came to the discovery that she hated committee meetings. This one had barely begun, and rather than being allowed to lay out the vision she and Aunt Dolly had for the school, the meeting had been taken over by Mr. Todd. One would assume he would be out of words, this being a Sunday and him having preached that morning. He'd boasted of delivering the sermon at St. George's in Hanover Square to a crowd of London's finest.

Philippa had attended a small chapel in Belgravia, near to where she had once worked as a paramour. She was not one for elaborate church rituals, for she felt it was too easy to become enamored of the pomp and pageantry rather than focus on worship. That and fewer people knew of her past at the small church, and didn't stare or whisper as the parishioners did when she attended church with Charlotte and Marcus at the aforementioned St. George's.

"I believe we should have set the criteria for admission long before this time." Mr. Todd skewed his mouth. "It is not as if we do not have an excellent template from which to work. The Magdalen Hospital has been most generous in sending us their requirements for entry. I say we should adopt exactly these terms." He pinned a paper to the table with his index finger.

Philippa counted to ten. Then fifteen. He had been arguing every point, always in favor of aping the Magdalen. "Sir, if we were merely going to mimic the Magdalen, which does, I agree, perform a fine service, we would simply have added our labors to theirs at their site rather than gone to the exertion of establishing our own charity. It is our desire to be distinguishable from the Magdalen and offer our aid in different, and dare I say, broader ways." Why couldn't the man understand?

"But it is most important that your successes outweigh your failures, especially at the outset of this venture. You should only admit those who are fairly close to redemption already, with the fewest hinderances, in order to, shall we say, boost your numbers? When people see the efficacy of your methods, they will be more inclined to give money and support the ministry. It is at that time, when more money is coming in, that you may broaden your approach to accepting those more at risk. You must trust me in this matter. I have more experience in the oversight of charity work than you."

If she were sitting beside him rather than across from him in the Haverly dining room, he might have patted her on the head.

Then she would have had to strike him.

With a carefully measured tone, she said through tight lips, "And I, sir, have more experience in the needs and lifestyle of those we will help than you, so perhaps you should trust *me* in this matter." *At least I hope I have more experience, though if most people knew the number and stripe of so-called gentlemen who had visited the house on King's Place, they might well be shocked.*

The reverend's face grew red, and his neck swelled against his collar. She took a perverse delight in opposing him. He'd spent the evening being obstructive, and someone needed to put him in his place.

"Please." Aunt Dolly reached for Philippa's hand. "I believe we would all do well to take each case on its own merits rather than maintain a list of predetermined requirements. I do not believe we should deny anyone seeking help, and in my estimation, a probationary period will sort the ladies out. Having run a refuge out of my own home, I have, perhaps, the *most* experience, both with being in need and being the one who provided aid, and I can tell you, those truly wanting help will stay and abide by the rules of the school. Those who do not will leave of their own accord, usually within a week. Most problems work themselves out if you give them grace and time."

"Most wise, Mrs. Stokes. If you do not mind," Marcus interjected, "might I look at the Magdalen Hospital's rules for admittance? Perhaps we are not so far apart in our philosophies?"

The dining room door opened, and Sir Bertrand Thorndike slipped through.

"My apologies, Your Grace, ladies, gentlemen." He slid into the first vacant chair, across and down the table from Philippa. It also happened to be next to the dowager, who leaned his way ever so slightly and sniffed. Like a trained bloodhound on the scent for liquor perhaps?

She must have detected nothing, for though she gave him a sidelong glance and pursed her lips at his tardiness, she turned her attention back to the discussion.

Marcus must have forbidden her to voice her every opinion this evening, for she had contributed little beyond fierce nods of approval at everything Mr. Todd had to say.

"Philippa, are there changes you would make to the Magdalen system of admittance?" Marcus asked, looking up from the pages.

"There are. Several." She consulted her own list.

"Please, speak freely."

He might come to regret that invitation, but Philippa did not intend to squander the opportunity. She loaded all her guns, determined to break through the reverend's stubborn lines. At the very least, he would have to sit quietly and listen for a time.

"First, the Magdalen only admits new students on the first Thursday of every month, and each case is decided by majority vote of a committee. I believe help should be offered no matter what day of the month it happens to be. Further, I believe those working at the school, Mrs. Stokes and I, primarily, should have say over those who are allowed inside. This will lessen the number of committee meetings required as well as give oversight to the people who will actually be working with the applicants rather than those more distant from the day-to-day running of the school.

"Second, each applicant to the Magdalen must have a reference from a family member or clergyman. I do not intend to ask for references. Most women in need cannot procure such a document, nor should they have to in order to qualify for aid. No woman should have to prove she is good enough to be helped.

"Third, the Magdalen is very strict on the type of woman they will admit. I do not intend to exclude those who are with child, nor those whose health may be failing." She held up her hand as the reverend leaned forward and opened his mouth.

"No, we do not intend to put the sick in amongst the healthy. I intend to have a pesthouse to quarantine the sick. One of the buildings on the property will be devoted to the treatment and convalescence of those who have a communicable disease. Once those ladies are well, they can move into the manor and begin their training."

"What you are proposing is . . . it's vastly beyond the scale of what was initially discussed." The dowager got in before the reverend. "You and Mrs. Stokes would have all the . . . *power*, and the committee would exist for what purpose? If we have no say over the admission policy or the standards, what would be the point of our existence?"

"Philippa, what role did you see the board having?" Marcus asked.

None. I didn't envision a committee or board looking over our shoulders. "Fundraising, financial oversight, input on the overall visions for the hospital. Handling the legal issues such as the lease. In other matters, those that involve the day-to-day workings of the school, those things that bring us into contact with those we serve, Mrs. Stokes and I would manage ourselves as we have done up to now."

"I see." He looked to Charlotte.

Her sister spoke up after being quiet all evening. "It seems feasible and even prudent that Philippa and Dorothy be in charge of the daily responsibilities at Eleos. Someone on the grounds must have the authority to make decisions. The board cannot convene for every little thing. Philippa and Dorothy are certainly more than capable. They have proven so in the work they have already begun."

Philippa wanted to hug Charlotte.

"Humph." The dowager shook her head. "I believe at the very least, Mr. Todd should have some say in the daily business of the school, as he will be in residence there too. He will be in charge of these women's souls, after all."

"I would be honored to assist you when potential—shall we call them students or patients? When new applicants arrive, to assess their fitness." Todd held up his hands. "I agree that anyone in need should be welcomed in, but after that probationary period Mrs. Stokes spoke of, an assessment would be in order. Physical and spiritual."

He was offering a compromise, but if she accepted, then she would be forced to allow his input . . . and once a man had input, it wasn't long before he dominated every decision.

She had vowed never to be under the power of another man for as long as she drew breath, and she wasn't about to change for the likes of Mr. Simon Todd.

Dolly gripped her wrist, pinching with her nails. "Go along to get along for now. We'll find ways to outmaneuver him if we have to." The whisper moved the hair at Philippa's temple.

"If you propose to have an infirmary, you will need a physician to attend," Charlotte said. "Or possibly more than one on a rotation, perhaps? Do you plan to have separate quarters for all newcomers? Must they be examined by a physician before being admitted to the main house?"

How humiliating for the women. Philippa had assumed she and Dolly would, through questions and observation, be able to ascertain if a woman needed treatment. They certainly had enough practice identifying such diseases.

Dolly nodded. "I agree that a physician or surgeon or apothecary would be an asset, but most of the women we will be treating do not trust men, nor are they eager to follow men's dictates. If we could find a woman well-versed in healing and midwifery, she could tend the infirmary and refer cases to a physician or apothecary as needed. Until such a healer is hired, I will see to diagnosing those who need special attention."

Tension built in Philippa's shoulders. This had all gotten so far out of control. Dolly's house of refuge at the end of King's Place had been solely their domain. They had not asked for oversight or input from those who had no notion what it was to be in the predicament of the women who sought sanctuary there.

Though the women only stayed at the refuge house for a day or two, a week at most, and then were back on the street, selling themselves once more to survive. If she wanted the scope of this work to expand to life-changing education and care, she and Dolly would have to invite more people into the process. But more decision-makers meant more bureaucracy and bickering, and thus far, had not resulted in helping any individuals.

Perhaps they were wrong to dream of a larger charitable institution. Perhaps they should be content with training a few girls here and there in domestic servanthood.

But that would mean continuing to live off Marcus and Charlotte's generosity.

And Philippa could no longer do that.

This entire process was more daunting and complicated than she had ever imagined. The committee had been pushing ideas around for nearly an hour, and nothing was decided yet.

As if Marcus had come to the same conclusion, he stood and took control of the meeting. "Let us confine ourselves to the material issues this evening. I do not want our efforts, especially those of Miss Cashel and Mrs. Stokes, to be bogged down in committee doings. I propose that admissions and the day-to-day running of Eleos School be under their control with occasional assistance of Mr. Todd as called upon. I further propose that Mrs. Stokes search for a woman skilled in healing to become a resident at the school, while Sir Bertrand will find a qualified physician or apothecary to oversee the infirmary on an as-needed basis."

Philippa glanced down the table. Sir Bertrand? Thus far he had contributed nothing but his presence to the meeting, and not even all of that, as he had been very late. Did he perhaps have connections to the medical field?

His brows went high at the directive from the duke, but he nodded and said nothing.

"I further propose that we apply to the Earl of Whitelock to send to Whitehaven for workers to repair the property. Evan has a veritable army of building and maintenance experts on the Whitehaven estate. If he can spare a few, the work at Eleos should go forward at a good pace and most economically. Asbury is content that I oversee the repairs, within his approved budget, and submit the receipts to him for payment upon completion. While we cannot expect to be fully staffed and occupied at once, a small group of students and workers should be able to move in within the fortnight, if not sooner, once we put workers to the task of making at least the manor house habitable."

"I will undertake that correspondence," Charlotte offered. "I'm certain Evan and Diana will want to help, even though they have already left the city for Whitehaven."

"What shall I do?" the dowager asked.

"I have a special task for you, madam. With the board's approval, I move that the dowager begin the planning of a fundraising subscription party, to be held here at Haverly House at the beginning of next Season. The guests will make donations to the hospital, and in exchange they will be treated to a lavish ball as well as a semiannual publication detailing Eleos's success and efforts and one tour of the facility per year. If they continue to donate, they will continue to be invited to the annual event. You may add persons to your planning committee, madam, and I will give you the budget for the preparations and execution. The guest list will be up to you and your committee."

The dowager's normally stern expression lightened with every word her son spoke. Philippa had to hand it to Marcus. He had created a task that suited his mother and would keep her busy and out of everyone's hair for the next many months. Next Season would not begin until after Christmas, half a year from now. With that much time to plan and organize, the party would be a rout.

"I know exactly whom I should ask." The older woman's gaze grew distant as she undoubtedly saw dancing couples and buffet tables emerging in her mind. "This will be the most coveted invitation of all of next Season."

How much money might they raise with such an effort?

Much better and probably more effective than charging people to come to church. Mr. Todd was still adamant on that count, and he cited the lease agreement for his arguments. Philippa could not say no and maintain the lease.

"Each of us have an assignment. Mr. Todd, I suggest you tell your fellow clergymen that the school will be open and accepting students in a fortnight. The church repairs will take longer and require trained craftsmen, but until then, you can hold services in the manor house's great hall."

A knock sounded on the dining room door, and Mr. Ffoulkes, Marcus's butler, slipped in. "Forgive me, Your Grace. There is someone here who desires to see Miss Cashel and Sir Bertrand. She says it is most urgent."

"Who is it, Ffoulkes?" Marcus asked. "We are nearly finished here. Can it not wait?"

"She says her name is Lydia, sir, and she says her friend, Nell, has been arrested for stealing the Prince Regent's jewels."

Chapter 7

Bertie bounded out of his chair at the butler's statement. "Arrested?" That was preposterous. Though he himself technically had no authority to arrest anyone, it was his investigation, and he should have been the one to determine when an arrest was necessary.

He sketched a bow to the ladies in the room and a quick nod to the duke and duchess. "Take me to the girl."

Miss Cashel nearly beat him to the door. "Where is she?" Once in the hall she called, "Lydia?"

"She's in the kitchen, ma'am." Mr. Ffoulkes hurried ahead of her to hold the door, and Bertie followed behind.

The girl sat huddled on a bench by the back door, a shawl clutched around her shoulders. Tears streaked her face, and her eyes were round as shillings.

"Oh, Miss Pippa, it's terrible. They took her away. They took Nell to prison." She slid off the bench to the floor, gripping Miss Cashel's skirt, face turned up in appeal.

"Shh, Lydia, calm yourself." Miss Cashel gripped the girl's shoulders and lifted her to the bench once more. She looked to the chef. "Mr. Lovellette, brew some tea and add some sugar."

The Haverly kitchen staff stood like statues in a gallery, but after a moment, the French cook stirred, his moustache twitching, and handed a maid a teakettle. "Water, *hâtez-vous*." He underscored his words with a "be quick about it" wave of his hand.

Miss Cashel took a kitchen towel off a drying rack above the girl's head and handed it to her. "Compose yourself. Dry your tears. We cannot help if you give way to hysterics."

Lydia mopped her cheeks. "Yes, Miss Pippa." She sniffed and blinked.

Bertie frowned. Was he surplus to requirements? Here he was, supposed to be in charge of this investigation and someone else had authorized the arrest of a suspect, and now Miss Cashel was commandeering his witness.

Stop playing second and exert yourself, man.

"Miss, you say she was arrested, but by whom? On whose authority?" he asked.

She swallowed hard. "Mr. Lingfield told the Prince Regent that the brooch was found in the scullery, and His Highness insisted that someone be arrested for it. Whoever was in that room last before it was found, he said, and that was Nell. She didn't do it. I know she didn't. I don't know how that brooch got into that tureen, but we didn't put it there. We tried to tell them, and no one would listen. The guards at the front gate took her away." She turned to Miss Cashel. "She didn't even have her shawl."

"Where did they take her?"

"I don't know. I tried to follow the wagon, but Mrs. Evans held me back. Said I couldn't do nothin' for her anyway." She screwed up her face again, and a small sob leaked out. "When no one was looking, I snuck out and ran all the way here. I knew you would help me, Miss Pippa. Nell ain't guilty of nothin' more than being a poor scully with nobody to speak for her. And now I can't go back to Carlton House because I ain't supposed to be out. Mrs. Evans won't let me back in if I return there, and if she does, Mr. Lingfield will clout me good and toss me out anyway."

Bertie recalled Lingfield's temper and his caustic treatment of his staff. How many times had these girls suffered the rough side of his tongue or the back of his hand?

"I assure you, you will be welcomed back to Carlton House, and

Mr. Lingfield will not lay a hand on you." His ire at the situation surprised him. In the past, he'd been quite adept at keeping feelings at bay, of existing only on the surface of situations like these and not getting involved. "But first, we must go to Newgate Prison and locate Nell. I do not know that I can get her released, not after the Prince Regent's order, but we can question her further and see to providing for some of her basic needs."

"You believe they took her to Newgate?" Miss Cashel asked.

"That is the logical choice. It is the closest gaol. The magistrate who would have issued the warrant in that area of London would have sent her to there. The prince would not bother with a warrant, but the jail warder would need one for his files, so he would no doubt procure one after the fact."

"I'm coming with you." Miss Cashel rose, her gown swishing, the candlelight gliding over her glossy hair.

"Newgate Prison is no place for a lady like you." She would stand out like a Grecian statue in a cow byre. Terrible things happened in a prison, awful sights, noxious smells . . . if he allowed her to come with him, he could not protect her from what she might encounter.

The look she gave him was indecipherable, then a wry laugh escaped her rosy lips. "I assure you, Sir Bertrand, I have been in worse places."

To his consternation, an actual blush heated his collar line. He was inclined to forget her origins, that she had only escaped the St. Giles rookery by becoming a courtesan.

"I would suggest you change for the journey then." He hated that embarrassment roughened his voice. Where was his famous aplomb? "I will fetch the carriage and tell His Grace where we are going."

She may spurn his efforts as unnecessary, but he would still try to protect Miss Cashel from the worst that Newgate had to offer.

The carriage was a bit crowded with Miss Cashel, the girl, and Mrs. Stokes joining him.

"Miss Pippa, what will happen to me now? What if he can't get me back into Mrs. Evans's and Mr. Lingfield's good graces?" Lydia wrung her chapped, red fingers, darting a look Bertie's direction.

"If Sir Bertrand says he can smooth things over, then you must trust him. However, if you would prefer a different situation, we will find one for you. I do not like it that Mr. Lingfield is making free with his slaps. I did not place you in a royal household to suffer abuse."

While it warmed Bertie that she spoke highly of his abilities, he did not miss the iron in her tone. She was no fonder of seeing young girls buffeted about than he.

Was this now his lot in life, visiting Newgate to question scullery maids? Not at all what he had envisioned when dreaming of leading his own team of agents. He disembarked from the carriage at the entrance to the prison. Not long before, he'd had to get his niece, Juliette, released from custody here. She'd protested the arrest of an innocent man and found herself in darbies for her trouble.

If he fought too hard against what the Prince Regent had done, he might find himself in a similar position. He had better tread carefully.

"We're here to see a prisoner in the women's gaol. Call up the warder, if you please." Bertie gave the man his card.

"Sir," the man held the card up to his lantern, glanced at Bertie's face, and nodded, his eyes widening. "We don't let people into the gaol at this hour."

"You will take us through to an interview room and bring the prisoner to us. I do not wish to question her in the cells." Perhaps that way, the women would not see the terrible conditions of the jail.

The guard scowled. "You're awful high in the instep for a fellow who's drug two women and a girl to this rathole."

"I'm acting upon the authority of the Prince Regent himself. Perhaps you would like me to disturb him, to tell him one of his jailers thinks so little of his regent that he would refuse his messenger?"

The man jerked. "No need for all that. This way, sir."

They followed him down a dark hall, open on one side to a courtyard, and into a cold, stone room with a bench, a pair of chairs, and a plain table. The guard lit two lamps from his lantern. "I have to lock the door, sir. It's protocol. I won't be long." He closed them in to go find the women's warder.

"This place is horrible," Miss Cashel said, hugging herself, her nose wrinkled against the smell. Dank straw, unwashed humans, and poor sanitation mingled into a miasma impossible to ignore.

And this was one of the nicer rooms in the complex. If she saw the state of the cells, she'd either faint or go on a crusade for prison reform.

Bertie had once gone undercover as a prisoner here to reveal an anarchist plot to blow up a shipping dock. It had been one of the longest, foulest fortnights of his life. Even now, being locked in this relatively safe and clean room made his muscles tighten.

Eventually, the clank of keys on a chain and heavy footsteps announced the arrival of the warder . . . or in this case, the wardress. A large, rather untidy woman held Nell by the elbow, glaring at her from the corner of her eye as if she expected the girl to try to overpower her at any second.

"Don't usually allow visitors this time of night. Make it quick." She shoved the girl into the room, then looked Sir Bertrand over, her expression changing from belligerent to surprised. "Sorry, sir. Didn't realize the tone of her guest. What's the likes of you want with a nothing like her, if I may be so bold as to ask?" Her mouth remained open after the question.

Nell rushed into Miss Cashel's embrace without a sound.

"You may ask, but our business is private. We will inform you when we're ready to leave." Bertie slid his gaze to the door and back to the wardress's face. A petty tyrant, given a bit of power over powerless people and prone to abuse, no doubt.

When she had gone, he turned to Nell. "Tell me what happened. Lydia gave us her account of events, but I would hear it from you."

The girl, her eyes red-rimmed, spoke from the protection of Miss Cashel's arms. "We cleaned up the broken soup tureen, and we went to bed. But this morning, Mr. Lingfield came to the scullery, and he brought a pair of footmen. Said His Highness knew the brooch had been found and was insisting someone be arrested. I was the last one in the room, but I swear I didn't put it there. I didn't even know it was there. If I had, I would have brought it to you myself."

She ducked her head, tears cutting through the dirt on her cheeks.

Miss Cashel guided the girl to one of the chairs and pulled the other alongside her. Lydia took a seat on the bench by the door, but Bertie preferred to stand. Memories of his time as a prisoner spy kept interfering with his thoughts. This poor girl. He had little doubt that the women were treated no better than the men in this heinous establishment.

And he had never been fond of confined spaces.

"Nell, I've questioned every servant in that house. No one seems to have had the opportunity to enter that room unnoticed except you two girls." He paced the stone floor. "You were the only one alone in there for any length of time. You're sure nobody came in? Not even for a minute?"

She stared at the floor and shrugged.

"Nell, what are you hiding?" Miss Cashel asked.

"Nothing," came the quick reply. "I didn't steal the jewels, and I didn't hide them in the scullery. I'd have to be a fool to hide them there. Who else would be suspected but us, leaving the brooch in the scullery?"

She had a point. Yet Marcus had said Miss Cashel had a finely honed ability to know when someone was lying. If she thought Nell was hiding something, it only confirmed what Bertie had sensed ever since he'd taken on this case.

"What else are you not telling us?" Bertie asked. "Do you know who stole the jewels? Are you protecting someone?"

She shook her head, but she shot a glance at the other maid.

"Lydia? Do you know anything?" He turned his attention to the girl. "Did you see something?"

Again a long look between them, and Nell shook her head a fraction of an inch.

"We should tell them," Lydia said, her voice low. "So you can get out of this place."

"No!" The panicked protest escaped Nell's lips, and her face paled. "Don't."

"If you don't tell, you will hang. Mr. Lingfield said so. If you steal something worth more than a shilling, you'll hang. That brooch is worth lots more than a shilling." Lydia turned to Miss Cashel. "I did see someone leaving by the ground floor door out to the stables, but it wasn't a servant." She raised her chin, her eyes both scared and defiant. "I think his name is Lord Pringle. He came and went quickly the day the jewels went missing, and again yesterday, and he came in through the servant's entrance. A lord like him should have come in the proper way and been announced to Mr. Lingfield, but he didn't. I saw him come in, and he was gone for maybe half an hour? We had finished washing up the breakfast dishes and had set to cutting vegetables for lunch. I had to go get more turnips from the cool store, and I saw him leave the house by the servant's yard door."

"Lord Pringle?" Bertie was familiar with the man. "No one reported him as being in the house. Why am I just hearing about it now?"

His voice must have been too loud, too stern, for Lydia cowered. Nell slumped, her face in her hands. "You should have kept quiet. You promised. You swore it."

"We didn't swear to protect someone who would steal and let you hang for it."

"What do you mean you swore?" Bertie asked.

"When we was hired." Nell scrubbed her hand beneath her nose. "Mr. Lingfield made us swear we would keep the secrets of the house. Who came and went, and anything we heard while we were working. He made us sign a paper that said if we told anything to anyone, we'd be sent to gaol. But I never told, and I'm in gaol anyway."

Was this why no one had been helpful when questioned? Bertie had gotten almost no information, and all the while Lingfield had sat beside him in the interviews, glaring at his staff, frightening them into silence.

He and Lingfield were going to have words.

"Did no one else notice this Mr. Pringle moving about?" he asked, dampening his ire and speaking more gently. It wasn't the girls' fault. They had only been keeping their word. No wonder nothing had leaked to the press about the theft. Every employee was scared rigid to divulge any secrets. More than just being fired, they would find themselves in the dock for treason.

Lydia shook her head and shrugged. "There's lots of ways to get around the house without being seen. His Highness prefers most of the servants stay hidden. If this man wanted, he could get most anywhere. All he'd have to do is avoid the footmen and upstairs maids."

This Bertie well knew, having tried to map out the labyrinth of passageways and back stairs at Carlton House. Still, if Lord Pringle had slipped in and out and only a chance trip for some turnips had discovered it, were there others who had done the same?

It seemed there could be more suspects moving furtively about the house, but Lord Pringle had sprung to the top of his list for the time being.

"Nell, I'm going to leave money here with the jailer to see that you get a blanket and some better food. And I'll try to get you released as soon as possible. I do not think you had anything to do with the theft, but it may take some time to get others to agree with me." Blaming a helpless young girl would suit some people nicely.

Especially whomever the real culprit was.

Philippa strode down the Oxford Road, her heels clacking on the walk. Her maid, Mary Rush, trailed behind, silent as always. Having had the freedom of traveling without a maid when she was a courtesan—after all, what could damage her reputation then?—Philippa was still not accustomed to having a chaperone along everywhere she went. Nor could she often entice the woman to engage in conversation beyond single-word answers.

But she was too tired and irritated to worry about that at the moment. She took her mood out on the pavement in quick, hard strides. Ever since visiting Nell in Newgate Prison the night before, her temper had simmered just below the surface. She had lain awake, her spirit as rumpled as the coverlet.

If word of Nell's arrest got to the ears of Mr. Asbury, would it nullify the lease for Eleos? As a graduate of Philippa and Aunt Dolly's program and with a placement at Carlton House, the girl's arrest would certainly qualify as bringing the school into bad repute.

Even if it did not nullify the lease, who would hire any of her girls if they acquired a reputation for purloining valuable items from their employers?

She skirted a costermonger selling hot pies, and another wheeling a barrel of ale which he sold by the mug. Antoinette's was along here somewhere. Philippa had never visited the modiste, but Diana Whitelock had recommended her as a possible place for one of the girls. Sarah Coventry, a seventeen-year-old from Cornwall who had come to Aunt Dolly for help, had proven herself quite adept with a needle, and Philippa hoped to find her a good employer to utilize those skills.

Ah, there it was. She found the green door and the sign with gold lettering above it. *Antoinette's: Modiste.*

"Antoinette" couldn't be less French if she tried. Still, it was the done thing for modistes, regardless of their origins, to adopt a French name. After all, the *ton* considered French fashion to be most desirable. "Frannie Cooper. You're Miss Cashel?" Mrs. Cooper was as English as kippers.

"I am. Thank you for seeing me." Philippa removed her gloves.

"Come into the workroom. We've no customers at the moment, and we've work enough for an army making dresses for folks leaving town for the summer months." The shop owner led the way past a pair of rather sumptuous dressing rooms to a sunny open space filled with tables, rolls of fabric, and drawings of gowns. Pattern pieces lay like snowdrifts, and shears, tailor's chalk, spools of thread and lace, and a bevy of industrious young ladies completed the picture.

The young ladies, all dressed in plain, dark gowns, bent over their work, needles flashing. One woman pinned pieces of fabric onto a dressmaker's form, and another worked a flat iron next to a small brazier.

Light streamed in the windows, and the place was bright and airy. This would be a good place to work, if only Mrs. Cooper would take Sarah.

After a brisk negotiation, which included specifics about wages, lodging, and a one-month trial, Philippa agreed to bring Sarah for a probationary period.

"I got a soft spot for girls like that. As long as she minds her business and doesn't do anything foolish, I'll see that she has a place. If she's as good as you say with garment making, she'll fit in fine. I own the building, left to me by my late husband, and I keep rooms upstairs for my girls. The rules are simple. No men, no drink, and no stepping out after dark."

"That is reasonable. She's a good seamstress, and she has no desire to go back to her old life."

"If she works out, maybe I'll call on you for other girls. You never know. Business is brisk, especially since the Countess of Whitelock became a patron. She's that stylish, and now everyone wants a dress from Antoinette's." Satisfaction laced the modiste's tone.

Diana Whitelock was one of the most *au courant* women in London, with an instinctive sense of color and design and excellent taste. Charlotte owed much to Diana's guidance when it came to her wardrobe, and Philippa had taken advantage of her expertise too.

She left the dressmaker's in a better frame of mind than she had entered, though Nell's predicament still troubled her.

Was Sir Bertrand Thorndike the man for the task of investigating the theft and Nell's wrongful arrest? What if he was not up to the requirements? Nell would be executed. Wouldn't this be better handled by a proper investigator like Mr. Swann? Or Marcus himself?

Her mood soured again.

It drifted through her thoughts that perhaps she should pray about it. She was rather new to the notion that God could and would help her. Charlotte and Marcus had been kind, teaching her about a God who did more than just punish on a whim. And Aunt Dolly spoke often of God's provision and direction in her life. Though Philippa was certain God had more important people to help, people who deserved His attention, who didn't have her dismal past to overcome, Charlotte insisted that He would hear Philippa when she prayed.

I've no practice at this, but God, if You could see fit and if You are not too busy, help us free Nell, and if it isn't too much to ask, if Mr. Asbury might not find out about what's happened, that would be best. I'm sure others better than me, like Charlotte or Aunt Dolly or Marcus would ask the same, so if You can't be bothered with the likes of me, You could listen to them. She paused. *Amen.*

How were you supposed to know if God even heard you? With so many people, so many prayers being said, and so many who were more worthy, better, more pious, and with cleaner pasts than her, any prayer she uttered would likely be at the very bottom of God's list of priorities.

Pedestrian traffic had increased on the Oxford Road, and she and her maid had to weave a bit. She gripped her reticule, not letting it dangle from her wrist. Cutpurses abounded in crowds like this.

It was nearing midday, and her stomach let her know she had only nibbled at her breakfast. She'd been too disquieted to think of food when it was offered. If she could find a carriage to hire, perhaps she could be at Haverly House before luncheon was over.

A quick movement caught her attention. Up the street a few paces, a man in a top hat and brown coat spoke with a girl of about twelve or thirteen summers. He leaned toward her, backing her against the wall. Her eyes were wide, and he loomed over her. She shook her head, but he nodded, inching closer.

She watched for a few moments. The man tried to touch the girl's face, and she flinched, her eyes screwed up and her mouth trembling. He motioned toward the alley behind her, and her shoulders slumped, her chin dropping.

Philippa had seen this too many times. She had been that child once, though thankfully not as young her first time. She inserted herself between them, shoving the man back, only able to do so because she had caught him off guard.

"Leave her be." She glared, watching him intently, every muscle tense.

He righted his hat and tugged on his lapels. "Get out of my way. This is none of your concern."

"I know what you're about, and I will not have it. Clear off. You cannot have this child." Indignation coated her words, banishing fear.

Passersby paused momentarily, then continued on, not wanting to see. Philippa's maid hung back, her hands covering her mouth.

The girl edged to the side, but Philippa put out her hand to keep the child behind her.

"Go, you predator. She's a child."

"She's my child," he shot back.

A pause. Had she misread the situation? "She's your daughter?" The girl looked nothing like him.

"Yes."

Without turning she asked, "Is that true, child?"

"No. I ain't his daughter." Her voice shook. "But you shouldn't have interfered. I have to do this. Me mam says I have to go with a gentleman if he asks."

"You do not."

"Perhaps you would rather take her place?" The man leered at her, sizing her up and down.

She reached into her reticule and removed the muff gun that Marcus had given her and trained her to use. Stepping close, she put the small barrel against the man's patterned waistcoat. "You will leave now. This pistol is small, but I am unlikely to miss. I cannot stop every man from preying upon women, and this child is barely even old enough to be considered a woman, but I can stop you here, right now."

The man froze, color draining from his face. "You've lost your reason," he croaked.

"Perhaps, but not my nerve. You might consider what happens to a man shot in the gut."

He backed up with a scowl, spun on his heel, and stalked away, disappearing into the crowd.

Quivers shot down her legs and up her spine as she returned the gun to her bag. Her nerve indeed. What had she been thinking? Marcus had given her the firearm for her protection, not to accost strangers on the High Street.

Yet what else could she have done? Turned a blind eye to the situation?

The girl looked ready to collapse. She had her hand on her throat, and her eyes darted as if looking for a way of escape.

"Easy, child. He's gone now."

"You don't know what you've done. Now I have to start again." Furrows appeared on her brow. Her shoulders slumped, and she scuffed her foot on the pavement. "If I don't find at least one gentleman before nightfall, I won't have anything to eat again."

"Start all over? You were looking for a . . . gentleman?" Philippa used the word loosely.

The child nodded. "I have to. There ain't nothing else I can do. My mam kicked me out of the house. She can't feed me no more. There's six younger than me. She said if I asked the right man, he'd have his way with me and leave me a coin."

Philippa closed her eyes, dismay washing over her, followed by gratitude that she'd gotten to this child in time. "What is your name?"

"Kate."

"I am Miss Cashel. How old are you?"

"I'll be twelve in a few months."

God save us all. She's a baby.

If the Earl of Tiptree had abandoned Philippa's mother a few years earlier, Philippa would have found herself in much the same situation.

"You're coming with me."

"Where?" Kate asked, tensed for flight once more.

This had been lining up to be the worst day of the young girl's life, and Philippa made a quick decision. "For the best day you've ever had."

"What do I have to do?" Her chin took on a wary, suspicious tilt.

"Bless you, child, you have to do nothing but enjoy yourself. We'll start with luncheon. I'm famished." Philippa offered her hand, and cautiously, Kate took it.

They found a pie cart and availed themselves of one each. Another vendor had boiled eggs, and a third, bottled cider. Carrying their parcels, they made their way to Cavendish Square, just north of the Oxford Road, and found a park bench beneath a spreading oak.

Kate licked her lips, holding the pie to her nose. "I never had a whole pork pie all to myself before." She bit into it, her eyes closing and a small moan escaping her.

Warmth spread through Philippa that someone could be pleased with such a small thing. Moving as she did in the more elevated strata of London Society, it seemed most of the people she met and mingled with had an insatiable appetite for pleasure, but rarely found satisfaction. A single pork pie, bought for a ha'penny, was more riches than this child had ever seen.

"Don't eat too quickly. I don't want you to make yourself ill."

Kate was thin to the point of emaciation. Her mother had probably despaired of feeding her, and only because of their desperate straits had she pushed the girl out to make her own way.

Philippa had made the choice herself before her mother had been forced to, but it had been no easier. Amelia Cashel had gone from pampered paramour to penniless poor in the space of a day. Keeping body and soul together had been more than she could accomplish, especially once she fell ill. Her heart had broken entirely when Philippa did what she had to in order to ensure their survival.

Amelia lived long enough to see her daughter escape that life, but not by many months. Philippa knew she would approve of today's mission, and the greater one of starting Eleos School.

When they had finished their food, using Philippa's handkerchief to tidy up, Kate rose and bobbed a curtsey. "Thank you, Miss." She put her hand on her middle. "I ain't had a full belly in a long time."

"We're not finished, Kate. There's more to do today." Philippa looked to her maid. "A dress, I believe, is in order, wouldn't you agree?"

Mary Rush nodded. "In a nice rose color perhaps? To complement her complexion?"

"A capital idea."

Kate currently wore a misshapen mud-brown dress that looked as if it had been cut down from a larger garment and then let out a time or two as she had grown. The hem straggled and waved enough to make a sailor seasick, and the bodice was made for someone more endowed than a spindly eleven-year-old.

"Back to Antoinette's?" the maid asked.

"Indeed."

Philippa kept her eye out for the man she had run off. He had been shamed, and men who had been shamed by a woman could lash out and attack from ambush, as she had reason to know. But they saw nothing more of the scoundrel.

Frannie Cooper took the measure of Kate and brought three ready-made garments from the workroom. "Any of these do?"

Kate made to touch one of the gowns, then pulled her hand back.

"Go on, child. Which one do you like?" Philippa asked. Mrs. Cooper had chosen wisely, for each was pretty without being ostentatious for a young girl of modest means.

Pale yellow, spring green, and the maid's choice of rose. All with cap sleeves and a bit of ribbon decoration.

"Why? Why are you doing this? You can't mean for me to have one of these? These are for ladies, not the likes of me." Kate wove her fingers together and twisted them at her waist.

"You're right to be cautious, child. Gifts from strangers can come with hidden obligations. But I assure you, this is a gift without any strings attached." *For the girl I used to be. And for the woman I hope you never become.*

She settled on the rose gown, and Philippa added a shawl, a petticoat, and a spencer. Mrs. Cooper provided a basin of warm water for a quick washing. A stop at a milliner's supplemented the outfit with a straw bonnet with a rose ribbon, and they found a receiver's shop that had a pair of practically new walking boots. "If we had more time, I would take you to a cobbler and get a pair made for you, but these will be better than what you have now."

Kate's old shoes, with slats of wood inside to cover the holes in the leather soles, went into the bin.

"Now, I believe a carriage ride to St. James's Park is next on the itinerary."

"I never rode in a carriage before." Kate wore a wondrous expression, as if she could not quite believe what was happening to her.

Philippa smiled. "Have you ever fed the ducks on the Serpentine? Or had ice cream at Gunter's? I believe we should attempt both before our day is through."

By the time they had finished their sweets at the famous shop on Berkeley Square, Kate looked ready to drop. Sated, but not serene.

"What happens to me now?" She touched the ribbon at her throat. "Today has been wonderful, the best in my whole life, just like you said, but I still ain't got no place to go."

"I have just the location for you, sweetling, and it will not involve you looking for a gentleman." Philippa and Mary Rush gathered their things. "One more carriage ride, then we'll find you a good supper and a clean, nice bed all to yourself."

Kate shook her head as if such a fantasy place could not really exist.

They journeyed to the new Earl of Aylswood's townhouse. Only weeks before, the earl had been plain old Mr. Daniel Swann, but his life had changed tremendously when the Prince Regent had invested him with the Aylswood title. Some said he should have had his rightful place as the heir to the Rotherhide title and estates, but he seemed content enough with his new peerage.

However, it wasn't the earl Philippa wished to see. Instead, she asked their carriage driver to head down the mews behind the townhouse, stopping before the section of stables belonging to the earl.

She asked the driver to wait, and she and Kate disembarked.

"What is this place?" Kate asked, her hand tightening in Philippa's.

"A house run by kind people who take in children like you." She knocked on the door beside the stable entrance.

An avalanche of footfalls sounded on the stairs behind the door, and small face peeked out. "Yes?" The girl had freckles and a halo of wispy curls that had escaped her braids.

"Is Mrs. Cadogan at home?"

The child, possibly eight years old?—looked Philippa up and down, transferred the look to Kate, and then the carriage.

"Who is it, Martha?" a woman's voice called from upstairs.

"A lady to see you. She's got a girl with her," Martha shouted over her shoulder.

The woman came downstairs, wiping her hands on her apron. She had blonde hair, nicely combed, and blue eyes. The scent of supper surrounded her as she moved.

"Don't keep them waiting in the mews, girl," she scolded, but softened the words by cupping the girl's head and smoothing her wayward curls. "I'm Mrs. Cadogan. What can I do for you?"

"My name is Miss Cashel, a friend of Lady Juliette Thorndike." Philippa inclined her head. "I understand you take in children in need."

"We do." Mrs. Cadogan looked the child over. "Sometimes."

"If we could speak privately?" Philippa inclined her head up the way. "Wait here, Kate."

When they could not be overheard, Philippa explained what had transpired that day. "I have no place to keep her at the moment. My current lodgings at the Duke of Haverly's residence are full to the eaves with people and servants, and I do not wish to impose upon them further. The new charity hospital, Eleos, will not be ready for residents for a few days at the earliest. If you could keep her until then, I will send for her. And I will pay for her upkeep." She reached into her reticule, bypassing the pistol, and producing some coins.

"Bless you for saving the poor mite. Of course she can stay. I will ask his lordship's mother, the viscountess, if there's a place for her in the Aylswood house. They're just setting up the staff, and perhaps they can use a scully or tweeny. She's the right age."

"That would be perfect. If they cannot take her, I will move her to Eleos, but it would be best if she could be placed right away."

"Never you worry. We know how to help young ones settle in."

They returned to the carriage, and Kate looked from Philippa to Mrs. Cadogan. "Am I to stay here?"

"Yes, love." Mrs. Cadogan smiled at the girl. "You'll stay with us for a bit. Martha, take Kate upstairs and show her where her she'll sleep. Sort out a nightdress for her and a comb and let her pick something from the toy box. Dinner needs my attention, so I'll be up soon."

Martha grinned and took Kate's hand, but Kate pulled away, diving toward Philippa and hugging her waist. "I wish I could go with you."

Philippa put her hand atop the girl's straw bonnet, surprised when tears pricked her eyes—she who guarded her heart against feeling anything that might make her vulnerable. "Kate, child, you will prosper here. Safe and well cared for. As you should be."

The girl lifted her face, tears hovering on her lower lashes, making her eyes seem bigger than ever. "You were right. This is the best day of my whole life."

As Philippa and the maid trundled away in the carriage, she thought, *I hope not, little one. I hope you have many and better days ahead.*

Chapter 8

"WHAT DO YOU KNOW OF Lord Pringle?" Bertie asked Marcus, taking a seat in the cramped, dark, secret room that was Marcus's office above Hatchard's.

"Pringle?" Marcus looked up from a folder. "Why?"

"Turns out, he was in Carlton House the morning the jewelry was stolen, and he might have had access to the scullery where the brooch was found." Bertie drummed his fingers on his knees. "Why does no one tell the truth in these matters? I questioned every staff member repeatedly, and not a one mentioned him. Surely someone saw him that morning. I only just managed to draw it out of the maid who is sitting in Newgate at the moment."

Marcus drew his hands down his face. "Philippa is convinced the girl is innocent. As I said before, she's a keen judge of character, and she can detect a lie quicker than anyone I know."

"I'm a fair hand at that myself, and I know that, while the maid may not be lying about stealing the jewels, she is concealing something. And the other scullery maid, Lydia, must know what it is. I've not been able to pry it out of either of them. Whatever it is, they're more afraid of telling it than anything I can do to them. Much like the rest of the servants at Carlton House. It seems the household manager, Mr. Lingfield, makes each employee swear an oath, on penalty of death by hanging for treason, not to reveal anything they see or hear in the house. Every employee is keeping their mouth shut. Those girls are petrified, but they know something."

Marcus narrowed his eyes. "They are in a rather vulnerable position. Do you believe they saw something they shouldn't or that they were participants in the crime?" He held up his hand when Bertie opened his mouth. "I know you believe the girls to be innocent, but what if they were coerced? Perhaps someone forced one or both of the girls to steal the jewels, slip them out of the house, and then made them lie about it or face the consequences, either of being arrested or being silenced by the real thief?"

"You see?" Bertie spread his hands. "This is why jewel theft should be a matter for Swann and the Bow Street Investigators, not an agent like me. Mr. Lingfield has such a stranglehold on the staff at Carlton House that not a whiff of this has gotten to the newspapers yet, but it's merely a matter of time. Anything concerning the Prince Regent is instantly news. I cannot believe the arrest of his valet for household thievery hasn't been shouted from every street corner, much less the theft of the jewels."

"I agree. Expect the news of the valet to break soon because the court records will be public. As to the jewel theft, it will be a test of Mr. Lingfield and the Prince Regent's dominance of the staff if it does not become common knowledge soon. Members of the press have noticed your presence at Carlton House and are speculating about it. Are you currying favor with the prince? Are you going to make a move into politics? Have you been added to his staff as an advisor or courtier? Lots of guessing and nosing about."

How did Marcus know these things?

"No one has approached me about it. And the last thing I would ever do would be to stand for Parliament." Bertie shook his head at such an absurd notion.

"The speculations as to the goings on at Carlton House will come soon, I imagine. The prince is working hard at refurbishing his image and at the same time gratifying his need for attention." Marcus tapped the front page of a newspaper on the corner of his desk. "The papers are full of his doings, entertaining various dignitaries, lavish parties, and what the prince is wearing to the Royal Opera—all information fed to the papers by the prince's staff and on his say-so, no doubt. Vacuous at best, but the public will read it."

"How can I investigate under these circumstances? Everyone is keeping secrets, and no one wants to be tried for treason. Should I go to the prince and tell him to make his staff divulge what they know?"

"One does not tell the Prince Regent what to do. If you want to accomplish something regarding His Highness, you must broach the subject as a question, ask for his insights, and then direct him toward the conclusion you seek, while making it seem as if it was all his idea to begin with." The jaded edge to Marcus's tone led Bertie to believe he had performed this maneuver on more than one occasion.

"As to the question you raised about involving Swann and Bow Street, I had a feeling this was coming. I agree that it is time he should be consulted on the theft; therefore, I have asked him to meet us here. Not that I don't think you are capable of solving this little mystery, but I do believe in using every tool at my disposal. Daniel knows how to keep his own counsel, and if the prince hadn't been so reluctant, I would have had Swann involved from the outset. I will not ask him to investigate, merely for his expertise, a bit of direction, as it were." Marcus leaned back in his chair, the leather squeaking. "I will not go against His Highness's wishes in making this a public matter, but I will avail myself of Daniel's experience in investigating crime, in his capacity as one of my part-time agents. The plans I have for you in the near future are coming to fruition, and I do not wish you bogged down in this investigation if it is not resolved quickly. If I need you to pivot to another assignment, I'm sure I can convince the Prince Regent to let Daniel run with the case."

Daniel had a growing reputation as the finest police investigator in the kingdom, in addition to being the newly promoted supervisor of detectives at Bow Street. "I look forward to his thoughts on the matter."

And to possibly jettisoning this investigation into his capable hands. "Does Daniel know Lord Pringle?"

"I have no idea. I don't know Pringle well. He's one of the Regent's courtiers, so he will have a file at the Home Office. I shall consult. Discreetly."

Bertie could count on Marcus's ability to gather information without drawing notice. He wouldn't put it past the duke to break into the Home Office after hours, purloin the required files, and appear at a dinner party or soiree a half hour later as if nothing untoward had occurred.

Soft footfalls on the stairs indicated Swann's arrival.

"Ah, right on time." Marcus glanced at the door. "I told him to come up despite the book being moved."

"Good day, Your Grace, Thorndike." Swann removed his hat and set it, brim up, on the table beside the door. He tossed his gloves into the crown.

"Swann . . . or should I call you Aylswood? How is the new title fitting?" Marcus asked.

"Like a coat that is a bit too snug, Your Grace." He shrugged his shoulders. "Which is how current fashion appears to be trending. It takes a valet and a strong footman to get me out of this garb."

His coat did fit as if painted on. Bertie tilted his head. "I have my tailor give a bit of extra room across the shoulders, else how would I conceal any weapons?"

"I shall have to have a word at my next fitting." Swann took the other chair, close by Bertie. Of course, there was no choice but to be close by in such a small space.

The scents of smoke, ink, and paper permeated the cramped room. No windows for anyone to spy through and only the one door at the top of a hidden staircase with no landing, making it harder to break into.

Adequate, but Bertie much preferred the War Room in the attic of his brother's house or the meeting room at Haverly's townhouse.

"What is it I can do for you, Your Grace?" Daniel asked. "A bit of sleuthing? Though where I will fit it in with my new responsibilities at Bow Street and in the peerage, I don't know."

"Not sleuthing, but your expertise in police matters. This must be kept confidential." Marcus's words held a gravity that focused Swann's attention on the duke. Bertie well knew the feeling. When Haverly spoke like that, the matter was serious.

"Of course."

"Even from Lady Juliette and the earl and countess."

Swann paused, and Bertie could imagine the internal wrestle. He was newly in love, newly engaged, and newly a peer. Beginning his relationship with his soon-to-be bride by keeping secrets from her and her parents would not sit well.

But the lives of agents for the Crown were filled with secrets, even from those one loved most. Sometimes *especially* from those one loved most. Yet another reason Bertie had not sought himself a bride. He did not wish the entanglement of keeping half his life concealed from a wife.

"You have my word," Swann finally said.

Bertie apprised him of the situation, beginning with being called to Carlton House and ending with his visit to the maid in prison. "I've done everything I can think of to track down the culprit, but I'm no closer than when first summoned to Carlton House. And the Prince Regent has set the clock ticking. He has demanded the capture of the thief and the restoration of the jewels before he returns to London. He's going to Tunbridge Wells for a fortnight, and will brook no argument as to his timeline."

As the information unfolded, Swann leaned forward, his eyes taking on an intense light. He reminded Bertie of a hound on a scent. The man was made to be an investigator.

"You've questioned everyone as to their movements in the house?"

"Yes, but the staff is extensive, and they seem to have free rein to go most anywhere in the house, especially when the prince is not in residence, which he wasn't at the time of the theft. Then there is the little matter of them being bound by secrecy by their employer. Gathering information is a true battle."

"That is both a drawback and a benefit. Too many people with access and opportunity, but more people to see someone commit the crime. Getting the information may be a matter of conferring with the Prince Regent and releasing his staff to speak freely with you." Daniel reached into his interior jacket pocket but withdrew his hand empty. "Another word to have with my tailor. No inner pocket for my notebook and pencil. I might as well be wearing banded hawsers."

"Marcus has suggested that approach with the prince as well, as long as I phrase it as a request and not a dictate. We searched the house twice. A maid later found the brooch in the scullery." Bertie reached into his pocket and withdrew the piece he had brought to show Marcus. "Sapphire and pearl. This alone is worth a hundred or more pounds. I was only recently apprised of the fact that Lord Pringle, courtier to the prince, was in the house at the time the jewelry was stolen and just before the brooch was found."

"I will discover what I can on Lord Pringle and inform you both of what I find. Do you have any advice for how Sir Bertrand should proceed with Pringle?" Marcus asked.

"The more information you can gather before you confront him, the better. Find out where he was in the house when the parure went missing. Find out if he had a motive to steal the jewels. Is he in debt? Have other things gone missing when he's been about? Track his movements, his relationships, and his habits. It's always very delicate when you center your attention on a peer, however minor. Society will prefer to believe the maid guilty. They will resist the idea of a peer being so crass as to rob the prince. You will have to be discreet and careful, mounting your evidence beyond doubt before you accuse someone." Daniel leveled his gaze at Bertie. "If word gets out that you're looking beyond the maid at a lord, you will meet with resistance."

Bertie nodded. "I heartily wish the prince had called upon you, rather than the agency, to sort this out. I've no experience in this area."

"Experience aside," Marcus said. "You are well equipped to see this through, Bertie. You're observant and intuitive, and you're brave enough to follow the investigation wherever it leads. Not one to bow to convention or politics and hide the truth."

The praise had what Bertie surmised was the desired effect in bolstering his flagging confidence.

"I am not ready to surrender just yet," he avowed. He did not want Marcus to think him a lightweight when it came to fulfilling a mission. "What other advice do you have?" he asked Daniel.

"I always find it useful to follow the paper. Any records associated with the creation and purchase of the jewels. Any paperwork that indicates a change in the household, the accounts, the staff, the movements of the prince's possessions. He was in Brighton when the jewels were delivered and stolen?"

"Yes." One of the few facts of which Bertie was certain.

"Get a list of which servants were with him. If it exists, a list of what items he took along. A list of gifts given to his former mistress, Mrs. Bascome, or others. Anything you can acquire regarding records. Often a clue is hiding in the paperwork. Ask my newest investigator, Owen Wilkinson. Many's the time I've put him on the paper trail, much to his disgust, as he would rather be pounding on doors and questioning suspects. But the answers we need are often in the tedium. Police work is predominately a willingness to sift through information."

Bertie sighed. He commiserated with this Wilkinson chap. He would rather be shadowing a suspected spy or breaking into a locked office in the middle of the night than studying pages of ephemera from Carlton House.

"I would assign Partridge to follow Lord Pringle. I will arrange for you and I, Thorndike, to meet Pringle at White's later this week." Marcus laced his fingers, propping his elbows on his chair arms.

"Is he a member of White's?" Bertie had not seen him there.

"Not yet, but I shall invite him to dine with us. In company, of course. I'm putting forward my brother-in-law, Charles, for membership. I will gather a handful of men, Pringle included, to dine, and you can begin to get a sense of whether you believe he is capable of theft."

Bertie was reminded once again that Marcus was a master spy, capable of manipulating circumstances to his liking and to suit his needs, with what seemed little effort.

Which meant he was quite capable of manipulating Bertie as well.

"Work is coming along nicely, is it not? I believe we shall be able to take up residence within the week if we're willing to live amongst the improvements for a time." Aunt Dolly stepped around a pile of saw-dust. "Even sooner if needs be. I would rather sleep rough here at the manor if it meant we could begin helping more women sooner."

Philippa wanted to pinch herself. This felt like a dream. They stood in the old baronial hall, the scents of fresh paint and new wood over-coming the previous smell of dust and neglect. The workers Marcus had hired had only been there three days and had already made great progress. "I fear we shall have to be ready sooner, as Mr. Todd is bring-ing applicants today to be interviewed. He is in quite the hurry to begin, isn't he? Are the sleeping chambers going to be ready?"

She had to speak over the sound of hammers and saws, the clack of lumber being stacked, and the tramp of boots. At least a dozen men were hard at work. At this rate . . .

"As long as we can get straw to fill the mattresses. I was able to purchase several lengths of ticking for a good price, and the Haverly seamstress and her assistant have been busy sewing on them the past two days. I suppose we can make pallets on the floor as a temporary measure."

"Where did you get money for yard goods?" It had been preying upon Philippa's mind, the expenses needed to get the place habitable. Mr. Asbury might be responsible for the cost of making the structure sound, but the furnishings and household goods were up to them to supply. And nearly all their reserves had gone into the first rent payment.

"I've been keeping a secret." Aunt Dolly looked back over her shoulder as she headed toward the staircase leading to the gallery.

"A secret?" She and her dear friend and mentor had no secrets from one another, did they?

"Follow me." At the top of the staircase, Aunt Dolly opened the door to one of the rooms. The hinges screeched, squealing as the door dragged on the wooden floor. The carpenters had not made it this far just yet. Inside the room, stacked boxes and furnishings took up nearly every inch of floor space.

Philippa leaned to one side to study an escritoire that looked familiar. She recognized a bedframe, and a porcelain ewer. "These are your things."

"Yes, I had them brought here."

"But what about your house on King's Place? These are the furnishings of your home." The home where Philippa had first met Mrs. Dorothy Stokes, former madam-turned-rescuer of fallen women. Philippa had been ensconced at a well-known "disorderly house" on King's Place a few doors down from Aunt Dolly's and had fled there when one of her clients beat her rather severely.

"I sold it. I will not need it. I will live here at Eleos, and we can use the money from the sale to purchase needed supplies. And whatever I have here"—she waved her hand toward the furnishings—"well, we can spread those out where needed."

"You cannot use the money for Eleos. That house, or the money from it, is to keep you in your declining years." Guilt smote Philippa.

"Nonsense. God will keep me in my declining years. In fact, He already has. He's provided Eleos. And you need not worry that I sold the house on King's Place for ill use. Since you and Lady Charlotte were rescued from that scoundrel Ratcliffe, the Duke of Haverly has made it his mission to clear out the brothels and turn that street into a respectable neighborhood. As a result, the value of my property went up quite a bit. I received a tidy sum for the house. A silk merchant bought it for his wife and family. The proceeds are more than enough to buy bedding for our new clients plus other essentials."

"I shouldn't allow you to do this. It's far too generous. What if the hospital fails? What will you do then?" Philippa well knew the precarious nature of an independent woman's finances. Especially one who had made her living as both of them had, however much in the past that might be. Aunt Dolly had no family on which she could rely. She had only herself and Philippa.

"I've learned over the years that though I might not know where my next ha'penny was coming from, God does. He will take care of me as He always has. I cannot put my trust in coins or men. Using the money from the house to help get the school up and running is what I am led to do. You would not want to contravene God's message to me, would you?"

If only Philippa could be as certain as Aunt Dolly when it came to God's benevolent care. If only He would speak to her as clearly as He did to some others. Though in one thing, she and Aunt Dolly were in agreement. Men were not to be trusted, not completely.

"Is anyone about?" A man's voice came up from the hall.

Philippa went to the balcony railing, which wobbled when she leaned on it. Backing up a step lest she tumble to the flagstones below, she recognized Mr. Todd standing in the entrance.

"Sir, we will be right down." Philippa resisted rolling her eyes. Why had Marcus made provision for the reverend to attend their applicant interviews? Though she had nothing against the man personally, she would rather be free of his interference, especially when it came to admitting women to the charity.

When they reached the ground floor, Mr. Todd was gazing up at the windows, his hands clasped behind his back, a large Bible clamped beneath his arm. "I see the dowager had her way as to color?" Two men stood atop a scaffold, applying a fresh coat of paint to the dingy plaster. She had to admit it did brighten and cheer up the place.

"The dowager often gets her way, and Mr. Asbury was no match for her. Still, it looks nice. Nothing like a new coat of paint to smarten up a room." Aunt Dolly offered her hand to him. "Thank you for meeting us here. I thought we might conduct interviews in the oratory. It's smaller and not as noisy as the hall, in addition to being the first room that was cleaned. You've brought our first applicants?" She looked around as if expecting them to appear.

"They are outside in the wagon. There are seven, drawn from the parishes of my colleagues." He frowned. "They certainly do not inspire confidence, if we were to judge by appearances, but with the speed at which things are occurring, I had no chance to, shall we say, weed through them before bringing them here."

Philippa bridled, stiffening, but Dolly put her hand on Philippa's forearm and squeezed.

"Well, as the Great Physician said, He did not come to heal the well, but the sick. If they were not in need and wanting help, they would not have come. Let's get them inside."

Mr. Todd had brought the women in a rough-sided, high-wheeled cart, as if they were sheep on the way to market. He did deign to help them down, however. Once they were all on solid ground, he went into the house.

"Ladies, there are some benches in the hall where you can sit. Perhaps we can get them something to quench their thirst?" Aunt Dolly motioned for them to precede her inside.

"Certainly." Philippa went in search of Clara, one of the girls she had been training and who was cleaning in the kitchen, to fetch some water.

When she returned to the main hall, Aunt Dolly was addressing the ladies. "We will speak with each of you privately. There is only one room habitable for sleeping at the moment, but we hope to have another two ready by nightfall. If you agree to what we're offering here, you can stay right away. It will not be luxurious, and you will be expected to pitch in and help with the work, but if you do not mind living in a house under repair, you will be safe, fed, and welcome."

Several had rolled bundles with them, an extra dress, a few trinkets perhaps? Probably all their worldly goods. They would most likely not argue with the conditions here.

"Would you like to go first?" Philippa asked a young girl on the end of the bench. Fifteen? Sixteen? A smattering of freckles and wide, brown eyes. She nodded, weariness in every line of her body.

Once in the oratory, Mr. Todd waited for the ladies to be seated before taking his own chair. "I shall merely listen if you do not mind. I have not conducted such interviews before and will hold my comments until I see how you ladies work together."

Philippa was nonplussed. He'd made his statement with none of the pomposity she had expected.

She chose the chair beside the young girl rather than taking a seat across the table from her. Hopefully, if the young woman did not feel she was getting a dressing down, she would be at ease.

Aunt Dolly opened an inkwell and took up the form Marcus had provided them to use as a registration form. "Your name?"

"Bridie. Bridie Jacobson."

"Your age?"

"Fourteen."

Even younger than Philippa had thought.

They went through the basic questions, and Bridie seemed to gain confidence. Until Aunt Dolly asked, "Have you ever been in an institution like Eleos or the Magdalen Hospital before?"

"I was in the Magdalen last winter." Wariness invaded Bridie's eyes.

Philippa's heart sank. The poor child had sought help or been placed there by her family at the tender age of thirteen?

Mr. Todd sat forward. "How long were you there?" It was the first he'd spoken during the interview.

Bridie shrugged, her shawl falling off her shoulder. "A few weeks. I didn't like it. And me mum needed me out earning something, else the little ones would starve."

"Why did you choose to come here then?" His frown made his words even sharper.

"My mum said the curate told her Eleos was different, that I would learn a skill so I could find work. Maybe sewing or child minding or cooking. And to read and write. Then I could help Mum feed the little'ns with my wages instead of what I've been doing. The curate said the parish would help my mum until I was trained proper and found work."

"I see." He lowered his brows. "I'm afraid the fact that you were unable to complete a program of rehabilitation in the past means a high likelihood of you failing this time as well. I have to advise against admitting Miss Jacobson at this time."

Philippa gave Aunt Dolly a startled glance and put her hand on Bridie's arm as the child made to rise. "I beg your pardon. It is not upon you to make such a decision, Mr. Todd. Mrs. Stokes and I are responsible for handling the admissions. You are here as a courtesy. Nowhere in our policies does it say someone cannot enter Eleos if they have partaken in another charitable cause."

He puffed out his cheeks, as if forced to make her see reason. "But you must show an excellent success rate in order to keep the lease with Micah Asbury. If you admit those who have already failed to reform, you set yourself up for repeated lack of success. We only want the candidates with the highest potential to succeed, especially at first. I'm only looking out for the future of the school. Miss Jacobson has had a bite from the reform apple, and she spit it out."

Philippa put her arm around Bridie's thin shoulders. "We will not turn anyone away. There will be the customary probation period for all new students, but no one will be denied admittance." How dare this man barge his way into their work. He hadn't the slightest clue what it was to be a woman in Bridie's situation, and here he was dividing sheep from goats as if he had authority.

"Then what is the purpose of the interview process?" he asked. "If everyone gains admittance, we're wasting our time here."

"It is merely for us to get to know each pupil, to ascertain their needs, and to set them up for a profitable time here." Aunt Dolly lifted one of the pages she'd been writing on. "Bridie, do you have any particular skills? Can you sew or tend children or care for animals?"

She shook her head. "I got a passel of little brothers and sisters, and I have watched them. Never held a needle in my life, and we never had enough money for livestock."

"Are you interested in cooking? Or gardening?"

"I would be interested in eating." She put her hand on her stomach. "Been a spell since I saw any victuals."

Philippa smiled and gave Bridie a squeeze. "There will be plenty of food for you soon. For the next few days, you will be given tasks to do that will help us get the facility functional. Cleaning, sorting, and carrying, mostly. During that time, you'll have regular meals and will live in our intake dorm. All our dormitories will be intake rooms at first, so you will not be separated from the other girls. The rules are simple here. No fighting or squabbling, each girl's locker is private so no dipping into their boxes, follow the timetable, be respectful, and do your best. Do you think you can abide by those rules?"

Bridie considered for a moment and then nodded.

"At no time are you a prisoner here. If you decide this isn't for you, you are welcome to leave. However, if you choose to leave and then wish to come back, there may not be a bed for you. We anticipate being full up soon. Weigh carefully if you decide to walk away. We want to give you every chance to succeed here, to give you skills and abilities to enable you to support yourself in a wholesome and honorable way. We will teach you and equip you, and we will seek to find a safe place of employment once you finish the course, but it will be upon you to work hard, learn much, and keep yourself out of trouble."

"Yes, ma'am." Bridie's eyes were round in her dirt-smudged face.

By the time they finished the last intake interview, Philippa was exhausted. Not that the interviews were taxing, but the weight of the women's stories was heavy. So much sorrow, so many cases of abuse and abandonment. She could not turn any away, not even the middle-aged woman clearly suffering a catching disease.

"We have an infirmary. It's a bit rough and ready, but you will remain there for treatment." Aunt Dolly rose. "I will take you there. Philippa, you will see Mr. Todd out?" She leveled a telling look at Philippa, clearly a warning to be polite.

As they reached the front door, the reverend shifted his Bible under his arm to pull on his gloves. "I have to say, I think you're making a mistake, especially with the syphilitic and the girl who rejected help before. You would not want your lease to be terminated if Asbury comes to hear of it."

His tone held a warning, and Philippa was reminded that Todd and Asbury were close friends. Asbury had insisted Mr. Todd be installed as spiritual mentor at Eleos, thus all but planting a spy in their midst.

"We cannot turn people away because we *think* they might fail. Innocent until proven guilty?"

"None of these women are innocent. Isn't that rather the point?"

She flinched at the barb. "Neither are they beyond redemption. As a man of God, surely you do not judge who is worthy of the gospel and who is not? Are we all not unworthy? If we were worthy or able to save ourselves, we would not need a Savior. Much the same way as we cannot clean ourselves up enough to be acceptable to Christ, I do not believe these women need to be polished and already reformed before being accepted here."

"We are told not to cast our pearls before swine too. I only want your school to prove a success. You act as if I am working counter to your own desires. I have vastly more experience than you in both biblical interpretation and charitable endeavors. It would behoove you to at least consider my counsel."

She took a deep breath, inwardly railing against his patronizing tone. "These ladies are not to be considered swine. I will grant you are the superior Bible scholar and that you have worked with many charities, but you must allow that I have more experience with our particular clientele. I hope you will allow us to do our work in the ways we have developed through being on the front lines, as it were. If our methods do not prove effective, we will consider other ways, but permit us to at least try them."

He frowned but nodded. "When will my own quarters be finished? I wish to be installed soon so as to take up my responsibilities as spiritual leader here."

"That you will have to ask the foreman. He has the schedule assembled for the repairs. The chapel will take the longest to be restored, as

I understand it, because it was more heavily damaged and not essential for us to begin inhabiting the property."

"Considering your open policy of admission, I believe the chapel is essential and cannot be finished soon enough."

Chapter 9

"There's something there. Lord Pringle has unusual habits." Partridge eyed the War Room. "This is quite the space."

Bertie waved a casual hand. "Everything an agent might need to keep his skills sharp. I thought it might be a good place to review and strategize." He pulled out a chair at the table beside the pinboards. Stacks of documents covered the surface of the table. Following Swann's advice to follow the paper, Bertie had organized his interview notes, the household accounts, and other ephemera he had been able to lay his hands on.

Though studying them had proven tedious, he did have a better idea of the inner workings of Carlton House. Bertie had never had the responsibility of running an estate or house, and the scope of the machinations daunted him. He had been toying with the idea of purchasing his own house in London, but was he ready for that? Living with Tristan and Melisande had meant he was an easily accessible member of their team and able to have a hand in training Juliette. But now that he was a leader, perhaps it was time to move out on his own.

After he solved this theft, he would think about it. With the social season coming to an end soon, there would be some houses for sale in the city.

"What habits of his did you find unusual?" Bertie asked Partridge. The big man took one of the chairs, and Bertie cast about his memory.

Had he ever seen Partridge sitting? Haverly's right-hand man when it came to spying and protection, Partridge was always on the move.

Marcus had once mentioned he'd freed Partridge from a prison in Spain during the war and that he'd become his batman and returned to England with him where they had worked together since. Partridge had seen a few things, and Bertie was honored that Marcus thought he was the man to lead a team with Partridge a member.

"He's nervous. And he leaves the house at odd hours. I watched his place two nights in a row, and both nights, well after midnight, he took himself out for a stroll. Odd thing is, he never left by the front or back door. He climbed out of an upper story window, using a trellis to get down."

"Most strange. Where did he go?"

"Odder still, he just walked. Never went into a building, never met up with another soul. Easy enough to follow because he never looked around as he went. Eyes forward, same pace, same route each night. Walked from Cavendish Square up the Mall, stood in front of St. James's Palace for a while, looking out over the park, and then returned to his home."

Bertie's senses tingled. "Was he looking for a signal? Is he perhaps a spy?"

"I looked for any odd markings on the buildings or lampposts or signal lights in the windows, but I saw nothing. Nor did he encounter anyone as he walked, no passing of notes. He carried nothing but his walking stick. I followed at about a hundred paces, keeping to the shadows, but neither night did I see anything suspicious beyond him being out of the house at that hour. And his choice of egress."

"Were you able to get into the house either night?"

"No, not with him roaming about. I thought it best to see where he went."

Bertie nodded. "Perhaps I will join you tonight, and you can chase him about the city while I get a look inside. Who lives there with him?"

"A wife and two daughters. The children are small." Partridge held his hand perpendicular to the floor at not much more than table height. "They have a nurse with them. Then the usual household staff." He shrugged. "Shouldn't be difficult to get in and have a nose around."

"Marcus looked into his dealings with the Prince Regent and sent a report. Pringle is a courtier, and from what I can ascertain, a sort of adviser on domestic policies?" Bertie riffled through one stack. "The prince, it seems, does not desire to read parliamentary papers for himself but rather relies on his courtiers to summarize and simplify things. Pringle covers commerce and taxation matters."

"He was in the house when the jewelry went missing?"

"Yes, though no one thought to mention it until days later." Bertie grimaced. "Evidently, no one considered that it might be him because he's a courtier. Only servants would steal, according to their thinking, so only servants needed to be accounted for."

He'd argued with Mr. Lingfield at length, but the secretary continued to insist that privacy trumped the investigation, and no staff member would be released from their oath of loyalty to keep quiet about what they heard and saw in the house. What secrets must be guarded so carefully? The regent had left for Tunbridge Wells, and the clock was ticking on the investigation. He was expected back by the twenty-sixth, by which time Bertie must prove the maid Nell innocent by catching the right culprit.

Partridge crossed his arms over his barrel chest. "Pringle leaves the house after midnight, but we'll want to be in place before then."

"I'll meet you at the end of his block at half ten, then."

Cavendish Square proved to be a busy place even at that hour. Carriages came and went, and across the expanse of the green, a party was in full sail at one of the townhouses. Candlelight blazed from every window, and music drifted on the air.

"If Pringle is invited to that party, it will be easy enough to get into his house, but we won't be able to track where he goes." Bertie followed Partridge around the corner into the shadows of the mews behind the row houses.

"No way to know if he's at the party until he doesn't come out the window after midnight." Partridge signaled toward an open stable door. "This one's empty and has a good view of the back of the house."

The stable was swept clean but still smelled of horse and grain and dust. Bertie, dressed in dark, loose clothing adequate for clandestine burglary, was careful not to brush against anything that might leave dust marks on his attire.

Partridge had no such qualms, leaning his massive shoulder against the wall a few feet back from the doorway, out of sight of anyone looking from a window.

Neither spoke. Each knew his role, and each was adept at waiting. Here in the mews, the music from across the square was faint, and the traffic sounds muffled. In the stall next door, a horse snorted and shuffled in the straw. At one point, a carriage rolled down the cobbled alleyway, past their hiding place.

After an age, Partridge stirred. Bertie stepped behind him. Three floors up, a leg protruded from the window followed by a hand, a shoulder, and then a head. Lord Pringle grasped the trellis beside the opening, and with remarkable agility, descended, dropping the final couple of feet to the cobbles and landing lightly. He wore no hat or cloak, and his boots were scuffed and dull. He'd managed to descend with a walking stick in his hand. Glancing quickly up and down the mews, he set off at a brisk pace.

Half a minute later, Partridge slipped out and followed, surprisingly silent for such a large man.

Bertie held in place, studying the back of the house. Not a single light showed, and the dark square where Pringle had emerged now had a white curtain hanging over the sill, twitching in the small gusts of night breeze wafting up the mews. Always tricky, entering a house where you didn't know the floor plan. Was that a dressing room or Pringle's bedchamber? Did he break with current trends of separate sleeping quarters from his wife? He had to assume Pringle had a valet. Did the man sleep nearby or on another floor?

He bounced lightly on his feet, readying himself, calling on his training and past experience. His heart thrummed with the challenge.

This was the destiny to which he had been born, the descendant of a long line of British spies and agents, well trained and capable.

He wouldn't give up this life for anything.

Certain no one was about, Bertie crossed the mews, slipped through the iron-barred gate into the small back garden, and up to the trellis. Some sort of ivied vine with small, pink flowers curled and tendrilled its way upward, but the structure itself seemed sturdy enough. With the agility of much practice, Bertie climbed, making sure of each hand and foothold before releasing the previous one.

Child's play. His head reached the level of the sill, and with eyes accustomed to the dark, he peered into the room, moving aside the gossamer film of the curtain.

Nothing moved inside. He picked out shelves and cupboards, a row of hats, a rack of walking sticks and umbrellas.

Pringle's dressing room.

No valet's cot.

Levering himself up, he sat on the sill and swung his legs inside. His custom-made footwear landed soundlessly on the wood floor. The shoes, created along the lines of an American Indian's moccasin, were soft and malleable, perfect for sneaking about on important missions.

A quick poke around showed a doorway into what must be Pringle's bedroom. He did not share a sleeping chamber with his wife, and the bed was unmussed. A pipe lay on a table beside a low-banked fire, and the lingering odor of tobacco hovered in the air. A newspaper lay on the chair by the table, along with a glass. Bertie picked up the stemware and sniffed. Sherry.

He returned to the dressing room and eased the door open. The hall was deserted and dark. Perfect. He closed the door.

Pulling a scarf off a hook, he laid it along the bottom of the door and returned to the bedroom to light a candle. In the dressing room, he set the candle atop a dresser and began opening drawers.

Handkerchiefs, shirts, cravats, small clothes . . . nothing unusual, nothing out of place. His valet might not sleep in the dressing room, but he kept a tidy closet.

Nothing of note, and certainly no sapphires and pearls.

Removing to the bedchamber, Bertie checked the bedside table and then began on the bookshelves. With the number of times he had been tasked with breaking into and searching a residence, he knew the proclivities of most people. They hid things in handy places, where they could check on them often.

"Eureka," he whispered. One of the books on the shelf was hollow. Hoping to find the missing jewels and end his case and Nell's incarceration, he lifted the tab concealing the cavity. The space held only three folded pages, each with a broken wax seal.

His heart sank. Still, if the pages were worth concealing, he should at least read them.

Bertie took them into the dressing room where he had ensured the candlelight wouldn't be seen under the door and perused the papers.

He may not have found the jewels, but he had found a reason Pringle might steal them. The motive leapt off the pages in black ink.

What to do now? Should he take the papers or leave them in situ? He would need to confront Lord Pringle with what he'd found, but not before reporting to Marcus. This might go higher and broader than Bertie was authorized to deal with, and he would not, in any case, make a move without Haverly's input.

Better take the papers, lest Pringle destroy them in the meantime. He tucked them into his breast pocket, returned the book to the shelf in the bedchamber, and snuffed the candle. Last thing, he returned the scarf to the hook, checking that all was as he had found it.

As he turned to the window, he heard a quiet but unmistakable scrape outside. The trellis shuddered. Someone was climbing up.

No place of concealment offered in the dressing room. Like a lintie, Bertie leapt for the bedchamber. Perhaps he could get into the hall and wait for a chance to sneak back through the dressing room or out the front door.

Problem. The bedchamber door had a bolt on the inside. Could he shoot it back without making noise?

In a split-second decision, Bertie lowered himself to the floor and rolled under the bed, allowing the bed skirt to fall into place and conceal him.

Of all the green mistakes, not shooting that bolt first thing and giving himself a second method of escape. It was a cardinal rule. If Juliette found out about this, she would have a hearty laugh at his expense. How often had he stressed to her she must ensure more than one way of escape without discovery when burgling a place?

Soft footfalls in the dressing room next door, the closing of the window, and then the brush of feet on the bedroom carpet. Rustles and movement, the glow of a newly lit candle, and overhead, the sag of the mattress on the ropes as Pringle sat on the bed.

Bertie's muscles clenched, and he turned his head to the side. How he hated confined spaces. A fine layer of dust lay on the floor all around him, and his movements had stirred it about. Pinching his nose to stave off the growing sneeze behind his eyes, he castigated himself. He must never breathe a word of this. Humiliation heated his face. Eventually, the urge to sneeze faded.

Partridge would know, though, when he wasn't waiting in the stables. Pringle could not have been gone as long this time as he had been the previous two nights. It had been barely a quarter of an hour since Bertie had climbed through the window.

Shoes thudded on the floor as Pringle removed them, clothes were tossed onto the chair beside the bed. Bertie imagined every step. A nightshirt and robe had been laid across the foot of the bed, and the rustle of clothing, the flap of covers being pulled back, and the squeak and sag of the ropes indicated Pringle was at last in bed.

A lean, and a puff, and the faint light around the bed skirt disappeared. Darkness settled, but Pringle did not. He rolled, he punched the pillows, he changed positions.

Bertie lay like a log, flat on his back, eyes straining to see in the dark. He daren't move, but the floor was hard, and his back complained after a while. If Pringle would just go to sleep—even better if he would start snoring. Then Bertie could make his escape.

Partridge had had no way to warn Bertie of Pringle's early return. Another thing they had left to chance. Another thing that was Bertie's fault.

However, he did have a new line of investigation to follow. If only he could remove himself from the bedchamber without being seen.

"I need to see Mr. Newbolt, please," Philippa said to the secretary.

"Do you have an appointment?" The man frowned and checked a calendar on his desk. Weak morning light filtered through the sheer drapes behind him, silhouetting him against the window.

"I do not. I believe he will wish to see me, however. Please tell him that Miss Cashel needs a word with him as soon as possible." She kept her tone level and professional, even as her insides quaked. Never had she anticipated being in this position. Yet what else could she do? She handed over her card.

The secretary frowned. "He is in today, but his schedule is quite full. I shall make inquiries."

She smiled her best thank-you smile, the one that usually opened doors for her, and took a seat in an armchair. An annoying tapping hit her ears, and she realized she was bouncing her foot.

Calm down, Pip.

I can't. I never thought I would see him again. Much less come begging a favor.

The secretary returned, holding the door open. "This way, Miss Cashel. Mr. Newbolt will see you now." His voice held a tinge of doubt and incredulity that she had been able to sway his employer so easily, and his eyes held supposition and conclusions that did not flatter Philippa in the least.

She rose slowly, keeping her chin high, and moved as gracefully as she knew how—which was quite graceful indeed. As she passed, she looked at him from the side of her eye. "Thank you."

He reddened, and she smothered a smile.

Walter Newbolt was on his feet behind his desk. He waited until the secretary had closed the door before he spoke. "Pippa, what a surprise. Come in. Sit. What can I do for you?"

He tugged at his cravat, shot his cuffs, and smoothed his hands down his waistcoat. He was fifty or so, with gray hair, pale blue eyes, and a longish face. Well groomed, pleasant, and with impeccable manners.

And at one time, he'd been one of her most consistent clients.

"Please, I no longer go by Pippa. Call me Philippa, or if it is easier, Miss Cashel will do." She took the chair before his desk, adjusting her skirts.

He took his seat and picked up a letter opener, twisting it in his hands. "I confess, it was quite a surprise when McDonald said you were waiting to see me. What is it I can do?"

"I am surprised to be here myself. When I left King's Place, I never expected to see my clients again." No sense denying their former relationship. Best to get that out of the way quickly. "However, I am in need of a barrister."

He frowned. "Are you in trouble?"

"No, not myself. A young girl under my care. She's been charged with theft and is currently in Newgate awaiting trial."

"I see." He looked at his hands. "What is it she's accused of taking?"

"What we say here is confidential?" she asked.

"Of course. For the purposes of this meeting, I shall consider you a client, protecting anything you say to me."

"Very well. Nothing I say to you must leave this office. The missing item is a valuable parure. And to make things worse, she's accused of stealing it from the Prince Regent himself. She is employed at Carlton House, and the jewelry has gone missing. A piece of it was found in the area of the house where Nell works, and she was arrested for the theft. She is completely innocent. I can vouch for that, but the overseer at Carlton House wanted the case closed quickly and has no interest in finding the real culprit."

"Carlton House? From the Prince Regent?" He leaned back, as if distancing himself from the issue.

"Please, Walter." She used his first name on purpose. "She has no one, and if she's found guilty, she will hang. She needs the best barrister to defend her."

"Legal defense is in its infancy. I have not had much practice. Are you certain I am the best one for this case? It sounds as if the verdict is a foregone conclusion." He put the point of the letter opener on the blotter, pressing the hilt into his palm to balance it.

"It certainly is if you do not help her. There are many working on her behalf and attempting to find the real culprit, but it seems the Prince Regent's household manager isn't looking any further than poor Nell." She smoothed her skirts. "I realize it is a cheek, me coming here and asking anything of you, and I know this case will not cover you in glory or in even proper remuneration, for I have few funds. But you are welcome to all the money I have to defend an innocent girl."

She hated that she was begging. Especially from a man with whom she shared a past.

"How is it that someone has been arrested, but I've heard nothing in the press?" he asked.

"I believe they have postponed publishing the actual charge to keep the prince's name out of things. They cannot conceal it forever, but for now, it is . . . what is it called? Sub judice?"

His brows shot up. "That is the correct term, though I am surprised you know it."

She smiled ruefully. "You spoke often of your work when we were together." Most men did. They talked of their families, their work, their concerns, their worries. As much as the primary reason for which they came to her, she was convinced that most men wanted someone to listen. She remembered much of what was said, which was how she'd been able to relay important information to Marcus from time to time.

Wariness entered his eyes. "If I refuse the case, will you make our past relationship public? My wife never knew about my trips to King's Place."

Her heart sank. "Mr. Newbolt, I would never blackmail you. I am no longer in that life, and I have no desire to have any ties to it. If I did not need a barrister or if I knew any other barrister who might take Nell's case, I would not be here now. You are free to accept the case or not, but I would not force you to take it by threats."

The ramifications of the life her father had forced her into through his abandonment seemed never to end. Like a boulder cast into a mill pond, the ripples raced out, causing her world to bob and toss as she grasped for a solid hold.

Never to be truly clean, never able to undo her past. Never worthy of regard.

Bitterness coated her tongue and her outlook.

She gathered her reticule and stood. "Good day, Mr. Newbolt. It is clear we cannot move beyond our former relationship. I shouldn't have come. If you do know of a barrister who might be willing to take Nell's case, please, send word to the Duke of Haverly's house on Berkeley Square."

His eyes widened. "So that's where you disappeared to. Haverly is keeping you now?"

"Not in the way you mean. The duke is my brother-in-law. As I said, I am no longer in that life. I run a charity hospital for unfortunate women. I am doing my best to separate myself from the life I used to live. I hope you are doing the same. Your wife deserves better."

His face reddened.

"I will give your case some thought. If I cannot take it, I will refer you to someone who can."

As Philippa entered Haverly House an hour later, she could not deny the discouragement weighing her down. Nell was in prison for something she had not done, and Philippa was powerless to help her. Sir Bertrand was working to find the real thief, but would he be in time?

Sir Bertrand Thorndike. What did she really know about him? The second son of a prestigious family, one of Marcus's many agents, and now a member of the board of directors of Eleos School. Though his only task related to Eleos up to now was to find the services of a physician or apothecary.

She would rather he focus on freeing Nell. They could find a medical man later. Sir Bertrand lived with his brother, the earl, and the countess, at least while they were in London. And he had managed to fool most of the *ton* into thinking he was a drunkard and a dilettante. Marcus thought highly enough of him to recommend him to the Prince Regent and to suggest that she, Philippa, join his team of agents.

He was handsome and well-dressed, and intelligence gleamed from his brown eyes. Was he intelligent enough to unravel Nell's predicament? If the maid was convicted . . . it didn't bear thinking about.

Charlotte came down the stairs, a book under her arm. "I didn't realize you would be home so soon. You must be exhausted. I wish you would let us help more with the setting up of the hospital. Come have a cup of tea. I was just upstairs reading to Thea and Betsy. They're so dear. They will enjoy going with us to the Haverly estate. Thea has a quick mind, and Betsy couldn't be any sweeter. She's taken quite a shine to the dowager. Her Grace practically blooms with the attention. How are things going at Eleos?"

Philippa had been so deep in thought about Sir Bertrand and Nell, she hadn't even removed her bonnet.

"I was not at Eleos," she said, pulling on the ribbon bow beneath her chin. "I went to see a barrister in hopes that he would take Nell's case and defend her against the theft charges."

Brows raised, Charlotte put her hand on Philippa's arm. "And did he agree?"

Philippa looked down at the touch. Being Charlotte's sister had taken getting used to. She was given to physical displays of affection, often bestowing a hug or kiss on Philippa's cheek in greeting, something to which Philippa was unaccustomed. Physical interaction that was not a transaction or abusive did not come as naturally to her as it did her sister.

Knowing Charlotte had grown up without physical displays of affection too, Philippa had to wonder. Was she being deliberate with her touches and hugs to make up for what she had missed? Or had Marcus's love changed her? Marcus was never shy of a touch, a hug, or a kiss for his wife, and though Charlotte may speak of the dowager blooming under Betsy's attention, it was Charlotte who had truly blossomed in response to her husband's affection.

Philippa put aside the empty longing such thoughts stirred and returned to her predicament. "He said he would consider it."

"I didn't realize you knew any barristers." Charlotte took the bonnet from Philippa's hand and set it on the round table in the middle of the foyer. She then threaded her arm through Philippa's and led her to the salon. "Come tell me about it, and there is news from our father's house too."

Philippa flinched, and Charlotte must have felt it, for she tightened her arm. "Do not worry. The physician has been to visit again, and he says Father is maintaining his hold on life. No movement or speech yet, but he's opened his eyes, and he can blink in response to questions."

Good for him. The old reprobate. If he couldn't talk, he couldn't say unkind things. Perhaps his wife would get some peace.

Such uncharitable thoughts. Perhaps it would be better not to think of him at all than to give such room in her head to unkindness.

"Does the physician expect him to recover?" She loosened Charlotte's hold and took a seat.

"I do not think he will ever be the same as he was." Charlotte set her book on the secretary and sat beside Philippa. "Mother seems to be holding up well, however. It's as if, with a bit of freedom to act, she's discovered a new confidence."

"That's good. It is pleasing when a woman is given the opportunity to show what she can do with her own intelligence and will. Certainly we hope to instill those same abilities in our students at Eleos."

Charlotte reached for the cord on the wall beside her chair and rang for a maid. "How did your interviews go? Did Mr. Todd bring many applicants?"

"He brought several, and we accepted them all. When I left, they had pitched in with a will to get the sleeping apartments cleaned and ready, and two of them had experience with cooking and joined Clara in the kitchen. I'm amazed at all that has been accomplished in just a few days. Did you know that Aunt Dolly sold her home on King's Place? And she's using the funds to purchase bedding and food for Eleos."

"I knew she asked Marcus to help her with the transaction. I did not know what she intended to spend the money on, though that sounds like her. She really has a heart for those women and the mission."

"I wish I felt Mr. Todd had the same. He seems more concerned with making a name for himself than changing their hearts and lives. He tried to interfere with the admission of several of the applicants, wanting only those who were not 'too far gone' in his estimation to reform. He said it was because a few early successes will garner positive attention for Eleos, which it will do, I suppose, but something feels wrong there. I wish Mr. Asbury had not foisted him upon us. I would have preferred to choose my own spiritual leader, one with some experience of helping unfortunate women."

"Perhaps he will grow into the position? As he sees your work and your treatment of the women? I'm certain it is all new to him, and he is a man, with a man's understanding. Sometimes, in earnestness to save a person's soul, a preacher can appear rather zealous. The stakes are so very high, a soul's eternal destination. If you can give him some time, perhaps that zeal can be channeled toward being supportive and guiding rather than pulpit-thumping and judgmental."

"You are a kind person, always looking for the best in people." Philippa studied her hands in her lap. Why couldn't she be more like her sister? Mostly, she found herself suspecting lies, looking for hidden agendas, and protecting herself from being hurt in her encounters with others.

The maid arrived, but before Charlotte could request a tea tray, Marcus swept into the room, his long strides covering the distance effortlessly.

"Philippa, you must come with me. Something has occurred at Carlton House."

Chapter 10

Bertie stared into the cupboard. Around him, the opulent, even decadent decor of the Carlton House library belied what he saw. The smell of leather, books, and beeswax polish surrounded him, but bitterness coated his tongue.

The maid, Lydia, lay in a tangled heap, spilling out of the cupboard, her hand lifeless on the rug, her hair half covering her face. Her white cap was gone, and one sleeve had been ripped from her dress. Her eyes, which had held such quick intelligence and light, were now dull and staring. Her skin, drained of color, might have been made of porcelain.

The horror of it settled low in his gut. He had known this girl, however briefly. Had felt a sense of protectiveness, of sympathy for her situation. Had been oddly proud of her for escaping her past and making a better life for herself. And now that life and all its promise had been snuffed out.

"Who found her?" He forced the words past his lips.

"I did. Such a shock." Mr. Todd dabbed his upper lip with his handkerchief. "I opened the door, and she just tumbled out."

Though he wanted to turn and flee, Bertie forced himself to squat on his heels beside the body. A sense of waters closing over his head, of being dragged under by a force too strong to combat, threatened to drown him.

Where was his aplomb? His ability to divorce himself from emotion?

Rage, fear, disgust, sorrow, and guilt warred inside him. How did he get here? He was a spy, not a policeman.

Dark bruises ringed the young woman's neck. She had clearly been strangled. He avoided looking into her lifeless eyes, lest they reflect the accusations he knew she would be justified in making. The murder and the theft had to be connected somehow, and if he had apprehended the thief sooner, this child would still be alive.

This was now a police matter. He must call in Daniel Swann and a proper investigator. Theft was one thing, murder entirely another. The Prince Regent would not be happy, but he also could not be seen to thwart justice.

Bertie straightened. "Lock every door. No one is allowed in or out without my permission. I want every person in the building assembled in the entry hall." The killer could be long gone, but he also might be still in the house. "I want a complete list this time of *every* person seen coming or going today. No exceptions, and I do not care about the secrecy agreement. I don't care if the person is a dustman or a royal duke, his name goes on the list. Get me Mr. Partridge. He should be at the side gate."

If Lingfield hadn't resisted giving the staff the freedom to tell the truth from the outset, would the thief even now be in Newgate, unable to murder young girls? What had Lydia known or seen? And was it the same secret he still felt Nell was hiding?

Nell. Clearly, she was not responsible for Lydia's murder. She was ensconced in the gaol. Would her friend's death be enough to get her released? Would it be enough to release her tongue?

Partridge entered the library. "Poor mite." He stared at the body, determination hardening his features. "What should I do?"

"Send for Haverly and send someone for Swann. Tell them we have a murder and to set in motion whoever needs to be called for such things. This is beyond our scope. Despite Lingfield and the Prince Regent wishing to keep this quiet, a murder cannot be quashed. I will begin questioning the staff. Don't tarry on your errands. I will need you here."

"Right, guv." Partridge didn't need telling twice, and he would do more than Bertie had asked, for certain.

Bertie turned to Todd. "Tell me everything. When did you find her? Why were you in the library? Did you touch her or move her at all?"

The reverend backed up and sagged into a chair, clutching his handkerchief. "I came to borrow a volume or two for my personal study. I'm preparing my first sermons to give at Eleos, and I wanted to confer with some scholars on a particular subject. Whitefield and Edwards, specifically." He motioned to a pair of leather-bound volumes on the table by the door. "Mr. Powell, the librarian, was not present, and I wished to leave a note that I had borrowed the books. His Highness has given me free run of the library, but I wanted to do Powell the courtesy of letting him know where the books had gone. But I couldn't find any paper in the desk. I thought it might be in the cupboard."

He shuddered, and Bertie imagined what a shock it must have been to have a body tumble out.

"I knew that girl. She was a maid here. Often when I was working here in the library, she would bring a tray of tea. Who would do such a thing to one so young as she? I saw the bruises. She's been murdered." Again his hands shook. "I am a man of letters, of theology. I've never encountered anything like this."

"Did you touch her?" Bertie asked, eager to get this interview over and remove Todd from the crime scene.

"No. Of course not. It was quite clear she was dead." He looked aghast at the very notion.

"What time was it when you found her?"

"I am not certain. I came to the house in the late morning, and I did a bit of reading . . . I had no idea she was in that cupboard, I assure you. Perhaps an hour, maybe less, when I decided to leave Mr. Powell the note."

"You may join the others in the main hall. If you think of anything that might help, I am certain the investigators at Bow Street would be appreciative."

"Bow Street?" He jerked and dabbed his temple. "Are you not the one in charge of the case?"

"When it was a theft, and a personal favor to the Prince Regent, I was in charge. Now that it is a murder, it is a matter for the authorities."

"I see. I'm sure you are correct. There will be no keeping this out of the papers, will there? I would not like to see my name attached to such goings on. I have my reputation to think of, and not only that, but the reputation of the new charity. No scandal can be attached to Eleos School."

This would certainly be considered scandal. The murder of a young maid at Carlton House who had been through Miss Cashel and Mrs. Stokes's training course.

"That is out of our hands. I do not think your reputation will be besmirched. After all, you merely found the body where the killer had tried to hide it."

Which was a curious thing. Why had the murderer stuffed the body in a cupboard where it was certain to be found? Time must have been a factor. Not being caught, nowhere else to hide the body, possibly a chance to come back to retrieve and dispose of it better later?

He shrugged. No longer his purview. Swann would take over the case or assign it to one of his investigators. Bertie could only hold the crime scene and make certain no one interfered until the proper authorities got here.

What would this mean to the Prince Regent? He had made little headway on the original theft and had certainly not earned any equity with the prince with his lack of results. Would Prinny put in the word to Marcus to end his career?

Todd hurried out, casting one last wide-eyed glance over his shoulder at the body.

Bertie followed him into the anteroom outside the library door. He marshaled his thoughts and went over what he knew and what he would tell Swann and Haverly when they arrived.

In the back of his mind was a thought he hadn't wanted to consider.

Had Lydia somehow been involved in the theft? Had her fellow thief killed her to keep her quiet? Could she have been coerced into stealing, or might she have entered willingly into the crime?

Swann arrived first, with his second-in-command, Ed Beck, and the newest investigator, Owen Wilkinson, in tow.

"Blimey," the young man said, but Bertie didn't know if he was commenting on the opulent surroundings or the body spilling from the cupboard. He wished he had covered Lydia, for he hated that she was now an object and evidence instead of a person.

Swann assessed the situation quickly. "Owen, go for Dr. Rosebreen. Tell him to come personally and not to send Mr. Foster. Then go out to Rhynwick Davies's place and have him meet us at Rosebreen's as soon as he can."

Wilkinson sketched a bow and left.

Bertie recounted what he knew as Swann and Beck squatted beside Lydia's body. "Strangled, either with hands or something else."

"Rosebreen will be able to tell us."

Mr. Beck took out his notebook and pencil.

"Victim's name?"

"Lydia. I do not know her last name. She is—was—a scullery maid here at Carlton House, and she is a former pupil of Miss Cashel and Mrs. Stokes at Haverly House."

Daniel Swann looked up at Bertie. "So she was a former streetwalker?"

"That's what I understand. She and another girl, Nell, were placed here by Miss Cashel to work as household staff. Nell is the maid who was arrested for theft, though I am certain she is not guilty."

"Explain for Mr. Beck."

Bertie noted Daniel's businesslike demeanor, detached and observant. As Bertie himself had been trained to be. Keeping one's wits in a stressful situation was vital in the spy game, and in investigative pursuits as well. He would do well to remember that. His emotions were much too high at the moment for professionalism.

Bertie gave a quick recital of events to the present.

"Can we get this poor girl out of the cupboard? Show her a bit of dignity and cover her?" Bertie asked.

"Not until Dr. Rosebreen arrives. He will take care of the body once we have gleaned everything possible from the scene," Mr. Beck said. He was an old hand at this too. While Daniel had been examining the body, Beck had been moving slowly about the room, eyes watchful, hands behind his back, his notebook ready should he spy something worth documenting.

When Daniel moved away from Lydia, Beck took his place, squatting on his heels, peering into the cupboard, examining everything visible.

"Though her dress is torn and her cap is missing, there's no sign of a struggle in the room. Do you think the murder happened elsewhere and the body brought here? Or the killer tidied up?" Bertie asked.

"It stands to reason the murder happened here. Why kill her somewhere else and stuff her into a cupboard in the library? There's too much chance of being seen, toting a dead body through the house. And if you were going to try it, there are better places to hide it than here." Daniel opened another cupboard, this one full of more leather-bound books. "How did the killer happen upon the one cupboard that had enough room to hide the body? They're all full but that one."

"So it had to be someone who had access to the library and a familiarity with the contents." That would limit the suspect pool some. Surely the laundress or the head groom would not have need to come here. He would have to ask Lingfield and Mrs. Evans for a list of those who would have reason to visit the library. Maids, footmen, the various library staff, visitors who, like Todd, had permission to use the collection. Not to mention Lingfield and Mrs. Evans as well.

The library door opened, and he turned. It was surely too soon for the doctor.

Marcus Haverly stood in the doorway, and at his elbow, Philippa Cashel.

The air drained from her lungs, and she reached with numb fingers for Marcus's elbow to steady herself.

Lydia.

Sweet, kind, funny Lydia.

Marcus had broken the news to her on the ride to Carlton House. She hadn't wanted to believe him, but seeing the girl's body on the library rug meant she could deny it no longer.

Someone had killed the child.

There were three men in the large room, Sir Bertrand, Mr. Swann—the Earl of Aylswood, she absently corrected herself—and another gentleman she did not know. The plush carpeting, the gleaming woodwork, the smell of rich leather all conspired to overwhelm her. The plasterwork scrolls on the ceiling, the tasteful tables, chairs, and sofas artfully arranged to be inviting, practically shouted against the abuse of a dead body in their midst.

Her mind cataloged her surroundings in an effort, she supposed, to grasp onto pedestrian thoughts, anything mundane, so she wouldn't have to think about the one thing roaring in her head.

If she had not placed Nell and Lydia in the Prince Regent's household, Nell would not be in prison facing a hangman's noose, and Lydia would still be alive.

"Who did this?" She forced the question through her stiff lips.

Sir Bertrand came over to her and Marcus. "Your Grace. Thank you for coming. Miss Cashel, there is no need for you to be here. You shouldn't come any farther." He looked down into her eyes, his own troubled. "This is nothing for a lady to witness."

A lady.

That he would consider her such . . .

She shook her head. "I must attend to her. She is my responsibility." A hard lump formed in her throat, and she blinked to stem the moisture forming there.

He put his hand on her arm, and she read both compassion and strength in his expression. "Miss Cashel, she is *our* responsibility. This will not go unanswered." He tightened his fingers for an instant before dropping his hand.

She nodded and moved forward when he stepped aside, oddly comforted by his assurance that she was not alone in this tragedy.

The child lay like an abandoned doll, her feet still in the cupboard, her hair spilled across the carpet. Philippa reached out to touch Lydia's white cheek.

"Don't," Sir Bertrand cut in. "Do not disturb her. Dr. Rosebreen, the coroner, will arrive soon, and everything must be as near to untouched as we can make it. There may be some evidence or information on her right now that moving her might disturb."

Guilt weighed so heavily on Philippa's shoulders that she felt it might press her through the floor. Why had she given in to pride, placing the girls at such a prestigious location as Carlton House? Why had she not heeded that warning in the back of her mind and removed them when the girls admitted they were afraid of Mr. Lingfield?

She straightened, grateful when Marcus gripped her elbow and helped her, for her knees resembled aspic. "Where is Mr. Lingfield?" she asked.

"With the rest of the staff in the front hall, I assume," Sir Bertrand said. "We're heading there as soon as the body is removed to begin questioning everyone and recording their movements. Is there something you wish to speak with him about?"

"The girls were afraid of him, and you witnessed his temper regarding the acquisitive valet. Perhaps Lydia exasperated him to the point where he"—she gulped—"throttled her?"

Sir Bertrand nodded. "We will question him. And everyone else. Each person will have to answer for his whereabouts. She was killed some time in the forenoon, after she had cleared away the breakfast dishes in the servant's dining hall. Thankfully, we have a smaller window of time to verify than the one for the stolen jewels."

"I want to be there when you question the staff," she said.

Before Sir Bertrand could answer—though he was already shaking his head—Marcus said, "An excellent idea. You may put your skills at perception to use."

Dr. Rosebreen arrived, a rather tatty-looking individual in a rumpled coat. He was quick, efficient, asked pertinent questions, and gave a quick report.

"She's definitely been strangled. I suspect I will find a broken bone at her throat. She's still got some warmth . . . rigor mortis has begun to set in about the face and neck. She's been dead three, maybe four hours at most." He motioned to his assistant, who had been introduced as Mr. Foster, to come forward with a shroud.

Philippa stood beside Marcus, her back to the windows that looked out onto the principle courtyard and Pall Mall. The men were gentle as they wrapped the body, for which she was grateful, and Mr. Beck assisted them with the removal.

Everything in her wanted to wind back the clock, to put the sand back in the hourglass, and return to that day when the offer of placing the girls in this gilded cage of a house had first occurred. She should have kept them with her at the Haverly townhouse where she could watch over them, keep them safe.

But the cachet of having "reformed" two girls to the point of being in royal domestic service had been so appealing. What a success story for their program. She had considered how it would help with raising funds for the school and how good it would look to those on the outside.

She had taken comfort that they would be together and that they would have Mrs. Evans to look out for them. Mrs. Evans, who had known Aunt Dolly when they were younger and who had been in favor of their efforts to help women in need.

Philippa accompanied Marcus and Sir Bertrand into a small anteroom off the library, where they set up an area to question the staff. Well, small in comparison to the library. The Haverly music room could easily fit into the space, she thought.

Delicate pastoral scenes decorated the wallpaper, and a large mirror sent her reflection back to her as a footman brought chairs and moved a table from beneath the mirror to the center of the room.

Mr. Beck requested paper, pen, and ink, and took a seat at the end of the table.

Marcus leaned down to whisper in her ear. "Will you be all right if I leave you here? I must compose a letter and get it couriered to His Highness at Tunbridge Wells. I will take it upon myself that I requested the help of Swann and Bow Street. That way no ill wind will blow back on Sir Bertrand."

"I will be fine. When the questioning of the most pertinent suspects is concluded, I will go to the scullery and gather Lydia's and Nell's belongings. Then I shall return to Eleos. One of the maids here will serve as my chaperone."

Philippa sat in a chair along the wall, behind Sir Bertrand and Mr. Swann. She would observe and hold her thoughts until each interviewee had left.

Mr. Lingfield was the first to be called, as befitted his status in the house. He strode in, impeccably dressed, eyes sharp, but there was a certain strain about his mouth.

"This is a dreadful thing. What will His Highness say? I cannot imagine." He fidgeted with his watch chain. "That something like this should have happened while he was away and the house was under my charge." He moistened his lips.

Was that a bruise on the back of his hand? A scratch on his wrist?

Philippa straightened, unable to look away from the marks. Someone being strangled would fight back, wouldn't she? Perhaps clawing, gripping the hands about her neck?

"Can you please account for your movements this morning between nine and the noon hour?" Sir Bertrand asked.

"Is that when it happened? The poor girl. Let's see, nine o'clock?" He looked at his hands in his lap, blinked, and quickly covered the discolored one with his opposite palm. "I was with the comptroller, going over the accounts of all the shopping and expenditures incurred when His Highness went to Brighton. The prince threw several lavish parties while at the seaside, and the accounts are now due to the butcher, the grocer, the chandler, the brewer, the confectioner . . . oh, the lists go on. It took us several hours. I was still with Nottingham—the comptroller—when the alarm was raised about that poor girl."

"And at no time did you or Mr. Nottingham step out of your office?" Mr. Swann asked.

"Well, yes, at about half ten, I was called away to attend an issue in the throne room. His Highness is having new curtains installed, and the fabric has arrived from Italy. The draper, out of an abundance of caution, wished to measure the windows and dais again before he began cutting and sewing. I was gone for perhaps three-quarters of an hour? Surely you do not suspect Mr. Nottingham of killing a scullery maid in my absence?"

Philippa noted the dry edge to Sir Bertrand's voice when he said, slowly, "No, I do not suspect Mr. Nottingham at this time. Did you encounter the scullery maid, Lydia, as you moved through the house?"

"I did not. I would assume she would have been at work in the scullery."

"Would she have had a reason to be in the library?"

"No. Unless she had been sent by the housekeeper with a tea tray, but Mrs. Evans tells me she sent her on no such errand." Mr. Lingfield tugged on his chin. "I shall have to speak with Mrs. Evans. Her staff has entirely too much leniency if they are gallivanting about the house rather than performing the duties for which they are handsomely paid."

Philippa could almost see his umbrage rise as his shoulders straightened and his chest puffed out. If he could lay the blame on someone else, perhaps he would not be blamed for such a catastrophe occurring on his watch.

"You may go. Do not speak with anyone still waiting to be questioned." Mr. Swann looked to Mr. Beck, who nodded.

"Sir," Philippa spoke for the first time. "Before you go, perhaps you would care to explain how you acquired the bruise and scrape on your left hand?"

He froze, half out of his chair, then looked down at his hand as if surprised it belonged to him. A dull red started at his collar, and his throat lurched.

Sir Bertrand's head swiveled to look at her over his shoulder, then turned to Lingfield again. "I would also like to know."

"Show us your hands." Mr. Swann's voice held an edge of steel.

The secretary stuck out his hands, palms up. "Surely you do not suspect—"

"The backs of your hands," Mr. Beck interrupted.

For a moment, Lingfield hesitated, then rotated his wrists. The bruise and scrape came into view. "It isn't what you think."

"Then what is it?" Sir Bertrand asked. "Because it would appear you strangled a young girl, but before she died, she fought you, bruising your hand and leaving that scrape."

Lingfield's eyes widened, and sweat popped out on his brow. "No. That isn't what happened. I—" He withdrew his hands, again covering the bruise with his palm. "I have a temper, yes, and when I was with the draper, a footman, who should have been helping with the measurements of the windows, instead decided to lean against a plinth holding a valuable marble bust. He nearly toppled the thing, and I am the one who would have had to explain to His Highness how it came to be damaged. I lashed out. I backhanded the footman, and my aim was not true. The blow landed first on his shoulder. His epaulet caused the scrape, and the blow caused the bruise." He grimaced. "I am not proud of my actions, but chastising a footman and killing a scullery maid are two vastly different things."

"Which footman?" Mr. Beck's skepticism filled the air.

Lingfield's eyes showed white. "G-g-green," he sputtered. "Call him in here. He'll tell you."

"We'll do that. You may go now."

When he had gone, Sir Bertrand looked over his shoulder at Philippa. "Your thoughts?"

"He could have done it, but he seems sure the footman will corroborate his story. Unless he murdered her in a fit of temper that overrode his judgment, I cannot see him as the killer. He's worried, but I did not sense he lied about anything."

"That is my conclusion as well. Let us hear from the footman."

The young man entered, his shoulders tense and his eyes clouded. Philippa studied him, noting the slight swelling along his jaw. She let out a slow breath.

Mr. Green recounted events that paired neatly with Mr. Lingfield's account. He had nearly broken a marble bust, and the secretary had struck him.

"Was my fault, sir," he said, with a ducked head. His hand came up to touch his jawline. "Sharpish with his tongue and quicker with his hands, is our Mr. Lingfield."

"Thank you. You may go."

"Not that Lingfield is completely absolved," Sir Bertrand said, "but we should, perhaps, move on. Should we call Mrs. Evans next?"

"I believe we should speak to Mr. Todd," Swann said. "He is the one who found the body, did he not? I always want to question the person who was first on the scene."

"Yes. I should warn you. He was quite shaken."

"I will go carefully." Swann rose and went to the door to call for Mr. Todd.

When Mr. Swann didn't return immediately, Philippa began to fidget. Had the preacher left the premises?

Swann eventually came back with Todd in tow. The parson looked composed, not at all as disturbed as Sir Bertrand had made out.

"I apologize for taking so long. Mr. Todd was praying with members of the staff who requested it." Swann flicked out the tails on his coat as he took his seat.

"As spiritual adviser to His Highness, I consider it part of my job to look after the souls of those in his employ. Much as I do those who work and attend Eleos." Todd nodded to Philippa, sharing a comradely smile as he took the chair across the table. He held his Bible in his lap. "Sir Bertrand, I must apologize for my flustered behavior when you first arrived. I'm afraid the shock of finding that poor girl upset me beyond what I am comfortable admitting. I am supposed to be wise and a voice of reason, able to keep calm in trying circumstances, but I was callow and near hysterical." He cleared his throat. "In any case, my apologies. What is it I may answer for you that will help you find the degenerate who did such a terrible thing?"

"We would like to confirm the statement you gave Sir Bertrand, if we could. What time did you arrive at Carlton House this morning?"

"After eleven, I believe. I went out very early to Eleos, to assess the progress on the manse. Things are coming together very quickly on the manor house, and it is my intention to take up residence at the school soon." He flicked a glance at Philippa. "I would wish the preacher's house came furnished and with appropriate staff, but since that is not the case, I have prevailed upon the good graces of my friends, who have been compiling household goods. Some of those were to be delivered today, and I wished to see to their placement. Unfortunately, not a thing has been done to my proposed quarters, so I was obliged to have the possessions stored in the front room of the manse. This will make cleaning and repairs more difficult, but what could I do?" His tone held guarded censure, and Philippa lifted her chin.

"The manor has priority, you must agree." She sweetened her voice to the point of causing sickness. "The women under our care must be our first concern, and since you have lodgings at the moment and most of them don't, I am certain you will see the fitness of tending to their housing and comfort before we concentrate upon our own?"

Mr. Beck tapped his fingers on the desk. "Perhaps we could stay with the topic at hand?"

"Ah, yes, forgive me." Mr. Todd turned his attention away from Philippa, effectively dismissing her point.

Sir Bertrand shot her a wry look, his index finger pressed lengthwise across his lips, his eyes speaking volumes as to what he thought of the man's desire for his needs to be placed above those of the students.

Philippa lowered her chin, warmed to have an ally.

"As I said, I had received permission from Mr. Powell to use the library and to even remove some volumes for my study as needed. I had two books of sermons to return and several more to peruse in preparation for my first service at Eleos. If you will check, the books I wanted to return are on the table to the right of the library door. Mr. Powell instructed me to leave them there. The books I wished to take with me are on a chair by the window. I was in the library for half an hour, perhaps three-quarters. I wanted to leave a note for the librarian, listing the books I was taking and asking if he had access to another title or two. When I opened the cupboard in search of paper, the girl's body tumbled out." His face tightened.

Philippa caught the way he clutched his Bible, his knuckles white as he clenched and unclenched around the edges of the Book. He was perhaps not as calm as he would have them believe. Though neither was she. Who could be calm under these circumstances?

"When you entered the library, did you notice anything awry? Anything that appeared disturbed or out of place?" Mr. Swann asked.

"Nothing. All was peaceful. I could just as easily have left the room without ever discovering the child. It was only chance that I opened that cupboard door."

"Had you ever seen the girl in the library before?"

"Yes, on more than one occasion, she was tasked with carrying in a tea tray. I usually ask one of the footmen to see to it, but the girl brought it, though that was not the first time I had seen her. She was introduced to me by Mr. Lingfield, she and the other one, as charity hires, an attempt at reformation. He suggested they might need extra spiritual guidance to keep them on the narrow path to redemption." He smoothed his Geneva bands with one hand. "I met with them a time or two, to pray and instruct. Much as I do with others on the staff. As I was doing when you called me in here."

Extra spiritual guidance? Again, guilt smote Philippa. She had put them here, a place where they were looked upon as charity hires. Singled out as needing extra watching, as though they were thieves or would tempt other employees to sin?

This must be what a parent felt like when their child was grown and it was time for them to launch out on their own. Wanting to keep them close but knowing they needed to move on.

Except this time, one fledgling was in gaol and the other was dead.

"Gentlemen, I can help no more. I have told you all I know, and I must be going. I have an appointment with the archbishop." The reverend rose. "Oh, and Sir Bertrand, I might know of someone who would be willing to take on the medical responsibilities at Eleos. He's a retired naval physician. He worked at Stonehouse in Plymouth during the war and is now seeking to retire to the London area to be near his daughter's family. I shall, if you approve, send him to your residence for an interview? Captain Wyvern knows him as well. An excellent man."

Sir Bertrand nodded, but he looked to Philippa. "When Miss Cashel and I can arrange a time to interview him together, I shall let you know."

A tinge of warmth surrounded her heart that he had included her in the process.

When Todd had gone, she stirred. "Gentlemen, I will excuse myself. I will go to the scullery and gather Nell's and Lydia's possessions."

The men rose when she did. Mr. Swann said, "If you find anything of note, you will inform us?"

"You mean the missing jewels?" she said through tight lips. "The girls did not steal them, and I do not expect to find them among their meager possessions."

"No. I mean anything that might give a hint as to who might want to murder Lydia or blame Nell," he said gently.

Heat swirled at her collar. "I beg your pardon. If I find anything, I will certainly inform you, but these girls were poor. They are unlikely to have anything of worth, either as evidence or monetarily."

It was eerie, walking through the big house with no one about. No footmen standing at doors, no courtiers, no sounds. The entire staff had been gathered in the great hall for questioning. When she descended to the ground floor, it was worse. No sounds coming from the kitchen or laundry as she passed.

Thankfully, she remembered the way to the scullery. It had been nearly a week since she had visited Nell and Lydia and found them well and happy enough in their new work. Wary of Mr. Lingfield, but not indicating there were any problems.

How had things gone wrong so quickly?

As the lowest of employees, they had slept on pallets in the scullery. Their beds were rolled and placed in a corner during the day, and each had a small box of personal possessions. Philippa went to them, raising them to the countertop to inspect the contents.

"Which box belongs to which girl?" There was no way of knowing without asking Nell, who was currently out of reach at Newgate.

A wooden comb, a hair ribbon, a handkerchief. A tiny bottle of scent. She unstoppered the bottle and sniffed. Lemon water.

At the bottom was the New Testament that each girl received from Aunt Dolly when they entered her protection. Philippa opened the front page to see Nell's name inked there. Nell's box then.

The other box, Lydia's, was much the same as to contents, with the addition of two folded pieces of paper. Philippa opened them, cheap foolscap with rough pencil lettering.

"Would you do me the honor of allowing me to walk you home from church this Sunday in the company of my mother?" she read aloud. The page was signed Harry Sloan.

The second was simpler. It held a pressed, dried flower, and was signed "Your favorite footman, H.S."

Philippa touched the fragile petals. Lydia had been a pretty girl. It was not surprising that she had garnered the attention of a young man. And this Harry Sloan seemed honorable enough on the face of things, asking her to walk home from church, and with a proper chaperone in his mother.

Harry must be beside himself upstairs in the front hall, waiting to be questioned.

Philippa gathered the belongings into one box, leaving the other, the pallets, and the spare dresses and aprons on the hooks behind the door. The clothing had been supplied by the housekeeper as part of their duties as scullery maids and did not belong to the girls.

She would find the footman Harry Sloan, express her condolences, and ask him about his whereabouts this morning.

⁂

"He's here, but he's in a state." Mrs. Sloan held open the door to their modest home. "Come in."

Philippa folded her parasol, shaking off the raindrops, and set it inside the door. Rain had begun to fall as she'd left Carlton House with the girls' possessions, and finding a cab to take her to the address Mr. Lingfield had given her had taken a fair while.

"He was in such a state at the news of the girl's death, I sent him home. This was before Sir Bertrand commanded everyone be held at Carlton House, so you can stop glaring at me." Lingfield had scowled at her. Still angry that she'd noticed his bruised hand and demanded an explanation?

The small sitting room was pleasant enough, with horsehair upholstery and plain walls hung with a few bits of needlework and a calendar from Fortnum & Mason's. A small brazier in the fireplace took the edge off the damp chill.

Harry Sloan sat in a chair, a blanket around his shoulders, staring into the coals.

"Harry, a lady here to see you." His mother turned, the lace rimming her cap limp at her temples. "I'm sorry, I don't remember your name."

"Miss Cashel. I've come from Carlton House to ask your son some questions."

Sloan winced and stirred, shaking his head and turning his face away from her. "Go away."

"I'm sorry, I cannot." Grief was a real thing, but Philippa didn't have time to indulge him or herself in the loss of Lydia. Nell was in the dock and Lydia was dead and the killer was roaming free. If Harry Sloan had any answers, she wanted them.

"Sir, I am very sorry for your loss. I understand you were quite fond of Lydia. She was my friend as well. However, she would not want you to wallow if you could be useful in finding who did this to her."

He met her eyes, his own awash with torment. "Fond of her?" His voice croaked. "I loved her. I wanted to marry her. She had finally agreed to meet me at church on Sunday and come here for a meal with Ma." His long fingers gripped the edges of the blanket.

His hair was wet. As was his livery. Had he walked here from Carlton House? No wonder his mother had draped him in the blanket.

"Sit, Miss Cashel. I was just heating up some cider. We don't run to tea in this house, too expensive, but hot cider will be just the thing on this wet day." Mrs. Sloan indicated the chair across from her son. "Take that wet pelisse off and lay it on the drying rack."

She did as bidden, leaning forward. "Mr. Sloan. Harry. I have to ask you, did Lydia tell you anything that might help us discover who did this? She was hiding something, but she wouldn't tell me."

He shook his head, raising a trembling hand to rub the back of his neck. "I knew something was troubling her, but she wouldn't say what. Only that there were powerful men in the house who thought they could do whatever they wanted. I asked her who, particularly, and she just shrugged. Said there were always going to be powerful men, and it was a smart girl who guarded herself against them."

"She was right." But that did not narrow anything down. Every male in the house would be considered more powerful than Lydia, except maybe the boot boy. "Did she fear anyone specifically? Mr. Lingfield?"

He blew out a long breath. "We all respect Lingfield. He runs a tight ship, but she didn't answer to him. Mrs. Evans oversaw her work and would bring her up to task if she slacked in anything. Same as I answer to the butler first, though Lingfield was more likely to chastise a footman who would be seen by the public than a little maid who was kept hidden in the scullery most of the time."

"But was she? In the scullery all the time? She spoke of being sent on errands throughout the house."

He paused, then nodded. "Especially first thing in the morning before the house was awake proper or the day servants arrived. Not all the servants are quartered at Carlton House. Some, like me, come in by day. It means we get paid more, since we don't get room and board. That helps me keep Ma here in her own home. She was most anxious to do that when Pa died."

Philippa nodded. How blessed Mrs. Sloan was to have a son to help keep her. "Where might Lydia have been sent that would bring her into contact with 'powerful men' in the house?"

"Mostly carrying water or coals to the bedrooms on the upper floors. Or more linens or trays of tea or chocolate. Courtiers sometimes stay the night, and overnight guests are often in the house when His Highness has entertained the day before. The staff is run ragged after a party, and the next morning, those who did not serve the evening before are called to help out."

Courtiers. Guests. Those with access to His Highness. It could be anyone.

Philippa gathered herself. "You cannot think of anyone who would want to harm her?"

"I've been thinking of nothing else." He leaned forward, letting the blanket drop, and clenching his hands in his damp, curly hair. "She must have seen something she shouldn't have or known something she shouldn't have. That's all I can figure."

Chapter 11

"Pringle was at Carlton House yesterday morning. He's still a viable suspect. Plus, there are the papers I found at his house." Bertie quelled the rush of embarrassment at the memory of being forced to hide under a suspect's bed for hours before he could escape. Lord Pringle absolutely wouldn't fall asleep deeply enough for Bertie to risk coming out of concealment. He'd lain on his back on the floor, listening to the tossing and turning, the muttering and fidgeting. Bertie had resigned himself to wait until morning when Pringle left the house, when the man finally settled and began snoring loud enough to rattle the windowpanes.

Mr. Partridge had been waiting in the empty stall, and he had been controlled enough not to laugh aloud at Bertie's predicament.

"Sorry, guv. He turned right around and headed back to the house before he'd covered half his usual distance. Dunno why, nothing happened to alarm him. He didn't see me following. I had no way of letting you know."

Bertie could only hope Partridge had kept his own counsel and not told Haverly.

"If those papers from Pringle's house aren't motive to steal valuable jewelry, I don't know what is." Bertie followed the duke up the stairs at White's, glancing into the bow window as he ascended. He stopped talking when the door opened and an attendant took their measure.

"Good evening, Your Grace, Sir Bertrand." The attendant inclined his snowy head, his pink scalp showing through as he scrutinized them from head to foot.

"Good evening, Maxwell. Full club tonight?" Haverly asked as he pulled off his gloves. He dropped them into his hat and handed the items to the footman waiting to receive them.

"It's very lively in the gaming rooms but quiet in the dining room." Maxwell spoke through clenched teeth, as he always did. It didn't appear he was angry or even displeased, it was just a curious mannerism all his own. Bertie wondered if the man's jaw relaxed in sleep, or if he dreamed of biting nails in two.

Bertie removed his hat and passed it and his walking stick to the same footman.

"My brother-in-law, the Earl of Rothwell, will be joining us for dinner, as well as Lord Pringle. My guests for the evening."

The club had strict rules about who could and could not dine within its walls. Each member was allowed two guests per month. Records were kept.

"Very good, Your Grace. I shall see them in when they arrive. Your usual table is waiting."

The masculine dining room was quiet, as Maxwell had said, but then again, it always was. Navy carpeting, dark wood, low lighting, and conversations more murmured than shouted. Lots of business transactions occurred in this room, and it was expected that the members would comport themselves with dignity. One could let one's hair down, so to speak, in the gaming rooms, but in the dining and reading rooms, decorum was expected.

Naturally, Marcus had the best table in the room. In the furthest corner from the door with comfortable, padded chairs, brass wall sconces with green shades, and gleaming white linens, the placement meant Marcus could have his back to the wall and a clear view of the entire room. Some of the tables had panels or screens around them, but Bertie surmised that Marcus would prefer to see who came and went, perhaps to gather whether someone was trying to overhear his conversations.

Anyone could hide behind a screen and listen, but no one could sneak up on Marcus at his preferred table at White's.

"Will you raise the issue with Pringle during dinner? With Lord Rothwell in attendance?" Bertie slid into the chair to Marcus's right.

"Rothwell will only be with us for the meal. Your brother is coming later to take him into the reading room while you and I talk to Pringle. I thought the dinner might put Pringle at his ease before we broach his particular difficulties." His eyes sharpened, and he smiled. "Ah, here they are now."

Rothwell, tall, spare, austere, led the way, with Lord Pringle behind. Bertie half rose and bowed to the earl and the lord, while they both inclined their heads to Haverly.

"Sit, gentlemen, please. Thank you for accepting my invitation."

Rothwell sat opposite Bertie and took the measure of the room. "I've been in many a fine officer's mess, but nothing like this. I felt I was being court-martialed by that old tar at the door. The Spanish Inquisition has nothing on that fellow." He smiled to indicate his teasing.

"He is very good at his job. Better than a portcullis, is our Maxwell." Haverly took the folded serviette from beside his place setting. "If the Loyalists would have had Maxwell at Scarborough, the castle never would have fallen to Cromwell's forces."

Food appeared, brought by silent servers. Wine was poured, and Bertie studied Lord Pringle without, hopefully, appearing to do so. He had to remind himself to go carefully on pretending to drink, as he was supposed to be cultivating a new, more sober demeanor. But after so many years of pretending, it took concentration. He had often used the cover of his drink to distract from his true intent. What other mannerism could he use to mask gathering information as a spy? Tristan, his brother, used lighthearted conversation. Melisande used good etiquette and stunning looks. Marcus was formidable and commanding with a streak of mercy.

Bertie would have to find something to hang his persona on if he couldn't be the drunk dilettante any longer.

Lord Pringle was presentable enough, with a narrow nose, sharp cheekbones, and ordinary brown eyes. He was well-dressed, about thirty-five, and mannerly, as a courtier should be. The son of a minor nobleman and a bishop's daughter, he had married well. His wife, like his mother, was also the daughter of a bishop.

"I was almost late leaving the house, Marcus," Rothwell said, cutting his mutton. "Thea, in spite of being told not to, had a go at sliding down the banister and landed in a heap at the bottom of the stairs. She was unhurt, but she narrowly missed hitting the dowager amidships, and your lady mother had a fit of the vapors."

A smile twitched the duke's lips. "I can imagine the near miss was more traumatic than a direct hit would have been?"

"It was certainly louder. Thea has been properly chastised, the dowager properly soothed with a tisane and smelling salts, and order restored. It would have been seen to quicker if my wife and yours could have composed themselves instead of laughing to near hysterics."

"I've come to believe," Marcus said as he shook his head, "that there is an inner hoyden in every woman, just trying to get out. Sophie and Charlotte, and evidently Thea, do not put much effort into concealing this fact."

"At any rate, Sophia tells me she is nearly done with the shopping that brought us to London. Of course, she couldn't wait to introduce the girls and the baby to your mother, but are you certain you wish us to travel on to Oxfordshire with you? I would think, after the maelstrom I've brought into your house, you would wish to send us back to Gateshead on a post chaise. I, for one, would not blame you."

"Of course we wish you to come to the estate. The girls will love it. But how have you effected such a change in my little sister? As a girl, she loved shopping and could never make up her mind about anything. How has she managed all her purchases in just a few days?"

"I believe she misses the country. And we are aware of the imposition of invading your home with seven additional family members. She wants to get out of the city and show the girls where she grew up."

Lord Pringle ate quietly, listening, but with a half-puzzled expression, as if glad to have been asked to join a duke, an earl, and a knight at an exclusive club, but uncertain as to why. Bertie wanted to squirm as he remembered being trapped beneath the man's bed waiting for him to drop off. And that he had stolen those papers from his room. If Pringle knew, he would probably challenge Bertie to a dual of honor.

After the sweets course, Bertie's brother approached the table. "Ah, Your Grace, I hope I am not too early?"

"On time as always, Tristan. Charles," Marcus spoke to his brother-in-law. "You know the Earl of Thorndike? He's asked for a meeting with you concerning a business opportunity if you'd be willing?"

"Of course." Rothwell slid his chair back. "Will you be joining us?"

"No, not tonight. Sir Bertrand and I have other business to discuss."

"Very well, thank you for a most enjoyable dinner." Rothwell bowed with military precision.

"We'll take some port in the reading room?" Tristan said as the two men walked away.

Lord Pringle folded his serviette. "Your Grace, thank you for the invitation to dine with you. It has been a pleasure."

"No need to rush off." Marcus's voice had changed from genial to commanding. "Sir Bertrand and I have a few questions for you regarding your comings and goings at Carlton House."

The color drained from Pringle's face, and his eyes widened. His throat lurched, and his breathing quickened. With a despairing look over his shoulder toward the door, he tried to compose himself. A lick of the lips, blinking, and a tight smile.

"Yes, Your Grace?" The sound was thin, and clearly his thoughts crashed like waves behind his nervous look.

"You are a courtier at Carlton House, with access to the Prince Regent and his business." Marcus began with the facts. "And you were present at the time the prince's property—a parure he intended as a gift—was stolen, as well as being in the house when the scullery maid, Lydia, was murdered."

Pringle's breath hitched in his throat, and he reached for his glass. "Yes, Your Grace. A terrible business." He gulped the last of his wine.

"I've questioned everyone in the house multiple times, but never you." Bertie toyed with the handle of his fork, not looking at Pringle directly. "How is it that you have not made yourself available? One would think you were avoiding me. I would not have known you were in the house when the jewels were stolen if the scullery maid hadn't mentioned seeing you leave the house that morning . . . by a back staircase." He let the implied question hang in the air.

Lord Pringle's hands disappeared under the edge of the table, and he sat back, his throat lurching. Searching for a plausible answer?

"Why didn't you go with the prince to Brighton? He took several other courtiers with him." The duke switched the point of attack, a tactic Bertie had seen him employ on several occasions. Keep the suspect off-balance, make him uncomfortable, and secrets would spill out. Marcus crossed his fork and knife on his plate and slid it to the side. He held up his hand when a server began to cross the room, shaking his head.

The server immediately turned on his heel, whispered to the head waiter, and took up his station by the kitchen door. They would not be interrupted by staff.

"He needed me to stay in London. I was told to monitor the market and a certain takeover move that one company was putting together for another and that might have ramifications for His Highness's investments. I was also entrusted with the dispatches and communications between Carlton House and Brighton while the prince was away."

"Did you see the jewels delivered to Carlton? Did you see Mr. Lingfield take possession of them?" Bertie asked.

He rolled his neck. "Yes. I was in the reception room when the jeweler arrived. I didn't know why he was there at first, but he was proud of the jewels and did open the case. But I never saw them after that."

"Can you account for your whereabouts between ten and three the day the jewels were stolen?" Bertie had not found anyone who had used Pringle as an alibi, claiming to have been with the man at the pertinent times.

No answer. Pressed lips, glance darting between Marcus and Bertie.

"Lord Pringle?" Marcus said. "You see why you must make an account for yourself. Unless you want suspicion to fall upon you."

"But they arrested one of the servants for the theft. She's in Newgate right now." The words were mumbled.

"That is true, but I believe wholeheartedly that she has been falsely accused. She now has a barrister, one Mr. Walter Newbolt, who has taken her case, and he intends, with our help, to prove she is innocent of the charges. This will be most easily accomplished by revealing the true thief. It would certainly help fill some holes in the fabric of the case if you were to tell us of your whereabouts at the crucial times."

Bertie's attention focused on Marcus. Nell had a barrister? How had that happened? Had Marcus called in a favor or two? A bit of the iron banding around his heart loosened at the thought that Nell would have legal help. The urgency of freeing her and finding justice for Lydia were both costing him sleep.

"But you cannot suspect me? Why would I steal from the Prince Regent?" Lord Pringle protested. "I was in the courtiers' workspace all morning, writing dispatches and going over market reports. I certainly wasn't rummaging through the prince's dressing room for a parure. I assumed the thing had been locked up or was under the care of one of the prince's body servants."

"Can anyone verify you were in the courtiers' offices? Did you send to the kitchen for tea or receive a caller or perhaps encounter a staff member?"

"I don't know. I suppose I must have." He rubbed his temples. "I can lose track of time when I'm working. My wife says a church bell could peal under my chair, and I would be oblivious if I'm concentrating on a task."

"How can you not know what you were doing at such an auspicious time? It was just over a week ago, a day before His Highness returned to London. You could not have needed to send any dispatches to the coast on that day for they would not have reached him, as he had already begun the journey back."

"He arrived days before he was expected, so I had no idea he was traveling. And if I had known I would need an alibi for that morning, I would have left the office door open and invited every footman and page to stroll through. I was working. The matters I am entrusted with are quite delicate in nature, and I was concentrating. I lost track of time and did not emerge until well after luncheon. The cook had to put together a cold plate for me. You can ask." Desperation coated his words.

"What about yesterday morning? You were also within Carlton House when the scullery maid, Lydia, was murdered." While Marcus continued his questioning, Bertie took a gallop around his mental notes of the movements of the staff on the day of the robbery. The cook had not mentioned the late meal, but perhaps it had been forgotten. It wasn't much of a detail, but one that could be verified.

"There were dozens of people in the house at that time."

"But you left before the body was discovered."

"I had an appointment." He spread his hands, white showing all around his eyes.

"Were you in the library at any point yesterday morning?"

"No. I've only been in the room perhaps twice in my life. My work is all one floor up, in the courtiers' rooms."

Bertie pressed his hands on the table and leaned forward. "I think you stole those jewels, and one or both of the scullery maids, whose workspace looks out on the side door you used to leave the house, saw you. When you realized you could be recognized, you killed Lydia. Nell is out of your reach at the moment, but you must have been desperate when you knew someone could put the jewels in your hands on the day they were thieved."

"No." Pringle pushed his chair back. "You've got it all wrong. I haven't stolen any jewels. Why would I? And I would never murder anyone, much less a girl barely older than a child. Why are you saying these preposterous things?"

Bertie looked to Marcus, who withdrew the folded pages Bertie had taken from the man's house. "As to why you would steal jewels, perhaps you remember these?"

If Pringle had been pale before, he was ashen now. "How did you get those?" A croak.

"It is of little consequence. What matters is that I have them now. You are in desperate need of money. The jewels would serve nicely to pay your blackmailer." The duke flicked open one of the buff-colored pages. "'You'll deliver what I want, or I will ruin you. All you value will be destroyed if you don't comply.'"

"Who sent these to you?" Bertie asked. "And how does he propose to ruin you if you refuse to pay?"

"I don't know who it is." Pringle jammed his thumb and forefinger against his closed eyes, taking ragged breaths. "Please, can you not just leave it be? This has nothing to do with what has happened to that maid, nor the stolen jewels."

Marcus leaned forward, but when Pringle did not open his eyes, the duke bumped the table, causing the crystal and cutlery to chime. "Pringle."

The man jerked and straightened, his lids snapping open.

"We cannot leave this alone. Surely you see that a man with such access to the Prince Regent, in such a position within the court as you, cannot allow blackmailers free rein. You will tell us everything. We are not trying to harm you. We want to help." By the end of his speech, the duke's voice had softened to one of reasonable persuasion. "Start at the beginning. When did the first letter arrive?"

Pringle appeared to take stock of his options, then reached for the lifeline Haverly was tossing him.

"About the time the jewels were stolen at Carlton House. The letter was delivered to my house by morning post." He touched his temple, stemming a bead of sweat. "I couldn't imagine who would send it or how they could possibly know . . ."

"Know what?"

He shook his head, his nostrils flaring.

"Man, if you do not tell us, how can we help you? It cannot be as bad as you think. You are not the first blackmail victim in history, not even the first that we have helped out of his trouble." Marcus stared at him, daring him to show some backbone.

Pringle's hands trembled, and he licked his lips. "I . . . I . . . It was madness, but I . . ." He groaned and closed his eyes. "I have been unfaithful to my wife," he whispered.

Bertie grimaced. Marital issues. Yet another reason to steer clear of that particular shoal. If one was not married, one could not have one's wife used against him in a blackmail scheme. He would defer to Marcus, the married man, to lead this part of the conversation.

"I see. With whom?"

"Do I have to say?" His eyes pleaded.

"I cannot identify your blackmailer and intercede if I do not know all the facts. Confess and be released from at least that much of your torment."

"Her name is Lady Durrow." He again wiped his temples. "I don't know what I was thinking. I love my wife. I really do. This will destroy her."

Marcus looked at Bertie, one brow raised, then back to Pringle. "Don't you mean this will destroy *you*? Your grandfather a bishop, your father-in-law, also a bishop? Not to mention your poor wife, as you said. Yes, her above all. And more than the injury you will cause your family, you will lose your position at Court if your infidelities become known. His Highness cannot afford more scandal, nor to alienate his few supporters in the church, not when he is doing all he can to find legal and moral grounds to divorce his own wife."

Pringle's shoulders slumped.

"What did the blackmailer want? How much money?" Bertie asked. "The papers do not say."

"He did not want money. If only it was money he desired."

Marcus drummed his fingers on the tabletop. "What did he want, man? Enough of this shilly-shallying. Spill it."

Pringle looked at the nearly deserted dining room, casting over each shoulder, before whispering. "He wanted access to the information in the dispatch boxes sent to Carlton House. Specifically, those related to commerce and the business takeover I was monitoring for the Prince Regent."

Bertie suppressed a low whistle. They had just jumped from the salacious to the treasonous.

For which he was thankful, as he had far more experience rooting out traitors.

Pringle continued. "That was what I was doing yesterday morning and on the morning the jewels went missing. Both times, I was alone in the courtiers' workroom, and I could gather the information the blackmailer wanted without risk of interruption. I have no idea where the jewels went nor who killed that poor girl. I was sorting out my own problems."

Your Honor, I could not have killed that maid, because I was too busy committing an act of treason to keep my wife and family from finding out I had been unfaithful.

As a defense, it wasn't great.

"Have you delivered the package? Where and how were you to transfer it?" Marcus asked.

"Not yet. The last note says to await instructions."

A satisfied smile touched the duke's lips. "I see. Then we may still apprehend the blackmailer."

Bertie had lost a suspect in the maid's murder, but he was on the trail of a traitor.

More proof that he was a better spy than a detective.

Chapter 12

It should have been a day of celebration, the long-awaited dedication and formal opening of Eleos School, but Philippa could not stop thinking of poor Lydia, and the role she, Philippa, might have played in her death.

The dowager had done well getting the word out to the *ton* and providing refreshments for the festivities to come.

However, there was the sermon to get through first. Chairs had been set on the freshly cut lawn, and a pulpit erected on a small dais. Mr. Todd, resplendent in the robes of his office, sat on the platform beside Marcus, Charles, Mr. Moody, Sir David, and Sir Bertrand, as the male members of the Eleos board. Charlotte, the dowager, Aunt Dolly, and Philippa sat on the front row, and on the opposite side of the aisle, the eleven women enrolled at Eleos took up the first two rows.

Behind them, nearly one hundred members of the *ton* and gentry, all the dowager could gather at this time of year, had come for the dedication. Her Grace was certain they would donate generously before they left today, filling the coffers of the hospital enough to feed and house the women for at least the next three months.

Philippa hoped so, because as of that morning, the charity had exactly three pounds, eleven shillings, and four pence to its name. Aunt Dolly had reminded her at breakfast that God promised to meet their needs, never more than that while they lived here on earth. As long as they had food, clothes, and shelter each day, they would give thanks.

Mr. Todd rose and approached the pulpit. "Let us pray."

Philippa followed along for a while, but the prayer was so long-winded, so full of grandiose words and not a little bit of pomposity, that she let her mind wander.

She had visited Nell in Newgate, but the child swore she knew nothing about who would kill Lydia.

"The only thing I didn't tell you was that Harry Sloan was sweet on Lydia. We thought you wouldn't approve, her having been a street-walker once and him being a few years older. She wasn't sure she would let him court her, but she was thinking about it. That's all we was hiding."

Her little face was tear streaked, and she was distraught at the news of Lydia's death. The brighter tracks through the dirt on her cheeks tore at Philippa's heart. Yet, the girl still refused to look her in the eye, keeping her head down, her hands gripped in her lap. Was it her distress, or what she was forced to endure in the prison that made her seem so evasive? Or did she hide something else?

"Has Mr. Newbolt been to see you about your case?" she asked.

Nell nodded. "He had ever so many questions, but I don't think he thinks we can win. He said the brooch in the tureen will be hard to overcome."

"We're still trying to find the real culprit, Nell. Don't give up hope."

"The man who stole the jewels is the same one who killed Lydia." Her face was downcast but accepting.

"How do you know?" Was she about to finally tell what was troubling her?

She shrugged. "Stands to reason, don't it? Whoever took those jewels hid that brooch in the tureen so someone else would be blamed. Lydia must have twigged who it was. She was always smarter than me. And he kilt her for it."

Nell had come to the same conclusion as Philippa and Sir Bertrand and Mr. Swann.

But Nell insisted over and over that she had nothing else to tell. At last, Philippa was forced to take her leave.

Aunt Dolly nudged Philippa, and she realized the prayer was over and she'd been sitting there with her eyes closed.

She looked up and locked eyes with Sir Bertrand. His gaze mocked her silently from his place on the dais, and for some odd reason, warmth spread through her at their nonverbal communication. She could not fault his efforts in finding the thief and killer. He had questioned everyone she would have. That neither of them had produced results was frustrating.

"True religion. What is it? We are told in the New Testament book of James, 'Pure religion and undefiled before God and the Father is this, to visit the fatherless and widows in their affliction, and to keep himself unspotted from the world.' Those of us who practice pure religion, undefiled before God, are tasked with aiding those who have fallen or who are in distress, whether through their own actions, or through the hand of God."

The reverend waved his hand toward the women who had come to Eleos for help. "We are also told, that if we sin, we are to confess that sin. God will cleanse sin, but only if we confess, repent, and turn away from our wicked ways."

Philippa tensed. Surely he would not shame them in front of this crowd.

"It is the mission of Eleos to extend the mission of God. To practice true religion. To aid those in affliction. To help those in need. To assist them in confessing their sins and equip them to turn their back on their wicked ways to follow a clean, righteous path.

"And to those of us who are already on that righteous path, what does God intend for us? Oh, you can give through compulsion or coercion, and God can use those gifts for His own good and His glory, but what does the apostle Paul tell us in his book to the Corinthians? 'But this I say, he which soweth sparingly shall reap also sparingly; and he which soweth bountifully shall reap also bountifully. Every man according as he purposeth in his heart, so let him give; not grudgingly, or of necessity: for God loveth a cheerful giver.'"

She eased the straightness of her back. He had come close to calling the ladies to task, but had skirted away from it. If he wanted to preach about giving generously, she was all for it. Thus far, everything he had said was true, based upon the Scriptures.

"Do you want to know God's love? First you must repent of your sins. But you also must give of the blessings you have received. You must give cheerfully, without counting the pence. I know those who parse their income precisely and refuse to give so much as a ha'penny more than their tithe, but is that how God treats us? Do we only receive a calculated amount of His love? Of His blessings? Of His salvation? Give as it has been given unto you. Help those who cannot help themselves. Be loved by God."

He went on for some time, but Philippa's mind wandered again.

To be loved. Something every human craved. At least for a time. She had craved her father's love. Then his actions had broken her heart to the point where she wasn't even certain what true love was. Was the love of God something to be earned by confession of sin and giving of money? Was she only worth to God what she could give? If that was the case, she was worth very little indeed.

Marcus and Charlotte. She loved them, didn't she? Charlotte had expressed that she loved Philippa, but somehow, Philippa had never been able to say the words back.

Too many people in her life had pretended affection or tried to purchase a form of it. She couldn't toss the word about flippantly.

Aunt Dolly. She mattered a great deal to Philippa. If there was anyone living that Philippa might be able to say she loved, surely it was Dorothy Stokes.

She had loved her mother. So, once upon a time, she had been capable of love.

But now, love was something for other people. Both the giving and the receiving.

The sermon finally ended, and the celebration began. Luncheon was laid on, with servants from the Haverly House tending the guests. The ladies who were enrolled in the school were treated as guests for once, something of which Philippa heartily approved.

Aunt Dolly was giving tours of the manor house, speaking especially of the improvements still needed to attain their vision.

"I, of course, will be installed in the manse, and preaching regularly at the chapel, once the building has been restored." Mr. Todd held a cup of cordial. "Work has begun on the chapel, courtesy of the funds given by congregations throughout London."

This was news to her. When had the work started? Which work was that, and was it under the direction of the architect, Isaiah Hoffman? Or had Todd gone ahead without board approval? She would have to inspect the chapel after their guests had gone.

"It's a lovely party." Charlotte looked over the guests milling on the lawn. "Whatever her faults may be, the dowager does know how to throw a fete. Mr. Moody has been tasked with taking the donations, and his smile is as broad as a melon. The ladies look nice today. Where did you get the dresses?"

"Antoinette's. Mrs. Cooper heard we could use some clothing, and she kindly donated dresses so the women could be presentable for the service. She has been very generous, and she has taken in two girls to train as seamstresses, with the prospect of hiring others in the future."

"What a blessing. I shall be sure to patronize her shop next Season to say thank you."

The ladies all sat in a row along the front of the building, dresses identical in pattern though different colors, with fichus, bonnets, and gloves. Modesty personified. They whispered amongst themselves, but none of the guests approached them. There were sidelong glances, and a few reddened cheeks, but no friendly advances.

Philippa excused herself from Charlotte and went to them.

"Have you gotten something to eat? The plum duff is particularly tasty." She smiled at Bridie.

The girl shook her head. "We thought it best to wait until all the guests were finished. They won't want to take food after we've been through. Afeared they might catch something, no doubt." She shrugged, but Philippa heard the hurt in her voice.

"Nonsense. Come with me, all of you." She took Bridie's hand and when she had risen, tucked it into the crook of her elbow. "Have you ever had raspberry cordial?"

They followed like ducklings, even the ones older than Philippa. Those serving the food were well used to helping train rescued girls and were polite. When the ladies had full plates and cups, Philippa ushered them back to their row of chairs in the shade of the manor house.

"Now, eat up, and try to relax. This will be over soon. If someone does approach, you are only required to be polite."

She had gone a few steps before Mr. Todd was at her side. "Miss Cashel, a good turnout, is it not? And Mr. Moody tells me people are being quite generous. Enough that the manse can move up the priority list, I am certain."

He carried his Bible tucked under his arm, sizable, with latches, though when he had preached, it had remained closed on the pulpit. Perhaps he had such a prodigious memory that he did not need to refer to notes or the Scriptures to quote it accurately? He carried the Book with his usual pomposity.

"The board will certainly have something to discuss, if the donations are as large as you hope. They set the spending priorities. The manse will have to come behind the supplies and equipment for the vocational training, not to mention the getting in of poultry and cattle. Then there is the little matter of daily food, medicine and supplies for the infirmary, books, paper, and ink for the education of the ladies. Firing for the stoves, bedding, candles . . ." She sighed. "Yes, that priority list is quite long."

His neck swelled as he hunched his shoulders in displeasure. "I was assured that a residence came with this appointment. I must be present if I am to minister to these women. You heard my sermon. They must repent if they wish to be forgiven for their considerable sins."

She stepped back. "They must repent to God, not to you. Your presence is not necessary to their forgiveness."

He scowled. "I have long sensed your animosity to my appointment here. Is it that you have things you, too, should confess? Micah Asbury invited me to be the chaplain here because he was concerned with the spiritual guidance of the students of Eleos. And quite possibly because he had reservations about the suitability of two such women as yourself and Mrs. Stokes being in charge of the rehabilitation of fallen women, seeing as you are both fallen women yourselves. You would do well to consider that I am a man of God, worthy of respect, and that a word from me to Micah would see you and this entire cohort tossed out on your derrieres."

She flinched as if slapped.

He looked over her shoulder. "Plaster a smile on your face. The dowager and His Grace are approaching. It would not do for them to think we are quarreling."

Philippa turned away from the reverend, but could not get any words out.

Mr. Todd had no such problems.

"Ah, Your Grace, you have outdone yourself. I had heard your social skills and planning were without peer, and it is true. You've brought the right people, the perfect menu, and even the best of English weather to make the day complete." He bowed over her hand.

Sir Bertrand, who was passing by, stopped to bow to the dowager and the duke. "Miss Cashel, if I might have a word?"

"I say," Todd began to ask before she could answer, "is the unpleasantness at Carlton House going to be resolved soon? Will I be allowed back in the library by tomorrow? I have some studying to do."

"We're working on it. Following a new lead, which is why I must speak with Miss Cashel." Sir Bertrand offered his arm to Philippa, and she took it, grateful to have a reason to leave the obsequious Mr. Todd.

"You have a new lead?"

"Alas, I do not. I merely observed that you were within a small mouse's whisker of striking the illustrious reverend across his jowly face and thought it best I intervene. You've done well here. I'll confess, I had my doubts as to the wisdom of the scale of this endeavor. Not that you and Mrs. Stokes couldn't make a go of it, but taking on a property of this size so early in the history of Eleos was a step of faith to be sure. But after today, I can see the potential. To try to grow by increments would take years."

She was distracted by the play of muscles beneath the sleeve of his coat. He was thin, wiry even, but his arm felt deceptively strong.

And he had a sense of humor, something she considered essential in a man's makeup. If one could laugh, even in the worst of situations, one could usually find a way out.

"I've wondered as to the wisdom of such a move myself. And thank you for saving me from embarrassing myself by striking a preacher. However much he might deserve it. He hangs over my head like the Sword of Damocles. Oh, my, I've been with Charlotte too much. Her history and mythology interests are invading my own speech."

"How is he like the sword?" Sir Bertrand asked, with a twist of his lips, proving that he was not only amused, but that he was well-read.

"He has given not-so-veiled hints that, at the mere mention of a word from him to Asbury, he could have us tossed off the property and the school shuttered forever."

"Really. He believes himself so powerful? I would suggest he not play those particular cards without a good reason. Marcus and Mr. Moody are no fools, and the lease has specific language in it now that could very well trip Mr. Todd up." He patted her hand on his arm, and oddly, she was comforted.

Silly thoughts. She was clearly not herself. No man's touch could move her.

"He's pushing hard for the manse to be restored ahead of the other work. I think that's what grates me the most. He always seems to be looking out for himself rather than those he serves."

"Yet, the church must believe in him. And he did serve aboard Charles Wyvern's ship during the war . . . as a chaplain, yes, but the earl speaks well enough of him."

"Perhaps he was a different man then." She could not imagine the notion, but felt she should at least try to be gracious lest Sir Bertrand think her a waspish old prune.

"We're all different than we used to be. Change is inevitable as we gain age, wisdom, and experience."

He spoke as if to himself. Was he different than he used to be? Did he, like her, have regrets? She supposed everyone must have some regrets about their past, though with his privilege, she did not think he had much to rue.

"Where does the investigation stand?" she asked, seeking firmer ground in the here and now. "I spoke with the footman, Harry Sloan, and went to see Nell again. Neither could help with any new information. Nell says the only secret they were keeping was that Harry had taken an interest in Lydia. Lydia had evidently told Harry that she had to be careful around powerful men at Carlton House. He did not know what to make of that, and she would not give him specifics."

Sir Bertrand considered this. "I suppose a girl in her position in the house would have to be careful around any man. She might have been speaking in generalities."

His arm tightened, and she noted that his hand was in a fist.

"If only those girls had been frank with us from the beginning, perhaps we could have gotten enough information from them to keep them both safe. I understand that Nell has a barrister now. Marcus's influence continues to grow."

"He's a powerful man." Philippa would not divulge that it was herself who had called on Newbolt. If she did, she would have to explain how she knew him and why he might do her a favor.

"I still think there is something Nell is hiding, but I cannot imagine what. Perhaps she has a potential beau amongst the staff too, and she fears censure if she tells me?" Philippa sighed. As always when working with girls who were so experienced at such a young age, the difficulty in unraveling the twists in their logic was often the most arduous part of their rehabilitation. At the very least, Lydia's death had cleared Nell of any guilt in Philippa's mind. She would never be involved in anything that would put her dearest friend in jeopardy.

"We should turn back. Mr. Todd has followed our every step. If we are not careful, people will be bandying our names about." He chuckled, but appeared unbothered.

"You would not like that. My reputation is not one with whom anyone in polite society would wish to be linked."

He stopped walking, looking down on her with a puzzled frown. "What nonsense are you spouting? Your name is associated with many respectable people already, myself included. Am I not on your board of directors? In any case, reputation and character are not to be confused. One is what people *think* you are, and one is what you *actually* are. I should know. The *ton* believes I am a dilettante with a weakness for drink. But in fact, I am a dilettante who does not actually care for the taste of wine or spirits." He quirked one eyebrow. "And it has been my experience that there are many in what London considers 'polite society' who have fine reputations, but their characters are riddled with rot."

They neared Mr. Todd once more, who had his ornate Bible held before him like a decorative breastplate. He reached into his inner pocket and withdrew a handkerchief. He dabbed his not-inconsiderable nose. "The guests are beginning to depart, and as board members, it would behoove us to at least make an appearance and thank them, do you not think?"

Philippa removed her hand from Sir Bertrand's arm, and he bowed to her.

She nodded to him. "By all means. Let us make an appearance. Thank you for your company, Sir Bertrand. I appreciate the information. I feel strongly that with you on the case, Nell will soon be out of prison and Lydia's killer will be caught. I shall help you all I can."

Mr. Todd frowned. No doubt he thought it not her place to have any doings with something as unsavory as a murder investigation. She would add it to his long list of things of which he disapproved where she was concerned.

As the guests drifted away to their carriages, those remaining went into the manor house. The dowager leaned on her cane and surveyed the improvements that had been made thus far.

"Not back to its original glory, but functional enough not to be an embarrassment."

"You were right, Your Grace," Philippa offered, deciding to be generous. "Repainting was the correct choice. The hall is fresh and welcoming now." And it was. The fresh paint lightened the space, and with clean windows, sunlight streamed in cheerfully.

"I believe a rug or two and some proper seating is all the room will need for now. Along with a few portraits of the original members of the board to hang on this long wall under the gallery. Perhaps we can have Hamish paint them." The dowager bustled away, busy with her own plans.

Philippa shook her head. Mr. Hamish Sinclair, who had married the dowager's widowed daughter-in-law, was more likely to paint the students at Eleos than the board members. He had made quite a name for himself with a series of paintings called "The Army of the Unseen." Tender and perceptive portraits of servants and workers and those who would not ordinarily sit for a painting.

The servants from Haverly House quietly went about the business of packing away the remaining food and supplies, carrying in the tables and chairs. The students were helping, each one pitching in, Philippa was grateful to see. This first group was going to be a good one.

"Several of the attendees today are going to take what they learned of Eleos back to their parishes. I expect we will have more referrals soon," Mr. Todd said. He rocked on his toes a bit. "An altogether profitable day. I believe my sermon had the desired results, and imagine how well things will go once we have regular services here for the public."

One would think the entire enterprise hinged on his involvement.

A chastening look from Aunt Dolly across the way told Philippa to compose her expression to one less disgruntled.

Mr. Moody, with a cashbox and ledger in his hands, beamed. "Today has been most rewarding, both in good will and in the till." He seemed pleased with his rhyme. "If everyone follows through on what they have pledged, we will receive more than three hundred pounds."

Three hundred? From a single day's efforts?

That would see to so many of the starting costs of Eleos, as well as give them a bit of a reserve. Marcus had advised keeping some funds back in order to have a cushion should some unexpected expense arise, and Philippa approved of this plan—she who had never had anything to hold in reserve.

When the rest left, Mr. Todd stayed on.

"Should we have our supper?" Philippa asked Aunt Dolly in a whisper. "What is he hanging about for?"

"It will not harm anything to invite him to share our meal, though it will be much more pedestrian fare than anything to which he is accustomed, I'm sure." Aunt Dolly shook her head. "And you might try being polite to him. No one wishes to be bristled at continually. If you want him to play on your team, you will have to befriend him. He's a better ally than enemy, I'm sure."

"Befriend him? That pompous, pious pain?"

Aunt Dolly's lips twitched. "Has it occurred to you that he might think you a bit of a pain, my dear? You reject his every suggestion before you've even considered it, merely because he was the one to voice it. You're cutting off your nose to spite your face. He was very helpful today, and we did raise quite a bit of money for the school. The people who came for his sermon seemed to like it quite a bit."

Philippa was properly chastened. An idea wasn't wrong just because Mr. Todd proposed it . . . but he did chafe her. Always so sure he was right and so condescending toward the women he was supposed to be helping.

After a simple dinner of bread, cheese, and milk, Todd finally took his leave. He carried a satchel with his church robes and Bible.

"Have you no carriage, sir?" Aunt Dolly asked.

"No. I'm merely walking to the village. I will stay at the inn tonight and take the stage into London tomorrow morning. Before I go, I will return at first light to inspect the manse and chapel."

When he had gone, Philippa was restless. She could not settle to anything. The ladies had all gone to bed, and Aunt Dolly was knitting away in the common room next to a single lamp.

"I believe I will go for a walk."

Aunt Dolly looked up. "At this time of night?"

"There's plenty of light. There's still a half-moon." She picked up her cloak. "I won't go far. I just need to work off this unease."

"Do not be long. I will stay up until you return."

"Don't do that. You have had a long day. No harm will come to me, and I promise not to leave the school grounds."

The air was brisk but not cold, and the moon shone bright enough to cast shadows. She lengthened her stride across the grass, trying to stir enough of a breeze to blow the cobwebs from her mind. Or was she trying to outpace her conscience?

So many worries, so many times recently that her ideas had been confronted. By Charlotte, by Marcus, by Aunt Dolly, by Mr. Todd. Even by Sir Bertrand Thorndike, of all people.

He had been surprisingly logical in his reasoning about reputation and character. And he truly cared about finding the person who had killed Lydia. Cared enough to set his personal pride aside and call in Mr. Swann and his detectives to help.

Not many men of Philippa's acquaintance would be willing to do that.

Her steps took her past the darkened manse, a two-story, stone cottage with a slate roof. The grass and bushes had been cut back, making the place look a bit more respectable. If only a kind parson with a growing family had been invited to serve here instead of Todd.

Beyond the parsonage stood the church. She had not been inside since the first day she had inspected the property, and that only briefly due to the unsafe nature of the building.

Todd had indicated that reconstruction had begun, but what had been done? If the Church of England's coffers would spread to fixing the church, perhaps they would also extend to the repairs necessary for the manse, and Eleos could save the expense.

The Gothic door stood open a foot. Had the workmen forgotten to close it? She pressed her hand on the rough, oak surface, and the portal swung open silently. Clearly the first repair had been done to the hinges.

Where was the key? Did Asbury have it? Or would they need a new lock installed once the church was finished?

Darkness gathered around the doorway, but a few steps inside, the moonlight penetrated through the reticulated windows at the end of the church. The delicate stone tracery cast shadows on the floor and altar.

Scaffolding had been raised in the nave, and the altar had been draped with sheets to protect the wood from falling debris.

The smell of rock dust and damp tickled her nose. Hewn stone blocks sat in rows in the aisle, and a plasterer's hawk and trowel lay beside a bucket on the floor.

Would beeswax and lemon polish bring back the woodwork? She trailed her hand along the ends of the pews. The rood screen that had originally divided the chancel and the nave had been moved to the west side of the chapel, now separating the baptismal font from the nave. So many rood screens across England had not survived. That there was one in this little abandoned chapel was an unexpected treasure.

Stacks of timber had been placed along the wall beneath the scaffolding, ready for lifting to the roof, high above. Moonlight seeped through a hole in the slate roof tiles, and she could hear the fluttering and cooing of doves in the eaves.

With so much work already underway, it would not be long before the church was habitable.

A light spot beneath the scaffolding caught her eye. A square of fabric. Had one of the workers dropped a handkerchief? She stooped beneath the cross braces and reached for it, and in that moment, the scaffolding creaked. Dust showered down, and with a crack, the structure gave way and tumbled to the floor.

Something hit her shoulder, driving her to the cold floor, and another something heavy pinned her legs. The air filled with dirt and dust, and she coughed, then one last heavy something hit her on the head. A shadow passed over her, and she heard . . . footsteps?

The moonlit space whirled, and she lost consciousness.

Chapter 13

Vauxhall Gardens was a quiet place on a Sunday night in mid-June. Not as bustling as it would have been on a weeknight at the height of the season. Bertie shrugged, loosening the muscles in his neck.

Waiting for something to happen was the most boring part of spy work, but the best way to catch a thief from ambush was to arrive far earlier than the thief would anticipate.

Swann and Beck were concealed across the way, opposite the iron bench Bertie studied. For extra insurance, the youngster Owen Wilkinson was stationed near the music stage.

The hedge in which Bertie had hidden himself prickled. Why had the blackmailer chosen this particular place within Vauxhall Gardens? There was too much open space for decent hiding places.

Which was perhaps the reason. The extortioner would have a clear view of the surroundings and be able to see when Lord Pringle dropped the documents at the assigned place and whether he had come alone as instructed.

This entire venture had been very last-minute. Bertie had only just returned from the dedication party at Eleos when Pringle had knocked on the Thorndike door, all but panting that the blackmailer had contacted him and given instructions for the drop.

Bertie sent word immediately to Swann, and the young detective-turned-earl had put into motion the plan they had come up with only the day before.

Owen Wilkinson proved quite useful. In case the blackmailer checked the envelope Pringle left, Owen had forged a handful of official-looking documents, stacked them together with plain stationery to make a satisfying bundle, and sealed the envelope with wax.

Bertie would have to remember Wilkinson's abilities should he have need of a forger in the future. He was building his own stable of resources, men and women he could call upon for specific skills should the need arise on one of his missions. An excellent forger would come in handy, he was sure.

Where was Lord Pringle? He would be late if he tarried. The instructions were clear. Leave the package on the middle bench opposite the music stage before midnight. Do not stay. If at any time the blackmailer felt he was being watched or that Pringle was not keeping to the plan, the deal was off, and Pringle's wife and family would know of his infidelity within twenty-four hours.

Lord Pringle had been a shaking, sweating mess when Bertie left him at the Water Gate to Vauxhall to wait until the prescribed hour and give Bertie, Swann, and Wilkinson time to find concealment.

The time was tight. If Bertie had been the blackmailer, he would have gone straight to his own hiding place after delivering the drop instructions, at least an hour before the appointed time of the exchange.

Though Bertie and Daniel had taken a cursory look, it was impossible, in the dark, to check every place, and they had not wanted to tip their hand. The half-moon cast enough light that one could see well enough to get around without a lantern. He fidgeted, not wishing to stir the hedge but itching at the poking of the leaves and twigs.

At last, he heard footsteps on the path. Slowly turning his head, he spied Lord Pringle's top hat and dull, golden waistcoat. The metallic threads in the fabric winked in the moonlight. He held the package beneath his arm and walked in a straight line toward the drop point.

He looked neither right nor left, and as he approached, his pace quickened until he was nearly trotting. He dropped the package on the bench with a slap. It promptly bounced off and landed on the walkway. Pringle had to round the bench and retrieve it before placing it on the bench and hurrying away.

So much for being casual. Anyone would assume he was up to something clandestine. Not even Juliette, at their first training, had been as obvious and clumsy.

Pringle's footsteps faded as he turned the corner beneath the covered walkway and headed toward the gate.

A bug buzzed in Bertie's ear, and he swatted it away, rustling the bushes. *Quiet, you fool.*

Nothing else stirred. Not for ages.

When his legs were feeling pins and needles from crouching and his back protested his hunched position, he finally heard footsteps.

Not the heavy tread of boots, but rather the lighter tap-tap of shoes.

He risked leaning out of the bushes and grimaced. A woman, cutting through the park, alone.

She hurried along the path, head down, bonnet concealing her face.

Not young. Not slim.

A dark dress, a dark bonnet. A midwife, heading to a birthing? A maid out of the house when she shouldn't be? A doxy on the way to an assignation? If so, he wished she would move along and not spoil their trap.

But she did not move on. She stopped at the bench, looked down at the package, then bent to pick it up.

She was ruining everything, this strange woman. They would have to stop her and hope to reset the trap before the blackmailer showed his face.

He struggled from the grasping hedge.

"You there, leave that be." He hissed a whisper. "Mind your own business and get out of here. This is none of your concern."

The woman gave a little shriek and turned, dropping the packet to the ground. Her bonnet slid back, and he saw her face in the moonlight.

"Mrs. Bascome?" The prince's former paramour? The first suspect in his theft case? "What are you doing here?"

She darted looks up and down the path, as if calculating her ability to outrun him.

Swann, Beck, and Wilkinson emerged from their hiding places, cutting off any hope of escape.

Her lips trembled, and she stooped for the packet. "Just passing through the park." She shrugged. So she was going to try to bluff her way out of this? Bertie shook his head. She had walked right up to the bench and picked up the papers. No innocent passerby would have done that.

Lord Pringle marched down the path toward them. With a scowl on his face, he snatched the envelope from the woman and towered over her. "You? You're the one who has been doing this to me? You backstabbing old cow."

Bertie felt as if he had missed a stair in the dark. Pringle had been instructed to go home after placing the packet, and here he was, storming into the situation.

"Mrs. Bascome? You are the blackmailer?" Bertie asked.

This made no sense. Why would she want inside information on commerce? Had someone coerced her into retrieving the stolen information?

"Who are you working for?" Swann asked, clearly following the same track as Bertie.

"Working for?" She found her tongue as her shoulders went back and her chin rose. "I work for no one," she spat.

"You are the blackmailer?" Bertie asked again. It had never entered his head that the culprit would be a woman, much less the former mistress of the Prince Regent.

"Perhaps we should take this discussion into more formal surroundings." Swann nodded to Wilkinson, who stepped forward with a pair of darbies.

"What do you think you're doing with those, child?" Mrs. Bascome snarled. "Don't come near me."

"How did you know? How did you find out about me and—" Pringle stopped.

"Your little tryst with Lady Durrow?" She bared her teeth. "Alicia Durrow and I have known one another for years, since long before she turned the head of Lord Durrow. She tells me everything. I knew the next day after you had been with her."

He hung his head.

"Madam, I am arresting you for the crimes of blackmail and treason. You will be taken to the Bow Street magistrate's court for questioning and arraignment. You will then be taken to Newgate Prison, where you will await your trial and hanging." Swann's voice brooked no argument, and Mrs. Bascome flinched.

"Hanging? Treason? What on earth are you on about? I have committed no treason," she protested.

Owen stepped forward and slapped the darbies on her, wrestling with her as she writhed. Pringle was the one who stepped in to force her to be still.

"Blackmailing a courtier to obtain private dispatch information is the definition of treason. What did you think would happen if you were caught?" Swann gripped her elbow and marched her up the path. "Owen, take charge of that packet, will you?"

Wilkinson nodded, tucking the envelope beneath his arm.

Bertie followed Swann, and Pringle fell into step with him.

"Is it over then?" he asked. "She won't be allowed to ruin me, will she?"

"You should go home, Lord Pringle. I do not know how far the ripples will reach, but I will not be able to keep this from His Highness, and news of her arrest will most likely be public knowledge by morning. We cannot control what she decides to disclose. You should prepare what you will say to the prince. He will want answers. I will not throw you beneath the carriage wheels, but there will certainly be repercussions. If His Highness asks, I will tell him you cooperated with our investigation fully and that no sensitive information changed hands, but he will draw his own conclusions as to your suitability for future service as a courtier."

Pringle's shoulders sagged. "I foresee many more late-night walks in my future. I could not sleep since the first blackmail note arrived, and only walking could settle my mind. With this hanging over my head . . ."

So Pringle's late night perambulations were the sign of a troubled mind. He had come perilously close to committing treason. Bertie foresaw many more sleepless nights in Pringle's future.

They parted from Pringle and Beck at the gate, and the trip across London in Cadogan's carriage, newly adorned with the Aylswood crest, was tense. Mrs. Bascome seemed to realize the seriousness of her situation and sat with arms crossed, jaw set, but eyes glistening with moisture. Owen sat beside her, and Swann and Bertie opposite.

"What did you intend to do with the information you were squeezing out of Lord Pringle?" Bertie asked.

She stared hard at him. "What do you think?"

"I cannot imagine. You are not a woman of commerce, so the information would do you little good. You know Lord Pringle, but how does ruining his career help you?"

"I do not care about Pringle. I do not care that he betrayed his wife. I do not care about his career. I do care about finding someone to keep me now that Prinny has kicked me out of Carlton House. If I could promise financial gain, I could interest someone of means who could profit from entering into a situation with me. I planned to continue the coercion of Pringle and keep the information coming."

"So this was all about feathering your nest? It had nothing to do with the stolen jewelry or the murder of the scullery maid?"

"Murder?" Her arms slacked, and her hands fell to her lap. "What murder? Of course I was not involved in any murder. You have lost your reason."

Bertie sat back. How would he explain this to the Prince Regent? He had found a potential traitor in one of his courtiers and a blackmailer in his former paramour, but he had not found a thief and killer in his household.

"Miss Cashel? Miss Cashel, are you dead?" The young voice reached through the throbbing clouds in Philippa's head.

The sound of stone scraping, of grit underfoot, and the creak of wood followed.

"Miss Cashel?" The voice said again. Why wouldn't she stop?

Leave me alone. Why does everything hurt? What happened?

"She's here! Help me! I can't get her out."

Shouting now. Who needed to be got out of what?

Philippa tried to move her hand, to raise it to her pounding head, but she couldn't stir. Something heavy lay across her chest, making breathing difficult. She tasted blood, coppery and unpleasant, and a wave of nausea swept over her.

Where was she? It was too dark to see much, and the air seemed thick with dust.

The smell was familiar . . . she had been walking . . . at night. In the chapel . . . and smelled stone dust.

Rubble poked her back, and she was cold. Had she fallen asleep in the chapel? On the floor?

Footsteps, rushing.

"Oh, Pippa, what have you done to yourself?"

Aunt Dolly's voice.

"I knew I shouldn't have let you come out alone so late at night. Bridie, bring that lantern. Are you hurt, child?"

Somehow having Aunt Dolly fuss and call her "child" comforted Philippa. Whatever had happened, Aunt Dolly would fix it. She relaxed a fraction.

Lantern light hit her in the eyes, and she winced, turning away.

"I . . . my head aches." The words came out on a croak, and she coughed in dust, which hurt abominably in her chest. "Hard to breathe."

"Let's get this beam off her. It's suffocating her. Girls, we must lift together. There isn't time to send to the village for help."

A beam?

Memory trickled back. The scaffolding. She had been stooping beneath it to pick up a handkerchief someone had dropped, and it had come crashing down on her.

Had she bumped the structure somehow and caused it to fall?

A memory tickled her mind . . . but then it evaporated. Something important? Uneasiness.

Though who wouldn't be uneasy in these circumstances. The pain in her head drove out everything else.

How long had she lain in the rubble? Every inch of her body ached, and the weight on her chest made breathing an agony.

"Protect her head. This scaffolding isn't stable. Ready now?" Aunt Dolly asked. "Lift."

The beam shifted, sliding across her chest, and thunking to the floor by her left hand. Sweet air, though tainted with dust, entered her lungs, and she coughed again. She touched her head, rolling slightly to her side, wincing but grateful to get off her back and the rough stones beneath her.

"Don't move too quickly. Assess things. You may have broken some bones." Aunt Dolly's hands supported her.

"Easy, Miss Cashel." Bridie put her hand under Philippa's arm to help her from beneath the still-teetering scaffolding. "But hurry."

Stone bits and splinters fell from Philippa's dress as she staggered to her feet, moving with the ladies to the middle of the chapel. She coughed, holding her head. Her hand came away wet.

"You've opened your head. Here." Aunt Dolly pulled a handkerchief from her sleeve and pressed it to Philippa's hairline. "Your lip is bleeding too."

Philippa walked hunched over, feeling like an eighty-year-old woman emerging from a clothes mangle.

"Mrs. Stokes was that worried when you didn't come back. She roused the whole house to come look for you." Bridie kept hold of

Philippa's arm. "We couldn't think where you'd gotten to. It's gone half three."

Philippa looked at the faces, pale in the lantern light. She had left for her walk not long after eleven. "I'm sorry to have caused you worry. Thank you for looking for me. I might have lain there all night." Her throat hurt, testament to the dust still residing there.

"Let this be a caution to all of you. The chapel is not to be entered until the work is completed." Aunt Dolly took Philippa's hand and put it over the handkerchief. "Hold that there. Now, let us return to the manor house where you all can get back to bed and I can treat Miss Cashel properly."

Bridie insisted upon helping Philippa clean up, and she did not seem the least squeamish when it came to cleaning and treating the cut to Philippa's head.

"Perhaps we have a budding healer or midwife in our midst," Aunt Dolly commented as she opened the medicinal chest. "Would you like to train for a healer, Bridie?"

"I never thought of it. I seen plenty of injuries and sickness, that's for sure." She dabbed at the cut, and Philippa tried not to wince. "You got a fat goose egg here, ma'am, but the bleeding's stopped. I don't think it will need sewing up."

Thank goodness. Philippa clutched a shawl about her shoulders, covering the nightdress Aunt Dolly had insisted she don.

"Here's a cuppa, love. Get it inside you." Aunt Dolly set the hot tea at Philippa's elbow. "Most things can be put right with a cup of tea and some rest."

"If that's all, I'll be finding my own bed, Mrs. Stokes." Bridie closed the hasp on the medicine chest. "Glad you weren't worse hurt, but like we was told, we all best stay away from the chapel until it's safe."

Properly chastened, Philippa nodded, blowing gently across the tea. She took a sip and flinched as the hot beverage touched a cut inside her cheek.

When they were alone, Aunt Dolly sat opposite her. "You were lucky not to have been killed. What happened? Did you stumble against the scaffolding?"

She tried to remember clearly past the continued ache in her head. "No. I saw something there. I thought it was a handkerchief. I bent to pick it up, heard a crack, and then it all tumbled down. I suppose I bumped the scaffolding as I bent over." Again, that odd feeling of something she should remember flitted through her mind, but she couldn't grasp it.

"Odd. I suppose we're blessed that a worker wasn't up there when it fell. He would have been killed, without doubt." Aunt Dolly shuddered. "Were you able to walk off your megrims before your accident?"

"I don't know. I suppose getting flattened by falling masonry and wood knocked my mood out of my head." She had been bothered, but now her fussing seemed irrelevant. "In that respect, I suppose the walk had the desired results. I was ruffled up about nothing, I'm sure."

She wasn't being entirely truthful, for she still felt a sense of unease from the day. Her eyelids began to droop.

"I put a sleeping draught in your tea to help with the aches and pains that are sure to linger after such a mishap." Aunt Dolly patted her hand. "Let me help you to your room."

Philippa, once stretched out beneath the blankets on her bed, grimaced in the darkness. Tea and rest might be Dolly's remedy, but her disquiet would not be calmed so easily.

Chapter 14

Bertie nudged the tea cart out of his way and sat at the desk in the War Room. He looked up at the wall with its charts and lists. What had once been a pinboard full of specifics and clues of cases and missions was now awash in wedding details.

The War Room had become a bride's bunker.

Juliette stood behind him, near the disguises wardrobe, juggling three balls in a triangular pattern while balancing on a low, narrow beam. At least in all the wedding stramash, she had not abandoned her training.

"I don't understand why you aren't traveling to Pensax with us tomorrow. You always come for the summer," she said.

"You've stated as much, several times," he said, still facing the pinboard. Guest lists, menus, trousseau items, travel arrangements. He shuddered. When and if he ever married, he would grab his bride and be off to Scotland. A quick trip to Gretna Green and they'd avoid drowning in details.

He rolled his eyes. As if he would ever get married. That ship had sailed long ago. At thirty-six, he was a bit in the sere and yellow to marry, too set in his ways.

"I've stated as much so often because you've yet to give me a satisfactory answer."

"I'm in the middle of a mission." A mission he hadn't made much headway in just yet.

"Yes, I know. I can only assume it's the same one that has been occupying Daniel this last week. Is it the murder of the maid at Carlton House, or is it the arrest of the blackmailing paramour?"

"How do you know about those things?" He swiveled in his chair. Surely Daniel had not told her, not after being warned by Haverly to keep it quiet.

She continued to juggle the balls, not wavering in her balance. "It's in the papers. Did you not see them on the breakfast table?"

He had not been to breakfast. He had been so late at Bow Street, questioning Una Bascome, that he had arrived home in the wee hours and fallen into bed. He had only awakened when his valet came into the bedchamber and opened the drapes. Bertie had grumbled, but it was the valet's duty to wake him if he slept past nine.

"If you were a proper young lady, you wouldn't read the newspapers. You're supposed to be too delicate for such an assault on your sensibilities." He voiced the widely held notion, though he did not ascribe to it himself, of course. Women were often tougher than men and always tougher than men gave them credit for.

"If I were a proper young lady, you would not have taught me to pick locks, pockets, and fights." She grinned, then sobered, catching the balls and stepping off the beam. "You will come for the wedding, won't you? In September?"

"I wouldn't miss it, chicken. I shall sit on the front row, beaming as if I had invented love and instigated the entire relationship between you and Daniel Swann." He bowed his head, one hand over his heart. "I shall be the perfect uncle and wedding guest."

"All right. I should not doubt you, but it's so disappointing that you are not coming home with us. Heild House will not be the same without you popping in and out. For all of my childhood you came and went like a summer storm, blowing fun into my life before gusting out again. Do you remember when you brought me that puppy? And he promptly chewed the leg on Mother's Hepplewhite chair?" She opened a drawer and put the balls inside.

Bertie put his hand to his head, shying away from the memory. "Not my best work, I'll agree. But he was a cute little thing."

"What will you do, rattling around this house all alone for weeks? Father is only leaving a small staff to keep the place up. Mr. Pultney is coming to help with the wedding preparations, and the new housekeeper, Mrs. Robyn, is coming too. You won't even have a cook."

"I am capable of looking after myself, you know. As to a cook, I shall solve that problem by dining at the club or eating street food. Or I can always accept invitations to dinner to those who live in the city year round."

"What are you really up to? Is it a mission that requires you to stay here? You don't have to tell me what it is, but if I knew you were working, I wouldn't mind so much." She took up her dagger and a whetstone, eyes intense as she sat across the table from him.

He hid a smile when she spit on the stone and began sharpening the knife. What proper lady of the *ton* would behave so vulgarly? Yet he was so proud of her, the way she had integrated her spy work into her life so well.

"Not a mission, Juliette. It's just that it's beyond time I grew out of my brother's shadow. I've been content to live in his houses, keep to his social calendar, and follow his lead because I was one of his team members and because it was easy. But I've been offered a position as a team leader myself, and I think I need to expand my horizons. While you are at Heild House and preparing for your marriage, I shall be here in London, looking for my own property."

The gentle scraping of metal on stone stopped.

"Your own property?" She blinked.

"Yes, you know. A house, a place to live. Somewhere to keep my things?" He winked, teasing her.

"You don't have any things. Beyond a nice wardrobe, that is. And you can keep your clothes here." She frowned, testing the edge of the blade.

"Then perhaps it is time I did acquire some belongings beyond stylish haberdashery." Though the thought made him quail. He liked being the footloose bachelor who could come or go as he wished with nothing on his mind but his next mission for the agency. Becoming a property owner meant household accounts, staff, and taxes. Furnishings, decorations . . . dishes . . . he flicked his gaze up at the lists peppering the pinboard. All the things Juliette was buying and preparing for her wedded life.

He must be out of his mind.

Juliette let the whetstone drop to her lap, her eyes wide. "Are you looking for a house because you intend to marry?" Her face spread in a grin. "Have you fallen in love with someone? Are you going to go courting? Who is she? Do I know her?"

Bertie shook his head, holding his hands up, palms out. "No, nothing like that. You have love and marriage on the brain. I happen to want my own place because I am a grown man and it is beyond time I established my own residence.

"It was convenient for all of us having me stay here while I was a member of Tristan's team, especially these last few months with you returning home and your parents being sent on so many missions. I had to step in. But you're going to marry now, and you'll be Daniel's problem from that moment on." He took the sting out of the words with another wink.

She made a face at him. "I think it would be marvelous if you would find someone to love. You would be an excellent husband and father. There are many women who could only hope you might look their way. Perhaps Mother and I could put our minds to the task of finding you a suitable bride. We could start next season." She laced her fingers, straightening her arms and pressing her palms out, as if limbering up for an effort.

He put on a horrified expression. "The only thing I think worse than jumping into the marriage mart is letting my sister-in-law and niece parade through my life with a barrage of candidates. If I ever were to marry, and that is a slim chance at best, I will do my own choosing, thank you all the same."

The door opened, and Melisande breezed in. She looked fresh and as young as the day he had first met her, though more than twenty years had passed. He had not yet left home for university. Younger than Juliette was now.

"Ah, there you are, Juliette. Agatha has called upon you this morning. Do you wish to receive? She knows it is inconvenient, what with us leaving for Heild House on the morrow, but she wanted one last yarn with you before you go." Melisande moved the tea cart back to its proper place.

Juliette hopped up, bussed her mother's offered cheek, and hurried down the stairs.

Melisande sighed and sank into a chair. She picked up Juliette's dagger and tested it before setting it down. "I don't remember having all that vigor at her age."

"You did, you know." He leaned back in his chair and put his feet on the edge of the desk. "You were a whirlwind. Nobody could outdance you at the assemblies, nobody could outride you on the hunt, and"—he grinned—"nobody could outtalk you at dinner."

She wrinkled her nose. "All right. I was a bit of a hoyden, I admit. I needed some polish and sophistication, which came with age and experience."

He shrugged. "Do you ever miss the old days of haring about, embracing every adventure, creating fun if there were no fun to be had?" He caught the wisp of longing in his words.

She studied him. "What has you feeling so nostalgic?"

Contemplating the ceiling, he considered. "I suppose it is because I informed Juliette that I will be looking to establish my own household in the coming weeks."

"Your what? Really? Are you looking to set up your nursery at last?" She beamed, clasping her hands beneath her chin and reminding him again of the girl she had been when they first met.

"I hate to pour water on your fancies, but no. As I told Juliette, I do not plan to marry or 'set up my nursery.'" He gave an exaggerated, mocking shudder. "It is merely that it is time for me to get on with my own life, separate from Tristan's. I'm going to lead my own team of agents, as I'm certain Haverly has told you. To do that, I will need to have my own dwelling, my own war room." He waved to the walls.

She tilted her head. "Is that the only reason? That you will be a team leader? No one here has made you feel surplus to requirements, have they? You know we adore having you live with us?"

"You have been nothing but gracious and hospitable from day one. No one could ask for a better sister." He smiled ruefully.

"If you're certain. I would not like you to ever feel you were unwelcome or that we were pushing you out. And you will continue to consider Heild House your home, won't you?" She leaned forward, her dark eyes earnest. "Does Tristan know of your plans?"

"I haven't mentioned it just yet. My current mission has kept me busy."

She nodded. "Mrs. Una Bascome, onetime paramour to the Prince Regent, trying to buy and sell secrets."

Once something was posted in the dailies, it was out for the world to see. He sighed. At least Pringle's name hadn't come into it yet. His career as a courtier was finished, but he had not actually committed treason. Perhaps the prince would spare the man's life.

"In any case, talk to Tristan before we leave. He might have some suggestions of a nice townhouse you could buy." She rose and patted his hand. "For now, I must continue to supervise the packing. Would you take all those"—she indicated the lists and charts on the pinboard—"and put them in a folder for me? I never knew what a large undertaking a wedding could be. I only remember being blissfully in love and letting my mother and yours take care of the details when I wedded Tristan." She hurried down the stairs.

As Bertie removed the pages from the pinboard, he stacked them idly.

Tristan and Melisande's wedding day. More than twenty years ago now. He had stood up with his brother at the altar.

It had been most bittersweet, for he had supported his brother with a heavy heart.

Tristan had married the only woman he, Bertie, had ever loved.

"Finally, a break in this case." Mr. Partridge strode down the dark street. "I hoped the receiver's shops and fences would be useful, but I had little confidence. It's difficult to move such expensive jewelry in London through a receiver. Better to take it to the Continent to dispose of it. Our quarry must be desperate."

"Your man still has the bracelet? And it's all in one piece? Not taken apart for the stones?" Bertie hurried to keep up.

"It is whole yet."

They hurried up Wells Street, the moonlight not as strong as it had been the night before in Vauxhall Gardens. A miasma of cooked vegetables, smoke, dirt, and refuse hung in the air. The narrow, cramped street confined Bertie. Almost as if he could reach out and touch the buildings on either side of the lane at the same time.

"What's the name of this place?"

"Hawthorne's."

Bertie ticked back through his memory. "Where Juliette and Daniel retrieved the jade dragon?"

"The same. The proprietor has been on the books as an informant ever since. Got him stitched up proper. He gives us information, and Daniel doesn't bung him into gaol for dealing in stolen goods."

Another useful contact to add to his growing list, Bertie mused as he navigated the cobbled street.

"Will he be open this time of night?"

Partridge shrugged his massive shoulders. "He lives above the shop, and he's expecting us."

They reached Hawthorne's, mid block. Three golden balls hung from a black, iron filigree arm jutting out over the street, the sign of a receiver's shop. The half-timbered building had a large window and a cantilevered second story, testament to its Tudor beginnings. Faint candlelight shone from the back of the shop, and when Partridge pounded his meaty fist against the door, shadows moved inside.

"Evening, Hawthorne," Partridge said to the beak-nosed man holding the candle.

"Come in, come in. Don't let folks see you loitering." The proprietor shuffled back and held the door.

The shop was crowded with cheap goods. Dishes, snuffboxes, shoes, shawls. As they wended their way through, Bertie was careful not to brush against anything, lest he topple it and find himself the new owner. He didn't wish to begin his collection of household goods with anything from this lot.

They reached the back, where a counter separated the end of the shop from the back wall, and here were the finer items. Jewelry, pistols, smaller paintings, all in a glass case, all under the watchful eye of the shopkeeper.

Partridge crossed his arms. "Tell this bloke what you told me."

Hawthorne scratched his prominent nose and set the candleholder on the case. "Dunno why I have to go over it again. If you think I like being a sneak, you can think again," he mumbled. Reaching beneath the counter, he came up with a bracelet.

A circlet of lustrous pearls and sapphires that looked almost black in the low light, joined by a winking setting of gold. Far and away a higher-toned piece than any in the jewelry case.

It exactly matched the brooch that had been found in the soup tureen in the scullery at Carlton House. Without a doubt from the same set.

"This gent comes in, looks the place over, and takes this out of his pocket." He placed the bracelet on the counter. "I knew right away it was a fine piece." From an inner pocket, he removed a jeweler's eyepiece, scooted the candle closer, and stuck the magnifier into his eye. "If you look here, you can see the maker's mark." He turned the piece, then stopped. "Rundell & Bridge."

The jeweler the Prince Regent preferred and who had delivered the parure to Carlton House personally.

"So I says to the man, 'Where did you get this?' I'm careful about where things come from, being watched by you lot like I am." He glared at Partridge, who stared impassively back.

"And?"

"He says it's a family piece, from his grandmother, and that he's fallen on a bit of hard times and needs to sell it right away." He relaxed his eye and the glass fell into his hand. "I knew that was a load of rubbish. This piece is new as a freshly minted shilling. No wear, no scuffs, no worn prongs, not even any dirt like you'd expect from a piece that had been in a family for a while."

"What did you do?"

"I remembered that you lot were looking for a parure of pearls and sapphires, and I figured I was looking at one of the pieces, so I hemmed and hawed, and I told the gent I didn't normally deal in anything so fine. I asked what he was looking to get for it. He said a hundred pounds." Hawthorne snickered. "Where did he think I was going to get my hands on a hundred ready pounds?" He surveyed his domain, the pewter shoe buckles, the faded woolen coats, the row of silver spoons.

A hundred pounds? That was a reasonable request. The entire parure had cost a thousand pounds, with the tiara and the necklace being by far the most expensive of the pieces. The brooch had been valued at fifty pounds.

"I told him I didn't have that sort of money, but that I could get it. I was putting him off, see? Figured I would come to you gents with it. I told him I would need to get the piece valued by someone else before I laid out that sort of brass, but if he came back in a couple of days, and if the piece was verified as genuine, I would have his money."

Smart. "What did he say to that?"

"He said it wasn't good enough, and that he'd go somewhere else. I didn't want to lose the piece, since I knew you was looking for it, so I made him an offer."

"Of?" Bertie asked.

"Fifty pounds. It was as much as I could get me hands on in a hurry."

"He obviously took the offer." Bertie indicated the bracelet in the receiver's hand.

"He did, but not right away. Shuffled about the shop, looked at a few things, and then came back to the counter and agreed. I had to go upstairs to my strongbox, but I had my son keep an eye on the shop. A great lad, he is. Nearly fifteen summers now." Pride evident in his voice. "I paid the man, and he took the money and left. But since I knew you were looking for him, I sent my boy, Charlie, to follow him. Told him to be sly about it and not get caught, but to see where this gent went."

Hope flared in Bertie's chest. "And where did he go?"

Hawthorne shook his head. "Charlie lost him when he got into a hired carriage. He was headed west on the Oxford Road."

Hope died like a damp squib. Too much of London lay west of here and could be accessed by the Oxford Road.

"What did the man look like, and did he sign your ledger book to complete the exchange?"

"He were about as tall as you, heavier though, and older. Hard to tell his hair color. Wore his hat the whole time, and I don't keep it too bright in here." He shrugged.

Probably to keep the patrons from seeing the quality of the goods they were purchasing.

"How was he dressed?"

"Not good, not bad. Ordinary. Like he might be a gentleman who had fallen on some lean times. Black coat, hat, cravat. Nothing special."

"How did he talk?" Partridge asked.

"Funny about that. He talked ordinary, but then sometimes fruity like a swell. Like he'd been to Eton." The receiver mimicked the customer, drawing his upper lip down and stiffening his posture. "Then it was like he remembered he was supposed to be slumming, and he'd drop back into plain speech again." He shrugged. "I see all kinds in here, and he ain't the first who was trying to hide who he was or that he needed a receiver. Folks are high and mighty when it comes to folks like me . . . until they need 'em."

Bertie compared the description against the employees of Carlton House, but it was too vague to draw any conclusions, especially if the man had been trying to conceal his identity. He remembered Daniel's advice to always check the paperwork.

"Let's look at the ledger."

Hawthorne opened the tattered book, flipped one page back, and then turned the ledger around on the counter so Bertie could see the line he indicated. "If you can read that, you're some kind of puzzle breaker."

Bertie moved the candle closer, careful not to drip wax on the page and looked at the scrawl next to where Hawthorne had written "Pearl and Sapphire Bracelet."

"He meant to disguise his name and handwriting too."

"He wrote with his left hand, if that helps. But it isn't rare. Lots of my customers can't write at all, and either I write in their name for them or they put an *X*."

But if this man spoke with an educated tone part of the time, he surely knew how to write his own name.

"I'll take the bracelet and return it to His Highness." Bertie held out his hand.

Hawthorne scowled and retreated. "What about my fifty pounds? I paid for this bauble, you know."

"I will see if the prince will reimburse you or perhaps pay you a reward for finding it."

"Not likely, not from what I hear of old Prinny. More likely to hear I had it and toss me in the bowels of Newgate. You will tell him I didn't have nothin' to do with the theft and that I helped you? I gotta get that money back, so either get it from the prince himself or catch this blackguard and get it off him. I ain't a charity, and I can't afford to be tossing about fifty pounds like some of you swells can. I lose that money, and I'm out of business." His brow crumpled, and his shaggy eyebrows arrowed together over his piercing eyes. "I'm not quizzing you. I need that money. I never supposed you wouldn't get it back for me."

"Easy, man. I will see what I can do. I am certain the prince will not wish to see you ruined when you've done him such a service. Give me time. His Highness is not in the city. When he returns, I'll meet with him." And hopefully have real progress to report on the case and not that things had gotten considerably worse.

Chapter 15

"Philippa, you must return to Haverly House where you can be cared for properly. Have you had a physician tend to you?" Charlotte sat on the edge of Philippa's bed. "And why did I not hear of what happened for two entire days?"

Philippa smiled ruefully, grimacing as she shifted on the mattress. "I didn't tell you because I didn't want you to worry and because I feel so foolish. I knew the chapel was unsafe. If one of the girls here had done something so unwise as to walk through a construction area late at night, I would have given her a good scold."

Charlotte leaned over and brushed aside Philippa's dark hair to examine the cut and bruise on her forehead. "I should give you that good scold right now, but I won't. Do you think you will have a scar?"

She considered this. Once upon a time, such a mark would have been disastrous. She would have tried to hide it with makeup or changed her hairstyle. A courtesan with a disfigurement could not expect to attract the highest-paying clients. But now what did it matter if she bore a mark? It would not change her mission of helping at-risk women in the slightest. "We shall have to see, I suppose."

"How do you feel? Where else does it hurt?" Charlotte asked.

"I feel exactly as if a pile of wood and stone had fallen on me." She smiled. "I ache all over, but nothing too grave. My headache has finally dimmed to a low throb, and my bruises are healing. You do not need to fuss." Though Philippa felt comforted that Charlotte cared enough to come to the school. She was not accustomed to people demonstrating true concern for her.

"I like coddling people I care about. Don't you know that by now?"

Charlotte had fussed over her plenty when one of Philippa's former clients had beaten her near to death. She had moved Philippa into her house, given her the best of care, and declared to the *ton* that she was not ashamed of her half sister. Charlotte's tender treatment had given Philippa the boldness to turn her back on her former way of life and to seek to change others' lives for the better.

Yet it also made Philippa feel guilty when someone safeguarded or nurtured her. She was so unworthy.

"If you will allow me to get up and dressed, I will behave like a proper hostess to a duchess." She pressed her hands to the mattress to sit up, but Charlotte gently restrained her.

"No, you won't. Mrs. Stokes says you are to linger here for at least one more day. And I want our doctor to attend you, just to make sure you are not hiding anything from me. You wince every time you take a deep breath. Are your ribs injured?"

Charlotte was perceptive. It did hurt to breathe deeply.

"No broken bones, I'm sure. I landed on some rather uncomfortable stones and lay there for a period of time, growing some fairly substantial bruises, but I am fine, truly, and I am certain that moving about is what I need."

"If you are brave enough to countermand Mrs. Dorothy Stokes, I am not. You must follow her dictates. Do you want her to be disappointed in you?" Charlotte raised her eyebrows.

"No, indeed," Philippa hastily agreed. A disappointed Aunt Dolly was much worse than an angry one. "It's just that I've grown accustomed to working, to being busy. Lying here gives me too much time to think."

"That's why I brought you a book to read." Charlotte reached into the satchel at her feet. "I thought you might enjoy this one. *Travels into*

Several Remote Nations of the World by Lemuel Gulliver. Actually, it's penned by Jonathan Swift, but it's written as if Mr. Gulliver were the author. Have you read it?"

Philippa shook her head, taking the leather-bound tome. She hid her sigh. Nowhere in her upbringing had there been the luxury of books, nor did she find the same sort of escape into them that Charlotte did, for reading didn't come as easily to her as it did to her sister.

"I am certain I shall enjoy it. Thank you for thinking of me as I convalesce." She would have to read it, else she would dishearten Charlotte, who demonstrated her love through gifting books. Perhaps she and the other girls could read aloud of an evening and soon pass through the story. At least this one did not appear to be a tome on Greek or Roman history, two subjects which fascinated Charlotte.

"I came to give you news of our father." Charlotte patted Philippa's hand and went to the chair on the other side of the rug.

Philippa's mouth tightened, and Charlotte must have noticed.

"Now, don't get into a pucker. You bristle the moment his name is raised. I know he is unkind, unloving, and unlikable, but he's also to be pitied. He's laid low, can no longer even speak, and he's soured every relationship he's ever had so that no one comes to visit him except myself."

"And whose fault is that? He has always had the opportunity to be kind, to be loving, to be likable. He is reaping what he has sown." Philippa eased upright and plumped the pillow at her back. She scooted up against it, which helped with her breathing, though it made her a bit dizzy at first.

Concern pinched the corners of Charlotte's eyes. "That is because he does not know anything about grace and forgiveness and the Source of true kindness. It amazes me that he could be so respected in the church, attending staunchly every week, and yet be so far from understanding the Scripture. He is reaping what he has sown, that is true, but we who have received the grace of salvation through Jesus know that those who have not are to be the most pitied."

Pitied. Philippa despised that word. She had been pitied—when she wasn't being castigated. Was the earl pitiable, or was he merely a disgrace as a lord, a man, and a father?

"He is not worthy of forgiveness."

"Who among us is?" Charlotte studied her with sober, jade eyes. "If our redemption depended upon our being worthy of it, we would either not need redeeming because we were already worthy, or we would miss out entirely because we are all unworthy and in need of redemption. Grace and forgiveness are a gift from God, not something we earn."

"But there are some who are worse than others. Or so I have been informed my entire life. You speak of grace and salvation, and I have put my trust in Him, and yet I always feel as if at any moment He will realize He made a mistake and has saved the wrong person. That He will consider my past and deem me unworthy of His forgiveness." The thought was out before Philippa could stop it, and she immediately felt shamed and exposed. Why couldn't she keep her fears to herself?

Charlotte was at her side again quickly, taking her hands. "You are never to think that, Pip. God knew you before He formed you, and He has called you His own. That is not a mistake. No one merits God's grace more than another, and certainly no one is beyond God's ability to save."

"But you have not done the things that I have done. You have not lived as I have lived. How can you say that we are the same when it comes to God's favor?"

Squeezing Philippa's hands, Charlotte considered. "Do not put limits on God's power. Do you not think that God is both good enough and capable? Or do you think yourself so special that the blood of Christ is not enough to save you? You have asked for forgiveness, have you not?"

"Many times." Was she wrong in her feelings of inadequacy and unworthiness? Dare she hope that Charlotte was correct that God had meant to save her, that she wasn't just sneaking into His grace?

"'If we confess our sins, He is faithful and just to forgive us our sins, and to cleanse us from all unrighteousness.' That's what Scripture says. You are cleansed because God says you are, and you are not to argue with God." Charlotte shook Philippa's hands and gave her an elder-sister look. "Which also means that if God can forgive anyone, He can also forgive our father, and it is not too late, not until he draws his final breath."

Philippa bunched her brow. "The earl is hardly likely to ask for forgiveness, is he? He hasn't been interested to this point, nor has he considered anything he has done to be in need of forgiving."

"Where there is life, there is hope. One good thing about his not being able to speak is that when I go visit him, I can talk and talk and talk, and there's nothing he can do about it." She grinned. "So I share the truth of the gospel. And I tell him I forgive him for the unkindness he has shown to me, to my mother, to your mother, to you."

That was a bridge too far for Philippa, extending forgiveness to the hard, unfeeling man who had caused her so much misery. "You are a better woman than I. Forgiveness does not enter my thinking when the Earl of Tiptree's name arises."

"We are told to forgive in the same manner as we have been forgiven by God." Charlotte released Philippa's hands and sat back, sadness drawing her mouth down. "I have heard it said that bitterness is like drinking a cup of poison and expecting your enemy to get sick. Your unforgiveness toward our father does not hurt him at all, but it is harming you. I wish you could find it in your heart to set down the weight of unforgiveness that you're carrying."

"That bitterness was all that kept me going for a long time. I do not wish to excuse his behavior."

"Forgiveness does not excuse behavior. Forgiveness keeps another person's behavior from destroying your own heart."

Philippa considered her sister's words. Only the fact that she knew Charlotte spoke out of a genuine concern for her kept her from snapping back. Charlotte had things for which she could forgive their father, but she had not suffered like Philippa and her mother had.

It was no easy thing to set that aside. She had lived with it for a long time.

Charlotte sighed, relaxing her shoulders. "At any rate, I wished to bring you news of him. He is much the same, and Mother has actually hired someone to care for him. A man who worked in a military hospital in Spain. He performs all Father's personal care, which spares Mother. I think Mother is surprising herself at how well she runs the house without Father's input and oversight. And it turns out, as she learned from their solicitor and their banker, that they are quite well off. Father has always been parsimonious and has stashed money away for years. Not that she's squandering funds, but she is spending what it takes to run the household and pay a decent wage to the staff."

"She had better hope he does not improve then, for if he does, she will bear the brunt of his wrath." Philippa shook her head. He was a miser with so much stashed away, and yet he had turned her and her mother out without so much as a second thought to starve and make their way however they could. "Perhaps she should preserve a bit of that coin in case he turns his back on her, should he recover."

"I am hoping that he will be a different man if he ever does improve. That his trial will have brought him some humility and gratitude. I pray for you and for him. I pray that if not a reconciliation, then at least a cessation of hostilities will be possible."

"If wishes were horses, beggars would ride." Philippa paused, regretting her sharp tone when she saw the hurt in Charlotte's eyes. "Oh, I do not mean to be churlish. You are right to hope. It is just that life has taught me that hoped-for things rarely come to pass. You are kind to come and see me, kind to visit . . . him." She refused to say his name. "And kind to pray for us both."

Charlotte resumed her seat in the chair. "I've brought other news, happier news. Marcus heard of the accident, and he was most distressed. He is quite fond of you, you know. He admires your strength of character, and has decided to take a bit of responsibility from your shoulders."

Strength of character. Her?

Which brought to mind what Sir Bertrand had said, that reputation had little to do with character. Sir Bertrand had been kind to her during the party. Come to think of it, he had been kind on every occasion on which they had met. And he never seemed to want anything in exchange, which was refreshing.

Scratch that, he had asked her to consider being a member of his espionage team for the agency.

But he had given her the choice entirely, not trying to sway her one way or another.

Which was rather nice of him.

She realized she was woolgathering and focused on what Charlotte was saying.

"Marcus has decided he will step in and take care of the chapel restoration. Yesterday, he had a meeting with the church leaders to set things right. He has hired additional workers, and they have already begun. The roof will be repaired in a few days, and the stonemasons are hard at work. The scaffolding will soon be removed. As to the glass for the windows, he's commissioned a glassworks to repair or replace whatever needs doing." She held up her hands. "Do not protest. It's for you, yes, but also for the ladies who will worship there. Asbury is paying for the basic work, and Marcus has taken on the extras. I couldn't stop him, nor did I wish to."

Philippa sagged against the pillows. "You and Marcus are like a high tide. There is nothing that can be done to stop you. How can I say thank you?"

"Just be happy, Philippa. You deserve to be happy."

Bertie put his elbow on the table in Haverly's meeting room, propping his cheek on his fist. "Neither the blackmailer nor the courtier had anything to do with the theft or the murder. The man who brought the bracelet to the receiver's shop remains a mystery. I took the receiver, Hawthorne by name, to Carlton House, and we paraded every staff member in the place by him. He recognized no one, and no one seemed to recognize him. Not a single guilty glance or frightened look amongst them."

Partridge stood near the door, apparently reluctant to sit in Marcus's presence.

Daniel sat opposite Bertie, his face glum.

"Cheer up, man. You'll see her again soon," Bertie said. His brother, sister-in-law, and niece had left for Pensax three days before, and Daniel had been at Thorndike House to say his goodbyes. One would think they were parting forever instead of just a few weeks, the way he had clung to Juliette's hand and whispered in her ear, looking at her with a dog's devotion.

Yet another reason to remain heart-whole. Love turned a man's brain into blancmange.

"Mrs. Bascome is being questioned by our own interrogators. I do not think her case will come to a public trial. Agents are combing through her life, but thus far," Marcus drummed his fingers on the table, "there has been no evidence that she has done anything like this in the past. She was thoroughly checked out when the Prince Regent first showed an interest in her, and as with all his paramours, she was watched while she was in residence at Carlton House. I did not think we would have to continue our surveillance after one was cast out, but perhaps we will."

"What happens to Pringle?" Bertie asked.

"He will no longer be a courtier, for certain. Though no information reached the wrong hands, the fact that he was subject to blackmail and planning on an act of treason is enough to get him removed from his place of service. After that, it is up to the prince to decide his fate."

"But I have made no progress in discovering the thief and murderer." Frustration twitched Bertie's shoulder muscles. "The prince will return to London in a matter of days, and I will have nothing to tell him. He will be inclined to remove me, not just from this case, but probably from the agency. If nothing else, he will regret the knighthood."

Not to mention how disappointed Haverly would be. This was to be a sort of trial run on his ability to lead, and Bertie was failing miserably.

What would he do if he failed? Would Haverly relegate him to his brother's shadow again? Or would he quit him altogether? Marcus had said he had something in the works for Bertie, but if he couldn't solve a simple theft, would the trust be broken and the opportunity evaporate?

If he didn't have the agency, what did he have? No real job, no real purpose beyond his work. A chilled sweat broke out across his shoulders. He was in a room of men he respected, and if he could not equal them in competence, he would not be able to look them in the eyes ever again.

"Dr. Rosebreen sent his report, as did Rhynwick Davies." Daniel opened a folder before him. "The girl was definitely strangled. No signs that someone interfered with her, so he does not believe that covering an assault was the motive. She did fight back, but there was no skin or other tissue beneath her fingernails. Rhynwick says what was found there could be accounted for in her job. Lye soap residue, and a bit of beeswax polish, but also black fibers. He did a few experiments, and he believes they are broadcloth as from a man's coat. Perhaps she clawed at a sleeve or lapel?" He looked up, concern for the girl's final moments clouding his eyes. "Rosebreen does not rule out that she was killed in the library. He believes the act was very quick. With there being nothing displaced in the library, nothing broken or moved, he thinks Lydia was quickly overpowered, killed, and hidden within a matter of minutes. Our killer is a man of some strength and a bit of height, and he wears a black coat."

"A black coat. That does not narrow down the field much. Every servant not in footman's livery at Carlton House wears a black coat. And any man younger than eighty would be able to overpower the maid. She was young and slight." Though the receiver had said the man who came to sell the bracelet had worn a black coat.

"It does give further proof that the footman, Harry Sloan, who had an attraction to our victim, was not her killer, as he would be in full livery, red coat and gold braid." Daniel shrugged. "Can we learn anything more about the seller who tried to pawn the bracelet?"

Partridge shook his head. "I questioned the receiver at length. If he knew more, he would have told me."

"Hawthorne continues to demand repayment, and I do not blame him. Fifty pounds is a considerable sum. I am surprised he had that amount to spend. If he knew anything that would help us recoup his losses, he would be forthcoming. At least I hope he would." Bertie frowned, leaning back and staring at the ceiling. "I suspect not all his dealings are aboveboard," he said wryly.

Partridge grunted, shifting his weight. "I can assure you they are not. But mostly petty things. He knows not to step too far afield, not with us watching him."

How many people did Marcus have in his employ, and how many people did he have under surveillance? Bertie hoped he never found out, because that would mean he was in charge of the agency, and he did not want that job. He had a modicum of ambition, but not that much. His new responsibilities were ill-fitting enough, as if he had not quite grown into them.

Would he ever?

A knock on the door had them all turning. Haverly's butler, Ffoulkes, greeted Partridge. "Your Grace, a Mr. Nighly from the Bank of England has called."

"I have no appointment with anyone from the bank." Marcus frowned.

"No, Your Grace. Mr. Nighly originally called asking to see the Earl of Rothwell, but now Lord Rothwell has asked if you will join them. The bank representative seems distressed, and if I may be so bold as to comment, his lordship is not best pleased."

"I see." Marcus rose. "I apologize, gentlemen. This will not take long, I hope, and we can get back to our meeting."

Bertie swiveled in his chair, tapping the arms. The case and all its bits and pieces crashed about in his head. Much like his leads, his thoughts evaporated the harder he chased them.

He had not accomplished a single thing that he had hoped to do this month, and the added responsibilities had only complicated his life. He had not found a place to rent or buy. He had not found a physician or surgeon to take on the duties at Eleos. He had not managed to convince Miss Cashel to join his team even on a limited basis.

Miss Cashel. The Duchess of Haverly had informed Bertie of the accident her sister had suffered Sunday evening. What had she been doing in the chapel at that time of night? She could have been killed by that weak scaffolding. She was on the mend, he was told, but she should have been more careful. She was the driving force behind the entire Eleos enterprise.

She was a leader. Setting her sights on a dream and pursuing it even in the face of hardship and unpopular opinion. And she had the ability to convey her vision and gather people to her who could help her attain that vision.

Did he possess that ability? Or was he destined to be a lieutenant forever, only suited to be a cog in his older brother's wheel? Was he worthy of leading others if he couldn't find justice for one murdered girl?

Leaning forward, he scrubbed his palms down his face and sighed.

"Nearly every case is like that," Daniel said, rereading the notes from Rosebreen and Rhynwick.

"Like what?"

"You feel you're getting absolutely nowhere, and you begin to doubt your ability as a detective, or in your case, an agent. No matter how many times you've solved a mystery or successfully completed a mission, you begin to think this will be the time when you will be outed as a fraud, that you cannot do it."

"It happens to you?" Bertie didn't know whether to feel comforted to know he was not alone, or if he should be dejected that he was so typical. "What do you do?"

Daniel shrugged. "I keep plugging away. I keep trying to fit pieces together, and thus far, almost every time, the case has broken loose in a place I didn't expect. It will happen. Just don't give up."

"Am I that easy to read?" Bertie chuckled ruefully.

"I've been through this a few times. Detection and spy work have some overlap, but there are distinctions. And I think everyone, except perhaps Marcus Haverly himself, has felt unworthy or defeated in the midst of a difficult task. And this is your first case as a leader." He gave a sympathetic nod. "I'm feeling a bit of the same myself at the moment. I don't think I ever appreciated what was entailed in the job of supervisor of investigators at Bow Street. I'm now overseeing men with much more experience than I, older men who have served longer. It's taking me some time and a bit of finesse to get them to accept me as their governor. Ed's been a big help, but if I'm going to be in charge, I have to own my mistakes and learn from them."

"Do you think I've made mistakes in this investigation?" Bertie could sympathize with those investigators at Bow Street. Here he was, asking someone ten years his junior, who had been a part-time spy for all of three or four months, to evaluate his performance.

"When you look back on a case, you always see things you could have done differently. If I had to pick out something to cavil at, I would say your mistake was in not telling the prince that the theft was a police matter and that if he wanted the jewels back, he should be less concerned with keeping the theft from the papers and more concerned with putting both unrealistic expectations and deadlines on you, who had never before handled a criminal investigation.

"You are capable, intelligent, and persistent, but to put such strictures on you, and have his own staff working against you with their secrecy vows—" He butted the papers together and closed the folder, then slid the postmortem file across the table to Bertie. "Of course, as Marcus is fond of saying, one does not say no to the Prince Regent. You've done well, all things considered. You've questioned everyone you could think of, examined the scenes where the crimes took place, chased leads, and gathered as much information as you could. You've managed to catch a treasonous blackmailer, and you've recovered two of the stolen jewelry pieces thus far. It's only a matter of time until you find the others *and* the man who murdered the maid. You only fail if you stop."

Bertie nodded. Sage advice from the young man. He would be a good match for Juliette. Like Daniel, once she got her teeth into a puzzle, she refused to let go. Both had a strong sense of justice and a desire to right things that were wrong.

Partridge had remained by the door, and he said, "Lord Aylswood is right. You've done all you could. We're not finished. We just have to kick over the right rock."

A long speech for Partridge.

The door opened and Marcus, Charles Wyvern, and another man came in, presumably the banker, Mr. Nighly. Bertie frowned. Were they being added to the meeting, or was this something entirely different? He had no time for interruptions.

"I am so sorry this has happened. I wasn't in the bank at the time. We had no idea the document wasn't authentic." The banker appeared near to fainting, talking as he came through the door.

"Please sit, and start from the beginning. This is the Earl of Aylswood. Lord Aylswood is the supervisor of investigators at Bow Street. And this is Sir Bertrand Thorndike. They will be most interested in hearing what you have to say." Marcus indicated Daniel and Bertie before pulling out a chair for the banker.

So, they were to be Aylswood and Sir Bertrand for this meeting. Presumably, Charles would be called Lord Rothwell. Bertie straightened. He should act like a gentleman if everyone was going to be formal.

Mr. Nighly dropped into the seat and reached for his handkerchief to mop his brow. Bertie was tempted to send for a glass of brandy for the poor man who appeared next door to collapse.

Ffoulkes had not been wrong in saying Lord Rothwell did not look pleased. The lines along the earl's mouth had deepened, and his brows bunched over his intense eyes.

"Your Grace," the banker began. "I was going through some papers that had accumulated on my desk in my absence. I had traveled to Tunbridge Wells to meet with His Highness on a little matter, and my subordinates had been tasked with keeping things in order in my department at the bank in my absence. It was only two days, but I handle quite a bit of bank business. As I was refreshing my memory on what had transpired while I was away, I noticed this small blot in the lettering on this document." He removed the paper from an envelope. "I thought it best to have the document rewritten so as not to be smudged. The Bank of England takes pride in the pristine presentation of all our documents." Mr. Nighly's chin went up a fraction, but his eyes were still distressed. "I called in here tonight for Lord Rothwell's signature on the new document as it is on my way home from the bank."

Rothwell paced behind Daniel, his hands clasped behind his back, and Bertie could imagine the man striding the quarterdeck on one of the ships he had commanded during the war.

"The only difficulty is, I have never seen that document before in my life. The original is a forgery." Rothwell bared his teeth. "How could the man take advantage of me this way? I trusted him. I have known him for years, though not closely."

"Of whom are we speaking," Bertie asked. "And what, exactly, did this man do?"

"Mr. Simon Todd," Marcus supplied. "The reverend has forged a document in which Lord Rothwell is to serve as a guarantor of an advancement of three thousand pounds from the Bank of England."

Bertie's eyes widened.

Rothwell shook his head. "I would never serve as guarantor of that much money, especially for a man I had not seen in nearly a decade. He served under my command for a period of time, and up until today, I would have counted him as my friend, but this is preposterous."

Daniel reached for the certificate. "When did he present this at the bank?"

"This previous Friday, the fourteenth," Nighly supplied. "As I said, I was not in the city at the time. But no one would expect a man of the church to lie."

Bertie's mind reeled. Mr. Todd. He had found a dead body in the Carlton House library in the morning, and gone to the Bank of England with a forged voucher the next afternoon?

Was the timing a coincidence? The reverend must have been planning the loan for some time. Was it, perhaps, in conjunction with Eleos? To finish the chapel there? Or the manse?

An unauthorized loan, fraudulently obtained.

What a scandal.

What will this do to the Eleos property lease if it is discovered? The thought flitted through his mind, along with his assurances to Miss Cashel that the school would be a success and that Marcus and the solicitors had taken precautions against any claim Mr. Asbury could make that they had violated the terms of the lease. How flippant that now sounded. But surely Asbury could not claim they had violated the lease when it was his insistence that saw Mr. Todd installed at Eleos in the first place.

They passed the document from one to another, and when Bertie examined it, he had to admit it was well done. Heavy paper, expensive ink, well written but for a blot in the forged Rothwell signature. If not for that one mistake . . . a hesitancy in wanting to get it right or a twinge of guilt . . . the crime may never have been discovered. If Todd had paid the money back as agreed, Rothwell would not have known his former ship chaplain had used his name to get the initial loan.

"I assume he received the requested amount?" Marcus asked. "And that it was Mr. Todd who received it and not someone masquerading as the reverend?"

"Yes, of course we advanced the money. Lord Rothwell's name is good for whatever he decides to put it to, and we had no qualms about his ability to pay the loan back, should it be required. In fact, due to Mr. Todd's association with the earl, he was given favorable terms on the loan as well. A full point below the going rate. And I have met Mr. Todd. My subordinate at the bank described him accurately. Of course, Mr. Todd had to return for the money on the next Monday. It was near to closing time when he brought the promissory note, and it takes time to assemble and count that much currency. My clerk said the reverend was not best pleased at the delay, but there was no hope for it. The vault had already been locked by that time."

Rothwell looked far from flattered at the strength of his reputation and credit at the bank. "Regardless of the esteem in which you regard my finances, I refuse to be liable for the three thousand pounds, nor the interest, however favorable the terms. I have been used fraudulently, and I will not be held to account for it."

"No, my lord. You will not be held liable, but the bank has been bilked out of the funds. I could very well lose my position over this." Nighly mopped his brow again.

"Have you confronted Mr. Todd yet?" Daniel asked.

"No, I did not know the document wasn't genuine until Lord Rothwell denied knowledge of it this very evening. I thought I was taking care of a routine matter until it all went awry." The man was practically sobbing.

Marcus motioned to Partridge, who slipped out the door without a sound. Within moments, Ffoulkes entered with a glass of brandy for the distraught banker, but Partridge himself did not return.

Gone to locate Mr. Todd? Bertie resisted the impulse to follow.

"We are going to investigate this matter. For now, calm yourself, go home, and do not speak of this to anyone." Marcus grasped Nighly's shoulder, giving it a small shake as if to tell him to pull himself together. "It will be up to Lord Rothwell if he wishes to pursue this as a criminal matter, and if he does, I am certain Lord Aylswood will see it done. We will locate and question Todd, and if he still has the money, we will retrieve it."

He escorted the banker to the door, where Ffoulkes waited to see him out.

Four days, Bertie considered. Todd had collected the funds four days ago. How likely was it that he still had the entire amount? One tended not to let the grass grow beneath one's boots when one had that sort of money, especially when obtained under false pretenses. Bertie moved Lydia's postmortem file in a circle on the polished tabletop as he thought.

Did the forgery and theft of the funds from the bank have anything to do with the jewelry theft and the murder at Carlton House?

As Daniel had told him before, there was no such thing as coincidence.

Bertie pushed back from the table. "I believe Aylswood and I have some work to do. Your Grace." He bowed to Marcus.

"Partridge has gone to notify Cadogan that we are ready to leave." Marcus's jawline tightened.

"We?" Bertie asked the duke.

"I have a personal interest in this matter. It is my sister's husband who has been defrauded."

Rothwell frowned. "I am coming with you. It is my name he used."

Bertie crossed looks with Daniel. Five men, all haring about London after dark looking for one clergyman?

When they reached the curb, Cadogan had Daniel's carriage door open, and the duke's carriage was pulled up behind. Partridge leapt out of the duke's carriage from where he'd ridden from the mews.

Bertie paused. "Does anyone know where Todd actually lives?"

"He was going to move into the manse at Eleos, but it isn't ready yet." Marcus swirled his cape over his shoulders in a graceful motion. "I suggest we split up. Bertie, you and Daniel go to his most recent parish and rouse the sexton. He should know where the reverend lodges. Charles and I will go to Carlton House and see if he is there, or if Mr. Lingfield knows his whereabouts. And Partridge, visit Eleos and have a look around. See if he's been there but don't alarm the ladies. It might be best if they didn't know you were there."

Chapter 16

"WHAT ARE THE ODDS THAT this forgery has nothing to do with the theft of the jewels?" Bertie asked as they bowled along toward St. James's Church in Clerkenwell.

"Slim. One must not jump to conclusions, but . . ." Daniel raised his eyebrows and shrugged. "There's no such thing—"

"—as a coincidence," Bertie finished.

"Still, when I first came to Bow Street and was partnered with Ed Beck, he cautioned me against narrowing my thoughts to one solution too early in a case. If you come to a determination too soon, you can be guilty of seeing evidence that isn't there. Of trying to make the facts fit your theory rather than the other way around. What do you know about Mr. Todd?"

Bertie cast through his encounters with the man. "He seems to have a rather high opinion of himself, but that is not a crime. He is in good standing with his church and only left the pulpit at St. James because he was appointed one of the Prince Regent's chaplains."

"That might be due to him being a good pastor and counselor, or that appointment might be a favor granted or a debt repaid by the prince. One never knows." Daniel leaned against the squabs.

"I see you've been to the tailor." Bertie flicked his finger toward Daniel's coat.

"I have, and yes, I am armed. As you instructed Juliette, I never go anywhere without a weapon."

"Did she mention the time she wore a pistol to a Venetian breakfast at her parents' house, and the thing nearly fell out from its binding onto the drawing room floor? She was chatting with the Dowager Duchess of Haverly. If you could have seen the panic in her eyes." Bertie laughed. "It was the day you met Jasper Finch. The day the Montgomery Mill exploded."

Daniel's gaze grew far away for a moment before he shuddered, as if returning to the present after a bad memory. "Not the best of days, though I have to admit, that investigation brought me several benefits. I met Rhynwick Davies, who has helped me on several cases now. I had no idea how beneficial someone interested in the sciences could be to investigative work."

"He did not provide much help in the death of Lydia the scullery maid," Bertie pointed out.

"Did he not? Does Mr. Todd wear a black coat?"

The question caught Bertie in the stomach. "Todd found the body."

"Did he find it because he knew where it was? Because perhaps he put it there?"

"But why would he kill a Carlton House maid? I found no evidence that they had dealings with one another beyond the normal running of the household. The housekeeper sent the maid with a tea tray upon occasion, but other than that, their paths did not cross."

"We shall have to ask the reverend when we find him."

The sexton of the church was a young man, earnest, with pale skin and orange hair.

"He isn't in service here any longer." He hitched his weight from one foot to the other, blinking owlishly. He stood in his doorway, lamplight glowing softly behind him. He seemed to remember his manners. "Would you like to come in? We're just toasting a bit of bread over the fire."

"No, thank you. We know Mr. Todd left this position, but we're looking for his place of lodging."

The man scratched the hair over his ear, looking back over his shoulder to where his wife and children clustered around the fireplace. They stared, silent and still, as if unused to callers at this time of night.

"He had rooms over on Allen Street. I can take you. Whenever anyone in the parish needed him outside of church, I was supposed to inform him, so I know where he lodges. I'll get my hat."

A night watchman, an elderly, bent-backed man whose lantern seemed as weak as his stride, looked up as they got out of the carriage on Allen Street.

"Who are ye, and what do ye want here tonight?" His querulous voice wavered, wrapped in trepidation.

"Rest easy, Mr. Dent." The sexton removed his hat. "It's me, Colin Brace. Looking for Mr. Todd. He still bides here, does he not?"

The old man swept the lantern toward the red door with the brass number six on it. "Last I knew. Seen him a few days ago, didn't I?"

"When was that?" Daniel asked, holding up his tipstaff with the Bow Street brass plate.

The man shuffled backward, nearly tripping on the step. "He in trouble?"

"Easy, man. We only wish to speak to him."

"I seen him maybe Sunday night? Thought he was coming home from services somewheres. It was an hour, maybe two into my watch."

"Thank you, good sir." Daniel stepped up to the door and knocked on it with his truncheon.

Bertie turned to the sexton. "Mr. Brace, thank you for your direction. If you will wait here, we'll return you to your home when we've finished."

"Never you mind. I'll find my way. It's a nice evening for a walk. I hope whatever you need Mr. Todd for, it isn't anything too serious. He was a good pastor for our church. Well thought of, and very smart. If he can help you with your inquiries, I know he will." Mr. Brace put his hands into his trouser pockets and walked away, a light whistle drifting back over his shoulder.

Bertie wondered if anyone knew the real Mr. Todd. A thief and possibly a murderer, but unsuspected because of his vocation.

The door opened, and they were ushered inside by a Mr. Gadshaw, who introduced himself as the owner of the building. When introduced to Lord Aylswood and Sir Bertrand Thorndike, however, his expression froze.

"Mr. Todd. Yes, he has rooms here, but he isn't home at present."

A tall case clock ticked away in the foyer, and a narrow set of stairs went up to the first floor along the right side of the entryway.

"Do you know when he will return?" Bertie asked.

"No, sir." The landlord was a man of about fifty years, and he wore a banyan over a shirt and trousers, as if he had been relaxing before his fire with a hot beverage before retiring for the night.

"When did you last see him?"

"He broke his fast with us on Monday morning as is his normal schedule, but he has not attended a meal since then, which makes me no nevermind, since he pays for board whether he eats here or not. He appeared to be in a hurry to go about his business for the day and left straightaway after the meal."

"Did you think it a matter of concern that one of your boarders had not appeared at a meal for four days?" Daniel asked.

"No, milord. Mr. Todd had been more erratic of late, since being appointed royal chaplain. And he informed me that at the end of the month, he would be leaving for new lodgings at a charity. When he left on Monday, he had a valise which looked quite heavy, but that was not unusual either, as he was always carrying books to and from Carlton House."

"He gave no indication where he was going on Monday morning?"

"No, milord. None. And I did not like to ask, for his work required him to keep his own counsel. People came to him for advice, and he went to help people sort out their problems. He always asked us to maintain their privacy."

"Did he ever have personal visitors? Friends who called?" Bertie asked.

Gadshaw gave it some thought. "Only one who visited, and he never invited him to dine. We do welcome guests, though the meal must be scheduled and paid for in advance." He shrugged. "We must charge a fair price, else we would be eaten right into the poor house."

"Who came to see him?" Daniel asked.

"A Mr. Asbury. I do not know more. I do not believe I ever heard his given name."

"May we see Mr. Todd's rooms, please?" Daniel asked.

Gadshaw hesitated. "He will not like that when he finds out. He's a private man, as I said."

"This is a serious matter. He has been missing for four days, and we must find him soon. There may be information in his rooms that would help us accomplish that. Where does he lodge?"

"Don't you need a warrant or something?"

"You are the owner of this establishment, are you not? If you give permission, we can enter any room in the house. If you refuse, we will have to wake a magistrate, come back in the middle of the night, and Mr. Todd, who may be in distress, will have to wait further for help. Do you want that on your conscience?" Bertie wasn't certain that he spoke the truth about how quickly they could summon a magistrate, but it sounded good. He doubted very much whether Todd was in any danger or distress, but a little uncertainty might be just the push this man needed to give them access.

"He has the rooms upstairs at the front of the house. A sitting room and bedroom. I'll show you."

Daniel shot Bertie a smile as they followed the landlord up the staircase. At the top of the stairs, one of the doors was open a crack, and a pale blue eye peeked through the opening. Bertie stared hard back, and the eavesdropper slammed the door.

Mr. Todd certainly had spacious accommodations. Gadshaw lit several candles from the one he had brought upstairs with him, and he stood in the doorway. "I shall have to remain present."

"We understand. We will be quick." Daniel went to the desk under the window.

Bertie opted for the sleeping chamber next door, under the assumption that secrets were often kept farthest from the entrance. Human nature.

The room smelled of bay rum and cloves. Several expensively bound books rested on a table. From the Carlton House library?

The wardrobe yielded several ecclesiastical robes but little else.

The bureau was much the same.

Cravats, stockings, small clothes, Geneva bands, everything he expected to find. Modest clothing for a respected clergyman.

"Sir Bertrand?" Daniel called.

When he reached the desk where Daniel stood, he looked at what his soon-to-be nephew-in-law held up to the candlelight.

"Practicing?" Bertie whispered, not wanting Gadshaw to overhear.

It was a paper, with lines identical to that which Bertie had read on the forged guarantee from the bank. Most telling was the copying of the signature of Charles Wyvern, Earl of Rothwell.

"He had a letter from the earl from which to practice." Daniel pointed to a missive, dated nearly ten years before. "An ordinary epistle from a dozen years ago, giving Todd a commendation. It appears Todd was looking for a reference for a new position and Charles supplied one."

The presence of the letter and the practice paper proved a few things. First, that Todd was, indeed, the one who took the money from the Bank of England, and second, that the letter gave him the means to copy the earl's signature, though he had not been very successful at it. Wyvern's scrawl looked a bit like the forged one, but if Bertie could tell the difference, Charles surely could.

"We will be taking these papers with us. Please, if Mr. Todd returns, do not mention our visit, but do send word to Bow Street immediately. Do you understand?" Daniel asked sternly. "If you inform Todd that we are looking for him, you will be obstructing a police investigation, and I will arrest you. You have stated that you know how to keep your own counsel about those who come to Todd for spiritual guidance. Extend that ability to cover our visit."

Gadshaw gaped for a moment, then nodded. "Won't say a word." He swallowed. "Is the reverend doing something he oughtn't?"

"Do you suspect something amiss?" Daniel's tone remained sharp.

"No, no. If he's involved in something, none of us here know what it might be." The landlord backed through the doorway and into the hall, as if wanting to distance himself from any whiff of wrongdoing.

When they returned to the carriage, Daniel spoke to Cadogan, his driver, before climbing in opposite Bertie.

"Remember how I said investigations tend to break out in unexpected directions just when you think you've hit a wall?" Daniel asked.

Chapter 17

"You say we have reason to hope?" Philippa followed the solicitor, Walter Newbolt, and Aunt Dolly into the small interview room at the prison.

Aunt Dolly went immediately to Nell, who slumped on the bench along the wall.

"Oh, child, look at you." She drew her into her embrace. "Have you not been eating? We've been sending food."

Nell let out a sob and relaxed into the older woman's embrace. "I try, but the other women take it from me. If I try to stop them, I get slapped . . . or worse." She spoke into Aunt Dolly's shoulder.

Fire coursed through Philippa's chest. Nell was skin and bones, and she no longer had her shoes. Had those been stolen from her too? What sort of place were the warders running, where girls like Nell were subjected to violence from the other inmates?

Mr. Newbolt set his case on the table and opened the latches. "Miss, if you could gather yourself, we need to speak." He removed an inkwell and two quills along with several sheets of foolscap. "There have been developments in your case, and I believe I can have the charges dropped before we go to trial on Monday morning."

Nell raised her head, her dark eyes glistening with tears. "You mean I can leave here? I ain't gonna be hanged?"

"I will request an audience with the judge, and if necessary, the Prince Regent himself, who is bringing these charges against you. A man brought part of the stolen parure in to a receiver's shop to try to sell this week, and though he has not been identified or apprehended, the piece has been confirmed as belonging to the set stolen from the Prince Regent. That, along with the murder of the maid, Lydia, has swung suspicion away from you. Evidence shows that her murderer was a male, and you certainly couldn't have been the killer, as you were incarcerated here at the time. I expect you to be free by Monday afternoon at the latest."

Philippa's eyes stung as Nell collapsed against Aunt Dolly once more. The desire to cry was odd, since Philippa rarely cried. She often wondered if all her more tender emotions had been cauterized by the things she had lived through. Perhaps there was a bit of softness left in her somewhere. She blinked, dispelling the moisture, not wishing to appear vulnerable in front of the barrister.

Aunt Dolly rested her chin on the girl's head, eyes closed, lips moving, and Philippa knew she was praying her thanks.

Sagging into a chair as her sore muscles twinged and her bruises protested, Philippa added her own silent prayer of thanks. Though she still bore the guilt of putting Nell and Lydia into the positions at Carlton House and though she still carried the burden of Lydia's murder, she would not have to carry Nell's death too.

"What should we do in the meantime?" she asked Mr. Newbolt. Monday seemed a far time off.

"I wish to organize my presentation to the judge, and I would like to go over a few of the more salient facts of the case with Miss Nell, once she composes herself." With a patient sigh, he reached into an inner pocket and withdrew a pristine linen square.

Aunt Dolly took it and pressed it into Nell's trembling hands. Though the girl hiccupped and gasped, she did sit up and mop her eyes.

"I have the timeline of events as you relayed them to me in our first interview, and I wish to verify these facts." Mr. Newbolt shuffled the pages and found what he sought. He tilted the paper to the shaft of daylight coming in through the high, barred window.

Each point he read aloud received a nod from Nell, but as he neared the end of the page, her chin went down. Her breath caught, and she mangled the handkerchief.

Philippa put out her hand to stop Mr. Newbolt. He looked up and paused. "What is it?"

"Nell," she said. "It is time to stop lying. Or, if you are not lying, then it is time to stop concealing things from us. I have known from the beginning you were hiding something. At first I thought it was about Lydia and Harry's budding relationship, but now I think it's something different. Lydia told Harry that she couldn't trust every man in the house, but she would not give specifics. Do you know who she was speaking of? Is it Mr. Lingfield? Did she fear the secretary?"

The girl swallowed, looking so vulnerable with her sunken cheeks and her collarbones sticking out like spars. Her straight, thin hair hung limply, and fear—no, more like terror—painted her expression.

"Lydia told me I could never tell. Never breathe a word of it, because no one would believe us, we would lose our jobs, and you might get into trouble for trying to help us. She said if we ever told, he would do what he said."

Philippa straightened. "Who? Who would do what he said?"

"I'm not safe in here, but if I tell you and I get out of here on Monday, I won't be safe out there." She shook her head.

"Nell, I am not going to let anything happen to you. I will protect you. And not just me. I have powerful friends. Friends like Mr. Newbolt here, who is looking after your legal case. Friends like the Duke of Haverly, like the Earl of Aylswood, who is the head of the Bow Street police force. Friends like Sir Bertrand Thorndike." She stopped, not able to say that he was an agent for the Crown. "These are some of the most powerful men in the kingdom. They will protect you from whomever it is who has threatened you. But they cannot do so if you won't tell us who the man is."

Again she shook her head. "They are not more powerful than he is. He said so."

Philippa paused. Surely it wasn't the Prince Regent of whom she spoke. He was the only man in the realm who truly could wield more power than Marcus Haverly, the royal dukes notwithstanding. They were ineffectual at best, certainly more concerned with their own selves than gathering support and influence.

"Is it His Highness?" she finally asked, dreading the answer.

"Prinny?" Nell clapped her hand over her mouth at getting caught using the sobriquet. Then she shook her head. "Mrs. Evans said we wasn't to call him that, but everyone does. No, we never had no dealings with His Highness. Only saw him a few times. We wasn't allowed in his part of the house. Sometimes, if his carriage was leaving from the stable yard, Lydia and me would climb up on the scullery counter to look out the high window to see him leave. Took two footmen and a tiger to get him up into the carriage sometimes, he's that large."

"If not the prince, then who threatened you?"

"The reverend," she whispered. "Mr. Todd."

Everything in Philippa stilled, and weakness traveled from her scalp to her soles. The weakness was quickly replaced by outrage. "What?" Her voice sounded loud as it echoed off the stone walls. "He threatened you? With what? Why?"

Aunt Dolly hugged Nell. "Perhaps if you lowered your voice and stopped firing questions, she might answer." She tilted the girl's head back and looked into her eyes. "You are not in trouble, Nell. Just tell us what you know."

"Mr. Todd, he would come to Carlton House and use the library there. Mrs. Evans sent Lydia with the tea tray a couple of times. Mrs. Evans used to complain that Mr. Todd was a nuisance, and didn't she have enough to see to without having to run up tea and biscuits all the time? I think she sent Lydia or me because she wanted him to know he was being a bother and not worth being served by a liveried footman."

Philippa pressed her lips together. Domestic servants did have ways of getting their own back on the people they served, subtle but effective.

"What happened?" she asked.

"Lydia took his tray up the last time, like she was told, but when she got back, she was shaking. She said she didn't knock on the door before coming in, and he had something in his hand. He spun around and slammed that big Bible he carries sometimes. When he turned back, he was real mad. Said she had interrupted him, and didn't she know to knock? If she ever did that again, he would have her removed from service. And if she ever told a soul what she'd seen, she would be sorry. He worked for God, and God was more powerful than the Prince Regent. He said God himself would be angry if Lydia did anything to harm his reputation."

The more Nell talked, the more Philippa's anger rose. Mr. Todd. The man who had "found" Lydia's body. Had he been concealing in his hand something of value that he had stolen from Carlton House? Could it have been part of the parure?

Threatening a young girl with a judgment from God? The arrogance of the man.

She needed to speak with Sir Bertrand Thorndike immediately.

Philippa hurried into the former drawing room at Eleos that she and Aunt Dolly had converted to an office.

"We are not the only ones looking for Mr. Todd." She tugged the ribbon holding her bonnet. "When we parted ways at the prison, I went to the Thorndike residence, but the staff there said that Sir Bertrand was not receiving. I could tell from the butler's demeanor that Sir Bertrand wasn't in the house, not just that he wasn't taking callers."

"That isn't unusual, for him not to be home at that time of day. What makes you think he's looking for the reverend?" Aunt Dolly asked. Sunlight streamed through the now-repaired and pristine window glass, illuminating the desk where she had spread accounts, receipts, and reports of repairs.

"Because I went to Charlotte's house in search of Marcus. He needs to know what Nell told us because, if he is of a mind to do so, he can get her released quicker than her barrister can. But Charlotte says Marcus sent word late last night that he would not be home, that he was with Sir Bertrand, and they were looking for Mr. Todd. She said Marcus was in a meeting with Sir Bertrand and Mr. Swann, and someone else arrived during the meeting. Then they all, along with the Earl of Rothwell, went haring off into the night. The visitor must have brought them some news that set them on Mr. Todd's trail."

"Perhaps they have already located and questioned him?" Aunt Dolly tapped the side of her index finger against her lips, deep in thought. "I'm so disturbed by what Nell told us. That a supposed man of God would threaten a young girl to the point she was terrified for her life."

"Not only threatened, I surmise. I think he killed Lydia. I think he stole those jewels and tried to frame the girls, and when only one was arrested, he killed the other. He must have been concealing the stolen jewels when Lydia came upon him in the library. He must have been sure she had caught him. I knew there was something off about him. And he was foisted on us by the owner of this property." She tugged off her gloves and tossed them into her bonnet. "I hope whatever avenue Sir Bertrand and Marcus are pursuing, they have proof enough to both free Nell and convict Todd."

"There is no one more capable than Marcus, and Sir Bertrand seems more than competent too. They will run him to earth, and they will arrest him if he's guilty. Until then, you're just in time to interview an applicant." Aunt Dolly searched a stack of papers and pulled out one that had been folded and still had a wax seal adhered to one edge.

"Did a woman arrive this morning?" Philippa hadn't seen anyone waiting in the great hall when she'd hurried through.

"Not a woman seeking aid. This applicant is for the infirmary position. He comes on the recommendation of the Earl of Rothwell, and he's a former naval surgeon who served under the earl's command. He is seeking a civilian position, and"—Aunt Dolly looked up, her eyes showing hope—"his wife of two years is a trained midwife. They are seeking a place where they can work together."

"A naval surgeon? And a midwife?" Medical abilities and someone familiar with women's needs?

"We would be spared the expense of a trained physician, but still have the medical knowledge and surgical abilities we need," Aunt Dolly said.

Philippa hadn't considered this. A surgeon did not command the pay of a physician, for they had less formal training and more apprenticeship instruction. Physicians often stayed aloof from patients, giving their opinions but not doing any of the actual doctoring. Surgeons treated wounds, dispensed medicines, cared for the sick and injured, all without the physician's price tag. And if he had been a naval surgeon, he was more than likely well-versed in treating some of the diseases more prevalent in their clientele.

Not to mention a midwife on the premises.

Nothing was certain, but they did seem the perfect applicants for the position.

Aunt Dolly held up the letter. "If they are suitable—and from this endorsement from the Earl of Rothwell, they should be—it would seem God has answered another of our prayers."

Philippa took a chair, letting her tippet slide from her shoulder. "On the surface they do seem suitable, but you will have to forgive my reticence to eagerly embrace anyone without a thorough investigation. Mr. Todd also came to us highly recommended. Didn't he, too, serve under the earl when he was a ship's captain?"

"To be fair, the earl had not served with Todd long, and the endorsement of Mr. Todd came from Mr. Asbury, not the earl," Aunt Dolly pointed out. "We will interview the couple ourselves. The only sticking point I can see is that they are hoping that there is a housing stipend that comes with the position. Are there any buildings on the property that would be suitable to lodge them?"

Philippa considered this. "There's the manse. If Todd is proven guilty, he will not need it, and it's already under repair."

"Where would we house the new minister?"

"I propose we do not have a full-time minister at the school. I've never been comfortable with charging admittance to services or being the vehicle that promoted Todd's career. I suggest we apply to the nearest ministerial college and offer the pulpit as a training ground for young men seeking to enter the pastorate. We can have small, private services for the women of the school, and they won't be made to feel like they are on display. If, in the future, a likely candidate applies to be the school's minister, we can see about sorting out housing at that time."

Aunt Dolly sat back, resting her hands on the arms of her chair. She wore a satisfied smile.

"What?"

"I'm proud of you."

Philippa raised her brows, but she could not deny the uprush of warmth. There had been men in her life who had been proud to have her on their arm because they thought her beautiful and that it would make other men jealous, but rarely had she heard that anyone was proud of her for *who* she was, not *what* she was.

"I'm proud of all you have accomplished here at Eleos and that you are looking to the future of this place. You are becoming adept at administration, at solving the problems that arise, and also at anticipating those that may come in the future. It does my heart good knowing that our ministry will continue in capable hands when I'm no longer here."

Philippa's heart constricted. She did not want to think of a time when Aunt Dolly would not be there. Dorothy Stokes had been her friend, mentor, stand-in mother, and blessing. Without her, Philippa would either still be living in the brothel, or worse, she would be dead. It was Aunt Dolly who had encouraged her to forge a relationship with Charlotte Haverly. Without that urging, Philippa would have continued to treat Charlotte with coldness and would have missed their loving relationship and the sense of family that she'd never had before. She would have been all alone when her mother died. She shook her head. Aunt Dolly wasn't going anywhere.

"May that day be long in the future. What time will this surgeon arrive for the interview, and what is his name?"

"Mr. Vickery. And the appointment is set for after the noon meal."

"That gives me time to check with the cook as to our provisions list. How are the coffers?"

The time before the meeting flew. Philippa saw to a dozen details, making an assessment of the pupils and their progress and answering letters. All the while, she prayed that Mr. Todd would be found and a confession wrung out of him. He would answer for his crimes, and Nell would go free.

She debated changing to greet their guests, wanting to make a good impression, but then shook her head. *Start as you mean to go on, Philippa Cashel. The Vickerys, should they agree to come here, will see you in ordinary garb most days. If they are hoping to be impressed and looking for haute couture, they have come to the wrong ministry.*

No word had come from Charlotte, who had promised to send for Philippa when Marcus returned. They must either be scouring the city for Mr. Todd, or they had apprehended him and were questioning him.

Please, God, let there be justice for Lydia and that Nell may be released from prison.

The prayer had been on her mind constantly, but for the first time, she really believed it might be possible.

She presented herself in the great hall as the surgeon's carriage came up the drive. He'd hired a barouche, and he helped his wife descend, solicitously. She was a small woman with smooth hair at her temples beneath her straw bonnet, and she was obviously with child.

"Mr. Vickery? I am Miss Philippa Cashel." She held out her hand.

"A pleasure. This is my wife, Matilda."

"And this is Mrs. Stokes. Together, we run Eleos." Which was true, now that it appeared Todd would no longer be putting his oar in.

Aunt Dolly took over the tour, answering questions and showing them the crofter's house they intended to use as an infirmary. "We'd prefer not to call it a pesthouse." She wrinkled her nose. "I do not like that term. Infirmary is more appealing, don't you think?"

Philippa followed the group, taking her measure of Mr. Vickery. He walked like a navy man, a slight roll to his step, his shoulders back.

Often he clasped his hands behind his back as he listened, a trait she had noticed in the Earl of Rothwell and in Rothwell's youngest ward, Betsy, when she aped him.

Mrs. Vickery nodded warmly. "I agree. Infirmary is a much nicer term. How many women do you anticipate being enrolled at one time when you are at full capacity?"

"We've currently a score of women, but eventually, we hope to be able to serve as many as fifty. Once all the rooms are finished and we have furnishings and funding for that number. As always with a charity, efforts rely on donations. We've recently had a nice influx of donors, so we're able to expand rather quickly." Aunt Dolly turned to Philippa. "Much of the credit for the fundraising must go to Miss Cashel. She has been at the forefront of our efforts to make people aware of Eleos and the work we are hoping to accomplish here."

"Admirable and sadly much-needed work." Mr. Vickery patted his wife's hand where it rested on his arm. "We have been looking for some worthy cause to which we can lend our aid."

"You said you were looking for either accommodations or a housing stipend?" Philippa asked.

"Yes, we would rather not live in the same place we work. I'm sure you understand. If there is no other option, I'm certain we will make do, but with a child due in the coming months and treating patients with various conditions, I feel it would be best if my family did not live in an infirmary."

"Of course. We do have a house that will most likely be available soon. It is on the other side of the manor, near the church. Repair work is nearly completed."

The walk took perhaps five minutes, and Mr. Vickery commented, "How pleasant to have such a short jaunt to work, but to still have some separation. You may even be able to have a garden, Matilda, love."

She smiled up at him. "To grow my medicinal herbs, not to mention some flowers."

Aunt Dolly had the key to the manse's front door. "As this was originally a manse, there's a glebe provided if you wish to keep a horse or a cow. We will soon have a dairy and a fowl house, and you will, of course, be welcome to what is produced there."

The door opened easily, testament to the workmen who had oiled the hinges.

"We were anticipating a minister living here, and he's brought some of his belongings, but there has been a change in his circumstances. His things will be cleared out soon." Philippa noted the crates and furnishings that had been stacked in the front room. The boxes were now open, the belongings strewn about, crates tipped on their sides.

She frowned. Had the workmen gone through them? Surely not. Not men sent by the Earl of Whitelock. Had Mr. Todd rummaged through his things, looking for something? When had he been here, and for what had he been searching?

"This is a charming cottage. Even more than we had hoped for. We are definitely interested in the position." Mr. Vickery met his wife's eyes, and she gave a nod and smile.

Aunt Dolly clasped her hands at her waist, but before she could say anything, Philippa spoke.

"Thank you for your interest. We will be contacting you in the coming days. I must, of course, consult with the board on such an important subject as filling this position." Though she was encouraged by what she had seen and heard from the Vickerys, caution told her to wait until Marcus could learn more about them before they brought them onto the staff.

Aunt Dolly made a low sound, but she nodded. "Yes, we will send a note soon. I have your address on your letter. Will you be reachable there for the next fortnight?"

"Yes. Of course. We look forward to hearing from you."

As they left the manse, Aunt Dolly locked the door behind her.

Philippa paused on the path. "Will you see the Vickerys back to their carriage? I would like to check on the progress in the church. The workmen have finished the major repairs, and now it is up to us to see to the cleaning and tidying up. I'd like to assess what we will need and how soon we can have our first service there."

She said her goodbyes to the surgeon and his wife and turned toward the church. When she had her mishap the previous Sunday, she'd lost a silver button from her gown. Hopefully it was somewhere on the floor near where she had fallen. She hadn't even realized it was gone until this morning when she had checked the dress over to see if it could be salvaged.

The path to the church was still overgrown, but signs of the comings and goings of the workmen were evident. The grass had been trampled, and carts and wagons had created ruts. Hopefully there would be some gravel left over from the front driveway to spread here, else they would be walking in mud to church on rainy Sundays.

Though that was not a problem today. The afternoon sun warmed her shoulders, and bees buzzed in the tall grass. She had a feeling that soon, when the difficulties with Mr. Todd were sorted, when Nell was released from prison and ensconced here at the school, things would become easier. They could settle down to the future she had planned, and there would be only minor problems to deal with.

She gazed up at the Norman bell tower, shading her eyes against the glare. No bells would ring there anytime soon. The original iron bells had been removed years ago, likely melted down to make cannons for the war against the French. It would be a long time before they could afford to replace them.

Stepping inside the church, she felt the temperature drop. The stone walls tended to hold on to the cool of the night, and the flagstone floor was always chilly. Any heat rose toward the exposed rafters high overhead.

She admired the quiet space. It really was a lovely church and would be nicer still when the scaffolding was removed. A breeze blew through the stone trefoil openings in the apse and clerestory. The workmen had removed the broken glass, but the new windows had yet to arrive.

The dowager had insisted that colored glass was the only proper glass for the church, though Charlotte had pointed out to her that Sir Christopher Wren had preferred clear glass for many of the windows of St. Paul's Cathedral.

In the end, because there were other battles to fight, Philippa had given the dowager her way. Not to mention, Philippa liked the way light through stained glass shattered into rainbows across the preacher and the congregation on a Sunday morning.

She went halfway up the aisle and turned to look at the rear wall where the balcony level sat, fifteen feet from the floor. The square block of the bell tower bisected the balcony so that there was only one row of seats across the middle, with three rows on either side of the tower.

This was where Mr. Todd had proposed the ladies of Eleos sit as a choir.

In the back, where they would not offend the attendees. To be called upon to perform a hymn or two, and otherwise to stay out of sight and be grateful.

Her blood simmered. Such an arrogant man.

When Marcus and Sir Bertrand ran him to earth, he would pay for far greater sins than being unkind to fallen women.

The workers had removed the broken pieces of stone and wood, and the grit and sawdust had been swept up. No sign of her silver button.

A shame, for it had been costly. Charlotte had purchased the dress for her from Antoinette's after Philippa had left her life as a courtesan. Much of her former wardrobe was unacceptable for her new life, and she'd wanted no reminders of the past.

Philippa did not miss the clothing, for it had always felt like a costume she donned, a persona that wasn't her. The real Philippa was that innocent child she had been before her circumstances so drastically changed.

Before her father had abandoned her.

Her father. The thought of him twisted her mouth into a grimace.

She had been mulling Charlotte's words about the poisonous bitterness of unforgiveness. How it did her father no harm but harmed her every day.

"I don't want to forgive him. He doesn't deserve it. It would feel as if I were releasing him from the responsibility of his actions." She spoke the words aloud but softly, as here, alone in the church, seemed a good time to speak with God.

"Yet it is as if I have surrendered my peace of mind to him. Thoughts of him make me angry, cause me to make bad decisions, and rob me of my peace. If I could wipe him from my memory altogether, I would. But since I cannot . . . since I cannot, the only way to be shut of him is to forgive him?" She eased onto the front pew, gripping her hands together in her lap. "You say we are to forgive those who spitefully use us. Forgive as we have been forgiven. Do not repay evil for evil. But if You want me to do this, it will have to be You working in me. Change my heart."

She sat still, and the beginnings of something akin to peace began to seep through her. A lightness inside that she had not felt before. She inhaled slowly, letting the air trickle through her nose as she closed her eyes.

May that peace and lightness never end.

A door creaked, and the low murmur of voices reached her. Male voices? Had the workmen returned? She hadn't thought they would be about today.

Disappointment wriggled through her. The moment had passed, that calm time of prayer and petition. The tangible had intruded. She should make herself known to the workers so they weren't startled when they came in.

The voices were coming from the chancel behind the pulpit. The only thing back there was the Lady Chapel. That room hadn't needed any repairs. What business would the workers have in there?

Her footsteps echoed on the stone floor as she rounded the elevated pulpit. She pushed open the thick, oak door into the Lady Chapel, the iron studs pressing into her palms.

In the gloom, someone knelt behind one of the crypts, the burial place of some long ago baron and his wife, while another man stood at the foot of the crypt.

"Who is here?" she asked, her voice echoing in the stone room.

Both men whirled to face her.

Mr. Todd and Mr. Asbury.

Todd's large Bible, which had been balancing on the edge of the crypt, tumbled to the floor. It slapped the ground, and the cover flew open, revealing, not pages of typeface, but a hollow container . . . hollow but not empty. A tiara and necklace of pearls and sapphires spilled out, winking in the sunlight from the high windows.

Chapter 18

"Where else can we look?" Bertie rolled his shoulders, loosening his tight muscles. "Who else can we contact who might know of his whereabouts? It's uncanny. Did he receive a tip that we were looking for him? Or did he always plan to pike off after he got the money from the bank?" Bertie rubbed at his neck. He always got stiff riding in carriages too long, and he and Daniel had been scouring the city for Mr. Todd all night and half the day.

None of Todd's associates in the church had seen him. No one at Carlton House, his rooming house, or any of the pubs or clubs where he was known to dine.

"He could not know we would be looking for him, because he had no way to know Mr. Nighly would have that guarantee of repayment rewritten and his forgery would be discovered." Daniel pinched the bridge of his nose.

The carriage slowed abruptly, and the coachman, Cadogan, began shouting. "Get out of the way, fool!"

Bertie lurched forward, reaching out to steady himself.

"Oh, it's you. Sorry, I didn't recognize you, Partridge," Cadogan said.

The door yanked open, and Mr. Partridge stuck his head inside the carriage.

"Been trying to find you all morning."

"Come aboard." Daniel slid over. "You have news?"

"Went to the school, didn't see anyone, but there's something odd at the preacher's house. Boxes piled in the front room, but someone's gone through them. Open, things on the floor. Looked like it was done in a hurry."

"You think it was Todd? Packing to escape?"

"Don't know. I didn't light a lamp. Didn't want it to be seen from the manor house. Can't tell when the boxes were opened." Partridge shrugged. "If he was there, I couldn't tell."

Daniel rapped on the ceiling of the carriage and Cadogan opened the sliding door.

"Take us across the river to Great Dover Street near the gaol. There's a manor there, Eleos School, it is now. But first, let Partridge out."

Bertie nodded. "Partridge, find Haverly and report, and have him meet us at Eleos. We'll go through the manse ourselves and perhaps that will tell us where Todd might be hiding."

The bulky agent dropped gracefully to the ground, the carriage lurching as his weight lifted from the springs.

Weariness dragged at Bertie's body and mind. Though he was hardly in his dotage at thirty-six, he wasn't as young as he used to be, and he didn't recover from being awake all night as he once had.

Daniel smothered a yawn. "I now know why Sir Michael did not spend much time in the field. There's too much to oversee at Bow Street for much lead chasing or suspect hunting. I'm grateful to have Ed Beck as my assistant supervisor, but I cannot put too much on him. It is my job, after all."

"Do you think you will like your new position? It's quite a change."

He shrugged. "Change is inevitable, isn't it? And it's not all bad. I'm trying to embrace the changes and see them as challenges. I'm learning new things every day, and I'm having to grow up and let go of some of the things that were holding me back. I know who my father was now, even if the *ton* doesn't recognize the relationship. I've laid aside old resentment, mended my relationship with my mother, and been promoted to a supervisory position. All improvements on my past. Not to mention an earldom and, best of all, a bride-to-be that is far above anyone I ever dreamed of loving."

By comparison, Bertie felt . . . stuck. As if he floated on the surface of things, doing his job, wearing his persona as a dandy . . . had he worn it so long that it had become more than a persona? Did he know how to be anything else?

Was that why he was reluctant to let go of his reputation as an idle drunk who frittered away his time going from one social engagement to the next?

Was that why he was reluctant to actually search for his own town-house?

The sound of the horse's hooves changed as they turned from the packed dirt of the road to the gravel of the Eleos drive.

What a difference another week had made. Bertie had not been to the school since the fundraiser, and much had been accomplished in the meantime. The trim on the house had been painted a pristine white, and the windows gleamed. The front door had a new coat of paint as well, glossy black. Some shrubs had been planted along the front of the house. The place looked lived in and cared for.

A carriage waited at the door, and Mrs. Stokes and a man and woman stood talking on the front porch.

"Sir Bertrand." Mrs. Stokes's face lit. "Miss Cashel and I were hoping to speak with you. We have news regarding the matter you were looking into."

He was grateful that she spoke circumspectly about the case, especially since he didn't know the couple beside her.

"We have some news for you as well."

Mrs. Stokes indicated her guests. "This is Mr. and Mrs. Vickery, acquaintances of the Earl of Rothwell. They've come to inquire about the medical position here at Eleos."

Bertie winced. He had asked Rothwell to find a suitable candidate, as he knew he would not find time for it until the investigation ended. Slacking in his role as a board member and still achieving nothing anywhere else.

"A pleasure." He nodded to the couple and turned to Mrs. Stokes. "We've come to look in the manse." And pray something in the house would give them a lead to follow.

Mr. Vickery drew his brows together. "We've just come from there."

Bertie exchanged a look at Daniel and asked Mr. Vickery, "Was Mr. Todd there? We'd like to speak with him."

"He was not. The place was empty but for some of his belongings."

Mrs. Stokes smiled at her guests. "We will not keep you any longer, Mr. Vickery. Look for a missive from us soon."

The moment the Vickerys were in the carriage, Mrs. Stokes gripped Bertie's forearm. "We went to Newgate Prison this morning with Mr. Newbolt, Nell's barrister. And Nell finally told us what she had been keeping secret. Mr. Todd threatened them. Lydia caught him secreting something away when she took a tea tray to him in the library, and he told her if she mentioned it to anyone, he'd see she was sorry. I think it was the parure, and I think he panicked that you were getting too close. I think he killed Lydia out of fear that she could identify him as the thief."

Bertie nodded. With what they knew of the fraud and Todd's access to Carlton House, as well as his "finding" Lydia's body . . . the black fibers too. It all added up. "We need to look in the manse at his belongings. We haven't been able to locate him, and there may be something in his possessions that would give us an indication where to look."

"You'll need the key." She took a looped string off her wrist with a heavy, iron key. "Philippa has gone to the church. She can tell you better what Nell said and what Philippa thinks happened at Carlton House."

"I'll start at the cottage. You find Miss Cashel and see what she knows." Daniel reached for the key.

They parted ways where the path forked to either the manse or the church, and when he arrived at the church, Bertie noticed changes here as well. Fresh mortar had been applied to the stone facade, but the windows with the glass removed looked like empty eyes on the clerestory. Scaffolding had been erected along the south side of the church.

The door dated to the time of the Normans, oiled oak with iron studs and straps, and a Gothic arch top. It stood ajar.

He entered the narthex beneath the bell tower, his boots echoing on the stone floor. The baptistry sat behind a rood screen to his right and the pulpit ahead and to the left. The room smelled of sawdust and stonework, though the workers had left the place clean. Once the work was finished and the inside scaffolding had been removed, he imagined it would smell of candlewax and furniture polish and reverberate with choral music and preaching.

But not the preaching of Mr. Simon Todd.

"Miss Cashel?" he called, his voice bouncing off the empty space.

A small sound came from behind the pulpit. A grunt or whimper?

He jogged up the aisle, curious as to what she was doing. Moving furniture? He rounded the raised pulpit. There was an open door into a small chapel.

"Miss Cashel?" he called again, approaching the opening. As his feet hit the threshold, he froze.

Reverend Simon Todd had his arm wrapped around Miss Cashel's waist, pinning her against him, while his other hand held a shiny steel blade to her throat. Her eyes were wide, and her mouth gaped a bit as her breath came in quick gasps.

At their feet, the reverend's Bible sprawled open on the floor, and the missing jewels spilled from a hidden compartment inside.

Bertie had no time to feel vindicated.

Mr. Asbury leapt from behind the door, swinging wildly at Bertie's head with a candlestick. He ducked, feeling the swoosh of air as it passed his temple.

With the instinct his training had given him, he lashed out, chopping his hand across Asbury's throat. The man dropped the candlestick with a clatter, clutching his neck, gagging and choking. Bertie followed up with a sound kick to the man's stomach, hard enough to lift him from the floor as he bent over trying to grab a breath.

"Get out. Get out of here," Todd spat, all pretense of being a pious gentleman gone. "I'm leaving this church, and you will not try to stop me or she's dead."

Bertie shoved Asbury out of his way. "Let her go. Why are you doing this?" He feigned ignorance. If Todd realized he knew about Lydia and the bank fraud, it could cause him to snap.

"You can see for yourself. You're not that dense." His eyes flicked to the jewels on the floor.

Asbury had crashed to his knees, holding his belly, hacking and spitting. Bertie had to keep an eye on him while also watching Todd. If only Swann had come with him to the church. Two against one was never his favorite odds.

"I can take those back to the prince, and we can just forget about this entire thing. I'll tell him I found them, but I couldn't determine who stole them." It was thin, but perhaps Todd would go for it.

"Don't be stupid. Now, get back. Get out of that doorway." He flicked the blade toward Bertie, but had it back at Miss Cashel's throat in a flash.

Bertie assessed the situation. There was no other way out of the side chapel, so he had the man cornered, but that was also causing the reverend to become more agitated. If he panicked, he could kill Miss Cashel before Bertie could move, much less try to prevent him.

"What about him?" Bertie asked, indicating Asbury.

"He's on his own. If he had been quicker, we would have gotten away clean." Todd's eyes blazed. "If he hadn't forced me to marry his spendthrift sister who racked up debts all over the city trying to be an aristocrat before running off to Italy with Princess Caroline and her hedonistic set, I wouldn't be in this mess."

A wife? Nothing in their investigation had indicated that Todd was married.

Bertie backed out of the doorway, keeping his hands in plain sight. If Todd felt less cornered, perhaps he would turn Miss Cashel loose.

"Pick up the jewels," Todd ordered Miss Cashel. He stooped with her, knife at the ready, as she scooped up the tiara, the necklace, and fished for the earrings. "Give them to me."

He shoved them into his coat pockets and grabbed her again. Not a handspan between them as he kept her clamped firmly against his chest and inched forward. He spared a scathing glance at Asbury, still incapacitated in the corner.

The fright in Miss Cashel's eyes angered Bertie. How dare this charlatan of a preacher put his hands on her, threaten her life?

One of his team members. His friend.

How could he get an advantage here?

Todd and Miss Cashel stepped out of the small chapel, and he kept his back to the wall as he edged down the aisle toward the bell tower.

Bertie kept pace with Todd, the backs of his legs brushing the ends of the pews. He was willing to let Todd get away with the jewels if it meant he turned loose of Philippa without hurting her. They could always catch up with the preacher again.

"This was supposed to be such a sweet position, living free at the school, taking donations, removing my administrative fee off the top. My debts would be paid, my nightmares would stop." A fleck of spittle formed at the corner of Todd's mouth. "But the dead girl won't leave me alone. She stalks my dreams. I've been afraid to sleep. I couldn't return to Carlton House. I tried. I tried to go back, to pretend nothing had happened, but I couldn't force myself to go inside. If I had never married Janet Asbury, who goes through money like water, I would not have needed to steal the jewels. I never anticipated their loss being discovered so soon. You were breathing down my neck within a day. I was trying to sell the jewels, and I was working the bank scam, and it was all colliding." He was nearly to the rood screen, a dozen steps from the bell tower.

Miss Cashel's eyes locked on Bertie's. Her skin was flushed, and her head braced against Todd's shoulder as far from the tip of the knife as she could get.

What should he do? Though only a few feet separated him from

Todd, Miss Cashel was firmly between them. Could he signal her to jerk away while he dove for the blade?

And where was Asbury? Bertie darted a look back the way they had come, then focused on the clergyman.

"Todd, do not add another murder to your already troubled conscience. Let the lady go. You were trying to protect your reputation. Trying to cover your losses, trying to keep the maid from revealing your theft. But imagine how people will think of you if you kill the patroness of a women's charity to save your own hide?"

"Who will care about her?" He snarled, giving Miss Cashel a shake. "She's filth. Oh, she may look beautiful on the outside, and she may try to cleanse her soul with good works, but she's condemned. All the women here are condemned. It would be fitting if I killed her. I tried to do it before, collapsing that scaffolding on her, but I failed. It's so much harder when it must look like an accident." His eyes were wild, his hair unkempt, and his actions jerky.

It has to be now.

As if she had read his mind, Philippa slammed her head backward into Todd's nose, thrust his arm away from herself, and shot forward.

Unfortunately, she collided with Bertie even as he was rushing forward, intent on knocking that knife away from her.

Todd's head hit the wall and the knife clattered to the floor, but he reeled away and ran for the door.

Bertie grappled with Miss Cashel to keep her from falling, then set her away from himself to pursue the reverend before he could escape into the countryside.

But rather than rush out the door, the reverend raced up the bell tower stairs.

Swann came inside the church as Todd's footfalls echoed up the tower.

"There's another one inside, and Miss Cashel. Make certain she is safe, and take Asbury into custody." Bertie barked the words out and leapt for the stairs.

As he flung himself upward, he reached under his coat to draw his pistol. The knife was on the floor downstairs, but he did not know if Todd had other weapons.

Dust flew down, and a piece of rotted railing bounced off the stairs. The workmen had not stabilized this staircase yet, and it rocked and cracked under his boots. He glimpsed Todd on the landings as they rose up and up, but he wasn't gaining on the man.

Eventually, the reverend would run out of *up*.

A trapdoor that led to where the bells had been housed lay open, and Bertie paused beneath it to catch his breath. He wasn't enamored of the idea of sticking his head through that hole, but he had no choice if he wanted to apprehend his quarry.

Time to put his skills at stealth to use. Calming his breathing and moving quietly, he crouched as close to the top stair as he could so he could burst into the room and hopefully catch Todd off guard.

Three, two, one! He shot through the doorway and threw himself to the side, pistol at the ready—

Just in time to see Simon Todd launch himself from the belfry with a desperate cry.

Bertie scrambled to his feet and rushed to the opening.

The sprawled body lay on the rutted dirt path, more than fifty feet below.

Daniel Swann emerged from the base of the tower and bent over the body, his pistol in his hand. He looked up and shook his head.

"You are certain you are not hurt?"

Sir Bertrand had asked her that question at least three times. He squatted beside the pew, his hair tousled and his clothes covered in dust.

He actually looked rather nice, rumpled and far from his urbane, suave self. His concern gave all the indications of being sincere.

She removed his handkerchief from her neck, checked that there was not too much blood, and returned it to the wound. It stung only slightly, and thankfully, should not need stitches. She had no desire to be Mr. Vickery's first patient at Eleos.

She looked about her at the empty church. Twice she had nearly lost her life here.

"Did you know Todd was the murderer?" she asked.

"I knew he was guilty of fraud, but not certain about him killing Lydia." He wiped his brow with his palm. "We were putting the pieces together all of last night."

"I learned from Nell why he would have killed Lydia, but did not know about the fraud. That must have been some revelation for the Earl of Rothwell." She tried to speak evenly, to ignore the quaking in her middle and the instability in her limbs.

"If we had been able to connect sooner . . . I apologize profusely for not forestalling all this. You could have been killed." His hand formed a fist on his thigh, and he pounded it lightly. "I do not think I am the right man to lead a team for Marcus. I always seem to be a half step behind. If I hadn't made the assumption that Mr. Todd was an honorable man, I might have stumbled onto him as the thief before he killed Lydia."

She lowered the handkerchief and balled it in her hand. "You are not to blame for that. Mr. Todd was an accomplished liar who took advantage of his position as a spiritual leader to fool everyone. I did not listen to my instincts either. I knew something was off about him, but I pushed my doubts down. And I am the one who put Nell and Lydia in the positions at Carlton House. I thought it would be a fillip for the reputation of the school. I should have listened to my heart about Todd and refused Asbury's conditions on the lease. Better to have walked away from it than to have brought such trouble here. I should have removed the girls from Carlton House when the jewels first went missing. They voiced concerns about Mr. Lingfield's temper, and they were furtive and secretive. If I had taken them away, Nell would not have been imprisoned, and Lydia would not have been murdered."

He reached for her hand, and the warmth of his touch comforted her. "If I am not to blame myself, then you are not to blame yourself either. None of us knew of Todd's debts, nor that he was related to Asbury through marriage. You are certain you are not hurt?" He touched her chin, turning her head so he could examine her wound. "I wish Mr. Vickery had not left. He could make certain no more damage has been done." He made a rueful sound. "Even in that, I fell short. I knew I couldn't lay my hands on a good medical man for the school, not in any kind of a timely manner, what with the case taking so much of my time, so I delegated the task to Rothwell."

His touch was gentle, so different from the way Todd had gripped her. "The Earl of Rothwell has made an excellent recommendation in the Vickerys. Marcus has told me often as we have gone about setting up Eleos, that a good leader does not try to do everything alone. A good leader finds the right people and allows them to do what they do best, which frees up the leader to focus on the areas in which they excel or the things that are most urgent. I believe the investigation was more urgent than finding a healer for the school, and you delegated the responsibility to someone you trusted to do the job."

"That's what a good leader does, is it?" He released her chin.

She shrugged and smiled. "That's what I tell myself, knowing that I cannot do everything myself, even though I like to try."

Daniel Swann came into the church, and Philippa withdrew her hand from Sir Bertrand's, but not, she suspected, before the falcon-eyed Mr. Swann noticed.

"The local magistrate has taken custody of the body and Mr. Asbury, who is protesting his innocence loudly and with many words. I've made my report. Dr. Rosebreen will collect the corpse and do his own postmortem, though there is little doubt as to how Mr. Todd died." Swann held out his handkerchief, open on his palm. "I've collected every jewel I could find in the long grass, and I've got Owen Wilkinson scouring for more, but I'm afraid the reverend landed on what remained of the parure."

Indeed, the pearls and sapphires, twisted gold, and broken chain on the linen handkerchief in no way resembled the beautiful craftsmanship of the original pieces. Perhaps the Prince Regent could take them back to the jeweler's to be remade.

"I should get back to the manor. Mrs. Stokes will be wondering what's become of me." Philippa reached for the pew back before her to assist in rising, but Sir Bertrand took her elbow as he rose powerfully to his feet.

"I've spoken with her, but asked her not to come into the church until we were sure it had been cleared as a crime scene," Mr. Swann said. "She seemed satisfied when I told her you were with Sir Bertrand." His tone had a bit of humor in it, and his eyes speculated as he looked from one to the other.

She wanted to roll her eyes. As if there would ever be anything more than a professional relationship between them. He was a member of the aristocracy. She was the illegitimate daughter of an earl, a woman with a very checkered past. Sir Bertrand was a gentleman with nice manners, but he had his choice of eligible women, and she was far from eligible.

"Sir Bertrand," Swann continued, "Mr. Partridge has brought a reply from Marcus. The duke cannot meet us here, but he would like a review of all matters on Monday afternoon. He does not believe the young maid will be released from Newgate until Monday. Tomorrow being Sunday, it's impossible to be in touch with the right people. He's also instructed Mr. Partridge to bring Miss Cashel to his home for an overnight stay. The duchess will want to confirm for herself that Miss Cashel has suffered no ill effects after her encounter with Mr. Todd."

"Fair enough." Sir Bertrand guided Philippa toward the door. "I shall tender you into the care of Mrs. Stokes, and I shall finish up the last bits of this investigation."

Mr. Swann went ahead of them, and they stepped out into the late afternoon sunshine. The estate spread before them, and as promised once they reached the manor, the Haverly carriage sat before the front door. Mr. Partridge waited, speaking with the coachman.

Sir Bertrand paused. "I must commend your bravery, Miss Cashel.

You did not panic in a situation that would have most women paralyzed. I have a feeling that had I not arrived when I did, you would have managed to extricate yourself from your aggressors somehow."

"I rather think I would have done no such thing. I think they would have killed me and gotten away. It was your arrival that convinced Todd that there would be no escape, so he got away from you the only way he could. I am grateful for your timing."

He smiled, and his lower lids crinkled in a friendly way. "Quits then?"

"Quits. Oh, and I have considered your offer of becoming a member of your team. I believe I shall acquiesce to your request. It might prove quite diverting in my staid life."

Was she mistaken, or, when he later handed her up into the carriage and passed her valise in beside her, did he actually give her a cheeky wink?

Chapter 19

"THE ENTIRE CITY IS ABUZZ with the story. You heard people at church this morning. Even the preacher referenced the situation." Philippa wanted to throw something. "Mr. Asbury believes the lease is now voided because of what occurred there, though he is responsible for much of it."

"Don't fret. Let Marcus and the solicitors work on it." Charlotte reached over and patted her hand.

"I won't sit still for this," the dowager chimed in, her bothersome foot resting on a tufted footstool. "I thought those solicitors made certain something like this couldn't happen. None of what occurred with Mr. Todd could be considered the fault of the school. It's an outrage, and if I wasn't leaving for our estate in less than a week, I would take up the fight myself."

If the dowager took on Mr. Asbury, she would burn him to the ground.

Philippa put her hand over her eyes, giving in to the despair she had been battling since arriving at Charlotte's last night. "Asbury's solicitors say he must sell the property as he is in serious need of funds at the moment. We are to vacate the property by the end of the month. One week from today."

"I'm so sorry, Pip." Charlotte rubbed her thumb on the back of Philippa's hand, a gesture that was surprisingly comforting, but in a different way than she had experienced from Sir Bertrand. "Marcus will fight it. And Sir Bertrand and Charles and our solicitors."

"At this point, I don't even know if I want them to. It might be throwing good money after bad. It was folly on my part to think I could reach so high as to have a proper school with nice facilities and staff and a clear vision for helping lots of women. Someone like me . . . Everything I touch turns to dust. I should have been content with smaller efforts. Why would God bless anything I did? I'm not worthy of His kind attention." The words were thick in her throat.

"Oh, balderdash." The dowager slapped open her fan. "I never heard such twaddle in all my born days."

Philippa dropped her hand from her eyes.

"Stop being so missish and dramatic and listen to me."

Philippa blinked. She opened her mouth to speak, but the dowager wasn't finished.

"Stop putting God in a little box, telling Him what He can and cannot do. You're not so important that you can thwart His plans. Eleos is bigger than you and this little hiccup in its short history. God's plans for this ministry are bigger than Mr. Asbury's puny claims." The dowager sniffed. "Pull yourself together and get on with things. If this manor house isn't where the school should be, then fine. The country is littered with manor houses, and there are more than a few aristocratic families in need of money who will lease them to us."

Philippa was so shocked at the sensible wisdom coming from the dowager that she wanted to laugh. As always, Her Grace, Honora Haverly had cut to the heart of the matter without mincing words.

"Well put, madam." Charlotte's voice sounded suspiciously as if she were smothering laughter too. "We'll do what we always do, rally together as a family and meet each challenge as it comes. We have a week before we're supposed to vacate the property, and in that time, I believe Marcus and the solicitors will either defeat the claims of Mr. Asbury, or we will find another property. In the short term, if we have to move, I am certain we can find at least a coaching inn to rent to house the ladies until we can find more suitable lodgings. There is some money in the charity coffers, and we can raise more. If God is behind the work, it will prosper. We just need to have faith."

Faith. A tenuous thread sometimes. But hadn't Philippa felt only the day before the peace of God in her heart when she began the first, tentative steps toward forgiving her father?

Which reminded her, she needed to take the appropriate action there if she wished to maintain that peace. "Charlotte, have you any plans for this afternoon?"

"I do not. Other than perhaps a nap. I'm growing tired more easily these days. I do not know if it is chasing after Anthony or growing this little one, or perhaps both." She touched her belly. "The staff are taking care of all the packing and preparations for going to Oxfordshire, but I feel tired just thinking of that carriage ride."

"Oh, then you should rest. I can go on my own."

"Where?" Charlotte asked.

Taking a slow, deep breath, Philippa framed words she had never thought she would say. "I would like to call on the Earl of Tiptree and his wife."

She did not miss the burst of joy in Charlotte's expression, nor the flash of concern and query that followed.

"What need have you to visit there?"

"I have had time to reflect, and there are some things I must say to him. Coming so close to being killed has that effect upon a person." She touched the small nick on her throat where Mr. Todd's dagger had pricked her. At Charlotte's insistence, one of the maids had brought an ointment from the still room, and Charlotte had dressed the cut herself before bed last night. Today, it was only a small mark, an inch or so long, already healing.

"I will accompany you. I can nap anytime."

Philippa was grateful Charlotte did not pepper her with questions on the ride to the Tiptree townhouse. She was too much in her own thoughts, trying to come up with the words she wanted to say to their father for any idle chat.

A maid showed them into the house, and Philippa noticed the changes since her last visit. A rug graced the entryway, and new brass sconces lit the space.

The countess came down the stairs, no longer wan and thin, but with color in her cheeks in a pretty blue dress with an ivory fichu tucked into the neckline. And bless her if she wasn't wearing a pair of garnet earrings.

"Mother, you look lovely. How is Father?" Charlotte asked, bussing her mother's cheek.

"Some better. The manservant I hired has done wonders. He seems to know just how to treat a patient who has suffered apoplexy."

"Has Father said anything? Has he been able to move?"

The countess spoke to Charlotte, but she looked at Philippa. "He can move some on his right side, but beyond a bit of garbled noise, no words. The longer he goes without being able to speak, the less the physician believes he will recover."

"Lady Tiptree," Philippa said. "I do not wish to cause you agitation, but I was hoping to speak to the earl. There are some things I need to say to him."

The woman's brow furrowed, and she plucked at the bracelet on her wrist. "He does become agitated when he's accosted. It's why I have stopped telling him about things I'm changing around the house. What he doesn't know, he cannot become disquieted about." She bit her lower lip, a twinkle invading her eyes.

Verona Tiptree was like a bird newly learned to fly. She'd had her wings clipped long enough by her overbearing husband, it seemed.

"I will not disquiet him. What I need to say is more for my sake than his. I will not be long."

"Come then." She started up the stairs.

The improvements extended here as well. Another long, plush rug lay in the hallway, and an ornamental table along one wall held a vase of flowers. New curtains graced the window at the end of the passage, and a maid paused and bobbed a curtsey to her mistress, balancing a pile of what appeared to be pristine new linens in her arms.

They entered the earl's bedchamber, and here there had been changes as well, however of a more utilitarian nature.

The earl sat in a Bath chair, a strap around his thin chest holding him in place. His arms lay on padded rests, and his feet, clad in carpet slippers, sat upon a footrest. Beside him, a squat, older man looked up from where he had been reading the newspaper aloud to his charge.

He rose immediately. "Milady?" he inquired.

"Hello, Mr. Stanley. We have visitors. Look, Joseph, it's Charlotte and Philippa." She paused. "Your daughters."

Charlotte's face showed her shock at her mother's words, and the countess shrugged. "I've abandoned any pretenses. If he will not acknowledge the truth, I will." She seated herself in a chair by the door. "Please, Miss Cashel, say what you wish. He will hear you. Whether he will understand you is another matter altogether."

Philippa's feet felt weighted as she crossed the room to stand before her father. *You can do this. You can forgive as you have been forgiven. You want peace in your heart, and this is the way to obtain it. Be an example for the women you hope to help.*

The words of the dowager, of Aunt Dolly, of Charlotte, who had all tried to speak truth into her life washed over her, but the loudest voice was the Scripture that had gone through her head as she sat in the chapel wrestling with herself.

"Father." Her throat felt tight and dry, and she swallowed to alleviate the stricture.

His eyes blazed, and his right hand twitched, the fingers flexing.

"Father, I came to say that I forgive you." The words came out in a rush, breathy and small, though they were momentous to her. "I forgive you for the way you treated my mother and me." She had wanted to list all his faults one by one, to chastise him with them, to "heap coals of fire upon his head," but that would not have healed her heart. "I wanted you to know that my forgiveness does not absolve you of the consequences of your actions or your need to repent before God, but it does free me of the effects of carrying around the burden of bitterness. Charlotte once told me that holding onto bitterness is like drinking a cup of poison and hoping your enemy got sick. She's right. I am laying aside my bitterness against you, with the help of Jesus."

The entire time she spoke, he never blinked, never flinched. And he never looked away. Had her words had any effect upon him?

It didn't matter, she realized. Her words truly were more for herself than for him anyway.

"Goodbye, Father. I do not expect we will see one another again. I pray that somewhere in there, the part of you that can still think and make decisions will consider the state of your soul and take steps to repent. Your eternity is staring you in the face, and if you are not a child of God, it is not too late."

She turned and crossed the room, her steps light, her mind free. Charlotte put her arm around Philippa's shoulder, hugging her into her side.

"I'm so proud of you, sister." Moisture glistened in her jade eyes.

She had risked speaking to her father, offering him forgiveness, even though he had not asked for it. He would no longer be the thief of her peace.

Marcus's expression gave nothing away, but then again, when did it ever? This time, he'd called for an Eleos board meeting, but rather than seat them around the dining table, he had chosen the more comfortable setting of the drawing room.

Philippa arrived barely on time, having been at the prison to receive Nell when she was released and then taking her across the river to Southwark and the Eleos property.

But how much longer would it be their property?

Sir Bertrand sat beside her on the pale green velvet settee. He appeared every inch the dandy gentleman in his stylish clothing and impeccable manners.

But she had seen him at his desperate, disheveled best. He had risked injury to save her, and to capture an evil man.

Marcus had risked his life to save her once too, back when she and

Charlotte had been kidnapped by an evil man. Her brother-in-law's gallantry had marked a change in her relationship with him, a depth of affection and trust that she shared with no other man.

Would Sir Bertrand's bravery in saving her mark a change in the way she saw him as well?

Men often had a presentable side they showed to the public to polish their image and a less savory side they displayed when they visited her place of business. And she scorned them for their duplicity.

But here was a man who was dual-natured for honorable reasons.

And she had agreed to work with him for those same reasons.

God, You have a strange way of doing things. Forgiveness of someone else to free myself. Me, vowing never to be under the control or leadership of a man ever again, and here I am signing up to work with Sir Bertrand Thorndike, of all people? What next? What other preconceived notion am I hanging on to that You are about to turn on its head?

She was finding herself having more conversations with God than ever. Another thing she would not have reckoned on just a few weeks ago. She brought her attention back to the room as everyone settled in and Marcus stood to talk.

"Thank you all for coming. I wanted to hold this meeting before we departed for our country estate, as there is much to discuss." He leaned against the mantel. "You are all probably aware that Mr. Asbury, though incarcerated as an accessory to theft and murder, is, through his solicitor, claiming that Eleos has violated the terms of the lease. He has, in fact, issued an order to vacate the property in less than a week."

Mr. Moody, who sat at the writing desk with his ever-ready quill, scowled.

Philippa's stomach tightened. If Asbury thought they would go without a fight, he was in for another think. He might be under the assumption that he could oust a poor group of women, but he did not know the stalwart nature of those women. She might have been despairing yesterday, but she had found her courage. He would not get rid of them that easily.

"When he is found guilty of his crimes, he will either spend years in prison, or he will be hanged. What use will he have for money or a manor house then?" Charlotte asked.

"He has a wife and children. He wants the money from the sale of the estate to go to them if he's executed. He wishes for them to emigrate to America. Their lives will not be easy if they stay in Britain. The sins of the fathers . . ."

He shook his head and returned to the conversation. "What our dear Mr. Asbury did not anticipate is the mercurial nature of our Prince Regent. He's returned early from Tunbridge Wells. Sir Bertrand and I were granted an audience this morning to inform him of all that has gone on regarding the investigation into the stolen jewels, the murder, and the subsequent death by his own devices of his spiritual adviser." Marcus's tone was as dry as attic dust.

"To say he was shocked would be mild. Outraged, certainly. Grateful that the case was brought to a conclusion? Absolutely. The Prince Regent is nothing if not flamboyant with his emotions. He will bring the might and power of his position to bear upon Asbury. I do not feel optimistic about his future.

"However, the prince is also grateful to those who do him a service. Sir Bertrand will not say this himself, so I will. When His Highness asked how he might repay him for his good work on the investigation, Sir Bertrand did not ask for anything that would benefit himself."

"Now, Haverly, there's no need to state it this way." Sir Bertrand shifted in his seat, his shoulder brushing Philippa's. "You worked out the negotiations."

"I also believe in credit where it is due. You could have asked anything of His Highness and probably received it, up to and including a peerage, if the prince's past form is to be taken into account. Instead, you asked for a school." Marcus strolled to stand behind his wife's chair. Charlotte put her hand over his when he rested it on her shoulder. "Sir Bertrand relayed to His Highness what he felt to be the unjust actions of Mr. Asbury in evicting Eleos from his property. In his typical broad-stroke fashion, the prince has declared his intention of purchasing the entire property and donating it to Eleos."

Philippa didn't realize she had gripped Sir Bertrand's hand until she caught Charlotte's inquiring gaze flicking to their clasped fingers and back up to Philippa's eyes.

She dropped his hand like a hot rock, heat pooling along her collarbones and rising. She was beyond blushing. What was wrong with her, forgetting herself so? She dared not meet Sir Bertrand's eyes.

The prince was gifting them the property? At the behest of Sir Bertrand.

"There is one stipulation, which I hope you will not balk at." Marcus looked at Philippa. "The prince would like you to name the school after his daughter, in light of her recent nuptials. He would like the charity to be known as The Princess Charlotte Eleos School for Women in Need."

She considered this. A small sacrifice if it meant they would have a property to call their own. They could save the rent money, and all improvements would belong to them.

"He added that Princess Charlotte would become the royal patron of the charity, if you so desire."

"Of course we accept. A royal patronage and the property donated?" The dowager tapped her cane on the carpet. "One would have to be a fool to struggle on alone rather than accept such a magnificent gift. Imagine how easy it will be to interest the *ton* in the work if we have the backing of Princess Charlotte and the Prince Regent? My fundraiser ball will grow even more desirable to attend if we can put on the invitation that Her Highness, Princess Charlotte, will be present."

Philippa looked at Aunt Dolly, who had her head tilted, her index finger on her cheek, as she considered. She returned Philippa's gaze. "I believe we should accept. How do we go about thanking His Highness for his generosity?"

"Sir Bertrand gave his thanks in person, but I believe having Mr. Moody draft a letter on our behalf and having it signed by the board members would be appropriate." Marcus nodded to the solicitor. "Mr. Moody visited Mr. Asbury in Newgate this afternoon to inform him of the prince's intentions." His expression went wry. "And we all know, one does not say no to the Prince Regent. I think the deal will be brokered quickly. The prince will offer a fair sum, Asbury will accept it for the sake of his family, and Eleos—we'll still call the school Eleos in our conversations—will flourish in Southwark. That is, if Philippa is amenable to the conditions of the bequest?"

All eyes turned to her, and she bit her lip. The scope of their work had grown so much bigger than just her and Aunt Dolly. As she looked from face to face, Marcus, Charlotte, the dowager, Mr. Moody, Aunt Dolly, the Earl of Rothwell, Sir David, and Sir Bertrand, she felt a sense of partnership. They were all there to help, to ensure the success of the charity that had begun in a small house on King's Place.

"It should not be my decision alone. We're all in this together. I would accept the terms."

"Then it's settled." The dowager sat back, satisfied.

They continued the meeting, covering such details as the hiring of Mr. Vickery as the school's medical adviser and the purchase of livestock for the cow byre and fowl house. Philippa, however, could hardly concentrate.

The property, gifted to them. No other stipulations but adding to the name. A royal patronage.

She wanted to laugh. Yet another way God had flipped something on its head.

"I would like to contribute something," Charles Wyvern said. "With the school being such a fair piece from the city, it would be convenient to have at least a horse and trap. I'm thankful that the money Mr. Todd stole from the bank using my name has been recovered. At least most of it. Sophie and I would like to donate a means of travel small enough that you ladies can drive yourselves if you wish. We are leaving for the Haverly estate tomorrow with the family, but I presume you, Sir Bertrand, who are staying in town for a few weeks, could procure a safe driving horse and proper vehicle?"

Sir Bertrand nodded. "It's possible that Whitelock might have a likely horse down at Whitehaven. A retired military horse of kind disposition. I shall inquire."

Marcus nodded. "An excellent idea. Ask about a mare called Sprite. She was a hackney horse for years here in London, older now, but loved her work. If they can spare her at Whitehaven, she could be just the fit."

The meeting broke up soon after, and Philippa stood in the graciously appointed foyer of Haverly House. Sir Bertrand took her spencer from the waiting butler and held it for her.

Odd the comfort she now felt in his presence. Never once had he referred to her past or made her feel as if she were somehow "less." The perfect gentleman, with a wry sense of humor and quick instincts.

And now her team leader.

The notion filled her with hope that they would work well together.

As she and Aunt Dolly crossed the Westminster Bridge on their way home in the hired carriage, she looked out across the river.

"I don't know what to think. What to feel. Did that meeting really occur?" Philippa shook her head. "I feel as if we lost a farthing and found a guinea."

Aunt Dolly's shoulders went up and she, too, shook her head. "I'm amazed, and yet, there is a Scripture passage that keeps running through my head."

"Which one?"

"It's from Ephesians, chapter three. 'Now unto Him that is able to do exceeding abundantly above all that we ask or think, according to the power that worketh in us, unto Him be glory in the church by Christ Jesus throughout all ages, world without end. Amen.'"

"'Above all that we ask or think,'" Philippa repeated. "That about sums things up. I never would have asked or even imagined I *could* ask for a blessing like this. God has been very good to us."

"That He has. He asked us to step out in faith, to risk failure, knowing that He would sustain us."

Philippa leaned back against the jostling of the carriage and closed her eyes.

Unto You be the glory, Lord.

Chapter 20

WHY DID MARCUS WANT TO meet in Southwark, of all places, but not at Eleos? Having some time before the appointment, Bertie asked the driver to let him out on Blackman Street. He walked past a tobacconist's, a saddler's, and a bookseller's. This area of London was growing quickly. He turned onto Horsemonger Lane, then strolled past the gaol and onto Bath Terrace where a row of new townhouses lined up like soldiers, shoulder to shoulder, all alike in white stucco made to look like stone.

More evidence of the growing middle class. Merchants and tradesmen wanting homes away from their workplaces.

The view wasn't the most flash, looking out on the back fence of the county gaol, but with a few trees and bushes, that could be remedied.

The street was perhaps a half mile north of the Eleos property.

At number sixteen, at the far end of the street, he stepped up onto the small porch and used the brass knocker on the black, lacquered door.

Marcus himself opened it. "Ah, right on time. Come in." He stepped aside and Bertie entered.

A nice expanse of parquet floor stretched ahead of him, and a graceful floating staircase curved to an upper floor. High overhead, a skylight let in the sunshine. Much nicer inside than he had thought.

But there wasn't a stick of furniture, a rug, or a painting to be seen. The place was empty as a shucked oyster shell.

"Whose house is this?" Bertie asked.

"Yours, soon, I hope." Marcus opened a pair of pocket doors in the left-hand wall. "It's for sale."

Bertie tried to cover his surprise with a bit of aplomb. "It's a bit far from my customary lodgings in Mayfair."

Marcus nodded, going to stand before the fireplace with his back to the mantel. He crossed his arms. "True, but the location means the price is reasonable. Mayfair comes with a hefty cost."

Bertie looked at the drawing room. High ceilings, large front windows, plasterwork cornices. He could imagine a furniture arrangement, drapes, pictures on the walls.

"I have read your report and Daniel's on the case. You've acquitted yourself well in the face of difficult challenges."

Bertie strolled over to the bare window and looked out across the field to the gaol. "If I had acted more quickly, if I had seen through Todd's lies, I might have saved Lydia's life."

"And if she had been forthcoming with Todd's threats instead of hiding them, you would have apprehended him before he could kill her. You've been at this game long enough to know that 'if onlys' are pointless. Learn and move on."

Learn and move on. But in what capacity? Had he shown enough to Marcus to be given his own team permanently? Had he passed this test?

"I have a new challenge for you to consider. Something I have been working on for some time, and I believe you are ready to embrace." Marcus's boots echoed on the floor.

"And what is that?" A new case would be nice, provided he could accomplish the task before he needed to go to Pensax and Juliette's wedding.

"It's big. And it's the reason I believe this is the perfect house for you. Come with me." The duke led the way to the front hall and up the stairs. Bertie followed, curious, his senses pricking, as they always did on the cusp of a new assignment.

They did not stop on the first floor but continued up past the second to the end of a narrow hall. "This way."

Bertie didn't see exactly what Marcus did, but the wall opened on silent hinges, the entire panel a doorway to a steep staircase.

Shades of Thorndike House, it was a hidden space.

At the top of the stairs, Marcus opened a door to reveal an open area with bare rafters and high, narrow windows under the eaves that let in light but kept anyone from seeing in. He motioned Bertie to step past him into the room.

"Do you think this will suffice as your own war room? Think your team could work here?"

Bertie drew in a breath so deep he felt dizzy. His own war room. In his own townhouse. With his own team.

"I think this might be suitable . . ." He gave a half grin.

"I'm going to be quite direct with you, because the time for plain speaking has come." Marcus still held the doorknob, and Bertie turned to look at him. When the duke got that tone in his voice, it paid to listen.

"For years I have suspected you were holding yourself back from your full potential. Content to be known as the Earl of Thorndike's little brother. Almost an appendage." Marcus looked contemplative. "I know how it can be for us second sons. I had my work at the agency to give me a sense of purpose, but my older brother wasn't involved in my work the way yours is. Nor"—he paused—"nor was I stuck in the past, never having gotten over my first love. I know you have no unseemly feelings for your sister-in-law now, but I know you loved her once. And you have some idea that unless or until you find a woman who captivates your heart as she once did a sixteen-year-old boy, you will remain a bachelor."

Bertie bristled. This was territory Marcus should stay out of. His feelings for Melisande, however they had changed over the years, were none of Marcus's affair. It had nothing to do with the work. He was entitled to a private life.

"Before you turn pugilist on me, hear me out." Marcus held up his hands, palms out. "It's time you made your own way, got out from under both your brother's leadership and your ties to the past."

"As you say, I no longer harbor those feelings for my sister-in-law."

"Yet you have not moved on. You have not found someone new to love."

"I do not need to be in love to do my job. I firmly believe being a bachelor improves my work. I've no one to think of besides myself. And now my team. I have clarity of thought because I have clarity of emotion."

"But what I am proposing will be enhanced if you have a spouse. Or at the very least, a fiancée."

A frown scrunched his brow. "What possible case can you send me on that would require me to be married? Or engaged? If you need a married man, there are several in the agency to call upon. My brother, for one."

"Your brother will not suit. It's you I need. I'm proposing a whole new adventure, a whole new life. I'm proposing that you purchase this townhouse, establish yourself as a resident of Southwark. Then I want you to stand for Parliament as the representative for this district."

The air rushed out of Bertie's lungs and the thoughts from his brain. Then the questions crashed in, one tumbling over the other like water rushing over a mill wheel.

Stand for Parliament? Him? He hated politics. He wasn't a diplomat. He was a spy, an agent, an excellent cat burglar. How could he use those skills as a member of Parliament? What about his newly formed team? What about Partridge and Miss Cashel?

Marcus wasn't finished. "I've been thinking for some time about this move for you. It would not be forever, one term, perhaps two, unless you acquired a taste for it. There's something afoot in the House of Commons, and I believe you and your team are the ones to get to the root of it."

"Stand for Parliament so I can work a case?" That made more sense. Though the idea of making speeches, of asking for votes, of currying favor . . . ugh. Was he prepared to go through that grinder? For a case?

"Yes, and because I believe you would be a good politician. You're adept at gathering knowledge, and you've proven resourceful and determined in every case you've undertaken. You care about people even while you pretend you do not. It is yet another reason for you to abandon the facade of drunken idleness. You will need to prove yourself, and quickly, as the by-election will take place soon." He waved his hand idly, as if he weren't outlining the biggest change in Bertie's life. "We can speak more of it once you've let the idea sink in, but first, there's the matter of this townhouse. Do you think it will be suitable?"

Suitable? It was perfect. Which sent a suspicious thought through his head.

"How long have you been planning this for me?"

Marcus shrugged and made a low noise in his throat. "Long enough to have had these townhouses built in a district I believe you can win, and this one custom designed so you could have this space in which to work. Since I became the head of the agency, in fact."

Bertie didn't know whether to be angry or impressed. The machinations of Marcus Haverly would put Machiavelli to shame.

"Say the word and the house is yours, and we'll begin the election process. We'll need to come up with some issues for you to espouse that will benefit the Southwark people." Marcus was speaking as he turned to go down the stairs. "There are only a handful of qualified voters in the district, which should make winning the election fairly simple. Southwark is a 'rotten borough.' It has been susceptible to corruption for some time, and I fear is teetering on the edge of that particular precipice again. I have some ideas on how we will persuade those voters and get you into office."

I imagine you do.

Bertie shook his head. Him. A member of Parliament.

But also the incentive of a new case.

Marcus knew him too well.

He never could resist a challenge.

Author's Note

The Reverend Simon Todd is based upon a real person from history, Reverend William Dodd, who served at the Magdalen Hospital and who tried to steal funds to support his lavish lifestyle.

It is estimated that there were over fifty thousand prostitutes in London at any given time during the Regency period. Hospitals like the Magdalen and the fictional Eleos sought to help and rehabilitate these women, giving them the tools they needed to make a better life for themselves.

As for the Bow Street investigators and forensic science at crime scenes, I have accelerated their capabilities (not too far, I hope) for the sake of the story.

Acknowledgments

As WITH EVERY BOOK, THERE is an army to thank. To my friends, Michelle Griep and Julie Klassen, thank you for your encouragement, for being such great sounding boards, and for joining me in my hare-brained schemes.

To my family, especially my husband, Peter, who supports my dreams and is so openly proud of my efforts, many, many thanks.

Thank you to the team at Kregel, particularly my editors, Janyre Tromp and Rachel Overton. You take what I send you and make it so much better!

Agents advocate for, encourage, teach, and keep their authors going in the directions they should, and mine is the best of the best. Thank you, Cynthia Ruchti of Books & Such.

Recommended Reading

If you're interested in learning more about the topics covered in this book, I recommend the following titles:

Comptson, H. F. B. *The Magdalen Hospital: The Story of a Great Charity*. London: Society for the Promotion of Christian Knowledge, 1917.

Deacon, Richard. *A History of the British Secret Service*. London: Panther Books, 1985.

DesJardien, Teresa. *Jane Austen Shopped Here*. Self-published, 2020.

Dodd, William. *An Account of the Rise, Progress and Present State of the Magdalen Hospital for the Reform of Penitent Prostitutes*. Miami, FL: Hard Press, 2019. Originally published 1763.

Horwood, Richard. *The A to Z of Regency London*. Lympne Castle, Kent: Harry Margary, 1985.

Queen's Gallery. *Carlton House: The Past Glories of George IV's Palace*. London: The Queen's Gallery, Buckingham Palace, 1991.